Emily Grimoire was born and raised in Hartford, Connecticut. After graduating with a degree in History from the prestigious Smith College, she found solace from the hustle and bustle of everyday life in her storytelling. In addition to her writing, Emily is known for her philanthropy and dedication to various charitable causes. She serves on the boards of several cultural institutions and volunteers as a docent at a local whaling museum. Despite her success, Emily remains devoted to her ungrateful daughter and a granddaughter who turned out much better than expected. *Impractical Magic* is her first book with Avon.

EMILY GRIMOIRE

IMPRACTICAL MAGIC

avon.

Published by AVON
A division of HarperCollins*Publishers* Ltd
1 London Bridge Street
London SE1 9GF

www.harpercollins.co.uk

HarperCollins*Publishers*
Macken House,
39/40 Mayor Street Upper,
Dublin 1
D01 C9W8
Ireland

A Paperback Original 2024
1
Copyright © Emily Grimoire 2024

Emily Grimoire asserts the moral right to
be identified as the author of this work.

A catalogue record for this book is available from the British Library.

ISBN: 978-0-00-871868-8

Set in Birka by HarperCollins*Publishers* India

Printed and bound in the UK using 100% Renewable
Electricity at CPI Group (UK) Ltd

"Reality is always poor, weak stuff compared to magic."

—Orson Welles

Chapter 1
Look Homeward, Witch

As her Uber wheezed its way over the hill, Scarlett sat in the back, nervously sipping a coffee she should never have bought at all. She had a knot in her stomach, and the venti cappuccino with double espresso only tied it tighter.

Scarlett peered suspiciously out the window. Down in the valley, Oak Haven hid coyly behind a veil of autumn leaves, which made a patchwork quilt of crimson, amber, and evergreen. But she could still make out the roofs of familiar buildings— the curlicue of smoke from the tea shop chimney, the steeple of the local church. The distant town looked cozy and familiar, but there was a certain tremor in the air—something pricked at the edges of Scarlett's vision. *Has something changed down there?* she wondered. *Is something wrong? Or does it just seem different because I am?*

Scarlett hadn't intended to return to Oak Haven until she was carried there in a pine box. But her sister Delilah's voicemail carried her trademark Don't Question Me tone, all urgency and veiled accusation. Was there a fire at the family inn? Was there a corpse? Several? Delilah didn't say.

The thought of returning home filled Scarlett with a nausea-inducing blend of gleeful anticipation and overwhelming dread. There was so much wonderful waiting for her down in that valley, and so much awful.

And then there was Nate, who was both.

"Excuse me, miss?" Marty the Uber driver tapped his phone. "My GPS seems to be on the fritz. The address you gave me isn't registering."

"Yeah," Scarlett said resignedly. "That'll happen. Don't worry. I know where I'm going, unfortunately."

"Sorry, what was that last part?"

"Nothing, Marty." The closer Scarlett got to home, the tighter that knot in her stomach became. *This is a mistake,* she thought. *No matter what Delilah said. I shouldn't have come back. I don't have the right. Not after what I did.*

But . . . Too late now. "Take the next left."

As the car approached the town center, Scarlett saw something shocking. Something appalling. Something she'd never seen in Oak Haven and never thought she'd see if she lived a thousand years.

A bright orange sign shaped like a diamond: ROAD WORK AHEAD.

"Road work?!"

"You're in New England," mansplained Marty. "There's always road work due to the harsh weather. It's just a part of living here."

"Yeah, I grew up here, I'm familiar with the weather. But road work doesn't exist in Oak Haven. We fix our roads with magic."

He laughed. "That sure would be nice, wouldn't it? Just get Glinda out here to snap her fingers?"

"I'm not joking. I'm a witch, my sisters are witches. All the women in Oak Haven are witches."

"Uh-huh, sure. Of course you are! I guess even the Yellow Brick Road gets the occasional pothole, huh?"

Whatever, Scarlett thought. It didn't matter if he believed her—he'd forget the entire conversation in about fifteen minutes. "Just take a right up here."

In a region known for its crisp autumn air and cozy clapboard houses and pumpkin-spice everything, Oak Haven was by far the crispest, the coziest, the spiciest. The trees didn't limit themselves to the basic orange, red, and yellow. No. In Oak Haven, trees turned sparkling apricot and twinkling sangria and shimmering bronze. And it wasn't just about the foliage. The fall days were the perfect mix of warm sun and cool breeze, the evenings just chilly enough to demand a favorite sweater. The storefronts were adorned with wreaths of dried leaves and corn husks, while scarecrows stood vigil at every corner. Scarlett's hometown boasted more cider-donut vendors per capita than anywhere in the United States. The air smelled vaguely of cloves all the time.

Oak Haven should have topped every leaf peeper's bucket list. There should've been photo spreads in glossy travel magazines and fawning television segments from Oprah Winfrey.

Instead, few tourists made their way to Oak Haven. And those who managed to stumble into it? They experienced a fit of geographical amnesia as soon as they left. Google's many attempts to map the area invariably failed. Local weather forecasters gave up talking about the village because they could never find it on their maps.

This collective forgetting was no accident. It was a spell. It

3

was the same sort of spell that made the trees so spectacular and the weather so perfect. It was a spell deliberately cast and immaculately maintained by the village's Elder Council of Witches. A council that Scarlett's family had led for centuries.

"Wow," Marty enthused. "This is gorgeous. Look at these cool old houses. Man, how is it I've never been here before?"

"You have," Scarlett said. "You just don't remember."

"No way! I'd definitely remember all this."

"Whatever you say." There was no arguing with the forgetting.

"So, if you don't mind my asking . . . how do you know about this place?"

"I grew up here."

"Really?! And you left? Why would anybody leave a paradise like this?"

"Well, that's a pretty personal question there, Marty." The truth burbled up inside Scarlett like heartburn. *You see, Marty,* she thought, *sometimes in life, a person makes a mistake so big—does a thing so unforgivable—that she can't go home again, ever, no matter how much she may want to. So, she moves to San Francisco and pretends everything is okay.* But Scarlett knew that was a little more honesty than Marty was prepared to handle. So instead, she went with her old standby—the answer she gave everyone who inquired why she hadn't been home in a decade. "My family is nuts." It wasn't true, but it usually shut people up.

Not Marty. "Aww, c'mon, that's no reason. Everyone's family is nuts in some way or another."

"Oh, sure. That's Tolstoy right? All families are nuts in their own way?" Again, this was a joke Scarlett kept in the chamber, ready to be fired whenever someone got a little too nosy. "But you see, my family isn't, like, *low-salt peanuts* nuts. My family is

4

full-on, *deluxe-roasted macadamias with wasabi peas* nuts." As always, this line left Scarlett with a sour feeling in her gut. They weren't so bad, her family. She actually liked them rather a lot. But that wasn't information she cared to share with Uber drivers.

"Sure, you say they're crazy, but in the end, family is family, and families should be together. Don't you think?"

"Together?" She laughed bitterly. "Trust me, bad things happen when we're together, Marty. Very bad things."

"Aw, I don't believe that. You know what they say: 'In times of test, family is best.'"

Good grief, she thought. *Of all the Ubers in all the world, I had to get into Dr. Phil's.*

The car steadily rumbled along the winding road, passing by quaint homes with white picket fences and vibrant gardens.

Finally, they reached Galloping Hill Road, which led directly to the quintet of cobblestone streets that passed for Oak Haven's "downtown." But first, the car had to traverse Bonfire Creek, its banks lined with goldenrod and asters. The creek made a mirror, doubling the images of autumn trees along its bank. The gentle waters flowed beneath a charming, if dubious-looking covered bridge with barn-red sides and a mansard roof.

With a certain trepidation, Marty allowed his car to slowly cross the bridge. The aged wooden planks of the bridge groaned and creaked under the weight of the vehicle, and the scent of damp wood permeated the air. Marty released a little "hmmph . . ." sound, clearly questioning the decision to trust the fate of his precious Kia Sorento with the cranky old bridge.

"We kids used to jump off this bridge all the time," Scarlett offered by way of distraction.

"Oh really . . . ?" He was staring out his window as the car rolled slowly forward, as if he could keep the bridge aloft by concentration alone.

"No, not really," she admitted. "Bonfire Creek is pretty shallow, and the adults always warned us that we'd bust our heads open if we tried it. I did manage it once though."

"Ah, good for you," said Marty, who could not possibly care less about anything that did not involve the safety of his Kia.

"Of course, my parents completely flipped and grounded me for about three months, but . . . I say, worth it. I'm the only one who ever dove off that roof."

But with a pang, Scarlett realized she hadn't been home in a decade. Maybe all the kids did it now. Maybe it was no big deal.

At last, the car was over the bridge and Marty could relax— sort of. He was probably already worrying about having to use the bridge again to get home.

As the Uber continued through the center of Oak Haven, Scarlett looked out the window and frowned. Something wasn't right, and it wasn't just the road work. All her favorite shops were still around: Spellbound Books; Henrietta's music store; the All Who Wander travel agency. The lampposts were adorned with fresh garlands of vibrant leaves, overflowing flower boxes boasted clusters of cheerful chrysanthemums, and street parking remained free as ever. Everything seemed fine, but . . . something was off. No children in the town square, jumping in piles of raked leaves. No jack-o'-lanterns grinning from the windows. And . . .

Oh! She realized with a start. *Where are the gourds?!*

In Oak Haven, autumn had always meant gourds. Gourds in every shop window, gourds piled in the town square, gourds everywhere you looked. There were gourds shaped like swans and UFOs. There were gourds with warts and gourds with wings, bicolored, tricolored, and multicolored, too. Gourds by the hundreds, by the thousands—a parliament of gourds, a berserk of gourds, a madness. A level of gourd-intensity that could only be achieved via multiple spells maintained by a coven of gourd-obsessed witches.

But as the Uber made its way down Main, Scarlett saw no berserk of gourds. In fact, she saw none whatsoever.

Then she noticed the weather. It was just . . . okay. Not perfect, a little cloudy. Just . . . fine. That's when she realized the gourds were just a symptom. The illness was normalcy.

Oak Haven looked like any other lovely, tastefully decorated New England village. It used to be an enchanted place. Now it was just a place.

Several days earlier, her sister Delilah had left an urgent voicemail, summoning Scarlett home immediately. At the time, Scarlett had just rolled her eyes, unable to imagine what her sister was all worked up about. But now, gazing out the window at her unrecognizably normal town, Delilah's cryptic message became alarmingly clear: there was a problem with magic in Oak Haven.

The voicemail had said, "Scarlett, come home. It's happening again." And then, almost as an afterthought, "Oh and Nate's been asking about you." *Click.*

***

Dropping Nate's name had been a cheap shot on Delilah's part.

The *will-they-or-won't-they* drama of teenage Scarlett and Nate had been closely followed by everyone in Oak Haven. After all, the two were children of the town's most prominent families,

7

the Melroses and the Williams. For that reason alone, many said that their union was fated from the start. And when witches tell you something is fate? They aren't kidding. To the elders of Oak Haven, the tale of Scarlett and Nate wasn't so much *will-they-or-won't-they* but *when-will-they-dammit.*

Alas, the witches misunderstood something fundamental about teenagers: if you want them to do something, the worst thing you can do is tell them they should. The more Scarlett and Nate were told they were meant to be, the more they clung to the "friend zone." The two were inseparable, yes, but platonically so—stubbornly, platonically so. They ignored the whispers, giggles, and side-eyes from all the opinionated observers in town, remaining steadfast in their commitment to chart their own, just-friends course.

And by the time Scarlett and Nate realized that the witches were probably right all along? It was far too late.

***

The Uber pulled up in front of a massive country inn with mansard roofs and wraparound porches and an unlikely number of turrets. There were elaborate gables and a giant bay window with images of the Salem witch trials in stained glass.

Marty just stared, his mouth half open. "What is this place?"

"My family business," Scarlett said, letting herself out of the car. "Aka the wholesale mixed-nut factory."

Marty got out to fetch Scarlett's luggage. No sooner had he popped open the trunk than there was a great crash from the hotel's highest turret. The crash was followed by a girlish shriek and the smashing of windows as a great plume of pumpkin-colored smoke shot out of the turret, circled the hotel, and lifted up into the sky. Day abruptly turned to night; there were lightning strikes and a clap of thunder, and a thousand gourds rained down. They tumbled onto the lawn and smashed across the sidewalk.

Then, the sun returned as quickly as it had gone. The birds went back to chirping, and Marty's Kia was covered in gourd guts.

Up in the turret, a young woman with an unruly cloud of white-blonde hair leaned out the smashed window. "Is everybody okay down—OH MY GOD," she squealed. "It's Scarlett! Scarlett's home! Scarlett! You're home!"

"That I am." The sight of her sister's goofy grin pushed all of Scarlett's dread to the side for a moment. She couldn't help but smile, too. She shouted up at the turret, "How's it going?"

"Terrible! There are no gourds in this dumb town."

"I noticed! You're working on a solution, I see."

"Yeah, well." Luna had a musical laugh. "Didn't go as planned. Don't move. I'll be right down. Don't you move!"

Marty gaped at Scarlett, then at his gourd-covered car, then at Scarlett again. "Family of mixed nuts, huh?"

"My baby sister Luna is the wasabi pea in that particular analogy."

"Was that . . . uh . . . I mean, is she . . ."

"Was that magic? Is she a witch?" Scarlett allowed herself to enjoy Marty's befuddlement. "Told you so."

"And . . . are you?"

"A retired witch," she admitted. "But now that I'm here, it's strangely tempting to dive right back in. Hey, maybe I could de-gourd your car for you?"

"You know," he said, slowly backing away, "I think I'm good. I'm overdue to visit the car wash."

"Suit yourself, Marty."

As the Uber hurried away, Scarlett gazed at her luggage, sitting in a puddle of exploded gourds. She glanced up at the porch, trying to force herself to approach.

Am I sure I want to do this?

Nope.

Is it too late to flee?

Luna's cheerful face appeared at the hotel's front door.

Yep.

Chapter 2
Anything You Can Do . . .

Luna galloped down the walkway. "Scaaaarlett!! You're here!" Her flying hug nearly knocked Scarlett over. "I'm so happy. I've missed you!"

"Lulu! I missed you too! Okay, okay, let go . . . I can't breathe!"

"No!" She squeezed even harder. "No, I want my ten years' worth of hugs."

"Sure, but not all at once."

Luna pulled back and peered suspiciously into her sister's eyes. "Why'd you stay away so long, anyway?"

"Me?! What about you? Why'd you stay away so long?"

"But . . . I haven't." Her baby sister made a face. "I mean . . . Yes, I travel all the time, and I'm not here very often. But I always come back for Christmas. You, on the other hand? Never."

Scarlett felt like she'd been punched—all this time, she'd assumed Luna was her partner in the Avoiding Oak Haven Club. It was quite a shock to find she was the club's sole member. "You come back?" she repeated numbly. "I didn't know that."

"Well, how could you, since you're never here? What's the trouble, Scar?" Luna squinted at her sister in her mischievous way, leaving it unclear whether she was kidding or not. "Are you mad at us?"

Scarlett gasped. "Oh no! Lulu, no! I've missed you so much. Even Grumpus in there—" she gestured at the inn. "I've even missed her."

"Then why don't you ever visit? Why never call, or write, or anything?"

Scarlett gazed into her sister's watery blue eyes and could feel her heart cracking. "I uh . . . It's just . . ." She shook her head and chuckled awkwardly. "It's been a long day. Can we do this later?"

"You got it!" Luna hoisted one of Scarlett's bags over her shoulder. "Let's go inside."

Scarlett picked up her other bag and followed. "Hey, how's everything in Ankara?"

"Ankara?" Luna looked confused. "Oh, Ankara! No, I don't live there anymore—Ankara was four addresses ago. I left there for Yokohama, then Easter Island, then—no, wait, five addresses. Ankara, then Yokohama, then Penguin, then Easter Island, and I flew here from Bo-Kaap yesterday."

Scarlett laughed. "I'm sorry, there's a place called Penguin?"

"It's in Tasmania, silly." Luna walked backward toward the porch and said with a sigh, "Boy, do we have a lot to catch up on!"

The first thing guests usually noticed about the lobby was the scent—a dependable potpourri of baked apples, cinnamon, and freshly brewed coffee. As a child growing up at the hotel, Scarlett had long assumed that this was what all air was supposed to smell like. But today, the smell was gone.

Everything else about the lobby appeared precisely as it always had. To the left, a semi-circle of overstuffed armchairs around a stone hearth, antique rag rugs scattered across the dark hardwood floor, and the old grandfather clock ticking rhythmically in the corner. To the right was a grand piano that had occupied that spot long before Scarlett was born. At the back sat a check-in counter with a polished marble top. Behind it, a grand wooden staircase led up to the inn's suites. A winding banister curved gracefully upwards—a banister that Scarlett and her sisters had slid down a thousand times.

"Wow." Scarlett looked around. "Place hasn't changed one bit."

"Mama likes what she likes—you know how it is."

"Smells wrong, though."

Luna nodded. "That's the first thing I noticed, too."

"Hello, Scarlett." Delilah, the eldest of the sisters, stood like a centurion behind the reception desk. "You look older."

"It's been ten years, and *that's* your opening line?" Scarlett put down her bag and cautiously approached. "I *am* older, Del. So are you. You look good, though."

"Honest labor suits me."

"Oh boy, here we go." Scarlett sighed. "Still behind that old desk, I see. I think you were standing there when I left, weren't you?"

"Well, *somebody* has to."

"Delilah," Scarlett said, "you asked me to come, remember?"

"I had very little confidence you would appear. Luna, you must be so pleased—Scarlett's here, so you've won your bet."

Scarlett frowned. "Wait . . . somebody was betting *against* me showing up?"

"Well . . ." Luna shrugged, embarrassed. "I bet that you'd come, that should count for something, right?"

"Who was betting against me?! Was it you, Del?"

"You know I never gamble."

"If not you, then—" Scarlett stopped abruptly, because the girls' mother entered the lobby from the dining room.

Scarlett's breath caught in her chest. Mama looked . . . old. She'd known that would happen, of course—parents age, it's part of the job. But still. Her hair, while still perfectly arranged, had gone gray. The lines in her face had deepened, and her shoulders had a certain curl, as though she was carrying a burden far heavier than she should bear.

It had been a long ten years.

Surprising Mama was nearly impossible, but the sight of Scarlett standing in the lobby certainly seemed to do the trick. "Scarlett?" she exclaimed. "What are you doing here?"

"Uh, wow, Mama. Nice to see you too . . ."

Luna flung her arm around her sister's shoulder. "Surprise! You get both of us now. All your girls back together."

"Yes, Scarlett, of course it's nice to see you. That's quite an interesting choice you've made with your hair."

And there it is, Scarlett thought. *How is it that I haven't been home in ten years, but I step across that threshold, and I'm immediately eighteen again, and no time has passed at all?* "Let's see, how long was that, Mama? Ten seconds before the first dig? You're slowing down in your old age."

"Don't be smart. Are you staying for the weekend?"

"The weekend?" Scarlett repeated. "I mean . . . I suppose I'm staying until whatever this situation is gets worked out."

"What situation? There's no situation! Delilah, are you telling people there's a—"

"Obviously there's a situation, Mama."

14

Scarlett said, "I saw road work on the way here. What's that about? Why isn't the Road Spellwork Committee out there fixing it?"

"Well, yes, we're having a minor hitch at the moment. It's—"

"A hitch!" Delilah exclaimed.

Mama shook her head. "Everything is fine—"

"It's really not . . ."

"—and Scarlett, you must be starving. Delilah, why don't we go see what the kitchen can whip up for our prodigal here?"

Delilah rolled her eyes. "Prodigals get all the applause." She stomped off to the kitchen.

A man in a green flannel work shirt, toolbox in hand, came jogging down the staircase into the lobby. Mama saw him first and smiled. "All set with the sink in 301?"

"Fixed," he said. "What else can I do?"

Mama gestured toward the grand piano, and the two approached it for a discussion.

Scarlett stared openly. The handyman had the broad shoulders of a rugby player and the confident jawline of a superhero. She recognized the voice as Nate's but the physique . . . how could it be? She grabbed her baby sister and dragged her across the room for a more private conversation. "Luna," she whispered. "What happened to Nate?"

"What do you mean, what happened? He's ten years older, is what happened—same as the rest of us."

"No, but . . . um . . ." Scarlett stammered. "My Nate had acne and braces and a concave nerd-boy chest—"

"All of which he outgrew, ding dong. And pretty handsomely, if you don't mind me saying."

"Mind you saying? Why would I mind you saying?"

Luna shook her head and laughed. "Because of the thing you guys had."

"There was no thing!" exclaimed Scarlett unconvincingly.

"Don't be daft. The Ross and Rachel-y thing. Will they, won't they, were they on a break, why is there a monkey, et cetera. Did you two ever get around to having an *actual* date? I can't remember, it's been so long now."

"C'mon, there was never any monkey. And Nate and I were friends—that was it."

"Exactly, you were friends like on *Friends*—see what you did there?"

"No way! There was no *Friends*-related . . . thing. That was just a fantasy circulated by all the old ladies in town."

"Okaayy. Sure." Luna's eyebrows danced skeptically. "Whatever, *Rachel*. I'm gonna go help with the food. If we leave it up to Delilah, we'll be eating some sort of quinoa-based gruel." Then she was gone.

Scarlett turned her attention to the piano, where Mama said, "All right, Nate, so you're clear on the task? The piano hasn't been moved in thirty years, so the casters may need some convincing."

"Consider it done," Nate said solemnly. "WD-40 is my friend."

She nodded and headed for the kitchen, while Nate crawled under the piano on his back, the better to inspect the casters.

Scarlett approached the piano slowly, like it was a bomb that might go off. "Hey, you."

Nate sat up, smacking his head on the underside of the piano. "Dammit!" He crawled out from under and stood, rubbing his forehead. "Scarlett. Of course the first time I see you involves a headache. Plus, I've lost a bet."

"You!" Scarlett exclaimed. "You bet against me?"

He shrugged. "Not one word in ten years. Felt like my odds were good."

"*Thanks a bunch* . . . Anyway . . . it's nice to see you, Nate."

"Uh, yeah."

They stared at each other for a beat, then quickly looked away.

"You uh, you look good," he said to the piano.

"Me, or the piano?"

He flushed, embarrassed. "I should get back to this—your mom wants the piano in the ballroom."

"Seriously though—why?"

"Apparently the Gilbert and Sullivan Society will be arriving soon, and they all need lots of space for . . . various . . . piano-related . . . . Oh I don't know, I'm just doing what your mom asked."

"I see. So, you are the very model of a modern major piano mover."

Nate sighed. "That's the third time I've heard that joke today."

"Buckle up, it's gonna be a long weekend. But why are you moving it when one of us could just—" She flicked her fingers, suggesting a spell.

"Please don't. Magic has been all . . . I dunno, weird lately. Anyway, I heard you gave up magic when you left town."

"True," Scarlett admitted. "Ten years without."

"Well, you've only been home for five minutes—maybe pace yourself."

"Maybe . . . or maybe, doing your job better than you can is the perfect way for me to kick off this visit."

"Did you see the gourds?" Nate pointed at the door. "Looks like a haunted house exploded out there."

17

"That's Luna, though; her spells are always crazy. Come on, let me move the piano for you."

"Delilah says there's something off with magic right now," Nate said. "She doesn't want it used in the hotel unless absolutely necessary."

Deep down, Scarlett knew that if Del was saying something was wrong, then it probably was. But she'd been away so long, spent so much time resisting her powers and pretending to be like everyone else . . . Finding herself among her own witchy kind, the urge to connect with that side of herself suddenly became irresistible. "C'mon, let me do this—consider it a homecoming gift from me to you."

Nate shook his head. "Your sister forbids it."

"In that case, I really want to do it."

"Scarlett, please don't . . ."

"I can move this piano better than you can, Nate."

"No, you can't."

"Yes, I can."

"No, you can't."

"Yes, I can.

"No, you—dammit, Scarlett, I'm not doing a duet with you. Cut it out."

"Watch me." She focused her energy on the piano and gave a graceful flick of her wrist.

"Scarlett, don't—"

The air turned somehow electric, and the piano shuddered. It raised six inches off the floor and hovered there as if awaiting further instruction. "Told you," she said smugly. "Everything's fine."

Everything was not fine. All eighty-eight keys lifted off the keyboard and soared around the lobby like a white-and-black snake. The keys played a quick rendition of "Für Elise" and then dropped to the floor like ivory-and-ebony raindrops. The rest of the piano heaved itself four feet higher in the air and then smashed itself to pieces on the floor.

Scarlett's jaw dropped open. *My God*, she thought, *I forgot how much I fucking hate it when Delilah is right.*

"Nice work, Scar." Nate sighed. "Welcome home."

Chapter 3
It's Going to be a Bumpy Night

The tuneful crash brought Delilah and Luna racing in from the kitchen.

Luna gasped. "The piano!"

"Seriously, Scarlett?" Delilah said angrily. "You've been here five minutes!"

"Oi, wot's all this bloomin' hubbub, then, eh?" An improbably tall, alarmingly thin man peered down from the first-floor landing. He wore a fuzzy hotel bathrobe, accessorized with an oversized top hat and a droopy mustache. His theatrical Cockney accent was only slightly more believable than Dick Van Dyke's. "Wot's 'appened to the peace and quiet of me 'ome away from 'ome?"

"It's okay, Max," Nate called out reassuringly. "Nothing to worry about, just a little . . . piano apocalypse. Everything's under control."

"It don't sound 'ardly controlled, now do it?!" said the mustached man.

"Just a little mishap. We're fine; you can go back to your room."

"All right then, I'm off," he huffed, "but if I'da wanted to stay at bleedin' Fawlty Towers, I wouldda bloody done it, right! You lot best sort it out, sharpish."

"Who the hell was that?" Scarlett asked.

"That's Max," replied Luna. "He's very sweet."

"*Sweet* is not the word I'd use," Delilah said. "He goes by Maximillian the Magnificent. He's been staying here the past few months."

"*Months?*" repeated Scarlett. "Since when does the inn have guests who stay for months?"

"Uhh, I dunno, Scar," Delilah said sarcastically. "Since we started having hardly any guests at all? Somewhere around there, I guess?"

"Maximillian thinks he's some kind of magician," Nate said. "And today he apparently also thinks he's English?"

Delilah corrected, "Technically speaking, he *is* a magician. The English part, I won't vouch for. Pretty sure he was Swedish yesterday. Regardless, he is a *right bloody pain in me arse, eh wot?*"

Scarlett frowned. "Since when do men in this town have magic?"

"Oh, I never said he had real magic. Maximillian is the non-powered, card-trick-performing, saw-the-lady-in-half type of magician."

Luna added, "He invited me to go see him at work tomorrow."

Nate wiggled his eyebrows. "He has a rabbit named Quentin."

"And he likes to play the piano in our lobby," said Delilah pointedly. "Or rather, he *used* to. But, *now*, thanks to Scarlett—"

"Oh my God, Del, it was an accident, obviously. I'm really sorry . . ."

"Nate," Delilah said, "didn't you tell her not to use—"

"Please," Nate snarked. "You think she listens to me?"

"Hey!" Scarlett exclaimed. "You gave me no indication *that* would happen!"

"What are you talking about, Scar? I literally said, *do not do magic*!"

"Sure, but you didn't make it clear how bad it would actually—"

"Are you kidding me?!" he interrupted.

As the bickering swirled around them, Delilah and Luna exchanged glances, and Luna grinned. "Nice to see some things never change."

"Everyone, pay attention to me now!" Zahir, the hotel chef, appeared in the doorway. He was pushing a wheeled cart, overburdened with platters and trays and tureens containing all manner of deliciousness. "Everyone to the dining room!"

Scarlett grinned and meant it for the first time since she'd arrived. "Zahir! I'm back, can you believe it?" Zahir was practically a brother to Scarlett and her sisters. His parents had been co-head chefs of the inn when they were kids, so Zahir had grown up alongside the Melrose girls—racing up and down the halls, terrorizing the guests. Now it seemed Zahir had stepped up to replace his parents and carry on the family tradition. Unlike certain other bad children Scarlett could name.

But as Scarlett moved to hug Zahir, Mama swooped in from the kitchen. "Ladies who have made messes need to address their messes before dining." She departed without pausing for any objections.

Delilah grinned like the cat who'd just inherited the entire canary factory. "No messes made by me. Guess I'm digging in first." She marched after Mama, leaving Scarlett at the mercy of the wrecked piano.

"Zahir," Scarlett said, "isn't it a little early for dinner? It's, like, four o'clock!"

He wrinkled up his forehead. "How many years has it been since you have had my family's cooking?"

"That would be ten," she admitted.

"Then I would have to say that your dinner is *extremely late*." That established, he turned and rolled his gorgeous-smelling cart into the dining room.

Luna was on her way outside to deal with the gourds on the lawn, but she turned back. "Just think of it as afternoon tea— we'll pretend we're Brrrrrrrrrritish!" She gave a perfectly royal curtsy and danced out the door.

"Hey," Nate called after her. "You want some garbage bags or . . . ?" But Luna was long gone. "Never mind, I guess." He bent down to pick up one of the larger pieces of the piano. He slung it over one shoulder like it was nothing. The sight set off a flutter in Scarlett's chest that she very much did *not* appreciate.

"You know, I'm not sure I understand this new Nate Williams," she said to him playfully. "Whatever happened to the ninety-eight-pound weakling who used to help me with my algebra homework?"

"Who used to *do* your algebra homework, you mean." He picked up a *second* plank of the piano to carry in his free hand. This was really getting ridiculous. "Wait here, I'm going to take these pieces down to the basement for safekeeping. I'm sure I can turn them into something useful—end tables or something. And I'll grab you a broom—you can start sweeping up the small pieces."

Nate turned to carry the piano rubble downstairs, unintentionally providing Scarlett with a view of his back, which was every bit as enticing as his front.

"Oh for crying out loud . . ." she muttered.

"What's that?" he called back.

"Nothing! Nothing at all . . ." Scarlett crossed her arms over

23

her chest and rocked back and forth on her heels. "Go on, go grab a broom for the witch . . . that's *so* original."

***

Nate brought the broom and a dustpan, and Scarlett set about tidying the floor while he made a pile of the remaining salvageable pieces.

"So, Nate," she said as casually as she could. "What are you doing here, anyway?"

"I help your mom out sometimes, no big deal."

"No, not here. I mean in Oak Haven. Didn't you want out of this town even more than I did? Whatever happened to *Mr. Get out of Dodge?*"

"Dunno, Scar. Whatever happened to *Ms. Stay Home Forever?*"

"Ouch." Scarlett took a step back, stung. "You know exactly what happened."

"You're right." Nate paused, then spoke more gently. "Shouldn't joke about all that."

They worked in silence for a while, awkwardness hanging over them like an indoor rain cloud. They were both relieved when Luna returned, brushing some remaining gourd guts off her dress.

"All done," she chirped.

"That quick?" Scarlett gazed at the appalling piano mess all over the floor.

Luna held the front door open so the other two could see her handiwork. She'd transformed all the smashed gourds into pumpkins and neatly lined them along the walkway. "You can't really see from here," she explained, "but if you go outside, you'll see they're all carved with the faces of famous topiarists."

With that, Luna went skipping into the dining room, no further questions permitted.

Scarlett and Nate were left staring. "Can you name a single famous topiarist?" she asked.

"I'm not sure I know what a topiarist is," Nate replied.

"Someone who designs ornamental plants—you know, topiaries?" Scarlett smiled slyly. "I mean, duh."

"Ohhhh," Nate said with a laugh. "A *topiarist*, why didn't I think of that? Well sure, of course there's tons of famous ones, there's . . . um . . . nah. Kidding. I have no clue."

"Some guy at Windsor Castle? Probably?"

Nate chuckled and went back to lumber stacking. "How's San Francisco these days? You guys have got, what . . . Alcatraz, Google, and terrible weather. Is that about the size of it?"

She grinned. "Perfect description—you've really nailed it."

"What's that saying? The coldest winter I ever knew was the summer I spent in San Francisco?"

"Yeah yeah yeah. Whoever said that was full of it." Scarlett emptied the dustpan into the trash and knelt down on the floor to gather up the escaped piano keys. "Seriously, I love it there. Lots of interesting people, great restaurants, very lively."

"By interesting people, you mean interesting witches?"

"No, not at all! I mean, I'm sure there are covens around; I just don't participate. Nope, I live a completely normal life. I work in an office, I bike everywhere, buy groceries, binge Netflix, sleep seven hours, and start over again."

Nate made a face. "Seriously? You *like* living like that?"

"I happen to *love* living like that!" But as soon as the words came out of her mouth, Scarlett knew she'd oversold it. "I mean, it's cool. It's good."

25

"Sounds horrible."

"I'm sorry, who are you again?" She stood up, ebony-and-ivory-filled hands on her hips. "So far as I know, you haven't left this town even once in your whole life, but you're going to stand there judging me? Like you know me or something?"

"I used to know you pretty well, Scar."

"You haven't seen me in ten years, *Nate*."

"Whose fault is that?"

Scarlett boggled at this. "Um, *both* of ours? I mean, who was it who couldn't wait to leave Oak Haven? *Deny thy father and refuse thy name*—that was supposed to be you, wasn't it? Who covered the walls of his bedroom with maps? Who had lists of every roadside attraction he was going to visit? Have you scratched the World's Largest Ball of Twine off your bucket list yet?"

"All right, fine." Nate raised his hands in surrender. "I haven't seen you for ten years—I'm not kicking things off with an argument. Let me finish up here and you go have dinner with your family. After all, *they* haven't seen you in a decade either."

Scarlett's eyes widened. "Wow, that was a shot! Somebody's been spending too much time with Delilah."

"Well, Delilah's been *here*, so yeah. I tend to spend time with people *who are here*."

"Fine, be like that." Scarlett stepped back, her arms raised in surrender. "Maybe consider whether this embittered Bette Davis routine of yours really matches with the whole Captain America look you're going for. But, you do you." She marched off toward the dining room.

Alone in the lobby, Nate gazed down at his neatly piled piano wreckage. "Huh," he muttered. "Me? Captain America?"

Chapter 4
Royale with Cheese

Scarlett paused at the threshold between lobby and dining room, realizing too late that she was about to go from dealing with Nate to dealing with her mother. Very much a "frying pan to fire" sort of situation.

Oh well, she thought. *I'm in it now . . .*

It was dinner time, and the Stargazer Inn should've been bustling with activity. After all, the inn wasn't just the best place in Oak Haven to stay, it was also the best place to dine. But instead, tonight an eerie silence hung in the air.

The fire in the massive stone fireplace crackled and spat, but there was no one for it to warm. The cheerful buttercup yellow of the wainscoting and countryside wallpaper felt cruelly out of place. Crisp white linens, vintage china, and gleaming cutlery sat untouched, patiently awaiting guests who never arrived.

"Zahir," Scarlett whispered to the chef. "Where is everybody?"

"I don't want to talk about it. Everyone, sit! Allow me to present the food."

The women sat down, instinctively arranging themselves in the same spots they'd occupied at every meal since the girls were out of high chairs: Mama at the far end, Delilah to her right, and Scarlett and Luna side by side on her left. The seat at the head of the table remained empty—that was Papa's chair and it would never be filled again. Scarlett angled her body toward her sister, away from Papa's chair; she knew wouldn't be able to swallow a single bite if she could see it.

"Tonight," Zahir announced, "I have prepared an autumnal feast for you all. Here we have pan-seared lobster medallions with a lemon-herb sauce, pumpkin gnocchi in sage brown butter, maple-glazed butternut squash, and a roasted vegetable medley with brussels sprouts, carrots, and parsnips. And for the prodigals, two special dishes to celebrate their return. For Luna, to honor her world travels, I offer Miso Lamb Empanadas with Harissa Yogurt and Tamarind Sauce—combining flavors from her recent addresses in Turkey, Japan, and Chile."

"Oh, Zahir!" She seemed touched and even a little misty. "Thank you."

"Welcome home. And for *that* one—" he pointed at Scarlett "—I have created what I call the Scarlett Special: a school of pan-seared sardines on a bed of couscous."

"Sounds great but, um." Scarlett frowned at her old friend. "Why is that a Scarlett Special, exactly?"

"Obviously, it is a reference to your most famous childhood exploit. You, diving off the covered bridge? Turning yourself into a school of fish on the way down?"

"That's so funny," she said, smiling. "I was just remembering that on the drive over here."

"Well, your notoriety has not diminished all these years later," Zahir replied. "Oh, by the way, the couscous represents the rocky bed of the river where you nearly cracked open your tiny fishy heads. Ladies, enjoy. Bon appétit!" He pushed the cart back through the dining room and into the kitchen.

"Well, Luna," Scarlett said amiably, "I guess I'll have to ask you to pass the sardines. I'm not really a fan, but if this dish is named after me, I can't refuse."

Luna put a single sardine on her plate—mostly out of solidarity—and passed it along. "I remember when you did that spell! We were all daring each other to jump off the bridge, but it was forbidden because the water was so shallow? Of course we all talked endlessly about doing it anyhow. The boys would brag that they'd be the first ones to jump. But inevitably we'd get up to the bridge and realize that it *did* look pretty shallow and the rocks *did* look pretty sharp . . . and we'd all chicken out. And then you suddenly said, 'Hang on! It's not too shallow if you're fish.' And over you went."

"Oh, that scared me." Delilah shuddered. "I thought you'd said, if you're *a* fish, not fish as a collective. I was picturing you turning yourself into a whale and beaching yourself on the riverbed."

"No, no, no," Scarlett said with a laugh. "Just teeny fishies!"

Mama put down her fork. "It's not funny."

"Mama, it was, what, about a dozen years ago? Seems like it all worked out."

"Worked out," Mama repeated archly. "Better to say you got away with it. If even one of those *teeny fishies* had swum away, rather than returning to join the others? If *just one* went off on its own? You would have been unable to reassemble yourself. You'd have been trapped in that state forever. You took a terrible risk that day, Scarlett. And why? To impress your friends? It was reckless and very selfish, if you ask me."

Scarlett glanced at her sisters, both of whom had eyebrows raised as if to say, *now you've done it*. She turned sheepishly to her mother. "I take it that's a no from you on the sardines then?"

Suddenly the lights flickered, and the room was transformed into Jack Rabbit Slim's from *Pulp Fiction*—a 1950s-style Hollywood diner in which the waitstaff dressed as dead celebrities. A waiter costumed as Buddy Holly stood at their table, impatiently demanding, "Who ordered the five-dollar shake?"

The lights flickered again and everything returned to normal—the quiet dining room restored to its usual self.

"Oh yeah, so . . ." Delilah said blandly. "*That's* happening."

At first glance the Stargazer dining room was a typical New England space in every way. But thanks to witchcraft, the room could be easily transformed into any type of venue a situation might require. Delilah told Scarlett that recently the dining room had served as a medieval jousting tournament for Mel Barnes's retirement party, a private Taylor Swift concert for the Friedman bat mitzvah, a red-and-gold festooned dining hall for the Chatterjee wedding, and the set of *Pulp Fiction* for the fortieth birthday of a visiting film buff. Anything was possible for the dining room—except, it seemed, remaining stable for a dependable length of time.

Delilah explained, "It keeps glitching. Any element of any venue we've created in the past has started showing up at random."

"Sounds . . . kind of exciting?" Scarlett suggested.

"Definitely not," her sister said grimly. "So there's that. Plus as you noticed there's no gourds downtown. The annual Gourd Materialization Festival was an utter catastrophe—everything they conjured immediately exploded. Gourd guts everywhere. And as you've probably noticed the lobby doesn't smell right— instead of our Cozy New England Inn scent, sometimes we get a whiff reminiscent of Office Supply Store, or Times Square After New Years, or Gerontology Wing of Local Hospital—that one's *super* charming."

"Sounds like, as the kids say, *our shit is fucked.*"

"*Language*, Scarlett," Mama said. She served some of the lobster medallions to herself and Luna. "We're having the occasional challenge with magic, is all."

"*Occasional challenge* doesn't begin to cover it," scoffed Delilah. "Scarlett, you saw the road work just outside of town. These massive potholes appeared, right? No big deal—the witches on the Road Spellwork Committee headed out to do the repairs. But the next morning, the holes were back. So they went out again, did the spell again, but the holes returned, even bigger. Next day, same thing. They finally had to call the county and ask for help. Not in hundreds of years has Oak Haven asked for help from the *county*. They didn't even remember we were here!"

"You are overdramatizing," Mama protested.

"Any suspects?" asked Luna. "What does the council say?"

"Everyone's confused. And panic is setting in. Magic has been bumpy for a few weeks now. Some ladies aren't even doing spells anymore. Did you notice the absence of magic downtown, Scarlett? How it's all sort of *average-looking* now? That's because some witches are afraid to cast anything." Delilah helped herself to some of Luna's honorary lamb dish. "Poor Polly—you remember her, right? She took over Spellbound Books when her mom retired. She's had terrible problems. She arrived one morning to find every book in the shop had been rewritten in

Mandarin. And I haven't even told you the worst thing that's happened. Last month, Zahir prepared one of his famous brunches—crepes, shakshuka, bagels with smoked salmon and caviar, honey cakes, and so on. Half of Oak Haven was here, lined up out the door, all of them drooling. But everything came out of the kitchen tasting exactly like Spam. Every single dish, from the cappuccinos to the coffee cake. *Everything*—no matter what Zahir did—everything tasted of Spam."

"Spam, spam, spam, spam . . ." Scarlett sang. "Spam spaaaaam spam . . ."

"It's not a joke!" Delilah exclaimed. "Zahir doesn't have powers—he did all that work by hand. And everything was ruined! That's why nobody comes to the restaurant anymore. He puts his whole soul into his food. Failing like that in front of the whole town? It broke him. He's a broken man. He hardly cooks these days—he only did this tonight because he was so happy to have the two of you back. These days it's Happy Panda takeout around here."

"Dear Lord, would you stop exaggerating, Delilah." Mama leaned forward in her seat. "Listen to me. You three are direct descendants of the founding mother of Oak Haven. Ever since, the Melroses have been one of the leading families of this town. Over and over again, Oak Haven has looked to us in times of trouble. It is essential that we all keep a brave face. If the three of you start running around with your hair on fire, you'll cause a panic."

Scarlett put down her fork. "I hate to even ask this, but . . . is it the trees again?"

"Of course it's the damn trees," Delilah said, while Mama said: "We don't know anything yet," at the same time.

On a small hill overlooking the town of Oak Haven sat a grove of ancient oak trees. Goodwife Virginia Melrose and the other town founders had chosen the site for their new settlement, specifically because of the enormous power of the oaks, which were easily a hundred years old even then. Over the centuries, that power had only grown along with the trees themselves—their thick, gnarled branches reaching upward and outward and even down, growing deep into the earth and then swooping back up toward the sun.

Ten years earlier, the trees had been poisoned, setting off a chain of catastrophes that ended with the death of Edward Melrose, the girls' father.

"This is exactly how everything started last time," Delilah said. "Remember? It was a few off-kilter spells at first, nothing serious—nothing to worry about, everyone said. But then more spells went wrong, then more, and then . . . Well, you all know what happened after that."

"You really think *we* should try to fix it?" Scarlett asked skeptically. "Last time we got involved—" She stopped herself before finishing the sentence. But all the women's eyes instinctively flicked toward the empty chair at their table.

"That was an accident," Mama said firmly. "It was not your fault, and you shouldn't blame yourselves."

"How can we not?" exclaimed Scarlett. "We were right there when—"

"Uh, sorry to interrupt." Nate leaned in the dining room entryway. "Lobby is all cleaned up. I'm gonna head home." He had removed his flannel and stood there in just his T-shirt. Scarlett thought she was being subtle in the way she snuck a glance at his exposed, muscle-bound arms . . . but then Luna reached over to push her chin upward to close her hanging jaw.

Mama turned to him and said, "Nate, won't you join us? Look at all this food—we'll never make a dent. We need your help."

Nate glanced at Scarlett and their eyes locked. But if Nate was looking for some kind of response, he wouldn't be getting one. Scarlett couldn't even breathe, much less speak.

The silence, although brief, was excruciatingly loud.

"Actually . . ." Nate broke eye contact, gazing down at his work boots instead. "I'm gonna let you folks catch up, have a little family time. I'll stop by tomorrow, Mrs. Melrose."

"As I keep saying," Mama called after him, "it's Kelly, Nate. You can call me Kelly!"

"I definitely can't, Mrs. Melrose," he hollered back.

After the front door closed behind him, Luna elbowed her sister in the ribs. "Scar! Why didn't you make him stay?! He clearly wanted your approval."

"I . . . uh." Scarlett shook her head like a puppy just out of the bath. "I don't know, I mean . . . He was rude to me earlier."

"Oh don't be childish," said Mama. "I'm sure that's not true."

"It is true! And, also, it's weird to see him again. My brain froze, I guess."

Delilah made a loud retching sound. "Somebody pass the wine."

Mama chuckled. "I confess, I'm relieved it's just us for tonight. Nate's right—we should get to know each other again." She reached for another serving of tagine. "So, Scarlett, tell us about your glamorous life in San Francisco. What have you been up to?"

"Yeah." Delilah drained the wine bottle into her glass. "What has kept you so busy that you haven't been home in ten years?"

"Now, Delilah . . ." Mama said warningly.

"Okay . . ." Scarlett began, "I work in brand management. My title is senior SEO analyst."

"*Senior*!" Luna exclaimed. "That sounds impressive. What does a senior SEO analyst do exactly?"

"It's a bit tricky to explain . . . Let's say, just as an example, that you wanted to advertise the inn online."

Delilah gasped. "We would never!"

"Of course not. It's just an—"

"Witches don't internet."

"I know that. I'm trying to—"

"The internet is full of so-called *wiccans*," Delilah muttered. "Sharing so-called spells on so-called FaceSpace."

"It's *not* called FaceSpace, and—"

"Amateurs who can't tell a pentagram from a pentacle."

Scarlett went to take a restorative sip of wine, only to see her wineglass glitch into a chalice of mead. "You know what," she sighed. "Never mind. I work in an office, Mama, doing office-y things." The glitch happened again and Scarlett's wine returned.

"*Delilah*." Mama frowned. "Let your sister finish. Go ahead, Scarlett. Let's say we wanted to internet the inn."

"Um . . ." Scarlett started to correct her but let it go. "Sure. My point is, if you had a website, it would be my job as SEO analyst to—"

"Senior analyst," corrected Luna proudly.

"*Senior*. Thanks, Luna. It would be my job to ensure that our inn would be the most visible one in the search results."

"Like a notoriety spell?" asked Luna. "To increase fame?"

"No," said Scarlett, her patience waning. "Bits of computer

35

code called spiders catalog all the sites on the internet, and it's my job to maximize the site's appeal to the spiders."

Luna clapped excitedly. "Oooh, insectomancy! I studied with a coven in Penguin who did amazing spellwork with weaver ants."

"Nope, that's not at all what—"

"I have a cape they made me, actually. An army of tiny seamstresses."

"There's no spellwork!" exclaimed Scarlett. "It's just good-old-fashioned, *non-magical work* work."

"Oh, my dear Luna," snarked Delilah, "you must realize that our sister doesn't think witches do *actual* work. Only non-magical work qualifies as work."

"Nooo," Scarlett groaned, "that's not what I meant."

Buddy Holly appeared at the table out of nowhere, demanding, "Do you want the goddamn five-dollar shake or not?!"

Scarlett put her head in her hands. "Oh my God, what a madhouse."

Mama sighed. "Let's have some more wine."

Chapter 5
The Golden Hour of Our Discontent

After dinner, Luna suggested they take a stroll around downtown—stretch their legs, maybe find dessert somewhere. Scarlett eagerly agreed; she was one part eager to get a look at Oak Haven, and three parts eager to get away from the stifling glare of her mother.

The setting sun cast long shadows across Oak Haven's cobblestone streets as the three sisters embarked on their outing. Now and then, a crisp breeze sent showers of crimson and gold leaves swirling all around them. Scarlett was happy to find that the town's scented air wasn't *completely* lost—now and again she picked up the familiar hints of cinnamon, apple cider, and woodsmoke. On Main Street, tiny lights twinkled merrily across all the doorways, casting a warm glow all around. Every shop window was a miniature fall-themed wonderland—yes, the gourds were noticeably absent, but in their place were charmingly costumed scarecrows, standing guard amidst colorful displays of Indian corn.

"Isn't it glorious?" Luna twirled beneath a canopy of amber leaves. "Autumn is the most magical time in Oak Haven. I always feel terrible when I can't get back for a visit this time of year."

"Agreed," Scarlett said. "It's like a storybook." She had missed this place terribly. The familiar sights and sounds of her hometown, the energy that pulsed through the air. She had sorely missed her sisters, too.

"The place looks like crap." Delilah could always be relied upon for a bracing dose of reality. "It's not even close to normal. The magic isn't working correctly and if you two weren't blinded by nostalgia, you'd see the signs everywhere. The bar is so low, a muggle could stumble over it."

"We haven't forgotten, Del," Luna said soothingly. "We're just trying to appreciate what's in front of us, is all."

Maybe Delilah is right, maybe I have set my standards to "muggle," Scarlett thought. But the autumnal vibe tugged at her heart regardless.

As they passed the bakery, Knead for Magic, the aromas of cider donuts and powdered sugar were overwhelming . . . and irresistible.

"C'mon!" Luna grabbed her sisters by the arm and dragged them to the door. "Dessert time!"

Delilah groaned. "How can you eat, after that meal we just had?"

"Always room for a sweet treat, Del. Come on."

"No." Delilah stomped her foot. "No, we're not going in. I absolutely forbid it."

***

Five minutes later, the sisters emerged from the bakery with three coffees and a bag of pumpkin beignets.

"I have visited so many places," Luna said, still chewing. "And I have never found anything like this."

"Come on," said Delilah, "let's head for the green."

As they walked, Scarlett asked Luna about all those places she'd visited. "Couldn't help noticing that I got the full Kelly Melrose interrogation about my job over dinner, and you got off scot-free. So tell us, world traveler and scholar of magic, what have you seen?"

"Oh, where to even begin . . ." she said wistfully. "It's so inspiring to see how many different magic systems there are in the world. No community is the same as any other. I spent time with a coven whose magic was based on intricate finger and hand positions, like a secret sign language. I studied a whole other magic system that's incantation-based, and the spells require these amazing concoctions of herbs. Totally different from Oak Haven where our magic is innate—it can't be taught, only channeled. We use our thoughts to focus the power of the oaks. It's all based on intent and concentration."

"Exactly." Delilah added, "That's why Scarlett is so bad at it."

"Haaaaaa ha ha, up yours." But Scarlett couldn't be mad. *She's right. I've always been lousy at the focus part. That's precisely why everything went so wrong back then.*

"You're not bad at it, Scar," Luna argued. "You probably just need to meditate more. Or try yoga, I don't know. Anyway, there are *so many* magic systems—you'd never believe it. I've visited places that derive all their power from the community's ancestors. Or take the Azores—their magic is derived from the water that's all around them. There's even a magical community in England centered around children with magic wands."

Delilah groaned loudly. "How can I forget? Those kids stayed at the inn one time—they were here on some kind of wizard-school field trip? It's a pointing-and-shouting school of magic. They're *very loud*."

"I don't get it," said Scarlett. "You keep saying 'kids,' but you mean girls, right?"

"No, there were boys, too. In fact, the boys were the loudest."

"But boys can't do magic."

"No, *boys in Oak Haven* can't do magic," Luna corrected. "Our system is matrilineal, but that doesn't mean all of them are."

"Yeesh." Scarlett wrinkled her nose. "Boys with magic. I assume it's mostly penis-enlargement spells."

Delilah high-fived her sister.

Luna shrugged. "It's not so odd, really. Think of Maximillian, the guest at the inn."

Scarlett and Delilah laughed heartily. "He's a *magician*," Delilah said disdainfully. "Magicians do *tricks*, not real magic."

"Exactly," Scarlett agreed. "Rabbits out of hats, ladies sawed in half, that sort of thing."

"Yes," Luna admitted. "*Some* magicians are pure theater. But not all of them."

"Come on, Lulu, be serious . . ."

Luna smiled patiently. "I'm telling you. The more I travel, and the more I learn about magic? The more I realize how little we actually understand."

Nearing the town green, the sisters passed Spellbound Books. In the window was a display of autumn-themed novels: *Breakfast at Tiffany's, Jane Eyre, Haunting of Hill House* . . . and of course, the always controversial *The Witches of Eastwick*.

"Honestly!" Delilah shook her head in annoyance. "I don't know why Polly insists on putting that one in the window."

Scarlett chuckled. "How many Oak Haven book groups do

you reckon have fallen apart in bitter arguments about *Witches of Eastwick*?"

"It's an absolutely disgraceful book!" Delilah exclaimed. "The witches give someone cancer in that book. We would never do that."

"True, *we* would never do that," Luna said carefully. "But who's to say some other witches wouldn't?"

Scarlett smiled. "That's kinda what fiction's all about, Del."

"Well, you say *tomato*, I say *despicable*." Delilah stomped away from the window.

Scarlett and Luna wiggled their eyebrows at each other. Luna threw her arm over her sister's shoulder, and they followed Delilah toward the town green.

***

On the green, a group of children were playing tag in and around the gazebo; their joyous shrieks echoed through the twilight. For a moment, the sisters paused to watch the kids at play. A pang of nostalgia tugged at Scarlett as she remembered being that age. She and her sisters had been inseparable. Full of boundless energy, they spent their days concocting potions in the woods and casting spells on unsuspecting butterflies. Back then, magic had seemed so simple—a source of wonder and amusement, a delicious secret binding them together.

We had no clue back then, Scarlett thought now. *We had no idea just how wrong it could go.*

Delilah broke their reverie. "We should visit the old woman."

"Ughhh," Scarlett moaned. "Come on. No, we shouldn't."

"It's a good idea, Scar." Luna wrapped one arm around each of her sisters. "We should remind ourselves what we're here for."

Opposite the gazebo stood the imposing statue of Oak Haven's founding mother, Goodwife Virginia Melrose. Cast in weathered bronze, the figure depicted a woman in flowing robes, with one hand outstretched as if casting a spell. Her expression was resolute, her gaze fixed on the horizon. The statue stood in testament to the unwavering determination that led to the founding of Oak Haven in 1682.

For Scarlett, the statue evoked a complex tapestry of emotions—admiration, sure, but also resentment, guilt, and a nagging, unwanted sense of responsibility.

"She looks so proud." Luna gazed up at their ancestor with a hint of awe. "A true pioneer. She led the Salem witches to freedom."

"Well, yeah," Scarlett replied, "she led the witches to freedom . . . but left the innocent women to hang. Nobody likes to remember that part. The witchfinders showed up and poof! Our ancestors disappeared into the woods. Nice for them, but not so nice for Elizabeth Howe, Susannah Martin, and all the other victims."

Her words hung heavy in the air. Their ancestors, heroic as they were in many ways, had abandoned their town—left Salem to the not-so-tender mercies of Cotton Mather and his crew of judges. It was a history they'd all had to grapple with in one way or another—a bloodstain on the otherwise valiant narrative of Oak Haven.

Luna sighed, a troubled look clouding her features. "It was complicated. It's not something I'm proud of, either. But those were desperate times. They had to make a choice."

"Well," Scarlett said, "seems to me they made a bad one."

Delilah's eyes flashed with anger. "Ohh yes, running away

from our problems is such a bad choice. Good thing *we'd* never do that. Right, Scarlett?"

Stung, Scarlett raised her hands in surrender. "Hey now! I get it. But I'm here now, aren't I?"

"*Finally*. You run off for ten years, leaving me to handle the inn on my own. *You're welcome*, by the way."

See, Scarlett thought, *this is exactly why I didn't want to be here. No amount of pumpkin beignets is worth this.*

Hoping to defuse the situation, Luna quickly offered, "You know, in the end, our ancestors did try to do the right thing. That's why Oak Haven takes in refugees, to try and make amends for having abandoned people in Salem."

"Ooh yes, *now* we're open to refugees." Delilah rolled her eyes. "That fixes absolutely everything, right?"

"Well, no," Luna admitted. "We can't change the past obviously, but the town has tried to—"

"Right, and has *Scarlett* tried? That's my point, Luna."

Scarlett sighed. "Delilah, like I said, I'm here, aren't I?"

"And the way you left Nate in the lurch, my God."

"Whoa. Don't drag Nate into this. If you're angry with me, fine—be angry with me. But you don't get to be angry on his behalf."

"Honestly, Scarlett," Delilah replied. "I don't know why you *don't* love this statue. Seems to me you live your life by the teachings of Goodwife Melrose: *When in doubt, bail.*"

"Del, come on now." Luna stepped forward, her voice soft but firm. "You're right, we shouldn't have left you to run the Stargazer all alone. I'm sorry I've been away so much and let everything here be your problem. And I'm sure Scarlett feels the same, too—don't you, Scarlett?"

Not at the moment, she thought. *At the moment I'm wishing I'd held out for two decades away instead of one.* But in the interests of peace, she just shrugged, muttering, "Yeah, of course. Sorry, Del."

Luna reached out and squeezed Delilah's hand. "We haven't been the best sisters," she admitted. With her free hand, she took Scarlett's—just like she had when they'd played Ring Around the Rosy as little girls. "But we're here now, and we're going to do whatever it takes to help you fix the magic."

Delilah's expression softened slightly, but the hurt remained. "You better."

***

Several hours later, Scarlett found herself in the childhood bedroom she'd shared with Luna. Her mother had left it untouched—a faded Panic! at the Disco poster still hung on the wall.

Flopping down on her old bed, Scarlett felt overwhelmed with longing for San Francisco. Was her apartment in Russian Hill only slightly larger than an Oak Haven closet? True. Was her rent *three times the cost* of an Oak Haven closet? Also true. But it was hers. She had her books and her plants and her favorite coffee mug with a chip in the handle. Scarlett was a grown-up in Russian Hill, living a grown-up life. One night in Oak Haven and she was a snotty teenager again. Bickering with Delilah, endlessly. Frustration with Mama, infinitely. Staring longingly at Nate and then looking away.

God, what an embarrassment I am. I've spent ten years wondering where Nate is, how he is, why he's never written me . . . then I finally get in a room with him and in five minutes we're arguing. And then he takes his shirt off and I'm drooling like some love-struck teenager. How did I devolve so far, so fast?!

Luna floated into the room in a frilly silk nightgown. She didn't literally float, of course, although she likely *could* if she wanted; her control of her powers had always been flawless. She rested gently on the bed beside Scarlett. "It will be all right, you know."

"You think? What's going on, Luna? Some spells go totally wrong, some work but then undo themselves, others just don't work at all. And that thing with Zahir's food . . . that wasn't even a spell—he doesn't use magic. It doesn't make a lick of sense how that one even happened."

"Ohhh, I know, Scar, it's a mess—I have no idea what we're going to do. But that's not what I was referring to. I meant it will be all right between you and Nate. I can feel it—this is your time, at last. I saw the way you two were looking at each other."

Scarlett made a face. "Nate? Never! He was only ever just a friend, Luna."

"Weren't you two about to go on a date, right before you left?"

"Ugh, fine. Yes we were." Scarlett sighed, not wanting to remember. "We were going to try an actual date. Which was an absurd idea, anyway—how do you suddenly start dating someone you've been friends with your whole life? It makes no sense at all. But then Papa . . . *happened* . . . and obviously we weren't going to date on the same day as his funeral. And then . . . then I realized I had to go."

"But why, though?" Luna asked. "That's what I've never understood."

Because it was my fault, Scarlett thought. *Because I'm to blame for Papa.* But when Scarlett looked into her baby sister's face, the words wouldn't come. "Because . . . sometimes you know it's time to go, and that was one of those times. Anyway, my life is in San Francisco now. I won't be sticking around Oak Haven long enough to get tangled up with Nate. No way."

"Sure, yes, of course. I'm sure you're right." Luna crossed the room and climbed into her own bed. With a snap of her fingers, the room went dark.

"Del doesn't want us to use magic," Scarlett reminded her.

"Oh bah, I can turn the lights out, surely. Sleep well, Scarlett. I'm so happy you're home with us."

"I'm happy to be with you—not sure about the *home* part."

After a long moment, Luna said, "You know, I'm just thinking . . . Perhaps I'll ask Nate out for coffee, myself."

Scarlett rolled her eyes. "Give me a break."

"But if you aren't interested, why not?"

"I know what you're doing."

"He seems lonely," Luna teased. "Sexy *and* lonely, quite a combination."

"You're not funny."

"Hmm, yes, I can picture us now, strolling down the street, arm in arm, me and my handyman . . ."

"You're a jerk, Luna."

In their quiet, dark bedroom, that treasury of all their childhood secrets, Luna giggled. "Love you too, Scar."

Chapter 6
Truth and Consequences

When Scarlett opened her eyes, the midday sun was streaming in the window and Luna's bed was already made. Scarlett hoisted herself up, rubbing her eyes. She had overslept. And there would be consequences.

"Shit."

She pulled on her fuzzy robe and wandered downstairs, hoping to find coffee. But the dining room had been cleared and all of Zahir's scrumptious breakfast offerings long put away. The only soul in the place was that magician, Maximillian the Magnificent. He sat by the window, at a table covered with books. He had a thick hardcover on his lap, and he would intently study a passage, then close his eyes. His lips would move, seemingly repeating what he'd just read. Then he'd look down at the page and begin the process again. Scarlett paused to watch him awhile. There was something hypnotic about it: read, close eyes, repeat the words; read, close eyes, repeat the words.

Zahir came bustling in from the kitchen, dropped off a gravy-smothered plate at Max's table, and headed back to his post.

Scarlett stopped him midway. "Hey," she whispered. "What's he doing?"

"No clue." Zahir sounded annoyed. "All I know is, he claims to be Canadian this morning, so he insisted I make him poutine."

"Oh yeah? If I claim to be a cop, can I get some coffee and a donut?"

"Absolutely not—I'm too busy with lunch prep. You want breakfast? Get up at breakfast time." And with that, Zahir was gone.

Since Max had paused his ritual to shovel some cheese curds down his gullet, Scarlett moseyed over to his table. "Morning, Mr. Magnificent. What's all the studying for? You taking night classes or something?"

He peered up at her with oddly cold eyes and tapped on the book he'd been reading: *Essential Facts About World War II*. "Tell me, witch: by what year had the *entirety* of Emperor Hirohito's army surrendered to the Allies?"

"Uh. Well . . . let me think . . . the war ended in 1945, right? So. Around then?"

Max made a buzzing sound. "Wrong! The *entire* army had not fully surrendered until the final soldier, Lieutenant Hiroo Onoda, gave himself up in 1974."

"Wow, impressive. You know your wars, huh?"

"I know all aboot it," said the magician, Canadianishly. "I know a whole lot of things, witch. And do you know how I know? Because we magicians? *We study*. We learn. We aren't like your kind, who sit around burning sage and waiting for the Muse to strike."

Offended, Scarlett made a face. "Sir, that's not at all how

witchcraft works. I don't know where you get your information, but we aren't just some—"

"*For example,*" he said, interrupting, "here is a fascinating tidbit that I just learned: Adolf Hitler had a nephew, William Patrick Hitler, who served in the U.S. Navy."

Scarlett couldn't help but laugh at that. "C'mon, there was a *Bill Hitler*?!"

"It's no joke, eh? He even won a medal."

Mama Melrose leaned into the dining room. "Scarlett, stop bothering our guests. I need to speak to you."

Oof, Scarlett thought. *This should be fun.* "Okay, Max, gotta go. Enjoy your studies."

"Don't you worry," said Max with a baffling degree of menace. "*I absolutely love trivia.*"

***

Behind the inn's reservation desk is a discreet door that leads to a small, low-ceilinged office—Mama's domain. Mostly the office was for bookkeeping and inn management, but it was also where she'd summon the girls for a stern talking-to when they misbehaved. Crowding the walls were framed paintings, tintypes, and photographs of many generations of Melroses. Whenever Scarlett received a summons—which was often, because of the three sisters, she was always the one misbehaving—she'd stare up at all those images and feel the weight of hundreds of years of disapproval.

She numbly followed her mother into the office now. As far as she could tell, nothing had changed in ten years. The ancestors looked just as disapproving as ever.

Mama assumed her position behind the desk, folded her

hands, and gazed at her middle daughter. "I assume you know why I've asked you here."

Scarlett sighed. This was classic Kelly Melrose: she'd wait, letting her guest squirm under her penetrating gaze, until the accused offered up a whole variety of reasons why they deserved to be in the hot seat. The worst part was, Mama rarely let the guilty party know whether or not she had confessed to the correct crime.

Scarlett sat up straight, trying to fight off the sensation of being twelve years old again. *I'm an adult now,* she reminded herself. *I am perfectly capable of having an adult conversation with my mother.* "This is about me accidentally destroying the piano, for which I apologize," she said firmly. "I suppose I'm just out of practice."

"No," her mother replied.

Scarlett tilted her head, confused. "No, it's not about the piano?"

"No, you're not out of practice."

"Of course I am. It's been ten years since I've—"

"Balderdash," said her mother. "You have been using magic whether you knew it or not."

Scarlett stared at her mother. "Absolutely not. This one time, I accidentally locked myself out of my apartment, and sure, I could have cast a spell to open the lock, but did I? No, I didn't. I sat in my hallway for four hours waiting for the locksmith."

"Oh well, congratulations—you sat in a hallway for no reason. What exactly did you prove, by doing that?"

Scarlett threw up her hands. "It's not about proving anything! You don't know everything, Mama. I'm sorry, but you don't. You haven't seen me in ten years."

"And I am to blame for that?"

"No, of course not. I'm just saying."

Mama leaned forward, a knowing look in her eye. "There are a fair number of rude people in San Francisco, right?"

"*What?!* Why are you bringing up San Francisco?"

"Just answer the question."

Scarlett rolled her eyes. "There's rude people everywhere . . . even in Oak Haven. Heck, even in this very room."

Her mother ignored the obvious attempt at provocation. "When you find yourself in a restaurant, and some moron is at the table next to you, babbling on his cellular phone about the latest start-ups, or kale futures, or whatever nonsense . . . what happens?"

"What do you even mean? Nothing happens."

"*Think*," Mama insisted, her gaze intense. "What happens, Scarlett?"

"Well . . . I guess . . . now that you mention it . . . I guess sometimes his uh, phone will . . ."

"Explode," Mama said, a note of triumph in her voice.

"God, no!"

"Melt?"

"No!" Scarlett exclaimed. "Good grief, what is wrong with you? I just mean . . . occasionally . . . the battery will die? Or the signal will drop? Or . . ." She trailed off, staring at her mother in disbelief. "You're not saying that's *me* doing it? Breaking some stranger's phone? Come on. Without trying?"

"All I can tell you is, phone-destroying spells were among the top ten most-cast spells last year."

Scarlett's eyes widened. "You know what the most-cast spells are?"

"Naturally, they are listed in the *Acta Diurna Magus*." The *Acta Diurna Magus* was an ancient witchcraft newsletter that had been in circulation since before the birth of Christ. There had been few prouder moments in the Melrose family than the day that Papa's article, "Ethics of Enchantment: Love Spells and Individual Agency" had been published in the newsletter. "Every issue contains a list of the most-cast spells, both globally and regionally. It's a way for us old ladies to keep up with what you young folks are doing. And one thing you're all doing, whether you realize it or not, is destroying the cellular phones of people who annoy you."

"But how can I be casting a spell without meaning to?"

Mama sighed, her expression softening. "Magic isn't something you do, Scarlett. It's not some hobby that you can opt to pursue or not pursue. *Magic is something you are.* You can deny it, ignore it, push it away . . . but magic is still there, alive in you. And if it isn't used? If it isn't nurtured and tended to? Well . . . like an ignored child, it's going to act out. Honestly? Given your ten years of magic repression, I'm amazed you haven't caused any significant accidents."

"No, of course not, I'd never—oh." Scarlett's mind flashed to an especially disastrous blind date about a year earlier; it began in a bowling alley and ended in an emergency room. "There might have been the occasional issue. I told myself it was a coincidence."

"Not coincidence. More like overflow. As far as my piano goes, I actually don't think it had anything to do with your lack of practice. It pains me to admit this, but I am slowly coming around to Delilah's opinion that something has gone wrong with magic."

"Delilah was always pretty sharp," Scarlett said. "You probably should have listened to her from the beginning."

"Delilah is absolutely sharp, but she is also an alarmist. Has been for some time."

"I don't see her that way."

"Oh *you don't*," Mama said, an edge in her voice. "Well, a less forgiving person than I might point out that you are hardly in a position to judge, having not spoken to her in a decade."

Scarlett took a deep breath, then exhaled. "Okay, you win, Mama."

"Funny, I don't feel like I've won anything. The truth is, Delilah has become a very pessimistic sort since her father passed. You do realize that, don't you? That *her* father died, just as much as your own father did? That you were not, in fact, the sole victim of that particular incident? And ever since, Delilah can be relied upon to find the absolute worst in every given situation. I've come to anticipate this quirk and I usually overlook it. But after Luna's failed gourd spell and your piano catastrophe, I've reconsidered . . . and I now fear Delilah is correct. And *this* is why I've asked you here." She ripped a page off a nearby notepad and slid it across the desk. "If magic is currently fragile, we must take steps to secure the inn and the safety of our guests. Thus, I need you to run an errand for me. Fetch these items from Williams Hardware."

Scarlett's heart sank. Late morning or not, it was far too early to deal with the hardware store. And on no coffee, no less. "Mama, please don't send me to Williams. You know I don't want to go over there right now. Send Del or Luna."

"Delilah and Luna awoke at a proper hour, enjoyed a proper breakfast, and went into town. Who knows, perhaps you'll run into them, *outside the hardware store*."

"But, Mama, that's not fair."

"Fair?! My child, I have seen a spell turn rain to sun. I have seen a spell turn old to young. But never have I seen a spell to turn the world to fair."

Scarlett sighed. *Well, there is a part of Oak Haven I haven't missed—my mother's aphorisms.* "Mama, come on . . ."

"*Now*, child." Mama pointed at the list like a threat.

Resigning herself to the inevitable, Scarlett accepted the shopping list. She stood up, stomped out of the office, and clambered up the stairs to get dressed. *I can't believe she's making me go to the hardware store with no shower and no coffee.*

But deep down, Scarlett knew: the consequence of oversleeping had arrived at last.

Because Nate runs the hardware store.

Chapter 7
Earl Thirteen

The story of Williams Hardware began some three hundred years ago and fifteen hundred miles away, with the pirate known as the Great Sea Wolf, Earl of Anglia, the Terror of Tortuga. Captured by the British Navy around 1700, the Great Sea Wolf managed a spectacular escape from his own execution, diving off the dock before he could be hanged. He was spared a briny demise due to the lucky arrival of a whaling ship, which was seeking out fresh hunting opportunities around Costa Rica. Alas, the ex-pirate's whaling career was cut short due to an unspecified role in a mutiny. He found himself a hunted man yet again. But the Great Sea Wolf got lucky a second time outside a tavern in New Bedford, where he met a witch, one Miss Sarah Williams of Oak Haven. Sarah Williams promptly tamed and then married the scurvy dog, bringing him home to begin their happily ever after in her hometown.

But, as the story goes, keeping an ex-pirate occupied proved a trickier job than Sarah had anticipated. That's when she realized that the witches of Oak Haven were sorely in need of a centralized place to store their magical supplies. Meanwhile, the husbands of Oak Haven were in need of projects to keep them busy around the house. And so it was that the Great Sea Wolf, Earl of Anglia, Terror of Tortuga, was transformed yet again— this time into Earl Williams, shopkeeper. Ever since, Williams Hardware had served the needs of DIY-ers, tradesmen, *and* the local witch community.

In the three hundred years that followed, the Williams family produced a long line of sons, all of them named Earl. To a man, the Earls were stalwart, honest . . . and mischievous, because pirate ways die hard. They also share the trait of exceptional longevity, due to marrying good-hearted witches who'd been disinclined to let them go. Currently there were five surviving Earls in Oak Haven. Earl Nine (age one hundred and twenty-one), Ten (age ninety-seven), and Eleven (age seventy-nine) spent their days in rocking chairs on the front porch of their family hardware store. Their primary occupations were coffee consumption, whittling, and arguing over the weather forecast—but they did manage a healthy sideline in the provision of unsolicited advice to passersby. Twelve, meanwhile, was a sprightly fifty-six and wouldn't be caught dead rocking the days away with those relics . . . not yet, anyway.

Then there was Thirteen. Earl Thirteen had proved himself to be the most rebellious Earl since the original. Years ago, the young scalawag caused an epic scandal in town when he rejected his birth name and insisted on choosing his own.

And the name he chose was Nate.

"What can we do?" Nine had said with a sigh. "Thirteen wants to be his own man. Truth be told, I understand where he's coming from. Me, I wish I'd been named Herman."

"Oh, Dad, you do not," scoffed Ten. "What nonsense."

Nate may have rejected his birth name, but he carried on the tradition of managing the family hardware store. And thanks to him, Williams Hardware remained an essential locale, both for all the witches who needed supplies and for all the Oak Haven husbands who simply needed an excuse to get out of the house.

A joyful shout emitted from the rocking chairs when Scarlett approached.

"Look who it is, Granddad!" said Eleven happily.

Nine pulled on his glasses to peer at the grown-up woman in front of him. "That's not our Scarlett, is it?"

"It can't be," said Ten slyly. "She was a tiny thing just yesterday."

Scarlett smiled. "It's me!"

The Earls hugged her and kissed her on the cheek and quizzed her on life outside Oak Haven, with many hints—both subtle and not-so—that it was well past time for her to return home and stay put. For a moment, Scarlett began to wonder if the Earls would ever let her leave . . . but their coffee cups soon emptied, and suddenly Nine declared, "Honey, go ask Nate for a refill, would you? Save me the trip."

"Of course, sir," she said. "I wouldn't want someone as frail as you exerting yourself."

"You watch yourself, miss," he said with a grin.

"I'm just teasing. You don't look a day over one hundred and five and you know it."

"Exactly why I always say every man should marry a witch."

***

The interior of Williams Hardware was a maze of shelves and cubbies, all packed with every gadget and gizmo that Oak Haven's DIY'ers might desire. A paint mixer and a key copier sat behind the counter, next to a sign featuring a magic wand in a red circle with a slash, and the words "NO SPELLS." Another sign with an arrow declared that lumber and gardening supplies were available out back. But what Scarlett didn't see, as she scanned the shelves, were the magical items required by her mother.

Oh no, she thought. *Has Williams gone normie too?*

"Hey there," said a voice behind her.

It was Nate. He'd cleaned up beautifully since she saw him last, and he wore a burgundy flannel shirt that complemented his dark brown eyes just perfectly and somehow made Scarlett want to throw up or cry or both.

"Can I help you with something?"

"Um." It took Scarlett a moment to remember what she was doing in Williams Hardware in the first place. "Oh! The Earls want more coffee."

"Aw, for crying out loud . . ." Nate sighed. "I keep telling them: 'Guys! This is not a diner. When I open a diner, you'll be the first to know.'"

"Also . . ." Scarlett gestured vaguely with her mother's shopping list. "Mama sent me for a few things. But, um, I don't see—"

"I moved all the magic supplies to the back room."

"Really? You treat magic like the adult section of a video store?"

"Had I ever been in a video store, I might get that reference. Basically I didn't want to risk selling some kind of powerful potion to a tourist. Easier to just keep it all out of their eyeline."

"Do tourists ever ask you about that NO SPELLS sign?"

He shrugged. "I tell them it refers to fainting spells."

"Really," Scarlett said with a laugh. "Do they buy that?"

"Do you think I care? Listen, I'm going to go refill the Earls." He moved toward the counter, where an archaic coffee maker sat beside the key-copying machine. "You can head on back; grab whatever you need."

Behind a door marked PRIVATE sat the second mission of Williams Hardware, beyond keeping husbands occupied: magical supplies. Scarlett grabbed one of the shopping baskets by the door and set about satisfying her mother's demands.

She began with the bulk herbs, which were collected in large barrels in the center of the room. The array of herbs lent the back room an indescribably funky smell that Scarlett couldn't decide if she loved or hated. Checking her mother's list, she helped herself to some dried sage, rosemary, and mugwort, plus rowan tree berries and dragon thorns, and something called iron thistle, which Scarlett had never even heard of but there it was, glinting away in its own barrel beside more typical thistles of the marsh and field.

Next Scarlett selected a number of rune candles, a satchel of obsidian dust, and a small box of shattered mirrors. Then she moved on to the shelves packed with little glass bottles: bottles of wishes, bottles of distilled emotion, even bottles of quietude, each gathered from a uniquely silent place.

As she shopped, Scarlett couldn't help remembering what Luna had said last night—about Nate, and how this was their time. On the one hand, it was an absurd idea. If anything was ever going to happen between them, it would've happened back when they were teenagers. She'd spent a decade building her life on the West Coast. It was too late for any nonsense here in Oak Haven. And not for nothing, but if their interaction yesterday was any indicator, they weren't capable of being in the same room without picking at each other.

On the other hand, he did look ridiculously good in burgundy . . .

The door opened and Nate poked his head in. "Need help finding anything?"

"Oh!" she said, startled. Nate had become a professional startler, so it seemed. "Umm . . ." She scanned her list to make sure she didn't miss anything. "I think I'm doing all right, actually."

"Do you need anything for plant magic?" Nate asked. "What do you ladies call it, horti-something?"

"Hortikinesis."

"Right. The last time magic went off, it was a problem with the oak trees, wasn't it?"

"It was, but . . ." Scarlett shrugged. "Nothing hortikinetical on my list. I'll tell you what, though: I sure hope it's *not* the trees this time. Fixing the trees was . . ." She sighed. "Fixing the trees broke everything else."

"Yeah, about that . . ." Nate said slowly. "I feel like I owe you an apology."

"You do?"

"Yesterday, you know . . . I hadn't seen you in ten years and practically the first thing out of my mouth was a dig about your dad, and making fun of San Francisco . . . It just . . . I don't know, I've been thinking about it, and it doesn't sit right with me, that I said that stuff."

Nate's apology sent a warmth spreading though Scarlett's chest. *No fair,* she thought, *you can't do a whole Tom-Hardy-as-lumberjack look and then be a sweetheart too.* "Aw, it's . . . it's okay. I mean . . . you're right, I *have* stayed away too long. And as for Dad, it's fine to mention him. After all, he died ten years ago."

"Yet you still blame yourself. Which is crazy, by the way."

"You know, there's nothing a gal loves more than being apologized to *and* immediately told she's crazy. Most guys do it in the other order, but . . ."

Nate flushed. "Oh man, I can't get this right at all, can I?"

"I'm sorry," she said, smiling. "I'm just teasing. And since we're apologizing . . . I'm sorry if I made you feel uncomfortable about joining us last night."

"Oh, no big deal."

"It was antisocial of me . . . I blame jet lag."

"Sure. San Francisco is a long trip."

"Yeah . . ." Scarlett looked into Nate's dark eyes, and they tricked her into saying something true. "It's a trip I was hoping you'd make. When I first got there? I'd be in a restaurant or something, and I'd suddenly think, oh, Nate would like this. But . . . I never heard from you."

"Well..." Nate hesitated. "I did think about it, I swear. But you've got to remember how risky it would be for me to leave Oak Haven. As a non-witch, I mean. I could end up with a pretty nasty case of amnesia."

"Yeah, yeah. The Forgetting Spell, I get it. Way, way too risky." She forced a laugh, hoping to play the moment off as a joke. "Funny though, how you used to talk about leaving all the time. World's largest ball of twine, right? Then we grew up and, come to find out . . . you're an Oak Haven lifer."

"Well . . ." He shrugged. "You always claimed that *you* were a lifer, and then you upped and left in the middle of the night."

"And then I sold my hair to buy you a watch chain, while you sold your watch to buy me a hair clip . . ."

"Yeah, pretty much." Nate gazed at her with a happy-sad sort of expression. "That sounds about right."

They stood together, close enough to touch, in a room full of magic. But ten long, silent years crowded in the room with them, and neither had the slightest clue what to say or do about any of it.

"Of course," Nate said finally, "if I *had* left, who would manage the care and feeding of the Earls? Who'd keep them in coffee and whittling supplies, if not me?"

"*Of course*," Scarlett repeated. "You're right—I had not considered the Earls."

"There you go."

"Won't someone please think of the Earls?"

When Nate grinned at her, Scarlett grinned back, and she suddenly realized that there were no bad feelings here, just complicated ones, and she didn't want the moment to ever end.

But then they heard the ringing of the cruel little bell on the front door.

"You have a customer," she said regretfully.

"Never stops," he replied.

"I guess I better go. Mama's waiting on all this gear. Do I pay you, or—"

"Nah, your mom's got a tab. So, uh. I'll see you. Around. I guess."

"I'll see you."

She moved to leave but Nate's voice stopped her. "Scar . . . You don't have to punish yourself, you know."

Scarlett turned back. "Punish myself, how?"

"San Francisco. Your whole *Exile on Lombard Street* thing. Living like some muggle instead of a witch? I mean, I get it, you felt responsible for your dad . . ."

"San Francisco's not a punishment."

"Working in some office? Sure sounds like self-inflicted punishment to me."

"It's great, I love my life there."

"Really?"

"My job is very—" Scarlett stopped herself. She could lie to her sisters, to her mother, she could even to herself, but somehow she couldn't bring herself to lie to him. "It's . . . occasionally . . . interesting . . . And occasionally . . . not so much. But all jobs involve a certain amount of drudgery, don't they?"

"I'm just saying, I've seen the so-called real world outside Oak Haven, and I know it's no picnic."

"Sure, but living in Oak Haven isn't always such a— Hang on one second. What do you mean, *you've* seen the so-called real world?"

Nate blanched. He looked away, seemingly at a loss to respond. "Uh. No, I just—"

"I'm sorry, are you saying you *have* left Oak Haven?" The warm and fuzzy feeling in Scarlett's chest turned cold and sharp. For years she'd been telling herself that Nate never visited her in San Francisco because the Forgetting Spell prevented him from leaving home. But apparently that wasn't the case? "So . . . you're saying you *did* take the risk."

"Well . . ."

"Just not for me."

"Scar, I—"

"Where'd you go, Nate? What were the fantastic sights you

left Oak Haven to see? Grand Canyon? Disney World, maybe? Or did you get all the way to the Golden Gate Bridge and then *not* call?"

"It wasn't remotely like that," Nate protested. "You're overreacting."

"Am I? Because what I'm hearing is that you *could* have left Oak Haven. You just *wouldn't* leave to visit me."

"No, that's not fair."

"Whatever, Nate. I have to go." She could feel tears pricking her eyes and there was no chance she'd let him see. "This room stinks to high heaven by the way—the least you could do is buy a fan." She left him standing there without looking back.

Nate sighed. "Ah shit."

Chapter 8
Sad Panda

Scarlett raced out of the store, barely managing to choke out a quick goodbye to the Earls and dash around the corner before the tears came. In the alley, she dropped her bag of supplies, crouched on the ground, and covered her face with her hands. Anger, shame, and no small amount of confusion washed over her.

I'm going to kill Luna when I get home, she thought. *All that jibber-jabber about how Nate and I should be together. I never should have let her get in my head like that.*

She took several deep breaths to compose herself.

I have no interest in Nate anyhow, she lied. *It's just as they say—I've put away childish things, and Nate was the most childish of them all. Plus there's plenty of men to date in San Francisco.*

That last bit was half true. There were, indeed, men for Scarlett to date in San Francisco. But all they could talk about was craft beer and technology stocks.

She sighed. *I probably just need coffee.*

Bending over to pick up her bag, Scarlett found herself face-to-face with a squirrel. The sight chilled her to the bone.

The squirrel was small and gray, with an unexceptionally fluffy tail. It held an acorn in its little paws. It was a skittering, chittering cliché of a squirrel.

But true Oak Haven squirrels were the size of small cats, with onyx-colored fur and majestic, almost peacock-like tails. Oak Haven squirrels traveled in packs. They were bad boys, a little risqué. Oak Haven squirrels were partial to bebop and clove cigarettes.

The most interesting aspect of Oak Haven squirrels was that no witch had created them. No spell had willed them into existence. As far as anyone could tell, the squirrels developed this way simply due to exposure to the ambient magic in the air of Oak Haven.

But now here was this horrid gray thing, this *basic bitch* of a squirrel, sitting in the alley and staring at Scarlett like *she* was the odd one.

What's happening to my town? she wondered. *This is not what I remember at all.*

Scarlett's musings were interrupted by the sharp voice of Delilah, who was standing at the edge of the alley, one hand on her hip. "You finally woke up, I see."

"Ha ha ha," Scarlett said. "Mama sent me to Williams and I had to face Nate. Thanks a lot for leaving me with *that* little assignment."

Her older sister shrugged. "Get up earlier—you'll get a better selection of chores. Come with me. I need to go talk to Polly."

Polly owned Spellbound Books, which was just across the street from where they were standing. But to Scarlett, it felt a thousand miles away. "Is there somewhere I can get a coffee? Breakfast had been put away by the time I got up, and I feel a headache coming on."

"Weren't you just at Williams Hardware?"

"Yeah?"

"Nate has the best coffee in Oak Haven."

"It's a hardware store."

"Be that as it may," Delilah replied, "Nate may have missed his calling. His coffee kicks the ass of that swill at Hexpresso Yourself."

"Well, no." Scarlett rolled her eyes. "I didn't think to get coffee *at the hardware store*."

"Let's visit Polly, maybe she has some caffeine for you."

Scarlett sighed. "God, I hope so."

***

Much like the inn, Spellbound Books had an inviting scent all its own—old paper and herbal teas, with a subtle hint of clove. But today, all of that was overwhelmed by the tang of sawdust and plaster.

Because Spellbound Books was in chaos.

The tiny shop was awash with ladders and table saws and buckets of nails. Tarps covered the shelves and the floors. A team of carpenters hurried in and out to the sounds of drilling and hammering. And in the center of the chaos stood Polly, the Melrose sisters' high-school frenemy.

Polly had been a year ahead of Delilah at school, and thus had always been well ahead of Scarlett—in academics, at witchcraft, at everything. She was the first to have a boyfriend, the school's top athlete, widely known around town as Handsome Bill. Polly was also the first to marry said boyfriend, the first to have a child. As far as Scarlett could tell, Polly had everything in hand, from her appearance to her magic, everything in place just as it should be. The other kids called her Triple P—Polly Practically Perfect. Everything went swimmingly for ole Triple P. Her life was practically perfect, all the time, always.

Until everything went to shit.

Until Handsome Bill turned cold for reasons no one could understand. Until Polly tearfully demanded a divorce. Until Handsome Bill poisoned the trees above Oak Haven and fled, never to return.

Ten years on, Scarlett was shocked to find Polly, the girl she'd envied more than any other, looking utterly discombobulated. Her face was pinched with worry, and gray hairs sprouted among the chestnut brown ringlets tumbling down her face.

"Hey, Polly . . ." Scarlett narrowly avoided colliding with a brawny gent carrying a pile of lumber. "What's going on here?"

Polly turned and gasped at the sight of the Melrose sisters. "Scarlett! Delilah! Oh, how good to see you. Is Luna here, too?"

"Not with us, but yes, she's in town."

"What a relief. We're in a state here as you can see. I hope you Melroses are ready to save us."

Scarlett and Delilah exchanged glances. "Uh, well we'll do our best."

"Have you got some coffee for Scarlett?" Del asked. "She's in a state, too."

Polly brought Scarlett and Delilah to her little back office; it was barely enough space for a desk and a couple of chairs, but at least it was quiet. Relatively quiet, anyway—the pounding of hammers and whining of drills reduced to a dull background noise.

Sitting there with her Doc Marten boots on the desk was Polly's fourteen-year-old daughter Violet. She wore oversized headphones, and her hoodie was pulled over her head as she gazed intently at her phone.

This time it was Scarlett's turn to gasp. "Is that . . ." She turned to Polly. "That can't be your little baby girl."

"That's what happens when you stay away for ten years, Scarlett. They grow."

"I see she has a phone?"

"And why not? The teens in town all have them." Polly sounded more than a little defensive. "I know it's addictive but with everything she's gone through with her dad, you could hardly expect me to say no."

"No, Polly," Scarlett said appeasingly. "I didn't mean it that way. I just meant: oh hey, we're doing cell phones in Oak Haven? Seems like the opposite of what the town is about, that's all. I mean, do you remember the arguments about allowing cable TV? My God, the way the elder witches flipped out? You'd have thought they were going to put a McDonald's in the middle of the green."

"Ughhh, Scarlett . . ." Delilah groaned. "You should have been here for the town meeting where we debated cell phones. The moment I saw a tower going up outside town, I wrote up a proposal that we create a spell to block the signal. But that would have involved the elders understanding what cell phones were in the first place."

"Oh no, I can just imagine." Scarlett chuckled. "I bet you made this whole pitch and they didn't know what the hell you were talking about."

"You heard Mama last night. *Witches don't internet.* That generation doesn't get it."

From what Scarlett recalled of last night's conversation,

Delilah wasn't exactly Steve Jobs, either. "Right," she said. "*They*, the old folks, do not get it. Unlike you, who thinks 5G is short for five grimoires."

"Well," Delilah huffed, "what *does* it mean, then?!"

To head off an argument, Polly offered, "How about I get you that coffee, Scar. Oh, Violet!" She banged on the desk to get her daughter's attention. "We have visitors. You know Delilah of course. This is her sister Scarlett. You've not seen her in a very long time."

Violet barely glanced up. "Hey."

"Hiiiiii," Scarlett said, too enthusiastically. "You were about yea high the last time we met—maybe five? Isn't that just—"

"Mom," the teen interrupted. "I ordered lo mein. I'm gonna wait for the delivery outside." Violet put her headphones back on and stalked out of the room.

Polly sighed. "That's my little charmer."

***

Huddled in the back office over coffee, Polly regaled Scarlett and Delilah with stories of her difficult past few months. The overnight translation of all the books into Mandarin was just the beginning of the trouble. No sooner had Polly gotten that sorted out than she discovered every single book had had its last chapter transposed with its first.

"Imagine opening up *Murder on the Orient Express* and the first words you see involve Poirot propounding his solutions! Or starting the *Da Vinci Code* by reading the epilogue. It was a catastrophe, an absolute catastrophe."

"Agreed," Scarlett said. "If you've started selling Dan Brown, things are way worse than I'd imagined."

"Don't be a snob," Delilah snapped. "He's very popular."

Scarlett made a face but dropped it. "Polly, any thoughts about who might be doing this to you?"

"Yeah, I can't help but notice that magic issues are at their worst in your store. Almost as if somebody was after you specifically?"

"After *me*?!" Polly Practically Perfect appeared altogether affronted. "Of course not! Spellbound is a jewel in Oak Haven's downtown. Who would try to hurt me, ever?"

"Your ex, obviously."

Polly's face turned hard. "Last I heard, Bill was on a shrimp trawler in the Gulf of Mexico. Anyway, it can't possibly be him."

"Why not?" Delilah said. "Why isn't he the prime suspect here? After all, he's the one who—"

"Because he's forgotten all about us, Delilah! That's how the spell works, isn't it? Non-witches forget all about Oak Haven. He doesn't know he married me, he doesn't know he has a daughter—imagine what that's like for Violet. You think I don't feel guilty enough, that the marriage didn't work out? Now my kid has to grow up with a father who wouldn't recognize her if she punched him in the face."

"She looks like she has a decent right hook," Scarlett said.

"Honestly? I wouldn't blame her. But it's not Bill. And I'm offended, frankly, that you seem to be accusing me of something. You can't possibly understand what it's been like. In the past weeks I've had books go entirely blank, I've had encyclopedias *disorganize* themselves out of alphabetical order. And there has been violence. One customer bought an illustrated copy of *Dracula* and the book tried to bite her while she was sleeping. Enough is enough. I'm done."

71

"Ahhhh," Scarlett said. "*That's* what all that drilling and sawing is about . . ."

"Exactly. I'm installing an entirely new magic prevention system in the store. Nate Williams has been carving the sigils that will power the spell. You remember Nate, don't you, Scarlett?"

Delilah let out a sarcastic little grunt.

"Of course," Scarlett said, trying to keep her voice neutral. "Good old Nate seems to be everywhere these days."

"Yes well." Polly's eyelashes fluttered coquettishly. "He's been wildly helpful in my time of need."

It was achingly clear to Scarlett what Polly meant by that particular remark.

She continued, "Once the prevention system is installed, there will be no more magic on the premises, period."

"Oh that seems extreme, Polly. And such a loss. I vividly remember coming to Story Hour back when we were kids. Your mom would read *Make Way for Ducklings* and actual ducklings would march around in front of us."

"Remember when she read *Pippi Longstocking*?" asked Delilah.

"Oh, that got wild." Scarlett laughed. "With the horse. Oh God, Polly, remember the horse? We can't let you give that up."

"I hate it, too," Polly said sadly. "But I don't have an option— I've been physically attacked by my own books. The David Beckham autobiography leapt off the shelf and kicked me in the head. And look at this." She rolled up the sleeve of her blouse. "Look at all the papercuts. Every time I sell something now, this happens."

There was a knock at the office door. "Excuse me, ma'am," said a male voice. "We need your input on the molding."

"Yes yes, I'm on my way . . ." Polly stood. "Scarlett. Delilah. I understand your concerns; I do. But I am just as desperate as you are to see things fixed. I don't *want* to forbid magic from this store—I just don't see any other option." She left the sisters alone in the office.

"I believe her," Scarlett said. "You?"

Delilah sighed. "I do. It's like she said, Bill has forgotten us by now. And anyway, he was too much of a nitwit for this. His big move was poisoning the oaks by hand. He couldn't pull off *vampire books*."

"So who did it then? Who is trying to sabotage us this time?"

"Not a clue." Delilah flung her arm over Scarlett's shoulder. "Let's go fetch Luna and head back to the Stargazer. I'm sure Mama's eager for whatever you got her at the store."

As they made their way out of the store, they passed young Violet, standing in the doorway. She gripped a paper bag stamped with the words HAPPY PANDA and stared out at the street as forlornly as only a fourteen-year-old girl can.

"Hey," Scarlett said to her, "you okay?"

"What do you care?" Violet snapped. She stomped away, across the street and toward the town green.

"Okaayy, 'little charmer,' indeed . . ." Scarlett glanced across the street at the hardware store; the Earls waved at her cheerfully, and she waved back.

A carpenter was nearby, rooting around in his tool bag for a replacement battery for his drill, and he laughed. "Don't mind her," he told Scarlett. "She's on her own little trip."

"Really," said Delilah. "What *trip* is that?"

"Well!" He seemed delighted to be asked about something that didn't involve molding. "That kid orders from Happy Panda every day. She stands out here, waiting for the delivery guy—of course, I say *guy* loosely. He's some pimply teenager from the next town over. And the girl is out here; she's putting on lip gloss or whatever they do these days. Fixing herself up, you know? Kid hands over the food, takes the money, gets back on the bike and leaves. She stands there just watching him go. Every day, same thing."

"Oh no." Scarlett suddenly understood. "He never remembers her. She waits here, every day, hoping today will somehow be different . . . And every day, he meets her for the first time."

Delilah shrugged, her curiosity already long gone. "It's an occupational hazard of living in Oak Haven. She should know that by now."

"I guess. Sucks, though." Scarlett glanced across the street at the hardware store. "It's hard out here for a witch."

Chapter 9
Abracadabra

On their way home, Scarlett and Delilah found Luna on the Oak Haven green. A group had gathered to watch a performance of Maximillian the Magnificent.

The town gazebo was festooned with balloons, streamers, and large handmade signs saying HAPPY BIRTHDAY NIGEL. Maximillian had turned the gazebo into a little stage, with a red velvet curtain and various magician props scattered around. Young children squirmed in the front of the crowd while their parents and more casual onlookers milled around at the back.

Scarlett and Delilah approached their sister, who had gotten herself a great view of the gazebo. "What's going on here?"

Luna grabbed Scarlett's arm without taking her eyes off Maximillian. "He's a wizard, I think!"

Delilah rolled her eyes and shook her head and sighed, all at once—the universal Big Sister expression for *I'm too old for this shit*. "Luna has been out in the wild too long—she's forgotten what magic tricks are."

"That's not a trick. *Look!*"

Maximillian reached out with an (apparently) empty hand to

pluck a coin from (apparently) thin air and drop it in a bucket. He repeated this several times before changing things up, pulling a coin from a little girl's hair, another from a little boy's shoe, and then he coughed out a third.

"It's called the Miser's Dream," Luna said approvingly.

"Yeah, I know," Scarlett said. "Anybody can learn that trick, Luna—literally anybody. The Miser's Dream is older than Earl Nine."

Delilah nodded. "And just as corny."

"Hush, both of you, you're embarrassing me."

Finding Luna at an event like this was to be expected—she'd always been intrigued by magic in any form, even "stage magic." But Luna was very much alone in her curiosity about magic. It was an article of faith among witches that stage magicians were charlatans. Witchcraft was innate—it could never be taught, only inherited. Stage magic, on the other hand, could be purchased at a joke shop or copied off YouTube videos. Witchcraft was real, went the general opinion, while stage magic was bullshit.

For that very reason, Scarlett was quite surprised to see young Violet among the audience in the park. If anyone was keen to cry "bullshit," it surely would be Polly's pissed-off kid. And yet there she was—perched on a bench, distractedly shoveling lo mein into her mouth. She didn't take her eyes off Maximillian.

Scarlett nudged Delilah. "Check out Angsty Teen over there."

"Wow," Delilah said. "I didn't know Violet was that interested in *anything* that couldn't fit inside her phone."

A pair of average grey squirrels went skittering past Violet's bench, chasing each other up the trunk of a nearby maple tree. She leaned over to whisper in Delilah's ear. "Squirrels."

Delilah understood. "They're horrible, aren't they?"

"Chilling. Do you think it's the trees?"

"That's the thing—"

Luna wheeled around. "Do you two mind?!"

Delilah rolled her eyes and guided Scarlett a few steps away. Meanwhile, Luna took a few steps in the opposite direction, hoping to make it clear she wasn't one with those grizzled cynics.

"*Anyway*," Del continued. "While you were sleeping, Luna and I visited the grove. Remember ten years ago, how sickly the trees looked?"

"Sure," Scarlett said. "They'd been poisoned."

"Right, well. Look at this." From her bag, Delilah removed a handful of oak tree leaves. They were firm, with a bright green color—darker on the top, lighter on the underside—with just a hint of autumn yellow tickling the edges. No discoloration or markings or bug bites. They were perfect.

Scarlett stared at the leaves for a moment. "The trees aren't sick."

"They don't appear to be."

"Then how do we explain the squirrels, Delilah? Or the potholes, or the failing spells. If we're not dealing with sick oak trees, then . . . what is it?"

"I don't know. But my first thought is: maybe something is indeed wrong with the trees, just not visibly. We're going back to the grove tonight. Luna's going to have a chat with them and see what they say."

"Excuse me," Scarlett said. "I'm sorry, what? Quick clarification. By *them*, you mean, Luna's going to chat with . . ."

"The oaks."

"The oaks. Right. My baby sister talks to trees. That's a completely ordinary thing for you to say."

"Apparently she studied with a coven in . . . oh nuts, where was it?" Delilah took a step toward her baby sister. "Luna," she said in a stage whisper, "where did you learn the tree-talking thing?"

"Bo-Kaap, in Cape Town," she said, never turning her eyes away from the stage. "They have baobab trees that are thousands of years old, and there's a spell where you can communicate with them. Now, will you shut up? Maximillian is about to do something interesting."

Scarlett nudged Delilah. "So she just talks to trees now."

"She's been busy. Traveling all over, learning all sorts of arcane magic."

"Oh my God . . ." Scarlett considered this. "Is *Luna* the most powerful of us now?"

"It's worse than that," Delilah said. "Mama says that Luna is the most powerful of *anyone*."

Luna turned to her sisters, her face flushed with joy. "He made a *rabbit* appear in his *hat*," she exclaimed. "A rabbit, Scarlett!"

"In his hat, Luna. I saw. Well done, Maximillian: you've mastered a feat achieved by any eighth-grade nerd with a top hat."

Delilah snickered. "Yeah, and *she's* supposedly the most powerful witch in the family—how about that."

Luna's eyes flashed. She stalked over to her sisters and said, "Now you listen to me. I have been all over the world, and I've seen all types of magic. Stage magicians are *not* entirely fake. When I was in Japan, I saw this young man do a trick with a plastic alligator and a cell phone, and I still have no idea how he did it without using genuine powers. Magicians are our cousins, and they deserve our respect." Luna turned her back and returned her full attention to the show.

Delilah rolled her eyes. "Well, she sure told us, huh." She impatiently checked her watch. "Is this thing done yet? We need to get home. Psst, hey, Luna. How much longer?"

Luna waved them off without turning around. "Go without me."

With a shrug, Delilah turned to Scarlett. "Let's go. There's something I want to show you."

***

"Look at it," Delilah said, disgusted. "Can you believe that?!"

They were standing at the corner of Main and West streets, and Delilah was pointing to the crosswalk ahead of them.

Unlike the parallel stripes seen in cities everywhere, Oak Haven crosswalks featured elaborate patterns of repeating circles, and within each circle was a complex maze.

At first glance, one might assume the intricate design was just one of those small-town quirks—like the "Garden of One Thousand Buddhas" in Arlee, Montana, or how Collinsville, Illinois, is home to the world's largest ketchup bottle. But Oak Haven's crosswalks are one piece of a massive, town-wide mosaic of enchanted sigils, elaborate carvings that generate a protective quilt of forgetfulness, keeping Oak Haven safe from the scrutiny of the outside world.

But this crosswalk had gouges all over it, like someone went at the designs with a sledgehammer.

"What the hell . . ." marveled Scarlett. "What happened to the sigils?"

"Excellent question. We're seeing this all over town."

Scarlett had heard about a lot of concerning developments in town since she'd arrived—the road work . . . the lack of gourds . . . the Spam incident. But they were small-bore, *things that make you go, huh,* types of changes. Even the squirrels, while certainly chilling, didn't feel existential. This was the first change that genuinely troubled her to her core. "Is this harming the Forgetting Spell?"

"Depends what you mean. This particular broken sigil, this *specific* one? No. The spell is cumulative. It's not just one sigil, it's thousands of separately carved— Now, hold on, wait one minute." Delilah abruptly turned an accusatory glare on her sister; Scarlett was alarmed to realize that Del had developed an expression nearly as intimidating as their mother's. The Melrose Scowl, they called it in town. Delilah had it mastered.

"What?! What's with the look? Don't give me that look."

Delilah continued giving the look. "You don't know how the Forgetting Spell works, do you? You have no idea."

"Of course I do. Don't be ridiculous. There are enchanted symbols all over Oak Haven—in sidewalks, over doorways, on moldings, in kitchen and bathroom tiles—and they cause outsiders and non-witches to forget about us."

"Yes, but *how*? How does it work, exactly? Prove to me you know how it works."

"Umm," Scarlett said. "It, uh, you know . . . works by . . . uh, making people . . . forget. Stuff."

"*Making people forget stuff.*" Delilah folded her arms across her chest, every bit the Teacher Who Isn't Angry Just Disappointed. "That's your final answer?"

"Well, what then? Jeez, I left town when I was eighteen!

Maybe I didn't learn every damn thing about this goofy place, okay? Stop being so smug and just tell me."

"The so-called Forgetting Spell doesn't make people *forget*, precisely. Instead, it interferes with the brain's ability to create new memories in the first place. All these sigils—all of these carvings all over town—are enchanted to subliminally broadcast tiny bits of useless trivia, over and over. One or two sigils would have no particular impact. But at scale? People whose brains aren't accustomed to the broadcast—meaning, anyone without magic who doesn't live here full-time—will find all their short-term memories replaced by nonsense. Maybe they suddenly know the lyrics to 'Goodbye Yellow Brick Road' but can't recall what they had for dinner. They'll remember that Chester Arthur was America's twenty-first president, or they'll suddenly know which film director has won the most Oscars, but somehow they *can't quite remember* that adorable little town with all the gourds."

"That's diabolical." Scarlett gazed down at the maze of circles beneath her feet. "Poorly named, though. The Forgetting Spell. Should be, like, the Hippocampus-Scrambling Trivia-Blast."

"I know," Delilah agreed. "For years I tried to get people to call it the Unremembering Spell, but that never took."

"Wait, though, I have a question: were the sigils trivia-based back in the eighteenth century, when they were first installed? Had trivia even been invented in the eighteenth century?"

"Have a listen. If you focus, you can hear the broadcasts yourself."

Scarlett knelt down in the crosswalk, laid her palm against one of the sigils, and closed her eyes. In a moment, she popped back up again, delighted. "Did you know: when Napoleon Bonaparte was in his mid-twenties, he wrote a romance novel?"

"Sure, *Clisson et Eugénie*," Delilah said, smiling. "There you go, question answered."

"Should we fix this one?" Scarlett moved to study the smashed-up part of the design.

"I've tried—there's another damaged sigil on the far side of the park. Instead of making it better, I made the damned thing disappear completely."

"Oof, because magic is acting crazy."

"Exactly," Delilah said sadly. "So I think we should leave it be. I just wanted you to see what we're up against."

Scarlett nodded grimly. She did see, and it was frightening. *Oak Haven without the Forgetting Spell. Oak Haven abruptly famous. Oak Haven on TikTok.*

She shuddered. "Let's go home."

Chapter 10
Anti-Hero

Mama unpacked the Williams bag and spread the supplies out on the counter. "Delilah." She handed her eldest a folded piece of parchment. "I'd like you to work up a protection spell for each room—this is the basic recipe. We've got a full house of light-opera fans arriving tomorrow, and I want to avoid any hiccups. Just ensure you keep the proportions of herbs correct, and you'll be fine."

"An individual spell for each room?" Delilah said, dismayed. "That's going to take hours."

"You best get started, then."

"Mama," Scarlett said carefully, "far be it from me to question you, but—"

Mama rolled her eyes. "Questioning me has never been *far* from you, Scarlett—your first word was, '*Really?*' What's your question?"

"If we're worried about spells backfiring, then . . . can't these also backfire?"

"Oh, I agree, it's an imperfect strategy, at best. But it *may* help and is certainly better than doing nothing."

"Canceling these reservations would be better, no? Just tell the Gilbert and Sullivan Society that we had to close. Why risk more Spam-related incidents or whatever?"

Delilah gathered up the spell ingredients in her arms. "Can't afford to cancel—we need the guests."

"*Afford*?! I don't want to sound like a brat but I never remember us worrying about affording anything, ever."

"Welcome to the twenty-first century, my dear," Mama said. "The power company waits for no man, or witch. Now, come Scarlett, help me with a little project in the dining room."

***

The *little project* awaiting Scarlett in the dining room was the same *little project* that had occupied her afternoons throughout childhood: assembling welcome baskets for guests.

Growing up at the inn, all three daughters had spent countless afternoons on this task, which Mama insisted be done by hand, not by magic. They'd stand around an enormous dining table, filling baskets with gourmet snacks, spellcasting supplies, bottles of wine, hangover cures . . . It made for an adorable little assembly line and, as the girls constantly pointed out, a flagrant violation of child labor laws. Somehow, their parents were never moved by that argument.

When she saw the pile of baskets waiting to be filled, the gifts waiting to be organized, the ribbons waiting to be tied . . . Scarlett sighed the bone-deep sigh of someone who'd just taken a time machine back to the least favorite moment of her childhood.

"Oh, don't fuss," Mama said. "There's only twenty to do—that's practically nothing. We'll be finished in no time."

"But . . . maybe I should go help Delilah with the protection spells?"

Mama raised an eyebrow. "You, who haven't cast a single spell in a decade, *except* for yesterday when you destroyed a piece of heirloom furniture? No, I think we'll let Delilah handle that. Grab a basket."

Scarlett and her mother worked in silence, occasionally broken by the chorus of "Cruel Summer" when the room glitched back and forth between the quaint dining room and the VIP suite of a Taylor Swift show.

"So," Mama finally said, "how was everything down at Williams? I bet the Earls were delighted to see you."

"Definitely." Scarlett focused on distributing the correct number of Zahir's tartlets into each basket. "They haven't aged a bit."

"Mmhmm . . . and how was Nate this morning?"

Scarlett mumbled noncommittally. Her cheeks burned remembering their argument. She knew it was stupid, but the revelation that he'd been willing to gamble with his memory by leaving Oak Haven . . . but not for her? It still stung.

Mama rightly interpreted Scarlett's waffling as a form of confession. "Well, that's no surprise. You two always did peck away like a pair of bickering geese."

"Yeah, I guess . . ."

"He's had a challenging few years, you know. He dated a bit, I think—not that Nate would share such information with the old witch who runs the inn. But I've seen him with female company now and again."

"*Thanks, Mama*," Scarlett muttered. "Thanks so much— that's great information to have."

"Nothing ever seemed to stick, of course. Seems like his mind was on someone else."

"Oh sure, someone else. Maybe he went traveling to *visit her*."

Mama frowned, confused. "Nate, travel?! Oh no. No, he's devoted to that store—he wouldn't leave it. No, there was only one time he's ever been away, and that was to rescue his father."

Scarlett slowly put down her armload of tarts and stared. "What?"

"Oh yes, what a drama that was. Nate's father is a twin. Did you not know that? Before your time, I suppose. Yes, so, the Williams family are reformed pirates—you know that part, of course. For hundreds of years, they only produced one child per generation, always male. No one knows why, though the assumption has always been that Earl One was under some sort of pirate curse. In any case, Nate's grandmother experienced a bit of a wobble, I guess you could say, and she had twin boys. Earl Twelve, otherwise known as Nate's father, and a second boy. After much debate they named him Viscount, because viscounts come after earls. Viz, as we called him—was a perfectly nice boy. I went to school with both twins; we're all about the same age. But I think Viz never quite felt at home in Oak Haven? The town wasn't big enough for two Williams boys, I suppose. When the twins turned eighteen, Viz left. But as the years passed, Nate's father couldn't cope with his twin having just disappeared like that, so he went looking for Viz and then things went very wrong . . . Anyway. Nate should tell you that part of the story; it isn't my place. But as I said: the only time Nate ever left Oak Haven is the one time he had to go rescue his father. That's the upshot."

Rescue his father? Scarlett's heart dropped. Shame washed

over her, replacing her earlier anger with a dull ache. All this time, she'd assumed the worst about Nate's intentions, never considering there might be a perfectly good explanation for him having left Oak Haven.

This is just like one of those internet posts, she thought. *Question: Am I the asshole? Answer: A resounding yes.*

"Nate's dad was in some sort of trouble," she repeated. "And he *had* to travel. He had no choice."

"That's what I just told you," Mama said, confused. "Why are you looking so—oh, Scarlett. What terrible thing have you said to that poor boy?"

The room glitched suddenly and Scarlett found herself onstage with Taylor. To the roar of the crowd, even Taylor had to agree that *it's her—Scarlett is the problem—it's her.*

The room glitched back, and Scarlett stood there like a wild animal caught in the trap of the Melrose Glare. Blessedly, voices in the lobby cut through the tension. Luna burst into the dining room with a flamboyant figure trailing behind her.

"Scarlett! Mama!" Luna chirped, a wide grin plastered across her face. "Behold. I present to you Maximillian the Magnificent!"

"*Mes belles dames,*" he said—suddenly and quite inexplicably French. He bowed, a flourish of his crimson cape sending dust motes dancing in the afternoon sun. Maximillian carried an overstuffed valise in one hand and a rabbit cage in the other.

"His performance in the park was astounding," Luna declared. "Scarlett, you really missed out."

"*Mais bien sur,*" Scarlett replied with a wry smile. Some animals have to chew off their own legs to escape traps—all Scarlett had to do to escape the Melrose Glare was to push Maximillian in front of it. "Of the millions of rabbits pulled out of hats throughout history, yours was definitely in the top five thousand."

Maximillian's smile didn't quite fade, but a bit of steel glinted in his eyes. "You seem quite bitter, my dear. Perhaps you should cast a cheerful spell to improve your mood? Or do you fear it would turn to *merde*, as all witches' spells in Oak Haven do these days?"

"Excuse me," Mama said frostily. "*What* did you just say?"

The temperature in the room seemed to drop ten degrees. *There it is,* thought Scarlett. *You're the one on the hook now, Max.*

Mama stepped forward, her voice low. "Perhaps, Maximillian, you should remember where you are, and choose your words with more care."

He blinked, momentarily taken aback. "I mean no offense. Magic is my trade and—"

"Tricks and lies are your trade, sir—just as they are with all your kind."

"Madame, *unlike witches*, I work very hard at perfecting my illusions. I am a consummate professional and my illusions are one hundred percent reliable, which is more than anyone in this room can say. I can only imagine how frustrated you all must be with the appalling chaos of late. But there is no need to take it out on an artisan such as myself." Maximillian turned dramatically, swooshing his cape as he made his way out of the dining room. "Please be so kind as to inform the chef I will be taking my evening repast in my suite."

With another flourish, he was gone.

"Mama." Luna joined her family at the gift-covered table. "That wasn't necessary. He's a tremendous talent."

"He's a tremendous gooney bird," Scarlett replied. "And . . . French, suddenly? He was Canadian this morning."

Mama rolled her eyes. "Russian a few days ago."

"What," Luna said, "You don't like diversity?"

"He is a ridiculous person," Mama declared.

"Witches are so prejudiced," Luna said. "You're such magic bigots."

Mama went over to her youngest girl and gave her an—arguably very condescending—pat on the shoulder. "I'm afraid you've been away from home too long, my dear. Nonetheless . . . you're right about Max in one sense. He is a well-behaved guest who pays in full every week. All of us—and I very much include myself—could bear to remember that."

"Max is just cranky because Oak Haven witches mistreat him so," Luna said. "You all have these wrongheaded notions about magicians being phony, and you treat them like they aren't even people. He was telling me about it on the walk home. Apparently, it's all the rage right now to hire him for cocktail parties; the witches sit around and mess up all of his tricks. To hear him tell it, humiliating magicians has replaced book groups as the number-one entertainment around here."

"I must admit," Mama chuckled, "it is amusing. Florie McNamara had a party last week and hired Maximillian to perform after dinner. When he reached into his hat to reveal that mangy rabbit of his, he pulled back an armful of black mambas instead."

Luna gasped. "Mama, that's terrible!"

"Pssh, she had an antidote spell ready—he never was in any real danger."

"Oh my God," Scarlett said, half-shocked and half-impressed. "You ladies are really getting spiky in your old age."

"It's not nice," Luna chastised, "and I can tell you it's really starting to get to him."

"Perhaps he should move along," suggested Scarlett. "Take his talents to Litchfield."

"All right, all right—that's enough," Mama said. "Luna, please go help your sister with the protection spells. We need a different one for each room and it's going to take a while."

"I will," Luna replied, "if you promise to be nice to Max from now on."

"I'll take it under advisement."

From the dining room, the witches could hear the front door to the inn swing open. "Hello? Anybody home?" The male voice in the lobby could only belong to one person: Nate.

Luna grinned wickedly. "Oh, Scarlett? It's for you."

Chapter 11
A Surprisingly Bangable Handyman

"I'm not going out there." Scarlett stepped back from the gift table, her mind racing. "Is something on fire in the kitchen? I think I smell something burning. . ."

Too late. Nate was standing by the threshold between the lobby and dining room. "Hey all," he said. "Where's this new piano I'm supposed to move?"

"Oh dear, I'm sorry," Mama sighed. "I should have let you know. I'm afraid we're still working on conjuring one."

"Sorry to hear," Nate said. "Chalk it up to those misbehaving oak trees, I guess."

"Afraid so." Mama turned to Scarlett. "Darling middle child, as Nathan has taken the time to stop by and see us, I suggest you go do what you know you need to do."

"Mama . . ."

"Go on. And don't dawdle—we have much to accomplish before you girls investigate the grove tonight. Go apologize for whatever it is you said."

"I didn't say anything."

Here came that Melrose Glare again. "It's all over your face, Scarlett."

"Nuh-uh!"

She turned to Luna for support, but Luna just shrugged. "Kinda is, Scar."

Scarlett folded her arms across her chest and gazed up at the ceiling for a moment. *This one's gonna sting.* "Hey, Nate, since you're here . . . Can I talk to you for a second?"

***

The back of the dining room looked out over a large stone patio. Beyond the patio sat about an acre of gardens, ringed with tall trees. In the center sat a large granite fountain, which, in better days, would send water jets arcing high into the air. The garden had once been a masterpiece of landscaping, with immaculate gravel paths winding through beds of fragrant roses and lavender shrubs. As a little girl, Scarlett used to chase the butterflies and hummingbirds that flitted from blossom to blossom. Today, the fountain was full of dry leaves, the blossoms just a memory.

Strolling around the yard, Scarlett was disturbed by the preponderance of unpulled weeds, untended shrubs, and unraked leaves. The once-immaculate garden, a source of Melrose pride and joy, was a specter of its past self. "She hasn't really kept it up, has she?"

"Well . . . your mother has a lot going on, especially since magic started glitching. And, uh . . ."

"*And*," Scarlett said, finishing what Nate didn't want to say, "tending the garden was always Papa's thing."

The back corner of the lot was the site of Papa's greatest love—his vegetable patch, where he'd spend uncountable hours from the first thaw to the first frost. Unlike her sisters, who never took to gardening, Scarlett had loved helping her father dig in the dirt. She'd enjoyed the affectionate labor involved in gardening, even without the use of magic. Although, from time to time, a *little* magic never hurt.

"I did my first spells out here." Scarlett led Nate to a cast-iron bench under a weeping willow tree. "Papa needed more earthworms for the garden, and I got to conjure them. Very basic spell, but I was only about five. The very idea of creating life like that was quite thrilling. A couple of years later, we had a bit of an aphid problem, so I was allowed to make ladybugs." She laughed at the memory. "I got completely obsessed with perfecting the number of black spots on their backs . . . Eventually, Papa explained that mommy and daddy ladybugs are perfectly capable of making their *own* baby ladybugs, and I'd best not go overboard."

"Quite an education to be had out here." Nate settled on one side of the bench. "You've got the birds, the bees, the bugs, the whole deal."

"Indeed, you can learn a lot in a garden . . ." Scarlett sat on the other end of the bench and stared straight ahead, not wanting to look at him for this next bit of conversation. "So listen . . . I'm a jerk."

Nate chuckled. "I mean . . . not most of the time?"

"No, yeah, I am . . . Mama told me about your father . . . and your secret uncle? Apparently?"

"Ohhh, I see. *That's* what this is about. Yeah, at the store this morning . . . you wouldn't give me a chance to explain."

"I kinda freaked out," Scarlett admitted.

"That's for sure."

"I was out of line. I don't know, it's like . . . I spent ten years becoming an adult, and then I get back here for five minutes, and I'm—"

"Seventeen all over again?"

"Ha, you're being generous. I think I was acting even younger than that. And listen." Here she turned to face him, hoping her words came out as sincerely as she intended. "I'm so sorry, Nate. I'm sorry about how I acted. And I'm really sorry about your dad . . . Is he okay?"

"Oh, my dad's fine." Nate frowned. "What did your mother tell you?"

"Just that you had to perform some sort of dramatic rescue?"

Nate laughed. "Wow . . . well. That's not the whole story. She told you about my uncle Viz?"

"Yeah. How'd that even happen? Hundreds of years of only-children and then twins suddenly?"

"Nobody ever admitted anything. But my grandmother may have resented the one-child rule. And she was a witch, so . . . maybe she cheated? In any case, it backfired because my dad was always considered the 'real' son. I'm told that everybody treated Viz like he was just this weird, gift-with-purchase kid. Not a bad boy, everybody said, but he just didn't fit in. So when he turned eighteen, he left. Which meant, of course, that he quickly forgot all about Oak Haven or that he had a family at all. Before he left, he told my dad he wanted to check out Texas, maybe work on a ranch. But that was all anybody knew."

"I don't remember you ever mentioning him while we were growing up."

"Are you kidding?" Nate said, making a face. "Big family secret. But then . . . I don't know what happened exactly. Dad hit middle age, and he just . . . he got it into his head that he should find his brother. Took several years to track him down, thanks to the Forgetting Spell."

"Sure. Because non-witches can leave Oak Haven and remember it, but not for very long."

"Exactly. Growing up in Oak Haven gives people like me and my dad a *little* resistance to the nonsense trivia . . . but it's weak. Non-witches like us can keep our memories solid for about three days, and then somewhere on day four, all this trivia starts buzzing around in our heads. Like, you try to remember a phone number, but all you can come up with is the fact that Martina Navratilova won Wimbledon a grand total of twenty times. It gets gradually worse, and by day six? Total amnesia. No recollection of the past at all. But Dad decided the risk was worth it, and he set out looking for Uncle Viz. Texas is a big place—even bigger when you can only search for three days at a time. So it took a while, but he did find him. And Dad started taking these trips out west to visit. Dad tried to convince Viz to come visit Oak Haven, but he wouldn't. Viz said he'd left for a reason, and even if he didn't remember what that reason was, he was going to trust himself that it must've been a good one."

Scarlett smiled. "That sounds exactly like something a rancher would say."

"Absolutely. Anyway, it kind of worked—Dad doing the visits. Then, a few years ago, he was headed home but only made it as far as Atlanta. Then his flight got delayed, and delayed some more, and then canceled. He ran out of time. We went to the airport to pick him up and found he never got on the plane."

"Oh my God. So . . . what . . . I mean, what happened?"

"Mom worked the witch connections—she knew somebody in Boston who knew someone in a coven in Savannah, I think it was. Just an all-points-magical bulletin, basically, looking for Dad. It turned out, he'd never left the airport. He got confused and missed his flight, and then he just stayed. I flew out to Atlanta to get him—found him sitting in a Macaroni Grill in Terminal 3. He had no idea who I was. That was the worst part. I walked up to him and said, 'Hey, Dad,' and it was just—" Nate gestured at his own face "—just blank. Nothing. It's one thing to be told, *oh, Dad has amnesia*, whatever. But to have him just look right through me like that?"

"Oh, Nate . . ." Scarlett reached over and squeezed his hand. "I'm so sorry."

"No, it's okay, he's all right now. But what sucked at the time was that my first reaction was to be mad. I was, like, *so so* mad at him, for a long time. It wasn't his fault—it's just that stupid Forgetting Spell. And, of course, I knew that, but . . ." He sighed. "I don't know. I couldn't get over that moment when he didn't know who I was."

"If he didn't recognize you, how did you get him to come home?"

"Mom planned for that. She wrote him a letter for me to give to him when I found him. I don't know what she wrote, but whatever it was, it was enough to convince him that he could trust me."

"But you say he's fine now, right?"

"Totally fine. It took a week or so, and Earl Twelve was back to his old self. Me, though . . . Not so much. It's so stupid because I know he didn't do anything wrong. But I still dream about that blank expression sometimes."

Scarlett studied Nate like a stranger—just a young man beside her on the bench, sitting there with his sadness. She felt like she was seeing him for the first time—seeing him as a real person. Not Nate, the surprisingly bangable handyman, or Nate, the over-idealized, never-quite-was boyfriend. Just Nate, a good guy. A good guy *and* a true friend, who she'd left in the lurch so long ago. "I should've been here."

"Nothing you could have done." Nate turned slowly, his gaze finally meeting hers. "I thought about getting in touch. I really did, but I couldn't bring myself to make that call. I mean . . ." He sighed, struggling to find the right words. "When you got so upset at the store today . . . I just wanted to say, *Scarlett, be serious. Do you really think I didn't want to visit you?!* Of course I wanted to visit you. Of course I did." His voice carried a level of frustration that took Scarlett by surprise. "I think about you all the time. About us . . . or about what *we* might've looked like if there had ever been one. But what am I supposed to do, visit you for three days at a stretch? That's what it would have been—just like my dad and my uncle. Three days, no more. Would that be enough for you? Because it wouldn't for me."

"Nate . . ."

As he gazed at her, Scar looked at his lips and suddenly the only thing she could think of was what it might be like to finally, finally kiss them after all these years.

"Scarlett? Were you about to say something?"

"Uh. Yeah. I . . . um." She turned away, hoping a thought—some thought, any thought—would return to her abruptly empty brain. "Look, I feel shitty about having just walked away from us being friends or whatever."

"Friends . . . *or whatever*?" Nate tilted in his head in the sexiest way—he really could be a bastard sometimes.

"Yeah . . ." Scarlett laughed awkwardly. "Uh, that was weird of me to say. I just meant that, uh, friends are extremely important. And old friends are even more so—I mean, there's a whole song about that, *make new friends and keep the old* and so on, and I don't know how long I'm even going to be in Oak Haven, but while I'm here, like, uh—why can't we be friends?"

Nate grinned. "*Why can't we be friends?* That's a song, too. Very musical conversation we're having. Okay, *friend*. Do you mind if I make a request?"

"Please," Scarlett said, a little desperately. "Please make a request so that I can somehow stop talking."

"I heard your mother say you and your sisters are checking out the oaks tonight. I was wondering . . . could I come along? I would really love to see that grove again."

"Of course. But I'm not following why you need to ask?"

"Right." Nate nodded. "This happened after you left. Yeah, they passed a law that non-witches such as myself aren't allowed in the grove."

"Ohh," Scarlett said, finally understanding. "Because of what Bill did."

"Exactly. Ole Bill really messed things up for the rest of us."

"Well, screw that guy," she declared happily. "Of course you can come . . . friend."

Nate nudged her shoulder with his own. "You got it, friend."

"Hey, uh. Since we're pals now and all . . . I have to ask you something."

"Go for it."

"Okay, I'm just curious . . ." Scarlett said hesitantly. "It's totally not important to me, but I'm just wondering . . . Polly?! I mean . . . really? You and the Triple P?"

Nate laughed. "What's wrong with Polly?"

"Nothing," she said. "I just don't see the two of you together, is all."

"Well, what'd you expect? What have you been picturing, all these years? Was I supposed to sit here and wait for you? Maybe take a picnic basket out to the woods and just sit there staring off into space, sighing a lot, writing wistful poetry: *Scarlett return to me?*"

"Oh my God, Nate, no! No, I'm so sorry. I never meant that you—" But then she realized his eyes were twinkling. "Oh, for fuck's sake. You're teasing me."

"You asked for it." He grinned. "No, there's nothing between me and Polly—that's the truth."

A little jolt of happiness went through her, which she decided it was best to ignore. "Well, I spoke to her at the store earlier, and she certainly implied otherwise."

"Bah." Nate stood up. "She was probably just trying to wind you up."

Or wishful thinking on her part, Scarlett thought.

"No," he continued. "I help out with repairs at the bookstore, is all. Same as I do with all the shops downtown. Which reminds me, I should get back. I didn't plan on being away from the store quite this long."

As they headed back toward the patio, Nate said, "But I mean . . . even if I *were* seeing Polly, it wouldn't matter to you anyway." He lifted an eyebrow. "Right? Since we're just friends?"

"Absolutely. Totally fine by me, friend. Bang away."

"Great, glad to have that understood." He gave her a playful tap on the arm. "So I'll see you tonight."

"See you tonight!" Scarlett grinned, feeling a thousand pounds lighter to have things settled with Nate. And if something deep inside nagged at her that *friends* was not the right description for them at all? Well, let that be a Future Scarlett problem. "Fight the power, break the law," she joked. "Come stare at trees with us."

Chapter 12
What Are You Doing With That Belt?

"I can't believe you invited him to stare at trees with us!"

It was midnight, and the sisters were standing at the base of the hill just outside of town. The night was chilly but clear, the moonlight casting a silvery glow across the hills. In the distance, the hoots of an owl echoed through the trees. Above them loomed the oak grove and, hopefully, answers about what was wrong with magic in Oak Haven.

Delilah snarled, "This is not date night, Scarlett!"

"*Date night* could not be further from my mind," Scarlett replied. "We had a nice chat earlier, and Nate and I are friends, period."

Both sisters groaned. Luna said, "That's absurd, Scar," while Delilah offered, "You're embarrassing."

A pair of headlights swept across the darkness: Nate's truck. The sisters waited as he parked and ambled over to join them. "Evening, everybody. Thanks for letting me join your Scooby-Doo gang for the evening."

"We're breaking a fairly serious rule here," Delilah noted.

Scarlett rolled her eyes. "It's a stupid rule—Nate's not

Handsome Bill, for crying out loud. He's not going to hurt anything."

"Don't worry," Nate assured the sisters. "Whatever you folks say goes. I'm happy just to be able to join you up there. I promise I won't get in the way."

Delilah emitted a little "humph" and headed up the hill first, with Luna behind. Scarlett and Nate hung back, then began the climb side by side.

"Beautiful clear night," he said.

"Cold, though." Scarlett hunched her shoulders against the chill—a typical posture for her in San Francisco. But here in Oak Haven, the imperfect weather was just another sign that something was wrong.

"Yeah," he agreed. "Cooler than usual. But just look at those stars."

It was a clear, cloudless evening, and the sky was positively crowded with stars, like a glittering carpet almost close enough to touch.

"Yeah," Scarlett said. "We never get stars like this in San Francisco, too much light pollution. Hey, remember when we used to sit on the roof of your dad's store and stargaze?"

"And you'd make up rude stories about the constellations."

"Oooh, Orion," Scarlett said in a sexy baby voice, "what are you doing with that belt?"

Nate laughed. "Yep, that's what I remember . . ."

When the group reached the grove's edge, Delilah suggested they conjure some light. "Be careful," she advised. "Nothing complicated."

"You okay with little old me using magic, Del?" Scarlett asked.

"Not really," Del shot back. "But go on, surprise me."

Luna conjured an antique lantern. Delilah turned the palm of her hand into a flashlight while Scarlett cast a torch that filled the space around her with flickering fire.

"Scarlett!" Luna gasped. "What are you doing?"

Delilah shook her head. "You're so bad at this, Scar."

"What?! What'd I do now?"

"You're gonna bring open flame into a grove of ancient trees in the middle of autumn," replied Delilah. "That sound like a good idea to you? Sparks everywhere? Are you completely stupid or what?"

"There's no sparks," Scarlett said defensively, "look how clean this casting is! And I won't drop it in a pile of leaves, for crying out loud."

Delilah exhaled sharply and headed off into the grove alone.

"*God, fine.*" Scarlett extinguished her flame and turned to her younger sister for sympathy. "What is her problem tonight?"

"She was a little harsh." Luna conjured a lantern for her sister, identical to her own. "But, Scar, it's true that you can be careless with fire sometimes. Remember the time you decided to make s'mores in our bedroom? Hey, Delilah, wait for me!" Luna hurried after her older sister.

"Wow." Nate chuckled. "You set a fire in your bedroom?"

"I was *six*. I mean, seriously?! Do I ever get to live that down?"

He laughed. "Probably not, no."

***

The foursome made their way to a clearing in the middle of the oak grove. Moonlight filtered through the sparse branches, casting odd patterns on fallen leaves underfoot. A damp, earthy scent hung in the air, tinged with a trace of something sickly sweet, like overripe fruit. In the center of the clearing sat the great-granddaddy oak—the largest and eldest of all, the one that had greeted the founders of Oak Haven and had stood vigil over the town across all the centuries.

"Nate," Delilah said quietly, "I'm going to have to ask you to stay back here."

"Sure. You do your thing; I'm just here soaking up the atmosphere."

Scarlett handed him her lantern and followed her sisters.

The witches circled the massive tree, studying its thick, strong branches and pointy leaves. Nothing was obviously wrong, but all the women could feel, in their hearts, that absolutely nothing was right.

"Okay, you two," Luna whispered. "I'm going to have that chat."

She knelt before the old giant, gently caressing its knotty trunk. From the folds of her cloak, Luna removed an elaborately carved wooden box. Inside the box were nine small candles. She removed one candle and, with a small flame that ignited off the tip of her index finger, melted one end of the candle and attached it to the tree.

Scarlett nudged her elder sister in the ribs. "Open flame. Alert, alert: there is an open flame in the woods."

"She's allowed," Delilah whispered back.

"Why is Luna allowed?"

"Luna is allowed to use flame because Luna never set her bedroom on fire."

"Six. Years. Old."

"Can you two stop?" Luna called over her shoulder. "Sacred ritual and all that?"

103

Delilah muttered, "She started it . . ."

Luna repeated the melting gesture with the rest of the candles, creating a small, glowing circle on the side of the oak. As she did so, she spoke gently in some ritualistic dialect Scarlett didn't recognize.

"What's that language she's speaking?" she whispered to Delilah.

"I believe it's a hortikinetic language."

"You say *a* hortikinetic language, meaning there's more than one?"

Delilah made a face. "There's loads. What, do you think seaweed speaks the same language as cacti? Duh."

"Wow, a whole world of hortikinetic languages . . . I doubt I could learn a hortikinetic language if I lived a thousand years."

Delilah agreed. "That's our baby sister for you."

"So impressive. Fucking Gandalf up in here."

Luna turned. "Guys, shh! I mean it."

"Sorry . . ."

Returning to her incantation, Luna reached out very slowly, placing her palm in the center of the circle of candles. After a moment, the bark around her hand began to glow.

Scarlett and Delilah watched in amazement as the glowing light spread from the bark to Luna's hand, then crept throughout her entire body. Luna whispered, and nodded, and whispered some more. The glow receded as gracefully as it had arrived. She blew out the candles, carefully removed them from the bark, and placed them back in the box. Luna picked up her lantern and returned to her sisters.

"What'd it say?" asked Scarlett. "What's the news from Treetown?"

"To be clear, trees don't speak English. They communicate through feelings and images. This oak showed me a *different* oak on the grove's western side. Something about the condition of that western tree is bothering all the other trees in the grove. When I tried to understand why, the oak showed me a strange insect, like a small dragonfly. Its wings lit up like a firefly, but a crimson light, not yellow. The image came to me accompanied by a tremendous sense of concern. Which is to say, whatever's going on with that western tree, the other trees are really unhappy about it."

"Sounds like some kind of magical infestation," Delilah suggested.

"Felt that way, too." Luna nodded. "The red dragonflies are upsetting the rest of the grove. Come, let's find the tree they're all so troubled by."

The two sisters hurried to the west, but Scarlett paused. "Sure," she muttered. "Let's go find the tree that all the other trees are scared of. What could go wrong?" She turned, gave Nate a little whistle, and pointed westward.

He approached her. "Are you sure your sisters want me coming along?"

"Never mind what they want. What I *don't* want is for you to get lost in the middle of a magic oak grove in the middle of the night."

"I, too, do not want that."

"Right, so stick with me, kid."

They made their way through the darkness side by side. The farther west they walked, the more Scarlett sensed a certain unnameable *wrongness* in the air.

Distracted by this thought, she put a foot wrong on a

fallen branch, which snapped under her weight, causing her to stumble. Nate reached out, wrapping his strong arm around her waist and righting her. He pulled her close, and she could smell the vague herbal scent of the hardware store's back room. His body radiated a gentle strength that warmed her, inside out.

It struck Scarlett suddenly that "Why Can't We Be Friends?" was a lousy song.

As they approached the far western edge of the grove, they confronted a peculiar and unsettling sight. One of the trees stood out starkly against the surrounding oaks, its oddness radiating across the grove like a malevolent beacon. Tiny, glowing dragonflies swarmed around, darted around the branches, leaving trails of red light in their wake. The tree seemed to pulse with an unnatural energy, the crimson glow beneath its bark writhing and undulating.

The air around the oak buzzed with the hum of the insects' wings—a disconcerting chorus that filled the otherwise silent grove. The insects' glowing bodies cast dancing shadows across the ground and nearby trees. These were no ordinary insects; they were magical parasites, feeding on the very essence of the oak and twisting and warping its power.

Luna had set up her candles around the tree's base; she was attempting the same hortikinetic conversation she'd had with the oak at the center of the grove. But this time, something was wrong. Her expression pinched and twisted, and her head tilted from side to side as though she was trying to understand the incomprehensible.

Nate stood close, one arm still around Scarlett's waist. "Is your sister okay?"

"None of this is okay . . ." A crease appeared across Scarlett's forehead, and her lips pressed together in a thin line. "I don't know, I've never seen her like this."

Luna emitted a low moan, which then rose in tone, octave by octave, becoming a yell and then a scream. Then, some invisible force sent her body flying backwards away from the tree and tossed her in a heap.

Scarlett and Delilah raced to Luna's side and knelt down beside her, saying, "Luna! Luna, are you all right?"

Dazed, Luna tried to sit up. "I'm all right . . . just a bit overwhelmed."

"Sweetie, what did you see?" Scarlett took Luna's hand and held it tight.

"Nothing that made any sense. It was just showing me nonsense images, and the harder I tried to piece the details together to make sense of things, the more confusing everything became. It was as if the tree *wanted* to communicate with me, but it couldn't put its thoughts together."

Nate sauntered over to the oak and rested his own hand on the trunk. "This tree is tripping balls."

"Who asked you?!" Delilah snapped.

"I'm just saying, you don't need to be a witch to feel the crazy coming off this thing."

"What are you even doing here? You have no business—"

"No, Del, stop," Luna said. "He's right. The tree is hallucinating."

Chapter 13
Tasmanian Weaver Ants

The three witches and Nate sat in a tight circle, a safe distance from the crimson-infected tree, with their lanterns piled in the middle, like a safely contained campfire.

"You're saying . . ." Scarlett was having trouble getting her head around this new information ". . . that tree is . . . high?"

"Not literally, of course." Luna shrugged. "But that's how it felt—like I was trying to have a heart-to-heart chat with a drunk. That oak was not making an ounce of sense, that's for sure. The dragonflies are interfering with the power of the tree, making its magic erratic and unpredictable. We're lucky it's only the one tree affected."

"For *now*," Delilah emphasized. "I don't want to think about the entire grove being under the influence of these flies. So, what's our next move?"

"A pot of coffee?" suggested Scarlett. "Or long showers sometimes help."

"How about a nice greasy cheeseburger?" Nate offered.

"Oh yeah, now you're talking."

Delilah rolled her eyes. "If you two aren't going to take this seriously, maybe you should go home."

"Sorry, Del."

"Hey, it's just our entire town's magic supply under threat. No need to get worked up about it."

"I said sorry, Del, jeez."

"It's imperative to cleanse this tree," Delilah said. "Luna, what do you suggest?"

"Hang on," Scarlett interrupted. "You mean right now? Shouldn't we get Mama, at least?"

Delilah frowned. "I am certainly not running home to *ask mommy* for permission to fix such a basic problem. Can you imagine her reaction? We'd never hear the end of it. No, we are three adult witches, Scarlett—even if you are out practice. We can handle a bunch of dragonflies. What do you say, Luna. Any suggestions?"

"Well . . . remember I was telling you about the weaver ants in Tasmania? They create these giant nests high in the trees. And what those witches do is conjure this very particular smoke that the ants absolutely hate. The smoke causes them to flee, and then you can kind of herd them where you want. I could create the smoke, and you two could cast a binding net all the way around the tree. The bugs will flee the smoke and fly right into the net."

"What sort of smoke will work?" Delilah asked.

"No clue—this is going to be trial and error. But I have to say, I agree with Delilah. I don't think we should wait around for the infestation to spread. Any minute now, those flies are going to decide the rest of the grove looks pretty tasty, and Oak Haven could lose control of magic completely."

Delilah nodded. "Okay, let's get started. Scarlett, why don't you and I set up over—"

"Hang on." Scarlett's eyes were wide and haunted. "Wait a second. What are we doing here?"

109

Her sisters look at one another, then back at Scarlett.

"Saving Oak Haven?" offered Luna.

"Seriously?! Am I the only one who remembers the last time we were out here, performing cooperative magic to 'save' Oak Haven?"

"Oh, Scarlett, no . . ."

"Come on!" Delilah exclaimed. "Completely different situation."

"How? How is it different, Delilah? Ten years ago, it was you, Luna, Mama, and me, right here in the grove, drawing some kind of nastiness out of the oak trees in order to save magic. Poison, back then, rather than bugs. We drew out the poison and . . . anybody remember what happened next?"

Luna shook her head sadly. "Please don't do this . . ."

"We drew it out, all right. Ooh boy, we drew that poison out of the trees and performed a transference spell to collect it in a *vessel*, back at the inn. And guess what that *vessel* turned out to be? Any takers?"

"Stop it, Scarlett!" Delilah stood up. "It was an accident."

"Yeah, Del. I never thought we poisoned our father *on purpose*. We just forgot to specify. *'Uh hey, Magic? Find a proper vessel for all that poison okay? Don't store it in the human vessel that's our dad, cool?* That was quite a whoopsie, wasn't it? And now, here we are, about to do the same goddamn thing all over again." Scarlett stood to face her older sister. "Tell me, Delilah, what do you reckon the unintended consequence will be this time?"

"Just go home, Scar. Luna and I can handle this on our own; no need for you to sully yourself with this."

"Go home?! Del, *you* called *me*, remember? You left that pathetic little message—"

". . . it wasn't pathetic . . ."

"—saying I had to get here immediately. But now that I'm here disagreeing with you, suddenly you don't want me involved."

"To be honest, Scar? After ten years apart, I'd forgotten how annoying you can be."

"Hey, enough!" Luna raised her arms like the referee she so often became when her sisters were together. "Del, we need Scarlett. Look at this tree—it's a hundred feet tall. A net of that size will only function with cooperative magic. Remember, we need to collect all the insects at once—if we lose even a couple, they'll just breed, and we'll be back where we started. And Scarlett, look . . . I understand what you're saying, okay? I hear you."

"Oh, you *hear me*," Scarlett groaned. "Wonderful. Therapy-speak, just what I need. You going to tell me that feelings aren't facts now?"

"Well, actually . . . The situation ten years ago was very different—I know it doesn't *feel* that way, but it was. That was a teleportation spell that went wrong, remember? We were trying to transfer physical matter across a distance. That's very difficult. We tried to specify what would become of that matter at the new location, and Papa accidentally got in the way."

"*Oh my God!* You're blaming him now?"

"Please, Scar, listen to me. I'm not blaming anybody. I'm saying this is very different and much simpler. We aren't transferring the insects through space. I'm going to chase them out of the tree, and you and Del will trap them. Period. Basic stuff. Okay? Del, are you okay?"

"*Fine*," Del said, although her tone suggested things were far from it.

"Scar?"

Scarlett stared up at the stars, then squeezed her eyes shut and tried to remember what Papa looked like.

"Scar, listen to me. The insects are devouring this tree and then they'll move on to another, and another. The longer we let this go, the larger an area we'll need to address, and the more complicated the spellwork will be. And if these dragonflies are allowed to take over the entire grove, who knows if magic will function at all. Which means, if you are concerned about risk, waiting to act is by far the riskiest choice. This moment, right now, is the least-risky time to do this."

She sighed. "All right. Luna the Litigator has talked me into doing her bidding."

"It's going to be fine." Luna gestured to Delilah, and the two of them walked slowly around the tree, marking out spots where sigils would be placed for the netting spell.

"Hey, pal." Nate gave Scarlett a friendly slug on the shoulder. "You all right?"

She sighed. "Sorry you had to see that."

"Don't even think about it. And listen, for what it's worth?" He leaned in to whisper. "I agree with you. If that helps."

She allowed herself another peek into those inviting black eyes of his. "It helps." She grabbed his hand and squeezed it hard. "Now please get back behind the tree line, so nothing happens to you."

***

Scarlett's stomach churned. Every instinct screamed that this was a terrible idea, and meanwhile the vague image of her father danced in her head. Papa had called, "Goodbye and good hunting, my angels," as his girls had headed out to the grove all those years ago. It was the last thing he'd ever said.

The memory of him had sent her running to the West Coast, had inspired her to avoid the covens of San Francisco, to play it safe, to be *normal*. Whenever she'd considered using magic to catch a cab, pay a bill, or clean the dishes, the memory of her father pulled her up short.

And look at me now, sitting under a goddamn magical oak with my sisters, my very own Glinda and Elphaba. What am I doing here?

"Okay, positions." Delilah's voice was clipped and businesslike. Either she wasn't thinking about Papa at all, or she was a much better actress than Scar had realized.

Scarlett and Delilah took their places, sitting cross-legged with their knees touching under the canopy of the infested oak. Luna stood beside them, holding a large tube that she'd conjured from thin air; it appeared to be some sort of didgeridoo. She'd also enchanted a dozen or so candles, which floated in the air at varying heights and cast a warm glow all around.

"Okay, that's cool," Scarlett admitted. "When this is over, you need to teach me how to do the floaty candle thing."

Luna frowned. "How do you *not know* the floaty candle thing? It's like a middle-school level spell."

"She was out in the garden all the time," Delilah recalled. "She was probably busy training her little ant army or whatever that was."

"Removing the ants from Mama's peonies was basically the only one of my spells she ever liked. So, are we doing this or what?"

Luna nodded. "You two start. I don't want to disturb the bugs until the net is up."

Delilah took Scarlett's hands in hers and closed her eyes. Scarlett hesitantly followed suit. With a disorienting jolt, she felt her sister's presence invading her mind. Delilah's fierce determination, tinged with an undercurrent of worry, nudged aside Scarlett's own mixed emotions.

But there was Papa's face again.

Focus, dammit!

Scarlett tried to push away the memory of her father. This spell required a unified flow of power, and her conflicting emotions were muddying the stream.

One by one, the sigils around the tree began to glow. Three beacons blinked into existence . . . then four . . . five . . . six. A faint outline of a shimmering net took shape above and all around them.

Luna began playing her didgeridoo. Low, mournful notes filled the clearing, and tendrils of hazy red smoke seeped from the instrument, coiling around the old tree trunk. But the red smoke didn't seem to disturb any of the insects. So Luna adjusted her spell and before long the smoke turned green . . . no luck either . . . then ochre.

Ah, ochre was the ticket. The tree itself seemed to shudder as all the frustrated insects spilled out of the tree.

But then, a thought came to Scarlett unbidden. A thought she hadn't allowed herself to have in a very, very long time.

Papa, I miss you.

The spell faltered. The sigils flickered and dimmed. The net wavered, its ephemeral strands twisting and straining.

"Scarlett, dammit!" Delilah's voice lashed out. "Focus!"

"No!" Luna's cry was sharp. "Oh no!"

Scarlett's eyes jolted open.

The net groaned, its shimmering outline snapping at several points. And then, in agonizingly slow motion, it began to tear itself apart.

"We're losing it!" Delilah yelled, her face pale.

Scarlett tried to pull herself together. She dove back into her own mind, searching for Delilah, desperate to weave their power back together. But it was too late. Another rip tore through the net, and the remaining vestiges dissolved into the night air.

The swarm broke free, casting their eerie crimson glow over the entire grove. The insects soared through the trees, diving-bombing one healthy branch after another. One by one, their crimson lights extinguished as they burrowed into their new hosts.

"Ohhh no," Scarlett whispered. "We've just made it so much worse."

Delilah stood up, murder in her eyes. "*You*, Scarlett. You made it fucking worse."

Chapter 14
Public Enemy No. 1

Morning arrived, unavoidably. Scarlett blinked awake, sunlight filtering through the gauzy pink curtains of her childhood bedroom. Her first emotion was a profound disappointment that she hadn't turned to stone or spontaneously combusted from the shame of last night.

Scarlett couldn't quite wrap her head around how badly she'd failed. Delilah had pleaded with Scarlett to return to Oak Haven but instead of being a helpful member of the family, she'd become a harbinger of chaos. All her long-forgotten childhood anxieties—that gnawing sense that she was always on the edge of a cliff, always just a few breaths away from messing everything up—clawed at her brain like a box of mad rats.

Maybe she should just disappear again. Leave Oak Haven, leave her family, before she could hurt them more. Might be the best thing for everyone.

The thought made her chest tighten. Because while fleeing the scene of the crime might, in fact, be best for everyone else, she knew it wouldn't be best for her. Running hadn't solved anything last time. Why would this be different? A decade's worth of time hadn't put an inch of distance between how badly she felt about what happened to Papa. Leaving now would just mean more ghosts to deal with later.

Besides, her family needed her—even if they hated her at the moment.

Ignoring the lump of dread in her throat, Scarlett forced herself out of bed. This was her mess, and she would have to face it.

While getting dressed, she heard strange honking sounds outside of her window—some high-pitched, like the noise of plastic toy trumpets, and others low, like broken kazoos. She pulled back the curtains in time to see an entire squadron of flamingos soaring over the inn. Meanwhile, a very unhappy-looking man bicycled past, hotly pursued by a single rain cloud that dumped water solely on him.

Excellent, Scarlett thought sarcastically. *Magic is in fantastic shape, I see. This should be a wonderful day.*

***

Downstairs, a cluster of bewildered-looking Gilbert and Sullivan aficionados had just arrived. The guests were an eclectic mix of what Scarlett expected to see—tweedy, easily startled academics mingling with glamorous *thea-tahh dahling* types—and some she absolutely didn't, like that pair of middle-aged men with long beards, Black Sabbath T-shirts and studded motorcycle leathers.

Delilah was behind the reception desk, checking everyone in with her trademark efficiency. "You're in room 308," she told an elderly couple. "Yes, there is an ice machine on that floor . . . No, we don't offer laundry service . . . Yes, I'm aware of the flamingos. There really isn't much we can do about them at the moment."

Scarlett noted her sister's clenched jaw and furrowed brow—not to mention her aura of barely suppressed rage—and hurried to help behind the counter.

"Good morning and welcome, Gilbert and Sullivan Society!" Scarlett announced loudly. "I trust that you are right, and we are right, and all is right as right can be?" Sotto voce, to Delilah's shoulder, Scarlett said, "Need any help?"

Delilah didn't even turn her head. "Not from you." Fake smile to the guests. "Enjoy your stay. Can I help the next people in line, please?"

Cold, Scarlett thought, *but not unjustified.* She turned to the coffee pot behind the counter, pouring herself a mug of liquid courage.

Meanwhile, Mama was at the front door with a small, wheeled bar cart. As long as Scarlett could remember, this was Mama's standard move whenever there was trouble at the inn. Complimentary cocktails always took the edge off.

"Good morning, gentlemen. Mimosa?" She handed each of the biker dudes an overfilled champagne flute. "We're so happy to have you at our inn."

The biker dudes didn't look especially happy to be at the inn. "We were coming up the street," said one. "And our Harleys turned into hogs. Not *hogs* like motorcycles—actual hogs. They both threw us off and ran away!"

"Yeah," affirmed the other. "What the hell is going on? And what are you gonna do about it?!"

"I'm so terribly sorry about the hogs." Mama smiled beatifically. "The town is having some troubles with anarchic magic at the moment, I'm afraid. I assure you, we will help you find your motorcycles posthaste. Please, enjoy some cocktails and don't worry at all."

"So, Del . . ." Scarlett said quietly to her sister, "I take it Mama knows about the magic situation."

"Everyone in Oak Haven *can't help* but know. It's so much worse than before. Everything is chaos. Now get lost. I'm busy."

"Scarlett!" Mama had just noticed Scarlett's presence, and she waved her over. "Come here a minute."

No fucking way, Scarlett thought. She had an epic scolding coming her way, but there was no chance she was ready to submit just yet. Instead, she pretended she hadn't heard her mother and dashed off to find Luna. Maybe her baby sister could offer a sliver of comfort.

Scarlett found her on the back patio. A determined frown creased Luna's brow as she sat cross-legged on a table, arms outstretched and chanting under her breath. Scarlett's heart sank when she realized what was happening. Luna was trying to conjure a piano for the Gilbert and Sullivan crew. Because the inn's piano had been destroyed.

Yet something else for me to feel terrible about.

Alas, every flick of Luna's wrist summoned forth something *other* than a piano. An accordion wheezed into existence, followed by a mournful set of bagpipes. A startled penguin appeared, squawking its disapproval before vanishing in a shimmer of blue light. It would've been funny if it had not been entirely Scarlett's fault.

Luna swore softly as yet another attempt conjured a dusty harp instead of the gleaming grand that the guests expected. Clearly, today was not a day for even the most basic of magic.

"Hey . . ." Scarlett said gently.

"Can we talk later, please," Luna replied. She didn't sound angry so much as fully absorbed in her task. An air of grim determination hovered all around her.

"Of course. I'll leave you to it." Scarlett backed away, but lingered at the French doors separating the patio from the dining room. She gazed out at the overgrown beds that used to be her father's garden. As a kid helping her dad, the garden had given her a sense of purpose. Now, every leaf, every blossom, seemed to whisper her failure.

"Papa . . ." she whispered miserably. "What do I do now?"

"Scarlett!" The sound of Mama's voice pulled Scarlett from her reverie; her mother, regal as ever, was standing in the dining room. "Scarlett, there you are."

"Here I am," she replied weakly. *Here it comes: the verbal flaying of a lifetime.* Scarlett leaned against the doorframe and waited for the enhanced interrogation to begin.

Instead, Mama just gazed at her daughter without speaking.

Scarlett tried to read her mother's expression. Was that anger? Disappointment? Something else? Scarlett couldn't tell. Mama had something to say—that was clear—but apparently, she wasn't ready to say it.

After a moment, Mama seemed to make a decision. Whatever emotions had been playing across her face were replaced by a purely businesslike expression. "Find Zahir in the kitchen and have him squeeze some more oranges for me. And fetch some champagne from the walk-in. Nate was kind enough to deliver a case but—"

"Wait, the hardware store stocks champagne now?"

"Of course not! The *market* stocks champagne, but it just so happens that Nate is one of those increasingly rare individuals who knows how to be helpful in a crisis."

Scarlett just shook her head. "Your ability to compliment one person and simultaneously insult everyone you've ever met will never cease to amaze."

"*Anyway*, he never appeared to restock my cart. I'm going to need it soon—those light-opera people drink like fish."

"Mama, wait. Can we talk about what happened last night? I just feel like—"

"Oh I know, your generation is very keen on *feelings*. But at the moment we have a lobby full of guests who *feel* tired, hungry, and unnerved by the number of flamingos soaring over our small New England town. What say we focus on our guests for the time being and worry about Scarlett's feelings at a more appropriate moment."

"But—"

"Feelings later, champagne now."

***

Weirdly happy to have been trusted with a job—*any* job—Scarlett headed for the kitchen. "Zahir, are you busy? Mama needs orange juice and champers."

Zahir stood alone in the Stargazer kitchen, feeding orange sections into a juicer one by one. The juicer's grrrrrr sound matched his expression perfectly.

"G'morning, Z." Scarlett hoisted herself up on the counter to sit beside him. "How's the juice business?"

Ignoring her greeting, Zahir thrust a half-filled juice glass in Scarlett's face. "Taste this."

She did. "Yum?" she offered encouragingly.

"Tastes like juice?"

"Yep."

"Not Spam?"

"Absolutely not."

"Are you sure," Zahir demanded. "You haven't just brushed your teeth or anything? That can change the flavor."

"Zahir, buddy. It's fine. I'm sure that Spam thing was just a one-time accident. After all, dinner the other night was *incredible*. Hey, I have an idea! There's a lot of folks in the lobby, so why don't you throw some omelets together or something?"

"Oh, sure." Zahir shrugged, sighed, and rolled his eyes all at once. "Easy for you to say."

"It wasn't your fault, Z. The Spam thing. There's a problem with the oak grove—it was nothing you did."

"It was nothing I did," he repeated. "And there's nothing I *can* do. I'm a master chef at the mercy of a bunch of trees. You know, that's what you witchy people forget. You walk around with all that power. You have no idea what it's like to just be . . ." He trailed off. "To just be."

"Hey, pal, you forget who you're talking to? I've spent ten years living as a muggle, remember?"

"Yeah, that was dumb of you."

"What do you know!" Scarlett exclaimed. "It's been fantastic!"

He grunted. "Liar."

"Steady there, Z."

"Scarlett, I know your family doesn't understand that job of yours, but I do—I read *Wired* magazine, okay? Your job is all long-tail keywords and crawlability and content optimization." He spat out the terms like they were Spam-flavored. "What an utter waste of your talent."

122

"First of all, it's more interesting than you're making it sound—"

"Bah!"

"—and secondly, I have absolutely zero talent as a witch. I proved that beyond a shadow of a doubt when I single-handedly destroyed the oak grove."

"Wait . . . *You* did this?"

"Last night, yeah. Delilah, Luna, Nate, and I went up there to try and fix the trees but—"

"Hang on," Zahir interrupted. "Nate?! What was Nate doing up there? That's illegal, you know."

"Oh, whatever—he just wanted to visit the grove, that's all."

"Uh-huh . . ." Zahir's eyebrows bopped up and down. "So that's back on, is it?"

"Back on? *What* is 'back on'?" Scarlett was confident she did an excellent performance of not understanding what he was alluding to.

"Gimme a break. You and Nate."

"There is no me and Nate. Where is he, anyway? Mama said he was back here."

Zahir reached for another orange. "He's in the walk-in."

"He's just . . . in the freezer? For how long?"

"What am I, your boyfriend-wrangler? I don't know. He took a case of champagne in there to chill, and he hasn't come out."

Scarlett frowned. "And you didn't think to look for him?"

Zahir grabbed more oranges and shook them at her. "Busy!"

"Right." She hopped off the counter. "Good talk, Zahir. You're the brother I never wanted."

He called to her as she walked away, "Back at you!"

Grrrrrr, said the juicer.

Scarlett yanked open the heavy stainless-steel door of the walk-in and stepped inside. As the door slammed behind her, she found herself standing on a street corner in New Orleans.

The air was thick with humidity and the scent of something deliciously spicy cooking nearby. Greenery dripped off the cast-iron balconies overhead. A cacophony of musicians blocked traffic on the street while tourists gathered to listen and dance and take pictures with their phones.

Scarlett spun around—the walk-in was gone.

Well, she thought. *This should be interesting.*

Chapter 15
Laissez Les Bon Temps Rouler

It wasn't the first time Scarlett had stepped through a portal. After all, portals had been her father's primary area of academic interest. But portals required a great deal of magical labor to create. They didn't just crop up at random.

Until now, apparently.

Across the street to her left, Scarlett spotted a group of street punks pottering around outside a grocery store. They were all tattoos, piercings, and Doc Marten boots, lost in a haze of patchouli and disaffection. And there among the punks was Nate. He was sitting on a case of champagne and drinking straight from one of the bottles.

She crossed the street and plonked down on the sidewalk beside him.

Nate handed Scarlett the bottle without speaking. She took a sip and handed the bottle back.

After a while he said, "We're in New Orleans."

Scarlett shrugged. "Seems like."

"I went into the walk-in . . . and now I'm here."

"Me too."

"Is this because of what happened at the grove last night?"

"Reckon so," she replied. "One tree was infected, and we had a few magic problems. Now all the trees are, and—"

"And magic is now just . . ." He made an explosion-like gesture.

"In anarchy," she said. "Yep."

He rolled his eyes. "*Cool.*"

They sat in silence for a long time, just listening to the music. The band was a motley collection of beat-up trumpets and trombones, accompanied by weathered banjos, a dented tuba, and a broken accordion. Kids with washboards and spoons kept the beat, more or less. The cumulative effect was sort of *Dixieland apocalypse*—which, Scarlett thought, felt appropriate under the circumstances.

Apocalypse. Her mind flashed to the magic supply room in Nate's store, and she winced. *Oh no . . . all those enchanted materials . . . He's sitting on the witchcraft equivalent of enriched uranium.* "Nate? How is your store? And all that magic in the back? Is everything . . . okay?"

"It ain't great. This morning, I heard all these banging noises coming from the back room, and then there was a sort of squelch, like if you dropped an octopus? Then I'm pretty sure I heard cats? I mean, *a lot* of cats. Followed by a sort of *rrr, rrr, rrr*-sound, like a car that can't get into gear. After that, let's see . . . oh yeah, after that came a screech—sort of a *caaaawwww!*—like an angry pterodactyl. I didn't dare even open the door—I just locked up and walked away. I figured your mom was going to be in trouble with all the guests showing up, so I picked up this champagne from the market and took it over there. She said, take it to the walk-in, so I opened the walk-in and . . ." He finished the champagne.

126

Scarlett wasn't sure whether to laugh or cry . . . maybe both. "Nate . . . I just . . . I don't even know what to say. I'm so sorry. I came back to Oak Haven to help and instead I've absolutely ruined everything."

"Oh, shut up."

"Pardon me?!"

"Sorry, I'm a little drunk. But still. I knew—when I saw all those dragonflies get loose last night, *I knew* today we'd be sitting here—well, not *here*, exactly, but we'd be sitting somewhere—talking about *ohhh boo hoo, Scarlett does everything wrong*. Just like with what happened to your father. You didn't cause that mess. But you, like, volunteered for crucifixion anyway. Exiling yourself for ten years over an accident."

"Okay, you are more than a little drunk."

"Absolutely. But I'm also right. Everything isn't all your fault, Scar. C'mon, I've got eleven more bottles of champagne here. Get drunk with me and stop being a martyr."

It was a more tempting offer than she wanted to admit. But Mama's words danced around in her brain. There they were, *feelings later* and *guests now*, doing a little tarantella to the sound of a Dixieland apocalypse.

Scarlett got up. "We can't. There's a bunch of guests at the hotel, and we have to take care of them first. Maybe later you can continue your dissertation on everything that's wrong with me."

Nate gazed up her, squinting into the sunshine. "I don't think everything is wrong with you, Scar . . . I think nearly everything is right with you. I mean . . . don't you know that?"

Your timing sucks, Nate Williams, she thought.

Scarlett held out her hand to pull him his feet. "Come on, time to go home. A bit of portal travel should sober you right up."

She led Nate through the tree-lined Jackson Square—past the fortune tellers and jazz combos and kids tap-dancing for quarters—to a narrow cobblestone alley. As soon as they stepped into the alley, the sun seemed to turn away, as if it didn't want to see what would happen next.

"What are we looking for, exactly?" he whispered.

"My father studied portals. Didn't you know that?"

"What kid knows what their friends' parents do all day?"

She smiled. "Fair enough. Well, Papa couldn't do magic, but he was a scholar of it, with a particular interest in portals. And he told me a story about this place—it's called Pirate Alley. The pirate Pierre Lafitte used to conduct business here."

"Wait," Nate asked. "Does this story involve my relatives?"

"Afraid not, no. This happened in the early 1800s—Earl One had long retired by that point. Anyway, Pierre's brother Jean would remain in the bay with their fleet of ships, while Pierre would come into town to make deals." She approached a nondescript wooden door, partway down the alley. "According to the story, Pierre got sick of traveling back and forth from the city to the bay. So, one of his many deals was with a local witch . . ." Scarlett rapped on the door with her knuckles, banging out a complicated rhythm ". . . to create a permanent, secret portal."

The door began to shimmer like a sidewalk in extreme heat.

"Your dad taught you how to do that?"

"He just told me the story." Scarlett smiled. "Mama knew the technique. Hold an image of the inn in your mind as we step through. Be very specific—we don't want to end up somewhere else by accident."

"Wait, portals work by thinking about where you'd rather be?"

"It's a big part of it. So do me a favor and hold a nice clear picture of the inn in your mind."

"Do we have to?" Nate wrinkled his nose. "I'd rather go hang out with Jean Lafitte."

"Nate!"

"Okay okay, just picturing the world's greatest hotel now . . ."

***

When their surroundings shuddered back into view, Scarlett and Nate found themselves standing in a luxurious, glass-enclosed shower. The shower head featured a state-of-the-art design with a dozen settings, ranging from mist to firehose. Scarlett hadn't been inside one of the inn bathrooms in a decade, but this level of luxury sure didn't feel right.

She gingerly opened the shower door to study their surroundings. Gold faucets. Gold toilet. The most enormous crystal chandelier she'd ever seen in a bathroom . . . well, the *only* crystal chandelier she'd ever seen in a bathroom.

In the distance, a male voice bellowed, "MELANNNNIAAAAA!"

She slammed the glass door so hard it nearly shattered. "Wrong hotel, wrong hotel—"

She turned to find Nate, laughing his ass off.

"Wait," she said. "Did you do this . . . ? On *purpose?*"

"I can't believe it actually worked!"

"*Oh my God.* You're not funny!" Scarlett began furiously tapping Mama's rhythm on the gold bathroom tiles. "Like, not even a little bit funny. If I can't get this open again, we are completely—"

129

From outside the bathroom, the bellow came again. "Dammit, Melania, are you upstairs?!"

The gilded wall shimmered, and Scarlett let out a relieved sigh. "Oh phew, here it is." She glared at Nate. "I should leave you here—you know that?"

He winked. "With this face? Nah, you couldn't."

Scarlett grabbed his arm. "C'mon, let's get out of here."

Chapter 16
Just the Two of Us

Another hotel, another bathroom shower. This time it was just an average hotel shower—no gold, and a curtain rather than a thick glass door.

Scarlett peeked out.

A woman screamed.

Scarlett screamed.

Nate shouted, "What the—?"

The shower curtain was ripped away, and they were confronted by an elderly woman in tweed, brandishing a samurai sword. Scarlett recognized her immediately as a member of the Gilbert and Sullivan Society—she'd seen her in the fretful crowd down in the lobby.

"Who are you? What are you doing here?" The lady wielded her sword in an awkward but not unthreatening manner. "And what have you done with my husband?!"

"Hey . . . everything is all right," Scarlett said as calmly as one can when on the wrong end of a samurai sword. "Madame, you saw me this morning, do you remember? When you were checking in?"

"Answer my questions!"

"Okay . . . I'm Scarlett Melrose, and my family runs this inn. This is Nate Williams. He owns the local hardware store, plus he's a part-time handyman and full-time pain in my backside."

"At your service," Nate offered.

The lady seemed to take only the tiniest comfort from this information, lowering her sword just slightly. "How did you end up in my shower?"

"Well, you've probably noticed that things are a bit complicated around town at the moment. We came through a portal from—you know what, that part doesn't matter. Anyway, it was purely accidental. We never meant to startle you."

"Did Bert go through a portal?"

"Bert?" Nate's forehead wrinkled.

"My husband Bert. He stepped into the bathroom earlier and disappeared. I've looked all over the inn. I can't find him anywhere. And now here you are. Did he go through a portal, do you think?"

Scarlett wasn't sure how to answer this in a way that would reduce the amount of sword-wielding. "Mmmm, perhaps? But if so, I'm sure he's fine."

"Ohhh yeah," Nate said. "Bert is completely fine at the bottom of a volcano or wherever he's ended up."

"What?!"

"He's kidding." Scarlett forced a laugh. "Such a kidder, our Nate—I mentioned how he was a pain in the backside, right? Now, erm, would you mind lowering your sword so we can exit this bathtub?"

Scarlett and Nate freed themselves from the clutches of Mrs. Bert and headed downstairs, only to find the lobby in an absolute uproar. Guests swarmed Delilah at the reception desk—making demands, asking questions, everyone in total panic. It seemed that Bert wasn't the only guest who'd gone missing.

"There you are!" Mama raced over to meet them at the bottom of the staircase. "What happened to you two?"

"Pro tip," Scarlett replied. "Don't use the walk-in. We ended up in the French Quarter."

"Oh for crying out loud." Mama sighed. "Well, I'll add that to our list of problems."

"What did we miss around here?"

"The doors . . ." Mama said despairingly.

"Really? Oh no. Nate, we missed the Doors."

He winked. "I've always been more of a Stones guy."

"Or the Who," suggested Scarlett.

"The Who?" Nate tilted his head in confusion. "Weren't they on second?"

"No, the Who was on first, What was on second, and I Don't Know was on third."

Mama sighed. "You two got into the champagne, didn't you?"

Scarlett and Nate made eye contact and giggled.

"Pull it together, both of you. As you two have already discovered, a number of doors have turned into portals overnight. Currently, Luna is on the hunt for the guests who've accidentally stepped through a portal and gotten lost. She's busy rescuing them; meanwhile, Delilah is managing their fretful companions. I need your help to prevent us from losing more guests."

"Sure, maybe there's a spell that could—"

"A spell?! Scarlett, we've got motorcycles turning into pigs and doors turning into portals. The last thing we need now is more magic. No, I have something far more traditional in mind.

Nate, please fetch your toolbox and some fresh locks from down in the supply closet."

"Of course, Mrs. Melrose," Nate said.

"We've been over this. Call me Kelly."

"We *have* been over it," he allowed, "and I really can't."

***

Mama stalked along the second-floor corridor, and Scarlett and Nate had to jog to keep up.

"Mama, will you please slow down . . ."

They came to a halt in front of Room 205. She handed Scarlett the room key and gestured for her to open it. "Just peek. Don't step inside or I'll have to go looking for you."

Scarlett shrugged and took the key. She opened Room 205 and leaned in, keeping her grip on the doorknob.

Instead of a quaint hotel room, she found herself gazing at Stonehenge.

A young woman cowered on the grass nearby, terrified and lost. She yelped when she saw Scarlett appear. "Who are you? Where am I? What's going on?"

"You're all right." Scarlett reached out to take the woman's hand and pull her back. "C'mon back—no sense hanging around out here."

The young woman allowed Scarlett to lead her across the threshold. "Oh, thank you . . ." She looked equally relieved and shocked to find herself on the second floor of the inn. "I . . . but . . . where am I now? How did I get here? I don't know what happened!"

Mama patted her on the arm. "I believe your companion is downstairs, quite upset. Go let him know you're all right." As the woman hurried down the hall, Mama called after her, "Help yourself to some champagne."

Scarlett chuckled. "Champagne makes everything better, quoth Mama Melrose."

"My dear, when you find a situation that is not improved by champagne, please inform."

"AA meetings?"

"You know." Mama put an irritated hand on her hip. "You're quite flippant for someone who caused all this madness." She pressed a piece of paper into her daughter's hand. "This is the list of the problem doors we've discovered so far. Please change all these locks—I'll see to the guests and place them in new rooms while we sort this out. Oh, and be sure to keep straight which new key goes with which door, or you'll cause yet another catastrophe, and you've done quite enough for today." Mama gave her middle daughter a healthy dose of the Melrose Scowl, then turned on her heel and stalked back toward the stairwell.

The Scowl never failed to make Scarlett feel as though she'd been shrunk down to about two feet tall. In fact, this feeling was so powerful that when Scarlett turned to look at Nate, part of her felt shocked that she was still tall enough to look him in the eye.

"You gotta give her credit," Nate said. "When your mom takes a shot at somebody, she doesn't miss."

"Yeah . . ." Scarlett said. "Suppose I had it coming."

He frowned. "What are you talking about? Scar, this isn't on you."

"Of course it is! You saw what happened last night."

"No way. If anything, you're the wronged party here." He opened the door to Room 205 and stared unblinkingly at the green, green grass of Salisbury Plain. "Huh. Yeah, I can see how your mother doesn't want guests in here." He knelt down to study the interior lock plate in the door.

Scarlett leaned against the wall beside Nate, not gazing at his broad shoulders and definitely not picturing the strong back underneath his flannel shirt. "What do you mean, wronged party? Delilah and I did that spell to trap all the dragonflies, and her half worked, but mine didn't because I got distracted. If I'd done my job, then—"

"Look, I may have been a little tipsy earlier, but I meant what I said. Think about it: you've have been out of the magic game for ten years, and your sisters drag you out to the scene of a hugely traumatic event from your past. And they expect you to, what, just come roaring back like you're Glinda the Good Witch? I was there in the grove, don't forget. You tried to tell them it was a bad idea, and they wouldn't listen to you. I'm Team Scarlett on this one."

She blushed. "You're a team of one, I'm afraid. You're playing solitaire."

"Here, hold these for me." Nate held out his hand, cupping four screws he'd removed from the door. As he dropped them into Scarlett's hand, their fingers brushed against each other. Their eyes locked, and Scarlett's breath caught in her chest.

"I would hope," Nate said, "that you're on your own team, at least."

"Yeah." Scarlett's voice came out in a breathy way that embarrassed her. "I suppose I am."

"Okay, then." He smiled. "It's you and me."

Chapter 17
That *Consumed With Dread* Look

Scarlett spent several pleasurable hours helping Nate change the locks on the doors that had become portals. The locks were old, a bit rusty, and none left their doors easily, but Nate always seemed to manage it. Every time Nate handed Scarlett a lock plate or a screw or some other bit of hardware, his hand would brush hers and she'd feel it all the way down to her toes.

Which is ridiculous, she chastised herself silently. *I'm not a teenager anymore.*

But she found herself eagerly awaiting those moments anyhow.

So far, they'd located four portals: the one to Stonehenge, another that led to the basement of the Sydney Opera House, another to a child's treehouse in Toad Suck, Arkansas, and finally the kitchen of Third Eye Restaurant in Kathmandu.

On the third floor, they came across Maximillian the Magnificent, who was sitting despondently on the floor at the far end of the hall.

"Let me guess," Scarlett called out as they approached. "You found another portal?"

He leapt to his feet. "*Nein! Guten tag!* It's fine. My room is fine."

"For crying out loud, he's German today," Scarlett muttered.

"Hey there, Max," Nate said. "Have you got a portal in there? Mrs. Melrose sent us here to change the locks, so nobody accidentally falls in."

"*Nein!* No portal!" Max smiled oddly—a forced-looking smile on a face unaccustomed to it. "Everything is excellent."

"Then, um, why are you sitting in the hall, Max?" Scarlett asked.

"I like the hall. Zis hall, *sie ist wunderbar! Und* my Quentin is napping, for which is required completely silence."

Scarlett and Nate eyeballed the magician suspiciously, then looked at each other, then back at him.

"You are sitting in the hall," Scarlett said, "so as not to disturb your rabbit?"

"Listen, buddy," Nate said in as chummy a tone as he could muster. "How about you let us have a look at your doors? We'll be super quiet, I promise. Just take a quick peek, just make sure everything is okay?"

"Absolutely *nein*!" Max declared. "My impedimenta are in zere. All ze tools of my trade. No non-magician may gaze upon these tools, it is *verboten*!"

"*Impedimenta*," Scarlett said, amused. "You mean your *props*? For your little *shows*?"

"I recognize your disdain, *und!* I am choosing not to acknowledge it. More important is my Quentin. Quentin requires his rest. I must insist you do no disturb him."

"Sure." Scarlett shrugged. "We'll leave you to it then."

She nudged Nate to suggest they move on, but he hesitated. "We should really check," he whispered.

"If he won't let us, he won't let us. C'mon, we have bigger problems."

138

"Okay . . ." Nate turned to Maximillian. "Max, please promise me . . . if you happen to find a portal in the shower, don't fall in."

"*Sehr gut!*" said the magician defiantly. "I would say *auf wiedersehen* except I have no desire to *sehen* you *wieder*."

***

On her mother's list, there was only one more door to fix: Room 317. "This says the room is unoccupied, which is a relief."

"Great." Nate nodded. "We'll change this last lock and then I should probably head back to the store. Everybody in town is going to be there looking for lock picks and tools and who knows what else."

"Yeah . . ." Scarlett's jolly mood faded as she remembered why everyone in Oak Haven would be lining up at the hardware store—to fix everything she had broken.

As they walked down the hall to the final room, Nate nudged her shoulder with his own. "Hey. I know that look."

"What look?"

"The look on your face right now. The *Consumed with Dread* look."

Scarlett frowned. "I don't have a Consumed with Dread look." She reached over and unlocked Room 317 with the hotel skeleton key. "Should we see where this portal goes? Maybe it's the Marianas Trench and I can just disappear there for—" the sight of what lay beyond the door brought her up short "—ever."

On the other side of the portal, impossibly white sand extended in all directions. A vast expanse of the ocean stretched out in the distance, rolling waves crashing against the shore. The sky was painted in a breathtaking display of fiery orange, melting into soft pinks and vibrant purples as the sun dipped below the horizon. A gentle breeze carried the whisper of the ocean and a salty fragrance Scarlett couldn't quite place.

As Nate took in the view, he let out a low whistle. "Whoa. Best portal yet, by a mile." He stretched out his arm across the transom, feeling the warm sun on his skin. "I bet the water's perfect." He peeked at Scarlett questioningly. "I don't suppose we could just . . ."

"Nate . . ." Oh, how Scarlett longed to leap into the waves with Nate at that moment. But she knew it didn't matter what she longed for. *Feelings later, champagne now*. "We can't. We're needed here. Besides, the portal could close while we're out there."

"Right, but . . . you got us home from New Orleans, didn't you?"

"I got lucky, because Papa told me about New Orleans. I don't know the location of every portal on Earth. We could easily get stranded on that beach."

His mischievous grin faded into something far softer. "Oh and that would be terrible."

"Yeah," she agreed softly. "Terrible."

"Well, let's visit the beach from right here. We'll just stand on the threshold and watch the sunset."

Scarlett hesitated. This felt dangerous, an indulgence in these chaotic times. At the same time, though, she didn't want to say no.

She edged beside him in the doorway. Standing so close, the feel of Nate's body beside her made her slightly dizzy.

Nate gazed out at the orange-streaked sky. "Hey . . . remember how your mom used to cast a movie screen in your back garden? She'd let all of us miscreants come over on Saturday nights?"

"Of course I remember." Scarlett chuckled. "Melrose Movie Night. All those old movies she'd show? Del and I used to beg

Mama to show something recent, but no. The closest we ever got to a 'current' movie was *The Princess Bride*, and that was only because my mother had a thing for Mandy Patinkin."

"Oh sure, who didn't? He was Inigo Montoya in *The Princess Bride*, for crying out loud! Wait a second—is *that* why we had to watch *Yentl* once a year? Because your mother was sweet on Mandy Patinkin?"

"Indeed, that was why. Still, *Princess Bride* was a good one."

"Fantastic." Nate nodded. "I loved that one. In fact, this one time, I was *this close* to starting a land war in Asia, and then I thought, wait—"

Scarlett laughed. "Don't do it!"

"Exactly! Vizzini says, don't do it."

"See? Melrose Movie Night wasn't just fun, it was educational."

"Definitely." Nate grinned. "Mostly what I remember is a lot of corny old beach flicks? That's what made me think of it now—this portal is bringing it all back. Surfing nuns, singing lifeguards . . . And a lot of Elvis movies, if I'm remembering right. *Blue Hawaii*, wasn't it?"

"Yes, and *Girls! Girls! Girls!* That was all Papa's doing. He was a big Elvis guy."

"Did you know, I've never seen a beach in person? Only in those movies. So I really loved Melrose Movie Night. Plus, I got to sit next to you."

"Aww . . ."

"Well, Scar, the thing about it was—you were *quiet*. So quiet. We sit down to watch a movie, and you'd go for ninety whole minutes without making fun of me."

Scarlett laughed. "And now, suddenly, *you're* constantly making fun of *me*!"

"Reckon, I owe you a few."

A silence stretched between them, not an uncomfortable one, but one that was heavy with unspoken questions and thoughts of roads not taken. Impulsively, Scarlett brushed his hand with hers. "Maybe someday you'll visit a real beach."

"Nothing like this in San Francisco, though, right?"

"I'll have you know, we do have beaches. Buuuut yeah, nothing like this. But we do have fog—I can offer you a whole lot of fog if you're interested."

Nate turned to her, and his expression held a touch of vulnerability now. "Fog can be nice, too."

Scarlett's heart pounded. In this stolen moment, with the world upside down, a reckless joy bubbled up within her.

He leaned in, his eyes questioning. It was a silent invitation, an offer to break through the barrier that had stood between them for so very long.

She closed her eyes. His lips met hers in a kiss as gentle and fleeting as the ocean breeze. It tasted like wishes.

But it was wrong, this flirting, this hinting at something more—not now, when their whole town was in turmoil and everyone's future uncertain. With a pang of regret, Scarlett pulled away.

Nate startled slightly, but then he nodded. "Yeah, you're right. Too much going on right now."

"It's just . . . I mean . . . you know how it is. I can't destroy my entire town *and* make out with you in the same twenty-four-hour period."

"Right." Nate smiled sadly. "Well, who knows? Maybe we'll come back when all this is over."

They gazed at one another for a heavy moment, and then with a last, lingering glance at the sunset, Scarlett stepped away from the door. Nate knelt down, took the screwdriver out of his tool bag, and got to work removing the final lock plate. "Listen, I meant what I said before. Try not to take it so hard about what happened. You didn't 'destroy your entire town,' as you put it. People don't blame you."

"That's very sweet, but it's also a huge lie. It's a given that the town blames the Melroses in general, and once the story gets out—which should take about twenty minutes—then they'll blame me in particular."

"Scar, if you feel like everyone views you as the person who caused the problem, then the thing to do is become the person who fixes it."

"Great idea, Nate—and how do I do that exactly?"

"Here, hold this hardware for me, would you? I have no idea how you fix it. Do you know anything about those dragonflies? If you can figure out how to get rid of them, you're golden. You just need some kind of magical exterminator, right?"

"I don't think that's a thing." Scarlett handed the new lock set to Nate without needing to be asked. "Here you go."

"Why thank you, intrepid assistant."

Nate smiled, and for a moment, all her feelings of dread wilted away.

"Hey, maybe you should talk to Aphra," he suggested.

"Aphra?"

"Yeah, she's got the yarn place on East Street? She's in my store all the time, looking for exotic herbs and weird items I didn't even realize I had. Who knows, maybe she has intel about bugs, too?"

"Hmm, I guess it couldn't hurt to ask. And I could definitely use a new friend at the moment."

Nate studied the lock plate to make sure he'd installed it correctly. "Not really a *new* friend, though—you know Aphra."

"Huh?! I don't remember that name. Oh God." She sighed. "On top of everything else, I'm forgetting people now?"

"Well, you know her and you don't, I guess. I'll let her explain it to you." Nate stood. "Okay, you try the new key—see how I did."

He'd done it perfectly, of course. Scarlett locked the door, then unlocked it and held it open. They stood side by side before the portal—all the trouble of Oak Haven behind them and a gleaming sunset ahead.

"It would be so easy to just step right through," she said longingly. "Evening at the beach. What do you say?"

He lifted an eyebrow. "A little skinny-dipping?"

"Nate!" She laughed girlishly. "Oh my God."

"Just kidding." He sighed. "I think I better get back to work."

"Yeah . . ." Scarlett closed the door and locked it. "Some other time."

"You want to come along to the store?" he asked. "I'll make coffee."

At that moment, nothing on Earth sounded more appealing than coffee with Nate . . . except for the bit where Scarlett would have to face everyone in town who'd been alarmed, damaged, or messed with by magic today. "I think I better stay here and help Mama," she said.

"Sure." He nodded. "I'll see you at the thing later. Everybody's gonna be there."

"The thing? What *thing* is happening tonight that I'm—oh! Oh, no. No, no, no, Nate, tell me they're not doing *that*."

"It's a town crisis," he said with a wink. "Of course, they're doing that."

144

Chapter 18
Oy, With the Flamingos Already

It was standing-room only at the Oak Haven town hall, where residents had gathered to discuss the ongoing magical calamity in their town. As town leaders, the Melroses had been key players at every meeting for centuries. Tonight, though, Delilah got to stay home and mind the hotel while Luna was still chasing a lost guest who'd stepped into his shower and ended up somewhere in Kathmandu. That left Scarlett with nothing better to do than attend. Mama announced she expected to see her middle child's face in the crowd, no matter what.

She skulked around the block a dozen times before forcing herself to go inside.

The large, wood-paneled meeting hall was lined with folding chairs, each one occupied. More people sat on the floor and leaned against the perimeter walls.

On a modest platform at the front of the room sat Oak Haven's Elder Council, composed of Mama Melrose and four other witches of a certain age. In the center of the platform was a podium occupied by Conrad Delmonico, Oak Haven's cardigan-beclad town selectman. Conrad loved the rules of order more than chefs love shallots, but the crowd was agitated and rowdy, and would not be governed—not by Conrad, nor by any rules of *any* order.

Scarlett snuck in the back as quietly as she could—holding her breath when the door loudly squeaked. She found an open spot against the back wall and scanned the room. Her mother was up front, of course, and she saw the Earls and their spouses in a clump in the far left corner. The backs of so many heads looked familiar, calling to a section of Scarlett's memory bank she hadn't accessed in a decade. Nate was over on the right— his face stood out to her as though lit by spotlight. For a half-second, Scarlett considered going over to sit beside him.

Trouble was, he wasn't alone.

He was sitting with Polly Practically Perfect and her Grumpy Goth daughter Violet. Polly leaned over to whisper in Nate's ear. He nodded and chuckled, then whispered a response.

What the hell?! Scarlett thought. *He told me he wasn't with her!*

He sure looked like he was with her. In fact, the little trio looked alarmingly like a family. *How dare he joke with me, gaze at me with those beautiful eyes and then kiss me,* she thought. But before Scarlett could climb all the way to the top of that particular high horse, Nate's earlier comments drifted into her mind: *What'd you expect? Was I supposed to sit here and wait for you?* And she sighed because, of course, he was right. She couldn't expect him to wait around for her. Nobody had the right to ask that of anyone.

Nate noticed her lurking by the back wall, and waved hello. Scarlett smiled weakly and half-waved back.

Suddenly the voice of a middle-aged man overwhelmed all

the other noise. "My gnomes are gone!" he bellowed. "They are gone, and I will have satisfaction!"

Conrad banged on the podium with his comically large gavel. "Please, please. Some order, I'm begging you. At the very least, introduce yourself for the official record." He pointed to his left, where there was a small table, chair, and transcription machine. No person actually sat at the transcription machine— the job was rendered moot when Mama Melrose had enchanted the machine to type on its own. Nevertheless, Conrad took great pride in his transcripts and was painfully aware that tonight's document would be one for the history books.

The angry man took a deep breath. "My name—*as if everyone in this room doesn't know*—is Samuel Chatterjee. Accompanying me is my wife, Belinda. Our gnomes are gone, and I have come here to demand that the elders do something about it!"

Conrad nodded sympathetically. "I completely understand, Samuel. We know the appalling frequency with which your gnomes become the focus of ill-mannered teenagers. But might I suggest, and I mean no offense, that given the current magical crisis we are facing, perhaps we should table your concerns about adolescent pranks until such time as—"

"No!" Sam Chatterjee stomped his foot. "My gnomes are not stolen. They are gone. They left. Early this morning, they packed their bags, called an Uber, and left."

"I'm sorry . . ." Conrad said slowly. "Your gnomes . . . packed?"

"It was brand-new luggage, too!" cried Belinda Chatterjee. "I got it special to take on my ladies' cruise to Bermuda next year."

"Right. Well . . . that does sound . . . potentially . . . magical . . . Err . . ." Conrad turned to the elders, desperately hoping someone would bail him out.

Mama Melrose stood. "Belinda. Sam. I am sorry for your loss. Please be assured that the council will see to it that your gnomes are returned or, if necessary, replaced."

"And the suitcases!" Belinda added.

"And the suitcases, yes."

A woman leapt to her feet; she cut a striking figure with coils of black hair piled on top of her head and a long, flowing robe in deep shades of purple and black. Her eyes glowed as if she knew something she shouldn't—maybe too many things. "Your feeble attempts at recompense are but a flickering candle against the vast darkness that threatens to engulf us all! Who among you shall take responsibility for the utter devastation wreaked upon my sanctum?"

Conrad sighed. "Louise, you must introduce yourself for the official—"

"Oh, this is too ridiculous." Louise's voice dripped with disdain. "I am Louise Demain, as you ignorant fools are well aware. My shop, Tout le Temps, and its sacred timepieces have been utterly shattered by the reckless actions of those who meddle with forces beyond their comprehension."

"Oh boo hoo," replied Samuel. "Whatever will Oak Haven do without its clock repair shop? Oh, I know—we'll all check the time on our phones like normal people."

Louise fixed her gaze on Samuel, her eyes burning with an otherworldly intensity. "Tout le Temps is far more than a mere shop, you blithering imbecile. It is a nexus of temporal energies, a bastion against the chaos that threatens to unravel the very fabric of reality. Oak Haven risks transformation into a prison of mundane horrors, a festering wound upon the face of reality, all due to the incompetence and hubris of those Melrose whelps."

The accusation hit Scarlett like a physical blow. As one of the three "whelps" in question, she longed to disappear from the meeting room, from Oak Haven, and from the planet entirely, if possible.

"Do you not understand the gravity of our circumstances?" Louise continued ominously. "Oak Haven is but a hairsbreadth from becoming . . . the next . . . *Jacksonville*!"

All fell silent as the crowd tried to process this dire proclamation from the town time witch. Louise's gaze swept the room, her voice dripping with contempt. "Yes, you gibbering simpletons. Jacksonville. I have spoken."

As Louise sat down, mutterings and nods of agreement rippled through the crowd. Louise and Samuel were far from the only residents who'd suffered from the jolt of surrealist magic that had swept across Oak Haven in the past twenty-four hours.

As whispers and complaints rippled through the crowd, Scarlett could feel accusing eyes flicking in her direction.

And the worst part? They weren't wrong.

Nate leaned over to make eye contact. *Ignore them,* he mouthed.

Scarlett could only roll her eyes in response. *What about Jacksonville?* she mouthed back. But Nate just shrugged.

Meanwhile up on the platform, Mama Melrose bristled. "The events of last night were unfortunate but completely accidental," she said firmly. "My girls went out to the grove with the expressed intention of *saving* our magic. I hasten to point out that this is far more than anyone else in this room has done."

A young witch stood to be recognized. Tall and rather literally *statuesque*—she looked like Venus de Milo got her arms back and promptly turned into Stevie Nicks—she immediately

149

commanded the boisterous crowd's attention. "For the record, my name is Aphra Pierre, and I run the yarn and fabric store on West Street."

Hang on, Scarlett thought. *That's Aphra?! Nate said I knew her . . . but he must be wrong. I would definitely remember someone so striking.*

Aphra continued. "I would like to point out that the Melrose family has heroically served this town for generations. If they say this was an accident that will soon be rectified, then I think we owe them the benefit of the doubt."

"What a kiss-ass!" hooted Belinda.

"Not at all. I'm just suggesting we put our pitchforks away for the moment."

Conrad nodded. "That's very wise, Aphra, thank you."

"You dare speak of wisdom, you fetus?!" Louise sneered at Aphra. "Does your pathetic little shop remain untouched by the eldritch forces that now run rampant through our streets? Or have you, too, borne witness to the unraveling of all that we hold dear?"

"Well, Louise, as a matter of fact, we've had our share of trouble today, too. Fabrics changing colors, some of my best wool turned back into a sheep, and some of the knitting needles have become polyamorous. But all of this is fixable."

"I'm sorry," Conrad said. "Your needles have what?!"

"Oh, it's . . . not worth a fuss, really, we should move on . . ." But when Aphra looked around the room, it was clear no one in the crowd was looking to move anywhere that didn't involve an explanation. "All right . . . I sell knitting needles, which usually come in pairs. Overnight, the needles seem to have collectively decided they want to see other people. As it were. Many of

150

the pairs have swapped, and there was a somewhat dramatic throuple with a quilting needle . . . Anyway, okay, yes—things are a bit chaotic at the store. But I wanted to say that we should focus less on blame and more on how we can move forward."

"Move forward?" Conrad cried. "With a town full of unpaired knitting needles?"

She shrugged. "Maybe the needles are happier this way, I don't know. Honestly, Conrad, the magic issues are a minor inconvenience in the long run."

"Says you," hollered Belinda Chatterjee. "You try going on holiday with no luggage!"

A man in a cheap suit stood to be heard. "Harold Fleming, accountant. Can we please discuss the flamingo droppings? They're all over my yard."

"Absolutely no one wants to hear about your droppings, Harold," shouted Louise.

"I got a pile of flamingo shit the size of a Hyundai!"

The hall erupted, everyone shouting over each other about their own magical mishaps. Conrad pounded away with his gavel, trying helplessly to restore order. His protests were drowned out by the cacophony of complaints.

Finally, Mama Melrose stood up and let out a piercing whistle that sliced through the noise. The crowd fell silent as she fixed Harold with a steely gaze.

"Harold Fleming, if you think your flamingo droppings are our most pressing issue, you are sorely mistaken. Oak Haven has far greater problems than the state of your yard."

Harold wilted under Mama Melrose's glare; with a mumbled apology, he melted back into his seat. The room fell into a tense silence as the gravity of the situation settled over them.

"My friends," Mama Melrose began, her voice resolute. "We are all facing challenges caused by this surge of anarchic magic in our town. But pointing fingers and dwelling on our individual troubles won't solve anything. We need to come together, share information, and work as a community to restore balance to Oak Haven."

A murmur of agreement rippled through the crowd . . . although, beneath the positive noises, it was also possible to hear Louise Demain muttering, "Naturally, that is exactly what the Melroses *would* say . . ."

"Investigative teams will be organized to look into each of these incidents," Mama Melrose declared. "And all your concerns will be addressed in due course. We will all need to work together to bring order back to Oak Haven. The town has faced far worse. And we will face this too—as a family. Even if some members of that family—" she lifted an eyebrow in Louise's direction "—need reminding what that means."

The energy in the room shifted. The group frustration remained, but now it was laced with a touch of stubborn Oak Haven resilience. As the meeting broke into smaller discussions, Scarlett finally was able to exhale.

Conrad leapt off the platform and went to check on his precious transcript. His moan of existential despair stopped everyone in their tracks.

"Whatever is wrong with you, Conrad?" asked Mama Melrose.

Conrad held up the transcript for everyone to see. It consisted of seven pages of single-spaced *ha ha ha ha no transcript for you ha ha ha ha no transcript for you ha ha ha ha* . . . The magic that controlled the transcription machine was, it seemed, just as chaotic as magic everywhere else.

Scarlett muttered, "I guess all work and no play makes Conrad a dull boy."

"Scarlett!" called Mama Melrose. She stepped off the platform and pushed through the crowd toward her daughter. "I'm pleased to see you." But before she could make her way across the room, a figure emerged to cut off Mama's approach.

"Miss Melrose, a word, if you please," puffed Harold Fleming. His cheeks were flushed with a mix of anger and exertion. "The droppings . . . it's quite bad. Truly very bad. And given your . . . *connection* . . . to this whole situation, it seems you owe me some assistance. Don't you think? Why don't you come with me and I can show you what—"

Just then an angel arrived in the form of Aphra Pierre, who stepped between Scarlett and Harold. "Sorry, Harry. Scarlett's not available right now. Please leave a message with the Flamingo Task Force, and they'll get in touch." She steered Scarlett toward the exit, ignoring Harold's spluttering protests.

Once outside, Scarlett finally managed a shaky laugh. "Oy, with the flamingos already."

"It's great to see you, Scar." Aphra wrapped her arm around Scarlett's and led her away from the town hall. "What do you say to a stiff cup of tea?"

Chapter 19
Where's Wallace?

Aphra pushed open the old, weathered door of Sometimes a Great Notion, and Scarlett followed her inside. She still wasn't certain she really knew this person, even though Nate said she did. But if someone—anyone—was inclined to be kind to Scarlett, this was not a moment she was inclined to say no.

Muted light spilled over shelves, casting long shadows that played across the floorboards. Like every shop in downtown Oak Haven, Aphra's place was decorated with a collection of scarecrows—but hers were far better-dressed than most, in velvet dresses with billowing sleeves, floppy hats and an impressive array of silk scarves.

"Why don't you have a seat by the window," Aphra said. "I'll fetch some tea."

Scarlett's footsteps fell softly on the worn wooden floorboards as she wove her way past aisles crammed with baskets overflowing with yarn, from the softest merino to the rustiest tweed. Over there were quilting fabrics in seemingly endless varieties; over here sat every color of thread imaginable. But in the very center of the shop was something curious: a thrown-together collection of basic-looking sacks, boxes, and what appeared to be cages. Both the objects and the display itself looked hastily made— very out of character with the effortless charm and perfection of the rest of the shop. But the sign beside them made sense of the mishmash: "Hand-Woven Magic-Dampeners: Safely Contain All Errant Magic."

Aha, Scarlett thought. *I expect there's been a run on those today, what with the grove in the state that it's in.* A pang of that same old guilt rose in her chest, but then she thought, *Well, at least my fuck-ups are good for business.*

She settled in an old chair, made welcoming by a collection of hand-stitched pillows. Looking around the store, she found it impossible to imagine the "hectic day" that Aphra had described at the town meeting—everything seemed so soothing and relaxed. You'd never know that just hours earlier, the store had been awash with wrongly colored yarn, broken-hearted needles, and a very confused sheep.

"That you, babe?" A woman's voice echoed from somewhere deep in the shop. "How'd the meeting go?"

"Yes, I'm home," Aphra responded. "I brought a friend back for tea."

Aphra returned from the back room, carrying a tray with a teapot, two well-loved mugs, a plate of cookies, and a half-pint bottle of whiskey. Accompanying her was a Black woman, her braided hair pulled back in a scarf. She wore sweatpants and a Stanford sweatshirt, yet still managed to look stylish.

"This is Scarlett," Aphra told her. "Scarlett, this is my wife, Dayo."

"You're one of the famous Melroses," Dayo said.

"I am," Scarlett replied. "More like *infamous*, at this point."

Dayo grinned. "Yeahhh, I was trying to be polite. Well, welcome home? I guess? Do you feel welcome?"

"At this precise moment, I do. But in general? Not so much."

"Have faith, I'm sure things will improve. Okay, I'll let you two catch up." Dayo turned and gave Aphra a kiss. "Don't be too long, babe."

"I won't, I promise," Aphra said.

Dayo went back upstairs, and Aphra settled in a chair opposite Scarlett. "We'll let that tea steep for a minute. Dayo is a bit impatient because tonight is usually the night we watch *The Wire*. I know, I know, that puts us *way* behind the times. But things move slowly in Oak Haven, as you probably recall. And we're very concerned about Wallace."

"You should be," Scarlett replied.

"Hey, no spoilers!"

"Sorry. Say, I couldn't help but notice your display of magic dampeners. I take it you don't just knit with yarn around here."

Aphra met her gaze with an amused smile. "With all due respect to yarn, it's one of the least interesting materials I use."

"You know, Aphra . . . I feel like Oak Haven has gotten a lot more interesting since I left."

"We have a speakeasy in town now."

Scarlett gasped, her eyes wide with disbelief. "We DO NOT."

"No word of a lie. Dayo runs it, in fact!"

"Really?! That's fantastic."

"Yeah . . . actually she and Zahir are talking about opening a real place. The speakeasy is really just a shack in the Chatterjees' back garden. But they want to do craft cocktails and pub food, that kind of thing. They're just having trouble finding the right location. But it'll happen. Hey—you stick around long enough, maybe Dayo will hire you."

"Well, all right." Scarlett grinned. "I will take that under advisement. Although, I think my mother would be pretty scandalized by a Melrose girl waiting tables. But my mother is down on pretty much everything."

"Right." Aphra smiled. "Tough old Kelly Melrose. Some things never change."

"Yeah, *some* don't . . ." She knew she had to ask Aphra how they knew each other. Still, Scarlett wasn't sure how to raise the issue without sounding as self-involved and forgetful as she apparently was. "But speaking of things changing . . . you . . . have changed? I guess?"

"Do you want a hint?" Aphra's eyes twinkled as she seemingly read Scarlett's mind. "I'll give you a hint if you like."

"I'm so embarrassed . . ."

"Don't be, I look a lot different. Your hint is: captain, Oak Haven High rugby team."

"Well, sure . . ." Scarlett's forehead wrinkled in confusion. "I remember the team, but our school didn't have a women's rugby team, so how could you have been . . . oh. Ohh! That was you?"

Aphra threw her head back and laughed. "That was me."

"You *do* look different! By which I mean fantastic. At the meeting tonight, I was like, *who's the knock-out?!*"

"Aww, shucks. Here, let me offer you some of this nectar." Aphra poured two cups of tea and then picked up the whiskey bottle, holding it in a sort of questioning way. "Yes?"

"Hell, yes."

"Excellent." She added a generous dollop to each teacup.

"So, here's the short version. One day, shortly after graduation, I made a significant discovery: I am fundamentally a klutz. I have no natural athletic ability whatsoever. Zero. Turned out, I was subconsciously using magic to *make myself into* the sports star my parents wanted me to be."

"You were casting spells without realizing it," Scarlett said thoughtfully.

"Yeah, I mean . . . does that sound weird?"

Scarlett grinned. "Not only does it *not* sound weird, but my mother recently informed me I apparently do the same thing. She says that back in San Francisco, I was not living 'magic-free,' as I told myself I was. But that in fact, I have been subconsciously casting all over the place."

"Whoa." Aphra laughed and lifted a closed fist. "Sisterhood of the Subconscious! Yeah, I was so desperate to fit in? The magic just happened, totally out of my control. Once I figured myself out, started presenting myself to the world the way I truly am on the inside, suddenly I could cast spells or not cast them, as I wanted. You know, the way magic is supposed to work."

"The way it *used to* work," Scarlett grumbled, "until I came to town."

"Oh, bosh—we were having magic problems before you got here."

"Aphra, what's all this I hear about Jacksonville? At the meeting tonight. What's-her-name, the time witch, said something about Oak Haven turning into Jacksonville."

"Bah, don't listen to her. She was being mean."

"No, come on," Scarlett urged. "What was she talking about?"

Aphra sighed. "Ahhh, well. Jacksonville, Florida, used to be home to some very *very* old oak trees. Old enough to support a whole lot of magic. There was a very powerful coven down there. And then the city came along and took out all the trees out to build— Oh, who knows? A shopping mall? Parking lots? Whatever, I have no idea. The point is, magic died out, the Jacksonville coven disappeared, and now that part of north Florida is mainly known for strip malls and traffic jams. But listen, don't let those town-hall biddies make you feel bad. That won't happen here. We'll fix this, don't worry."

Scarlett nodded. "Nate suggested that you might be a good person to ask about these flies?"

"*Nate* suggested that, did he? And how are *Nate and Scarlett* doing these days? The inquiring minds of Oak Haven long to know."

"Nothing to tell."

"Mmhm. Well, that sounds like a fib to me. And as far as the insects go . . . The scuttlebutt around town today was it's some sort of dangerous dragonfly?"

"They're shaped like dragonflies, but much smaller. And they glow bright red."

Aphra shuddered. "I don't like the sound of that. Have you looked them up in the *Myrmex Arcana*?"

"Was that a double album by King Crimson?"

"Ha, no. It's a reference work about all sorts of magical creepy-crawlies from across time. If there's any known information about those flies, the *Myrmex Arcana* will have it. I'm sure Polly has a copy over at the bookstore."

"Ohh, goody." Scarlett sighed. "A trip to the bookstore . . ."

Aphra tilted her head, curious. "I thought you and Polly were friends. No?"

"We are, it's just . . . Nothing. Forget it."

Aphra made a face. "Not nothing."

"Yeah it's . . . I mean . . . Argh! Okay. Fine. I'm just gonna ask you. Polly and Nate. Are they a thing or what? He says they aren't, and when he's *with me*, he sure acts like they aren't. But they looked very *thing-like* at the town meeting tonight. What do you think?"

"Aha! At last, we have arrived at the root of the matter." Aphra added a bit more whiskey to their teacups. "Well, since you asked what I think, I shall tell you. I think that Polly is a charming woman in the prime of life who was left in the lurch by her blockhead of an ex and forced to raise a troubled teen on her own. I think that Nate is a handsome, capable, and highly eligible bachelor with a good heart and an appropriate level of respect for women. And so, I think it's quite natural that Nate is absolute fucking catnip to Ms. Triple P, and honestly, who can blame her."

Scarlett stared down at her tea-and-whiskey concoction, wishing it were made entirely of whiskey.

"I also think . . ." Aphra leaned across the table to take Scarlett's hand in hers ". . . that Nate has only ever really loved one person. Then and now. But *she left him*. Remember that bit? If she came back—and I mean came back to stay—I think that Nate would no longer be able to so much as remember Polly's name."

Scarlett looked up to find Aphra's emerald green eyes staring straight into hers.

"What I'm saying is: it's in your court, my friend."

***

Over a little more tea and whiskey, the old friends reminisced and joked and made the world feel right again. But then came an impatient call from upstairs.

"Babe! I am pushing play on this episode in five minutes! With or without you."

Aphra chuckled. "Duty calls, I'm afraid . . ."

"Perfectly okay." Scarlett stood. "I should go before it gets any later. Maybe Polly will open the bookstore for me, to get a look at that . . . what was it called?"

"*Myrmex Arcana.*"

"That's the one. You never know: if I go back to the inn with some actionable information? Maybe my sisters will cut me some slack."

"Worth a shot," Aphra smiled. "C'mon, let me walk you out."

"Bye, Dayo—nice to meet you!" Scarlett hollered upstairs. "I'm giving you your wife back now."

"Thank you kindly," came the reply.

Aphra unlocked the door, and the old friends embraced. "It's so good to have you back. I hope you'll consider staying. San Francisco doesn't deserve you."

Scarlett had to laugh. "Right now, Oak Haven wants me to get what I deserve, so we'll have to see. And listen . . . Aphra . . . I just want to say . . ."

"What's up, hon?"

She paused, not sure how to find the words. "I guess I just wanted to say . . . I'm sorry."

Aphra frowned. "Not the magic thing again! We've covered that."

"No, I mean, about when we were growing up. Like . . . you and I used to hang out and . . . . and you must have been struggling. Right? You were dealing with this huge identity issue, and it must have been hard. And I had no clue. I never thought for a second what might have been going on with you."

"Oh, Scarlett. Look, first of all—as far as me being a struggling teenager, show me one who isn't. Right? We all had stuff to deal with. We were just kids—it wasn't your job to figure *me* out any more than the other way around. And anyway, what were you supposed to say? *Hey, have you considered that maybe you are miserable living as a boy, and all that spellcasting is just subconscious overcompensation?* Come on! That was *my* journey to go on. Mine. Okay?"

"Okay." Scarlett impulsively hugged Aphra again.

"Now go, find that book. And be nice to Polly when you see her. She's had a rough time. I mean, talk about struggling teens! Have you tried to have a conversation with her daughter Violet?"

"I have yet to successfully make eye contact with Violet. Much less conversation."

"That's what I'm talking about."

Scarlett left Aphra standing in the doorway, but she only walked a few steps down the sidewalk before turning back. "Hey, Aphra! I thought of something else to apologize for."

Aphra shook her head and laughed. "I'm going to need you to stop saying *I'm sorry* about every damn thing, Scar."

"No, you'll like this one. You're a good friend, and I'm sorry I've stayed away so long."

"Aha . . ." she said with a warm smile. "Now *that* apology, I will accept."

Chapter 20
Nevermore

It was getting late, and the well-behaved witches of Oak Haven had all gone home. Scarlett, on the other hand, ambled along the lonely streets toward the park. She studied the sigils carved into the streets, crosswalks, and doorways as she went. She lacked her sister Del's instincts about whether the sigils were functioning properly or not. But it worried her.

Nothing else in this town is functioning properly, she thought. *What happens if these sigils lose their tiny minds, too? How long until some developer replaces our grove with a shopping mall?* Aphra had projected such confidence that Oak Haven would never go the way of Jacksonville. It was a feeling Scarlett sorely wished she could share.

The CLOSED sign was posted at the bookstore, but there were dim lights on in the shop. Scarlett glanced across the street at Williams Hardware, which was likewise closed but had lights on anyway. She wondered whether Polly was visiting Nate's shop or he hers.

How sweet. Two small-town shopkeepers, situated right across the road from each other. Maybe they used to be rivals and are now falling in love. That's how it works in movies, right?

Feeling annoyed—partially at them but mostly at herself for caring so much—Scarlett gave a brisk knock on the bookstore's door.

The door swung open.

"Hello?" Scarlett stepped gingerly over the threshold. "Anybody home?"

No response arrived. The store was dimly lit and deathly silent.

She made her way past the construction area by the entrance—the piles of lumber and bags of unmixed concrete, the table saw awaiting its next victim. There were abandoned coffee cups and scattered sawdust on the floor. Scarlett could see that all the old sigils had been removed, but most had yet to be replaced by anything new. Whatever Polly was hoping to accomplish in terms of keeping magic out of the store, she hadn't done it yet.

"Anybody here?" she called again. "It's Scarlett! I'm just looking for a book—Aphra suggested you might have it. The *Myrmex Arcana*? So, I'm just going to look around if that's . . ." She sighed and stopped yelling. "Stop talking to yourself, Scar."

The shelves along the front of the store were all covered with tarps, which made it tricky to figure out which books were kept where. Then it occurred to Scarlett that well-loved books and best-sellers tended to populate the front: a reference book about magical insects would probably be shelved somewhere at the back. She made her way through the store, her eyes darting left and right in search of a reference section.

In the labyrinth of shelves, Scarlett scarcely noticed the shadows deepening, the air taking on a strange, briny smell. A loud noise startled her—it came from somewhere in Classics of Literature. She turned a corner to find a heavy hardback had somehow landed on the floor as if it had jumped off the shelf on its own. She approached it slowly—feeling a bit sheepish for fearing a book. It was a thick, leatherbound copy of the *Greatest Works of Jules Verne*. The book flipped itself open, pages turning on their own.

A massive, papery form unfurled from the open book—a giant squid formed from Jules Verne's own printed words, its monstrous eye fixed squarely on her. Scarlett screamed as a tentacle, impossibly long and assembled from the book's pages, whipped out and coiled around her waist.

She gasped, the weight of the enchanted paper crushing her. The squid, its beak snapping menacingly, dragged her back toward the book.

Scarlett grabbed the side of a shelf and hung on tight, trying to keep calm and focus her powers, willing the tentacle to loosen its grip. The monstrous limb twitched, and the paper relaxed momentarily but then clamped down with renewed pressure. Tiny printed letters dug into her skin.

That's ink, she thought angrily. *Ink is not supposed to be sharp!*

Which gave her an idea.

She focused her power on the ink, turning it liquid and slippery. She began wriggling, hoping to free herself, when two more tentacles joined the first. The more Scarlett struggled, the more entangled she became.

"I will not die at the hands of an old book," she cried out. "Let me go, you overwritten pile of—"

Paper, she thought. This is just enchanted paper.

Scarlett snapped, and a spark leapt from her fingertips. Success! Tiny crackles of flame danced along the tentacle, singeing the edges of the pages. The squid recoiled, allowing her to scramble free.

"Ha!" she pointed at the squid. "Haaaaaa ha ha!"

Her pride was short-lived. An errant spark had landed on a nearby shelf, and now flames licked at old, dry book bindings. The fire spread with alarming speed, filling the air with choking smoke.

You can be careless with fire sometimes, Luna had said.

Goddammit.

A fresh tentacle snapped from the book, coiling around Scarlett's feet. She leapt away, grabbing for as high a shelf as she could reach and pulling downward. A pile of books crashed atop the tentacle, and the squid gave a high-pitched squeal.

Scarlett glanced around in desperation. The heat was rising. The fire made its way to the construction area, consuming lumber and books with equal enthusiasm.

From the smoke, Scarlett heard three voices. "All for one and one for all!"

The Three Musketeers materialized amidst the rising flames, composed of the very paper and words that Alexandre Dumas had used to create them. Ever the tactician, Athos climbed atop a bookshelf to assess the situation. Porthos, with a bellow, waded through the smoke, the bulk of his papery form thus far resistant to the heat. In a flash of white paper, Aramis brought down his gleaming blade, severing one of the tentacles.

Disoriented, the squid thrashed wildly. Books rained from shelves, their pages scattering like burning moths. The Musketeers' swords flashed, slicing through the creature. Still, the squid's pages mended themselves as quickly as the Musketeers could attack.

Suddenly, a strange rumbling swept through the shop. The flames wavered, and a great wave, formed of book pages, surged from a copy of *Jaws* that had fallen off a shelf in Contemporary Fiction. Riding the wave's crest was a fishing boat, the *Orca*, its sides dripping with ocean-soaked text. As the wave crashed over the battle, a man sang out, *"Farewell and adieu to you fair Spanish ladies. Farewell and adieu to you, ladies of Spain!"* The wave swept the squid away in a deluge of seawater-splashed paper. Then everything dissolved back into the chaotic arrangement of scattered books and wrecked shelves. The Musketeers' battle cry faded as they disappeared back into their novel.

Scarlett coughed, struggling to breathe in the smoke-filled air. Despite the wave, the flames continued to spread, consuming books and shelves with terrifying intensity. It sickened her to realize that this fire was her doing, yet another of her failures.

Luna was right—I am dangerous.

Scarlett glanced at the shop's front door, wondering if she could make it past the flames and out onto the street. She saw a shadow moving outside the shop window—then the shadow took form.

It was Nate.

He charged into the store, brandishing a cherry-red fire extinguisher from Williams. Fear and guilt warred within Scarlett, with an unexpected flare of something else—something hot and undeniable at the sight of him.

"Scarlett, what in hell are you doing here?!" He moved with determination, the extinguisher spewing a white cloud as he fought the flames. "Are you okay?"

"I am now," she called out. "But when Polly sees this, she's gonna literally kill me."

Nate sprayed foam across the burning shelves. "I'll tell her it was my fault."

"You'd do that for me?"

He paused, turning to look at her. "I'd do anything for you. Don't you know that?"

She wanted to go to him, but the air was thick, her vision blurring. Scarlett stumbled, landing on a pile of books. As she pulled herself to standing, she felt a change in the air—a new danger sending vibrations through the smoke. Nearby books shivered and danced upon the shelves, pages rustling with an eerie rhythm.

"Scarlett, watch out!" Nate's warning came just as a creature emerged, a grotesque mix of ink and paper. It was Edgar Allan Poe's raven made monstrous, horrifying—its form dripping midnight ink, its talons gleaming with the sharp edges of razor-thin pages.

The raven shrieked and swooped at Scarlett. She tried to conjure a hasty, protective shield, but it shattered like glass.

Nate charged. He swung the empty extinguisher, striking at the raven's papery wings. The giant bird screeched in rage, flapping wildly. He flung his body at a nearby bookcase, pulling it down with a thunderous crash and pinning the raven beneath. Loose pages scattered, showering the room with a flurry of old tales and biting words.

Scarlett lunged forward, seizing her chance. She focused her power to draw out the bird's essence, pulling Poe's very words out of the creature and into the air. The monster thrashed, its papery form dissolving in a whirlwind of swirling text.

But it wasn't enough. With an ear-jolting shriek, the raven wrenched itself free and aimed its sharpened talons straight at

Scarlett. Nate leapt at the bird, putting his own body between her and the creature, a shield of flesh and blood. With one final, desperate surge of magic, Scarlett yanked out the raven's remaining essence, which exploded in a ball of pages, letters, and evil black ink.

The impact knocked them both to the floor. The extinguisher clattered away, and they landed hard, a tangle of limbs and flying paper.

"Nate, are you—" The words caught in her throat. He was on top of her, solid and strong, his chest heaving from exertion. They were surrounded by smoldering books, the air heavy with the scent of old paper and smoke.

His eyes, dark and fierce, locked on to hers. The chaotic room seemed to swirl around them. "Don't worry," he breathed. "I've got you."

Scarlett's heart frantically battered her chest. Desire, wild and undeniable, flared hot inside her, born of danger and adrenaline, of shared battles and unspoken longings.

Nate cupped her face with his hand, his thumb stroking her cheekbone. "Scarlett . . . I . . ."

His touch ignited a longing in her, a need that overrode the danger, the fire, her own common sense . . . everything. With a gasp, she pulled him toward her.

His lips met hers, hard and urgent. Scarlett arched into the kiss, her body melting against his, every inch of her clamoring for more. His hands moved along her body, pulling her into him—a desperate, hungry claiming.

This was madness. This was exactly what she wanted.

They shifted, rolling together across the damaged books, a tangle of limbs and ragged breaths, hands exploring each other in the darkness. Scarlett tore at his shirt, and he at hers, both desperate to feel their skin against one another. If there was fire, it was in them now.

Just then, a voice shattered the spell like a bucket of icy water thrown over their writhing limbs.

"What the hell is going on?" Polly stood in the doorway, eyes wider than ever, staring in outrage at the disheveled pair. "What in the hell are you people doing here? What have you done to my store?!"

Scarlett gasped, her face flushing crimson as she scrambled upright, hastily pulling her blouse back into place.

Nate, though sheepish, held a flicker of defiance in his eyes. The wreckage, the burning embers, Polly's fury . . . none of it could change what had just happened. He reached for Scarlett's hand.

"I'm so sorry, Polly," he said, a half-smile playing on his lips. "But please believe this is all my fault."

Chapter 21
Emergency Management

As the bookstore smoldered, Scarlett, Nate, and Polly convened awkwardly on the corner outside, awaiting the emergency team. None of the three spoke; none of the three so much as glanced at the others. Scarlett knew she ought to ask Polly if there was a copy of *Myrmex Arcana* in the store . . . *But hell,* she thought, *I can't even look her in the eye. How can I ask for a favor after all this?*

So the three just stood there together, silently waiting. It took the emergency services van about ten minutes to arrive, and it was the longest ten minutes of their lives.

Normally the fine ladies of the Oak Haven Emergency Magic Service (EMS) strode into any calamity with full confidence that there was no trouble so dire that magic couldn't fix it. But in the course of this very long day, they'd been run ragged on a seemingly endless number of confusing and intractable problems. The quartet of uniformed witches tumbled out of their van looking weary and very much in need of a few hours' rest. It hurt Scarlett's heart to know she was the one keeping them busy.

The EMS team leader was Priti Chatterjee, adult daughter

of the angry gnome-owners from the town meeting. She greeted Polly and Nate with reassuring smiles. Scarlett, on the other hand, received a whoop and a big hug. "Scarlett, you're back! Look at you! Aw, man, so great to see you."

"You too, Priti! Sorry, it's under these circumstances."

"Oh bah." She waved off Scarlett's apology. "It's the job. Hey, Ellen," she said to one of the other women, "would you unload the gear, please?" Priti flung an arm around Scarlett's shoulder and guided her away from the others. "So, how are you doing these days, anyway?"

"I'm all right. Today has been a little hardcore, that's for sure."

"You can say that again. Been rough all over, due to that grove situation."

Oh, you mean, my complete and utter fuck-up that could destroy the whole town, Scarlett thought. *That old thing?*

To change the subject, she said, "Hey, congratulations on your wedding. Mama told me you had it at the Stargazer. Who's the lucky guy?"

"Thanks! His name is Raj. Handsome, funny, makes a bad-ass cheesecake—you know, all the important stuff. We started dating when I was working in Boston. When he proposed, I told him I'd only say yes if he gave up the city and moved back here."

"And how is he taking to his new life as a non-powered spouse in Oak Haven?"

"You kidding?" Priti laughed. "Fucking thrilled. Back in Boston, Raj worked fourteen-hour days at a law firm. Now he reads two books a week, builds model airplanes, and hangs out with the Earls over at the hardware store."

"*Living the Life of Raj*, sounds like."

"You know it. So Scar, listen . . ." Priti's tone turned serious as she directed her attention to the bookstore window. "This is quite a mess, huh? Can you tell me what happened?"

"Sure, I came into the store looking for a book, and instead, one attacked me. A couple, actually."

Priti nodded. "I think there was a *Dracula* situation recently, wasn't there?"

"That's what I heard, that a copy of *Dracula* bit someone. But this was different: a squid physically left the pages of a book to come after me. And we struggled, and then I realized it was made of paper, and then . . ." she gestured helplessly at the charred store ". . . *that*."

"Gotcha. Well, we're going to head inside and check things out, and make sure they're safe." Priti strode back to her colleagues at the van. "Squad, let's gear up."

"Hang on, Priti? Can I ask you a favor?"

"Uh, sure? I've only been on duty for fifteen hours with no break, but yeah, please let me do you a favor."

"I know, I'm so sorry, it's just . . . I came here to pick up a book called *Myrmex Arcana*. Aphra says it might have information about the dragonflies infesting the grove. But then the squid happened, and everything got a bit crazy—" she forced herself not to glance at Nate "—and I never found the book. I can't ask Polly because . . . well, I can't."

"Right, too embarrassed to speak to the owner of the bookstore you've nearly burned down. Got it." Priti hoisted her pack over one shoulder. "You want me, EMS team leader and certified emergency response volunteer, to play librarian for you."

"I wouldn't ask if it weren't important. I mean, I could go in myself if you'd prefer that I—"

"All right, all right. Keep your shirt on, Melrose. I'll keep an eye out, and if I see it—that's *if*, mind you—I'll grab it."

Priti strode over to her team. "Everybody ready? Now, I want you all to keep your wits about you. Who knows if Polly had a copy of *The Necronomicon* in there."

"I didn't," Polly offered. "But I did have *Silence of the Lambs*, so . . ." She shrugged.

"Good tip," Nedra replied. "Polly, would you consult with us here? Let us know where the most dangerous sections are? No fava beans and chianti for us tonight."

Polly reluctantly joined the EMS team as they ventured into the store. Left alone on the dark street, Nate laid a gentle hand on Scarlett's elbow. "You okay?"

"Yeah, yeah of course. You?"

"I'm fine." He smiled shyly. "A little frustrated, maybe."

Scarlett felt herself blushing so intensely, she was certain it could be seen from space. "That was a little . . . uh . . ."

"Yeah." Nate chuckled. "It was a little *uh*."

What do you think you're doing, Melrose? she chastised herself. *You can't do this—you don't deserve a man like this. You can't do the things you've done and then have him.*

"I think the situation just got away from us," she said suddenly. "I mean, don't you think? You know, with the inferno and the ink monsters and all . . ." A wave of shame swept over her, and the words spilled out in an unstoppable flood of awkwardness and guilt. "I mean . . . that's not what we want, right? I don't live here; I'm not sticking around. And you don't want to *ever* leave, apparently. So, you know, what is the point? We don't even make any sense; it was just a big mistake."

"*Mistake*," he repeated dully. His expression was unreadable. "*What was the point*. Yeah. I guess there's no point."

"Well, *no point* sounds a bit harsh. I just meant that—"

"No," Nate interrupted. "No, of course you're right. There's no point to us at all. Anyway, glad you're okay, I should get going." He stalked across the street.

"Nate, no, hang on, that's not—"

He threw Williams' front door open, slammed it behind him, and disappeared inside.

"Oh goddammit," Scarlett said quietly. "Dammit, dammit, dammit."

"Don't worry about it," said a sarcastic voice behind her. "Men suck anyway."

She turned. Violet was sitting on the sidewalk outside the bookstore, staring up at her. Scarlett stared back, waiting for the teenager to say something else.

A few moments passed, and it occurred to Scarlett that the teenager was not going to say a damned thing. Scarlett walked over and sat down beside her.

"Violet, I just want you to know . . . the fire was an accident caused by magic being in anarchy. But we're going to fix it. Between the EMS team and Nate's handyman skills and my . . . well . . . my overwhelming sense of guilt, I guess . . . we're going to restore every page to every book in your mom's wonderful store."

"Fuck that place," Violet muttered. "I'm only sorry you didn't burn the whole thing to the ground."

"Well, hang on, I didn't *do it* in the sense that you're suggesting."

"I don't care. Maybe if the store fails, my mother will finally

175

leave this stupid town. Maybe then I could find a guy to like who can remember that I exist. Hey, maybe we can even find my dad. Not that he'd know he's my dad. But still, *I'd* know he was my dad, at least. That would be something."

Scarlett took a beat before responding, taken aback by Violet's honesty. Her first thought was that Handsome Bill's main contribution to Violet was his attractive DNA, and that, given his selfish behavior, good genes were about all the parenting she ought to expect from the guy. But she tried to think of something more positive to say. "I wouldn't be so quick to write off Oak Haven if I were you. It's pretty great."

"What are you talking about? *You left*. You're, like, *famous* for how hard you left."

"Yeah, well . . . I suppose that makes me pretty qualified to talk about life on the outside, now, doesn't it? Violet, the rest of the world is . . . well, it's got some good aspects, for sure. A lot of the food delivery guys are very handsome."

"Shut up. You're not funny."

"But it's not your home. In San Francisco, I'm always pretending witches aren't real. That might seem like no big thing, but it's trickier than you think. I basically have to lie about my entire life. I can't talk about the Turkey Trot we have downtown every Thanksgiving, which I adore. I can't tell the story about how my mother conjured an actual unicorn for my fifth birthday. Or about the time Luna and I tried to fly, and we ended up stuck on the church steeple."

"Well, lucky you to have so many adorable memories about your delightful childhood in Oak Haven. Some of us didn't get that."

"Violet, listen—"

176

"Whatever." She stood up. "Happy Panda closes at midnight. I'm gonna go order while I still can."

***

Scarlett sat alone outside the store, the smell of smoke in her hair, the sound of Violet's anger in her ears, and the memory of Nate's hands still warm on her skin. She looked over at the hardware store—everything was dark. If she was going to fix things with him, it would have to wait until tomorrow now.

But . . . do I even want to fix things? Maybe Nate being mad at me keeps everything simpler. After all, I should be focused on Oak Haven, not him. Plus, the more tangled up we get, the harder it will be to leave when all this is over.

Shouting and children's laughter emerged from inside the store. Suddenly, a gaggle of Victorian ruffians made of paper and text came barreling outside and took off down the street. Priti was right behind them, shouting, "Hey! Hey, get back here, you little bastards!"

But, the paper-children had the energy of fiction, while Priti was an actual human who'd been on the clock for fifteen hours. She gave up the chase and ambled back to the bookstore, defeated. Seeing Scarlett waiting by the building, Priti shrugged. "The Artful Dodger and his pals got away from us."

Ellen the EMS volunteer appeared in the doorway. "Those little shits took my wallet!"

"So . . ." Scarlett stood and joined them. "How's it going in there?"

"We're getting it done," Priti said tiredly. "But we have to shut the magic down one shelf at a time, so it's slow. Slower than a bunch of pickpockets, unfortunately."

"Can I help?" Scarlett offered.

"Nah. Thanks, but we have a system. Hey, Ellen—hand me that thing, would you?"

Ellen returned to the store and reemerged with a thick leather-bound book, which she handed to Scarlett. "Ta da," she said tiredly as she handed her the *Myrmex Arcana*.

"Ohh wonderful! This book is going to be so helpful. Thank you both so, so much!" Scarlett accepted the book eagerly and flicked through the pages. "Now we'll have everything fixed in— oh." She sighed. "Oh, for fuck's sake."

Priti frowned. "What's wrong?"

"Oh, you know," Scarlett said resignedly. "Nothing is ever easy."

Chapter 22
Ain't That a Kick in the Head

Scarlett headed back toward the inn, lugging the ancient magical text and about a hundred pounds of guilt and regret about a hundred different things.

Magic is in chaos because of me. The town's iconic bookstore is a smoking ruin because of me. The EMS team is about to collapse from overwork because of me. Nate is mad because of me. It seems as though Violet might be upset because of me, too? Scarlett wasn't sure whether to take the hit on that last one or not.

Passing Hexpresso Yourself, Scarlett was surprised to see the lights still on. On the chalkboard outside was the jaunty announcement: QUIZ NIGHT! SHOW OFF YOUR MAD TRIVIA SKILLZ! Despite the hour, the coffee shop was still busy—eight or so customers enjoying their cappuccinos and biscotti, electronica remixes of bossa nova classics on the stereo.

It's so late, Scarlett mused. *I hope they serve decaf . . .*

And also, *Does anyone* truly *enjoy biscotti?*

She moved on, returning her thoughts to self-reproach, when something struck her as odd. She turned around and returned to the coffee shop window.

Top hats.

All the customers wore top hats—both the men and the women—and some also wore flowing black capes. A few patrons clustered around the counter, their top hats bobbing in animated conversation. Another patron sat at a table, surrounded by several onlookers, brandishing a deck of cards with practiced ease.

Hexpresso Yourself is a magician hangout . . . she realized. *But how can Oak Haven have enough magicians to warrant a magician hangout? And they all love a quiz night? What the hell is going on?*

She stared at the coffee shop for a long moment, debating whether or not to go in and investigate. But the exhausted side of Scarlett quickly won out over her curious side. *I'll leave those weirdos to their trivia night,* she thought. *The* Myrmex Arcana *is more important . . . for now, anyway.*

***

Well past midnight, the lobby of the Stargazer Inn was a dim but inviting sanctuary, a fire still crackling in the old fireplace. Delilah sat hunched over the reception desk, the firelight accentuating the worry lines on her brow. A map of Oak Haven lay sprawled before her, dotted with notes in her neat hand, dutifully recording every reported magical incident in town. Beside her, Luna paced back and forth, deep in thought and humming a Gilbert and Sullivan tune.

As the door creaked open, a gust of chilly October air swirled into the room. Scarlett stepped inside and headed immediately for an overstuffed armchair by the hearth. She stretched her tired limbs and let the woodsmoke wash over her. The smell was more innocent, somehow, than the burning-book stench that was still in every pore.

"Nice of you to finally show up!" Delilah snapped. "Where have you been all night?"

"I've been a busy little bee." She held out the heavy reference book. "Got you this."

Luna drifted closer, tilting her head curiously like a bird sizing up a worm. "What is this, exactly?"

"*Myrmex Arcana*. Supposedly, if any book has information on the dragonflies, it will be this one. Trouble is . . . I have no idea what language it's in, or if that even is a language at all." She held it out for Luna. "What do you say, Einstein? Can you make anything of this?"

Luna plunked down on the floor and flipped through, her face lighting up like a child at her first Christmas. "Wowwowwow . . . Multiple hortikinetic languages here . . . Oh, and I think this bit is Sumerian cuneiform . . . And this might be . . . Enochian? Maybe? This is . . . just . . . wow."

"Is that a yes? Translation-wise?"

"Not off the top of my head, that's for sure. I can work on it, though."

"Let me get this straight, Scarlett," Delilah said. "It took you all night to track down what amounts to a major research project *for someone else to complete*. Do I understand correctly?"

"Oh, will you relax? I've been all over town tonight. I attended the town meeting on your behalf—*you're welcome*. Then I had some tea-flavored whiskey with Aphra. She's the one who suggested the book. Then I went to Spellbound to acquire said book, and then I got attacked by an enchanted giant squid, but don't worry because the Three Musketeers and Captain Quint from *Jaws* were on the case, and then there was the small matter of a raging fire in the bookstore, which was *not* my fault no matter what you may hear in the coming days, and then I almost had sex with Nate in, ironically, the DIY section, and then—"

"Stop." Luna tossed the priceless book onto the rug. "You what?"

Delilah leaned forward, her usual sternness melting away. "Yeah, I'm going to need to hear more."

"Alas . . ." Scarlett felt a rush of heat to her cheeks, a mix of leftover adrenaline and embarrassment. "There is no more. It *almost* happened, but it didn't, because Polly walked in—which was unforgettably horrible—and anyway, it's never going to happen again because afterward, I acted like a complete moron and as usual I said exactly the wrong thing and now Nate's furious and I've ruined everything. It's all over; that's the story, the end."

"Scar . . ." Luna rose up on her knees and took Scarlett's hands in hers. "I'm sure you didn't ruin it."

"Oh, of course she did," Delilah practically shouted. "This is Scarlett we're talking about."

Scarlett reluctantly met Luna's inquisitive stare. They gazed into each other's eyes, and Luna seemed to read every humiliating detail of Scarlett's evening.

After a long silence, Luna said, very gently and with great love, "You really fucked it up, didn't you?"

"Oh yeah." Scarlett nodded. "Really badly."

The sisters chuckled, which turned to laughter and then to a helpless hysterical giggling.

"I'm such an idiot." Scarlett wiped tears of laughter from her eyes.

Luna had to do the same. "You really are . . ."

Over at the desk, Del could only shake her head—when the

two of them got going, there was nothing to be done but wait it out. She grabbed a box of tissues from behind the counter and tossed it in the general direction of the couch.

When the giggling fits had more or less passed, Luna dabbed her eyes and said, "Seriously . . . I'm sure you can make up with him."

"Oof, I dunno . . . You weren't there."

"He'll forgive you," she said. "Knowing Nate, he's forgiven you already."

"Yeah," Delilah agreed. "He's always been dumb like that."

Scarlett rolled her eyes. "Thanks for your support, Del—much appreciated. I will say, though . . . I'll never think of the term DIY in quite the same way again."

"DIY, huh." Luna giggled. "Were power tools involved?"

"Oh, ew. Stop." Delilah made a face. "New topic please."

"Happy to oblige," Scarlett said. "So, why is a group of magicians hanging out at the coffee place right now? Hell, why is a group of magicians in Oak Haven at all?"

"Good question," Delilah said. "I have noticed more of those morons in town lately."

"Del . . ." Lula tutted. "We don't want to be prejudiced, do we?"

"Well, I'm sorry, but they're weird. With the outfits and the 'alakazams!' or whatever?"

Luna sighed. "So, I guess the answer is yes, we do want to be prejudiced . . ."

Scarlett had to smile at her tender-hearted baby sister. "I'm sorry, I'm not trying to be an anti-magician. It just struck me as odd, is all. Probably nothing—never mind. Say, what did I miss around here tonight?"

"Well!" Delilah said. "Zahir managed to pull off a steak dinner for the guests. Which went great *until* the steaks all turned back into several very angry cows—the upshot being, everyone in this hotel is vegetarian now. Then, in Room 206, some of the Gilbert and Sullivan people had their sheet music begin spontaneously performing itself. And the entire inn was treated to a full-volume performance of 'He's an Englishman,' over and over, for . . . what was it, Luna, about two hours? We finally managed to catch the sheet music and throw it in the fire."

"*For he himself has saiiiid it* . . ." Scarlett sang.

"He's *making us regreeeet it* . . ." Delilah sang back. "*He'd better shut up sooooon, or I'll send him to the moooon.*"

Scarlett applauded. "Good improv!"

"*Improv?* Hardly, I had two goddamn hours to think about it."

The inn's entrance bell jangled and the heavy oak door swung open, revealing Polly, her face contorted with a mix of fury and weariness. Her arms were full of hastily packed luggage, precious belongings tossed in shopping bags. Violet trailed behind unhelpfully, hooded sweatshirt pulled low over her face. Just a sullen shadow, her eyes glued to her phone.

Polly's gaze landed on Scarlett with the force of an Arctic blast. She dumped her bags on the floor with a thud. "Well, well, well . . . look what the kraken dragged in."

"Hah," Scarlett said awkwardly. "Haaaah . . . very good. Listen, Polly, again, I'm so sorry about the bookstore—"

Polly cut her off with a dismissive wave. "Save it." She directed her attention to the front desk. "Delilah, this is hardly how I expected my evening to go. And I truly am sorry to impose . . . but I'm afraid we are in need of a place to stay."

"Of course," Luna said. "Whatever we can do to help—you don't even need to ask."

Polly nodded, a flicker of warmth softening the harsh lines of her face. "Thank you both. It's just that the EMS team placed powerful wards all around the bookstore, plus there's all the smoke damage . . ." She glanced quickly at Scarlett, then back to Delilah. "Since Violet and I reside above the shop, well . . . we're essentially homeless. I hope you have a vacancy?"

"For you, always!" Luna stepped forward, throwing her arms around Polly for a supportive squeeze. "Don't give it another thought. We have a lovely suite overlooking the back garden that will be perfect for you and Violet. Let's get you settled right away." Luna scooped up an armload of Polly's luggage and headed upstairs without waiting for a reply.

***

Scarlett knew that, out of all the Melrose sisters, Polly would least appreciate any help from her. So, with that in mind, Scarlett made her way up to bed. It had been quite the clusterfuck of a day. But despite it all, the thing she couldn't get out of her head was the hurt expression on Nate's face, right before he stormed off and left her standing alone by the burning bookstore.

Everything I said came out totally wrong. What had happened between us didn't mean nothing. *It meant . . .*

Scarlett sighed. She didn't know what it meant. Because if meant *something*, that suggested she was supposed to *do* something about it. But what could she possibly do? Stay in Oak Haven to be with him? That was impossible. After everything she'd done, starting with her monumental screw-up ten years ago, and compounded by even more mistakes now? It simply couldn't be—she didn't deserve this place, or him.

On her way to bed, she passed the third floor and paused on the stairs—did she hear a party at the end of the hall? She made her way discreetly down the hall and listened. Music was coming from behind Maximillian's door—something swanky and nostalgic by Dean Martin. Scarlett could hear muffled conversation. Ice cubes rattling in drinks.

A little after-hours gathering, chez Maximillian the Magnificent, Scarlett thought. *What are you up to, Max?*

Chapter 23
Funkytown

Sunlight streamed through the windows of the Stargazer Inn dining room, illuminating the remains of a hearty breakfast buffet. A few guests from the Gilbert and Sullivan Society lingered over their eggs and nursed their coffees, their conversations punctuated by the occasional shift in the room's decor. The dining room shimmered and warped, transforming momentarily into Studio 54—Donna Summer blaring, a dizzying swirl of flashing lights all around. A moment later, the room morphed into a Hawaiian luau, with a roasted pig on a spit and hula dancers swaying. Then, with a final flicker, it settled back into its familiar New England charm, although a faint scent of coconut oil lingered in the air. The guests had all gotten used to these changes—their conversations barely missed a beat as the room bounced from a fabulous disco to Waikiki Beach and then back to the familiar paneling and floral wallpaper.

Scarlett came downstairs, bleary-eyed but determined not to miss another breakfast. She spotted her mother, Luna, and Delilah at a table, surrounded by the remnants of their meals. Before joining them, she headed for the buffet, piling her plate with scrambled eggs, bacon, toast, and a mountain of fruit. Scarlett plunked down at the family table, allowing the scent of coffee and the gentle hum of conversation to wash over her.

"Good morning, Scarlett." Her mother was occupied with the morning paper and didn't look up.

"Morning, sleepyhead," Luna chirped. "Welcome to the land of the living."

Delilah wasted no time on pleasantries. "Luna managed a rough translation of a page from the *Myrmex Arcana*. Seems these red flies have a somewhat biblical origin."

Curious, Scarlett leaned in. "Tell me."

"According to the book," Luna explained, "the dragonflies date back to Ancient Egypt. Remember all the insect plagues in the Book of Exodus? Gnats, flies, locusts? *Myrmex Arcana* speculates that our flies may have been created in response, conjured by Jannes and Jambres, two sorcerers employed by the Pharaoh. But it seems their plan backfired. Their flies render all magic unpredictable and surreal—"

"Yeah, no shit," Scarlett injected.

"Right, which makes them a pretty self-defeating weapon. They create chaos instead of control."

"So, who brought these nasties back? And why'd target us?"

"That's what we've been trying to figure out." Delilah sighed.

With a sudden jolt, the inn's wallpaper dissolved into a dizzying swirl of neon graffiti. The overhead lights vanished, replaced by a rotating disco ball that cast fractured shards of light across the room. The air filled with the pulsing beat of perennial roller-rink favorite, "Funkytown." For a heart-stopping moment, the Melroses found themselves clinging to the edge of their chairs as roller-skaters whizzed past in a blur of neon leg warmers and spandex.

"This is an old one," Mama Melrose shouted over the din. "I think we conjured this for Earl Twelve's twelfth birthday."

Abruptly, the roller rink was gone, and the dining room was just as it had ever been.

Scarlett sighed and took a sip of her coffee. "Okay, as we were saying . . . Who's unhappy in Oak Haven? Who has a bone to pick with us?"

"What about the town meeting, Scar?" Luna asked. "Did you notice anyone who seemed . . . agitated? Bellicose?"

"*Bellicose*, wow . . ." The town meeting felt like a lifetime ago. Scarlett racked her brain, trying to recall faces from just the night before. "The Chatterjees were pretty worked up about their missing gnomes, but mostly they seemed grumpy, not vengeful. This one guy was losing his mind over flamingo poop, but that didn't seem . . . Oh wait. What about that time witch? She was a bit bellicose, maybe?"

"Ehh." Mama's face soured. "Louise Demain. I wouldn't put this past her."

"Now, Mama," Delilah said. "Is Louise truly bellicose? Or just French?"

"I don't know this Louise person," Luna offered, "but a time witch seems an unlikely culprit. They have far stronger weapons at their disposal than dragonflies. And they aren't this subtle. I've encountered time witches before, and trust me, if they're mad at you, you know it."

"True," Mama conceded. "Still, a conversation couldn't hurt. Perhaps she'll have some thoughts about how to solve this problem. It would certainly massage her ego if one of us went to her for help. Scarlett, why don't you pay her a visit?"

"Me?" exclaimed Scarlett. "Why me?"

"Well, Delilah has the inn to run, and Luna must continue with the *Myrmex Arcana* translation, and I hate Louise Demain. That leaves you. Besides, what else do you have to do today beyond mooning over Nate Williams?"

Scarlett felt her cheeks flush. "I'm not mooning! In fact, Nate and I aren't on the best terms at the moment and that's probably exactly how it should be. As I have *plenty* of other things to do."

"Such as?" Mama raised an eyebrow.

"Well." Scarlett pushed her eggs around her plate. "I thought I'd hike up to the grove, check on things, look for clues. And I was going to stop by the bookstore to see if I could help with the clean-up. And, you know . . ." She looked up to find her family staring at her expectantly. "Fine," she sighed. "I was going to check on Nate, yes. But *not* because I'm mooning. He's got that whole magic storeroom at the hardware store—anything could be going wrong with all that magic, literally anything. It's quite dangerous. Honestly, Mama, I don't know why you aren't taking that particular situation more seriously. And as a Melrose, I feel like it's our duty to—"

The Melrose women exchanged amused glances. Delilah snickered openly.

"Oh shut up, all of you." Scarlett's face was as pink as the grapefruit on her mother's plate.

"Louise first," Mama said reasonably. "Nate Williams can wait."

"Fine," Scarlett agreed. "I'll do it. But there's something else." She leaned forward, her voice barely a whisper. "Last night, when I was heading to bed, I heard noises coming from Maximillian's room."

Luna's eyes widened with interest. "Really? What was it?"

"Music, conversation, ice clinking in glasses. It sounded like he was having a little gathering."

"Err, he's allowed to have company, isn't he?" Luna smiled. "In fact, I think it's lovely that Maximillian is making friends. He seems like such a lonely soul."

"Lonely?" Delilah scoffed. "He's as lonely as a peacock in a mirror factory."

Scarlett shook her head. "It's not just that. It seemed more like a secret meeting than a party."

"*Oh, please.*" Delilah shot back. "Secret meeting to do what?"

But Scarlett pressed on. "And it's not just Max. I saw a bunch of magicians at the coffee shop, and I just—"

"No, *bunch* sounds all wrong," Delilah interrupted. "What's the collective noun for magicians? An *ensemble* of magicians?"

Luna replied, "Maybe a *troupe* of magicians?"

"What about, like, a *sorcery* of magicians?"

"Ughhh," Scarlett groaned, "will you two cut it out?"

"Ummm," Luna said thoughtfully, "a *spellcraft* of magicians?"

Delilah shook her head. "Not quite."

From behind her newspaper, Mama announced definitively, "A *conjuration* of magicians."

"Boom!" said Luna. "That's perfect."

"Can we please move on?" Scarlett begged. "I saw a *bunch* of magicians—yeah, I said *bunch*, deal with it—at the coffee shop last night, all dressed in top hats and capes. And it was all very odd."

Delilah rolled her eyes. "Magicians are always odd, Scarlett. It's in their job description."

"But what are they all doing here?"

"Maybe they're here for the foliage," Luna suggested, her tone hopeful. "Max did say he loves autumn."

Scarlett wasn't convinced. "It's more than that. There's something . . . off with them. I can feel it."

"Don't be ridiculous," Delilah scoffed.

Mama lowered her newspaper. "Now, girls, let's not be hasty. Instinct is important, Scarlett. Just be careful not to let your imagination run away with you. But for now, how about that visit to Louise . . . ?"

***

Scarlett crossed Main Street, the crisp autumn air carrying the mingled scents of cinnamon, woodsmoke . . . and swimming pools?! A clear reminder that magic remained as drunk as ever. Her destination was on the far side of the green: Tout le Temps, Louise Demain's enigmatic clock repair shop.

A towering grandfather clock stood sentinel beside the door, its intricate gears and pendulums gleaming in the morning sun. The shop's display window was a chaotic jumble of old-world timekeeping devices—a sundial in weathered brass, an hourglass filled with sparkling sand, and a meticulously carved water clock bubbling merrily.

Scarlett entered the shop, the bell above the door announcing her presence. The air was heavy with the scent of incense and aged parchment, mingling with the metallic tang of old gears and springs. Flickering oil lamps provided the only light, casting even innocent objects in ominous shadow. The shop was a labyrinth of clocks, each one ticking and tocking in its own rhythm.

One massive clock dominated the entire side wall: an

192

astronomical clock dating back to medieval times. The clock was a complex marvel of intricate dials, moving parts, and an elaborately carved housing. Its primary face displayed the hour, but surrounding it were smaller dials and displays, showing the positions of celestial bodies and the signs of the zodiac. Small wooden figures appeared and disappeared, marking the passing of time. Periodically, the clock would "ding" or "dong" without any clear motivation.

A customer stood at the counter. Scarlett recognized him as one of the Gilbert and Sullivan troupe staying at the inn. He held out a cracked smartwatch with a hopeful expression and called out. "Hello? Is anyone here?"

Chapter 24
Timey-Wimey Gibberish

Louise Demain seemed to materialize from the shadows. Her violet eyes narrowed as she took in the customer and judged him wanting. Scarlett stood by the doorway waiting her turn.

"What eldritch abomination hast thou brought before me?" Her voice was a chilling contralto with just a hint of French accent along the edges. "Another pitiful millennial's broken toy?"

"Um, yeah, well . . ." the actor stammered, "I thought you might be able to fix it?"

Louise let out a sharp, mean laugh. "Fix it? Why would I deign to mend such a trifling bauble?"

"You . . . run a clock repair store? And this is a—"

"This is the flotsam of a society consumed by its own hubris. This abomination of plastic and lithium shall endure long after the great cosmic beast has ground your name to dust in the eternal void. Begone from my sight, lest your insignificance offend me further. Go sing an elegy to Siri."

The man turned and looked to Scarlett for help, but she could only shrug. *You're on your own, pal.* He stormed out of the store. The bell tinkled a mocking goodbye.

"And you?" Louise's voice dripped with condescension. "What worthless specks of dust have you dragged in for my inspection?"

"Well, you know, the philosophers in the band Kansas teach us that *we all* amount to dust in the wind, ultimately. But . . . I'm assuming . . . you . . . probably don't know that song. Anyway. I'm Scarlett Melrose? I saw you briefly at the town meeting."

Louise arched a perfectly sculpted eyebrow. "Ahh, yes. Another scion of the accursed Melrose lineage. Come to prostrate yourself before me, I assume? Seek thou absolution for your family's ineptitude? Though I doubt even the most abject apologies could hope to mend the shattered fragments of my irreplaceable relics."

"Not exactly. I'm looking for information."

"Oh, so you've finally realized the gravity of the situation. How typical of the Melroses, always a step behind."

Scarlett ignored the jab. "My sister translated a page from the *Myrmex Arcana*." She related Luna's discovery of the dragonflies' Egyptian origins.

Louise listened intently, her expression turning to fury when Scarlett mentioned what Luna had said about the sorcerers Jannes and Jambres. "Idiots!" she barked. "They were idiots! They dared to meddle with forces beyond their feeble comprehension. I bore witness to their pathetic attempts to stand against the inexorable flow of time. I saw them stand athwart the march of history yelling stop, and history's laughter mocked them eternally."

"Wait . . ." Scarlett was taken aback by Louise's firsthand account. "You were there? During . . . Exodus?!"

Louise laughed. "Child, I have borne witness to the birth of galaxies and the heat death of the universe itself. Your insect infestation is but a fleeting annoyance in the grand tapestry of cosmic events."

"Well, that's good news, then. If you find the insects to be no big deal, you can tell me how to get rid of them."

Louise tilted her head, studying Scarlett with an unnerving intensity. "The answer lies not in fighting the flies, but in understanding their purpose. They are scavengers of chaos, drawn to the frayed edges of time. To banish them, you must restore the balance."

Scarlett's frustration began to bubble over. "But how? We don't know where to begin, and you're giving me gibberish about the frayed edges of time?!"

A cryptic smile played on Louise's lips. She circled Scarlett, her robe swishing like the whisper of eldritch secrets. The only sound was the discordant tick-tick-tick of a hundred clocks, each a cacophonous herald of different moments in time. "The answer lies shrouded in plain sight, yet your mortal perceptions are too limited to grasp its true nature. The flies were manifested by magic, and only by magic will they be undone."

"Okay, I'm with you so far. Magic such as . . . ?"

Louise leaned in close, her breath a searing whisper against Scarlett's ear. "Riddle me this, Scarlett Melrose: what eldritch equation balances the scales of morality? How many acts of virtue shall erase a single transgression?"

Scarlett slowly turned. "What do you mean by that?"

"I mean what I say. Can a bad deed be undone by good?"

Just then, a cuckoo clock struck thirteen, and a little wooden bird exploded out of the clock's tiny wooden door with a loud screech, over and over.

Scarlett felt suddenly as though the floor had dropped out

from under her—as though the first part of this conversation had been the "upward" part of the rollercoaster and she was now plunging down at inexorable speed. She backed away from Louise. "What do you mean a bad deed? Why would you say that to me?"

"Oh, the Great Tomes of Time lay bare the secrets of your soul, child. You are no mystery to me."

Staring into the eyes of the time witch was like gazing into the most hateful mirror imaginable. Memories of her father began to flood her mind. "It was an accident . . . I just made a mistake. I would never intentionally hurt Papa."

Louise stepped back, a wicked grin on her face. "Did I suggest otherwise?"

"Lady . . ." Scarlett could feel tears pricking her eyes, but no way was she giving this witch the satisfaction. "I don't know what you want from me!"

"From you? What could I possibly gain from one so insignificant? But for your audacity in crossing the threshold of my sanctum, I shall impart upon you a single truth: the key to unraveling this infestation lies within your very being. Quite literally, I might add."

"I don't understand."

"In due course, the revelation shall make itself known to you." Her eyes glittered with a hint of malice. "Of course . . . a sacrifice may be required. A ritual that embodies both unity and transformation. But heed my warning, Scarlett Melrose. The road ahead is fraught with unspeakable peril, and the consequences of failure are higher than you can possibly imagine."

With that, Louise retreated into her back room, leaving Scarlett standing alone in a pile of timey-wimey gibberish.

As Scarlett departed the shop, the grandfather clock chimed the hour.

"Yeah, yeah, yeah," she muttered. "Time's a tickin'. I get it."

*****

Scarlett hurried away from Tout le Temps, hoping to put as much distance between herself and the creeptastic Louise Demain as possible. But she only made it to the corner before she had to pause and gather herself. She pressed a hand to her chest; her heart was pounding frantically. She took a deep breath, then another. The crisp autumn air filled her lungs, but it did little to calm her racing thoughts.

There on the street, her mind kept circling back to Louise's cryptic words. The time witch seemed to know Scarlett's worst secret—the guilt she carried over her father's death. It was as if she had peered directly into Scarlett's soul.

How could she possibly know? She's never met me before . . . barely even heard of me. She didn't even live in Oak Haven when it happened.

Scarlett felt horribly exposed and vulnerable. The pain of that fateful night was suddenly so raw, the wound still fresh, despite all the time that had passed.

Oh, she realized. *Maybe that's it. To a time witch, no time has passed at all. To her, I'm still the eighteen-year-old who just killed my dad.*

Shaking her head, Scarlett tried to push her guilt away and focus on the clues Louise had offered. The answer to the infestation lay "literally" within her. *What the hell does that mean?* And the idea of a sacrifice being required? That sent a chill down her spine. What more could she possibly give?

Lost in thought, Scarlett almost didn't notice the two figures passing by on the far side of the street. But when she saw them, her eyes widened in surprise. It was Violet and Maximillian, walking along, side by side.

Max seemed to be playing the role of kindly professor lecturing a favorite student. Violet hung on to Max's every word, nodding away like a bobblehead in a joke shop.

What the hell? Scarlett thought. *Violet doesn't listen to* anybody.

Seeing Violet in the company of a magician sent alarm bells ringing in Scarlett's head. *Magicians can't be trusted,* she thought, *but does Violet understand that?*

She knew she had to follow them. Scarlett crossed the street, keeping a safe distance behind the unlikely pair. She ducked behind trees and mailboxes, but she wasn't going to let them get away. Her heart pounded in her chest as she drew closer.

Violet and Max turned a corner. Scarlett quickened her pace, ready to confront them and demand answers. But as she rounded the same corner, she skidded to a halt.

Her eyes searched an empty street.

No sign of them anywhere—they'd simply disappeared. Scarlett spun around, checking every direction, but to no avail. They were gone.

Chapter 25
Dumb Kids

Defeated, Scarlett made her way back to the inn. Her dread grew as she imagined the conversations she was about to have. She'd report having seen Maximillian with Violet and, inevitably, Luna would declare that Max was too much of a sweetheart to be involved in anything questionable. Delilah would retort that Max was too much of a moron. Mama would stare at her newspaper and say, "Hmm." And that would be it.

Her report on the conversation with Louise was just as predictable. *The time witch says the solution is within me,* Scarlett would say, *quite literally.* Luna would smile kindly and say, *Well, isn't that interesting, I wonder what it means.* Delilah would snark, *In that case you should pull out a kidney and feed it to the flies; see where that gets you.* Mama would say, "Hmm."

Scarlett realized she didn't want to talk to her family about these problems. She wanted to talk to the sole member of Team Scarlett.

The question was: did he want to talk to her?

***

Scarlett argued with herself the whole way to Williams Hardware. *Stay away,* said her logical side. *Don't make up with him. Let him be angry. It's good for him to be angry because it will hurt him less when you leave.*

On the other hand, offered her emotional side, *I hate that he's upset with me. We're finally friends after ten years apart! I can't leave things like this.* A weak counterargument, perhaps. Yet somehow, a winning one.

As she approached the store, Scarlett's gut told her that, as usual, things would somehow be more complicated than she'd expected.

Her gut was correct. She could hear the shouting from out on the street.

The Earls were there on the porch, manning their rocking chairs. But instead of the usual chatter, they all sat very still and quiet, not wanting to miss a word of the quarrel happening inside.

Earl Eleven smiled brightly at Scarlett and gestured that she should join them on the porch . . . but quietly.

She knelt beside Earl Nine's chair and whispered, "What's up?"

"That's Dave Injabire in there—do you know the Injabires?"

She shook her head no.

"Must've moved in after you left," whispered Eleven. "Nice family."

"Very nice family." Nine nodded.

"Lovely family," Ten agreed. "But Dave's wife Linda apparently cast a spell on her garden . . ."

"Uh-oh," Scarlett said.

Nine's eyebrows did a little dance. "Very uh-oh, indeed."

"She meant well—she knows we're all low on gourds, and she wanted to produce some good-sized ones, just to contribute."

"She wanted to pitch in," added Ten. "Such a nice family."

Scarlett whispered, "I take it the spell didn't work out?"

Her answer arrived from inside the store, as Dave Injabire hollered to the heavens. "The gourds are bigger than our house. They grew and grew and grew, and now I've lost track of Linda entirely. She's underneath a damned pumpkin somewhere!"

The Earls melted into a fit of giggling. "I've lost track of Linda entirely," Nine repeated.

"Hooo, Linda, where are you?" Eleven tittered. "Which pumpkin are you under? Is it this one? Nope. Is it that one?"

"Shhh," Scarlett whispered, resisting a strong urge to join in. "Stop—she could be hurt."

The door flew open, and Dave burst out, his arms loaded with shovels. "I can't believe this town is so poorly run that—" Suddenly, he noticed Scarlett on the porch. "Oh, look! You're a Melrose, aren't you?! How perfect."

Scarlett stood. "Mr. Injabire, sir, I'm so sorry about your garden. Is there anything I—"

"Anything you can do?! Do you want to come dig pumpkins and help me locate my wife? No? Then stay out of it." He stormed off the porch.

"Sorry again . . ." she called after him. "And maybe tell your wife no more spells for now, okay? Just until we get the grove sorted out."

He turned back to glare at her. "Spells are part of our lives. Spells are why we immigrated to this ridiculous town in the first place. No spells? We'd be better off back in Kigali!" Dave turned and stalked off down the street, muttering.

"He has a point." Nate was lingering in the doorway. "Magic is a part of folks' daily lives. Without it, they don't know how to do anything."

Scarlett turned to look at him. *My God, those cheekbones . . . he needs to stop with those cheekbones.* "Everyone can get by for a few more days, surely."

He shrugged. "Get by? I guess. But do you know how many calls I've had from people who can't get their Wi-Fi to work without using magic?"

"A lot of calls." Nine nodded.

"So many calls," agreed Eleven.

"Discontent is rising, Scar. That's all I'm saying."

"Right," Scarlett said. "Okay, noted. Look . . . can we talk?" She glanced at the porch full of old men. "Somewhere private?"

He gazed at Scarlett, but she couldn't interpret his expression. Was there any warmth in it? Or was he still upset by her idiotic babblings outside the bookstore? "Unfortunately, I don't think I can leave right now. As I said, a lot of calls about the Wi-Fi."

"Why, though? You run the hardware store! How did you become the town IT guy on top of everything else?"

Nate frowned. "Maybe if we had *someone* living in Oak Haven who has actual real-world experience with the internet . . ."

"Oh, that's not fair!"

"Hey you two," interrupted Ten. "The fellas and I have got things handled here. "Why don't you kids go get yourselves some grog?"

Scarlett laughed. "*Grog*?! Listen, you scurvy dog, it's barely noon!"

"Oh, you know what they say," replied Eleven. "It's always happy hour in Tortuga."

"I don't know," Nate hesitated. "Some other time would be better. I just think—"

"We won't hear of it!" Nine picked up his cane and smacked it on the porch like a giant judge's gavel. "Thirteen, you get that gal out of here. We insist!"

"Really? You've really got the whole hardware store handled without me?"

"Consider it handled," announced his grandfather.

"Done and dusted," said his great-grandfather.

His great-great-grandfather agreed. "Get off our lawn, you dumb kids."

***

Scarlett followed Nate off the porch and down the quiet street. The autumn air was crisp, and the trees were lit up with brilliant fall colors. Scarlett didn't care about Del's complaints that they "just aren't as pretty" as usual—she'd been in California for ten years. The oranges, yellows, and reds of these New England trees were plenty appealing to her eyes. Of course, occasionally, she'd also notice a tree that was purple or spotted or plaid . . . because there was no chance that Oak Haven would let Scarlett forget it was in trouble, not even for a minute.

As they walked along the cobblestones, Scarlett glanced sideways at Nate. "Okay." She took a deep breath. "I'm just going to dive right in here, get it out in the open. Last night . . . You see . . . I was embarrassed. We got so swept away, and everything was really overwhelming and . . . I mean, not for nothing, but I nearly got eaten by a squid? Maybe a gal isn't exactly at her best after that? And suddenly there you are, and there I am . . . and *there we are*, if you know what I mean . . . and then there's . . .

204

Polly? Polly, of all people?! I just felt so exposed and . . . caught off guard, I guess? And . . . I said dumb things I didn't mean."

Nate stopped walking and turned to face her. "I know," he said gently. "I felt pretty exposed, myself. I also said dumb things I didn't mean."

"What happened . . . it didn't mean *nothing* to me. I don't know what it meant, to be totally honest. But *nothing* is definitely not it."

"I know that, too." He reached out for her. "C'mere."

Scarlett let Nate pull her into his arms. She melted against his broad chest, the steady thump of his heart calming her racing pulse.

"I've missed you," she whispered. "So much."

"I've missed you too," he murmured. They stood together for a long moment, the years between them falling away.

She tilted her head up to look at him. His eyes searched her face, a question in them. She nodded almost imperceptibly.

Nate leaned in and kissed her, soft and tentative at first. When she responded, the kiss deepened, years of longing and heartache pouring out.

Finally, Scarlett pulled back to look up at him, her palms resting against his chest. But this time, instead of longing, there was laughter—at themselves, at their own weakness. "I guess this is going to keep happening, huh?"

"I guess so." He grabbed her hand and pulled her along. "Come on, I want to take you somewhere."

Chapter 26
An Occurrence at Bonfire Creek Bridge

Nate led Scarlett down Galloping Hill Road. The crisp autumn air filled their lungs as they walked, fallen leaves crunching underfoot. Afternoon sunlight slanted through the branches of the towering maples, casting a warm glow along the path.

They walked in comfortable silence, their steps falling into a familiar rhythm. *Maybe coming back wasn't such a bad idea after all,* she thought. She inhaled deeply, realizing that the air smelled like home. The thought sent pangs of joy *and* sorrow through her. Home. It was a word she hadn't dared to use in connection with Oak Haven for a long time. She didn't deserve it—not after what had happened with Papa. But as she walked, feeling the warmth of Nate's hand in hers, Scarlett allowed herself a moment of hope that perhaps she might earn her way back, one day.

At the edge of town, the road narrowed as they approached the covered bridge over Bonfire Creek. The old red bridge stood out like a beacon against the vibrant foliage.

Nate helped her down the bank, which was checkered with smooth stones and late-blooming wildflowers. They settled on a large, flat rock and listened to the water bubbling and churning over the stones. Scarlett drew in a deep breath, savoring the peace.

"Ah yes," she sighed. "Here we are at the site of my greatest triumph—my infamous dive over the bridge."

"The School of Scarlett, as it is often called."

Scarlett looked at him, surprised. "Is it called that?"

"No," Nate admitted with a grin. "No, I call it that. Because, you know, of the fish."

Scarlett laughed. "Right, yeah, I got the pun. Hey, has anybody else ever . . . you know . . ." She made a diving gesture with a matching whooshing sound.

"No way." Nate shook his head emphatically. "In fact, every year all the kids in Oak Haven have to listen to a presentation from your mother about how witches should never turn themselves into wild animals—and *especially* not groups of wild animals— and especially *especially* not groups of low-intelligence wild animals that are likely to wander off."

"Oh my goodness!" Scarlett had no trouble envisioning that lecture, having endured it many times herself. "I'm so sorry for those kids."

"Yep. Not everybody can say they've had the impact on their hometown that you have," he joked.

"I guess not." She smiled. She was enjoying getting to know this new person, this adult Nate. He was as sweet and funny as his teenaged self, but there was a sturdiness to him now. A seriousness, but not in a bad way—a seriousness of purpose.

"This is where I was going to take you all those years ago," he said softly. "On our date. The date that wasn't."

Scarlett's eyes widened. "Oh no, really?!"

"Yeah." A wistful smile played on his lips. "I was going to pack a picnic basket. Steal a couple of beers from my dad."

"Wow, you were gonna pull out all the stops, huh?"

"Oh yeah, I had a whole pine-y, Heathcliff-y thing going on back then."

"If Heathcliff had just brought Cathy a couple of beers, that whole mess might have turned out differently." Scarlett impulsively reached out and grasped Nate's hand. "I'm sorry I missed out on our date. I truly am."

"Me too." He squeezed her hand back. "But you couldn't help it."

"No, I couldn't. Not after what happened to Papa. Still, though. I hate that it happened that way." To lighten the mood, she added, "I'm also sorry I can't just conjure us a picnic basket right now. But the way things are going . . ."

"Oh yeah, best not. We don't want to end up like poor Linda Injabire."

"Hey, speaking of the . . . uh . . . the current mess . . ." Scarlett began.

Nate raised an eyebrow. "Yes?"

"I had the dubious honor of conversing with Madame Louise Demain today."

"Oh boy. How'd that go?"

"She scared the shit out of me," Scarlett admitted.

"Yeah, that'll happen. Look, the thing you need to understand is that she treats everybody that way. FedEx won't deliver to her house anymore because she insists on telling the drivers when they're going to die. That's just Louise."

"Well, what do you think of her otherwise? Like, beyond her charming personality. Is she smart?"

"She's a time witch." Nate shrugged. "They don't make dumb ones. Why do you ask?"

Scarlett sighed. "Because she indicated that I, personally, am supposed to fix the infestation and save magic. That the power is within me . . . *literally*."

"What, like, in your kidneys?"

"See, I knew somebody was going to make that exact joke."

"Sorry." He chuckled. "All joking aside, what do you think she meant?"

Scarlett shook her head. "No idea. But I'll tell you what . . . as creepy as Louise was, something even weirder happened when I left the shop." She paused, taking a deep breath. "I saw Violet with that magician, Maximillian. I don't like the look of that little partnership at all. Maximillian makes me nervous. I don't care that Luna thinks he's a sweetheart or that Del thinks he's an idiot. I'm starting to think both my sisters are wrong."

"To be honest, Scar, the whole *witches versus magicians* thing . . . I've never really understood it. Seems to me like your kind and magician kind are all in the same business, basically. I mean, aren't you?"

"Well, what I've always been told—and, of course, Mama has a whole speech on this; she'd lecture us over and over—is that witchcraft is a way of being, while magic is a hobby."

"In other words, you all think they're fakers and they all think you're snobs."

"Essentially." Scarlett chuckled. "Yep, that's the long and the short of it."

"You know, it's just occurring to me now, but . . ." Nate's expression darkened. "I've had a weirdly large number of magicians in the hardware store lately. They come in all the time now—always different ones, too. Never the same face twice."

"Are they trying to get into the magic storeroom? Because that could be trouble."

He shook his head. "No, nothing like that. Very ordinary purchases. Brackets. Nails and screws. Tins of paint. Like they're redecorating."

Scarlett shook her head, unease rising in her stomach. "I don't like it."

Nate looked at her, concern in his eyes. "What do we do?"

Scarlett sighed, feeling the weight of the situation pressing down on her. "I don't know. It seems like Max may be the leader, so maybe I need information on him? Or maybe Violet is the weak link . . . You spend time with her and Polly, right? Would Violet talk to you?"

He shook his head. "Polly had me over for dinner last week? I asked Violet to pass the salt and she said, 'Fuck off, you're not my real dad!'"

"Bah," Scarlett joked, "You're no use to me at all."

Nate placed a reassuring hand on her shoulder. "Let me know if I can help . . . as long as it doesn't involve communicating with teenage girls."

Scarlett smiled, a warmth spreading through her at his touch. "You did, just by sitting here with me. I hated the feeling I had after the bookstore—like I'd lost a friend."

Nate's eyes softened, his voice gentle. "You didn't. You couldn't."

Spending time with Nate made Scarlett feel a hundred times lighter—so light she was almost giddy. She impulsively reached out to stroke the side of his face. It had been so long since she'd felt this connection, this ease and comfort in another person's presence. Their conversation flowed like the creek beside them, filled with shared memories and a sense of new possibilities.

Scarlett started to wonder if maybe she could face what happened to Papa, if she could face it with Nate.

She leaned in closer, drawn in by the warmth of his gaze and the gentle curve of his lips. Nate met her halfway, his hand reaching up to cup her cheek. Their lips met in a tentative kiss. This wasn't the overwhelming loss of control she'd felt in the bookstore; this was serene, unafraid—like something that was meant to be. As if every unspoken longing, every stolen glance, every missed opportunity had culminated in this single, perfect moment. As if a missing part of herself had finally clicked into place.

They lingered in their kiss for a moment, feeling like time had stopped. When they finally pulled apart, both were slightly flushed.

"Wow," Nate breathed. "That was . . ."

"Yeah," Scarlett agreed, a shy smile on her face. She snaked her arms around his neck, pulling him closer as she lost herself in the sensation of his lips on hers. Nate's fingers threaded through her hair, his touch sending shivers through her body.

She moaned softly as Nate deepened the kiss, and a delicious shiver danced down her spine. His hand roamed down her back, seeking and finding the bare skin beneath her sweater. Her breath hitched as he nipped at her lower lip, a playful exploration that sent a jolt of desire through her. The taste of him was intoxicating, a blend of cinnamon and woodsmoke. She pulled him closer, her body yearning for the press of his against hers. Every touch, every brush of his tongue, was a delicious exploration, a promise of more to come. Scarlett felt a sweet ache bloom in her core, a yearning that intensified with every passing moment.

She rested her forehead against Nate's, her eyes fluttering open to meet his gaze.

"I've never stopped thinking about you." His voice was a low rumble that resonated in her own chest. "I've thought of you every single day."

She leaned in, their lips meeting again. Scarlett savored every sensation, every shared breath. She wanted to disappear into this moment forever, to live out her life in it. A moment with no guilt or regret, nothing to explain or repair.

But as she sank into this reverie, she unwillingly found the wizened face of Louise Demain staring back at her.

Scarlett broke away, feeling like she'd been stabbed. "Nate?" she asked. "How many good things does it take to make up for a bad thing?"

Nate's confusion was written all over his face. "What does that mean?"

"It means what I said. It means itself. How many?"

"Well . . ." He was struggling to understand how Scarlett had leapt from the best kiss of their lives to a question like that. "I guess I don't think good and bad work quite like that. It's not a barter system."

Her heart sank. "No. No, you're right. Of course not."

Louise's terrible wisdom washed over Scarlett, turning her stomach sour. No matter how many good deeds she performed, nothing could undo the terrible thing she did to Papa.

"I don't know what I was thinking," she said, suddenly panicked. "I could never stay here."

Nate's eyes widened, a flicker of hope in their depths. "Wait, what does that mean? Were you thinking that you *might* stay?"

"But I can't, Nate. I can't possibly." Scarlett pulled away— being so close to him was impossibly painful. "I don't get to come home and have some *happily ever after* with you. Not after what I did. I don't deserve it."

He reached for her, his face creased with worry. "I don't know what you're talking about. You haven't done anything."

"You don't know!" She stood and moved farther away. Staring out at the creek, she longed to turn herself into a school of fish and swim away. Forever, this time.

"Scarlett, I don't understand. Everything was so good about ten seconds ago. What the hell—"

She whirled around, her eyes brimming with tears. "When I'm with you, I manage to forget somehow. I forget everything that happened, and I just want to dive into you."

"Well, I encourage that. Let's work on that angle for a minute."

"I can't possibly stay here, Nate! I can't face them—my mother, my sisters . . . I can't do it."

"Scarlett, I don't know what you mean. You seem to be getting along pretty well, actually. You are facing them—don't you see that? You've come home, you've faced them, and it's fine."

"That's only because they don't know!"

"Don't know what? What are you—"

"That I killed my father." She covered her face and sobbed.

"Oh, Scarlett . . ." Nate just stared at her for a long moment, looking like he might cry, too. "That's not what happened."

"You don't know," she blubbered. "You weren't there."

The sound of footsteps and voices on the road spared Scarlett having to continue. A group of townsfolk were ambling by, headed for the covered bridge. They could only be headed to one place: the grove. Scarlett turned her back, so no one would see her cry.

"Something is happening." She wiped away her tears with a clenched fist. "We should go."

Chapter 27
Rasputins

The grove wasn't far from town, a gentle uphill walk on a winding path Scarlett had trod since childhood. The path cut through fields of goldenrod, their blooms fading to rusty brown, their fragrance a bittersweet mix of honey and decay. As she and Nate walked in silence up the hill, Scarlett pulled herself together as best she could—pushing down all the anguish that Nate had unintentionally released.

It doesn't matter, she told herself. *Nothing that happened between us matters because nothing about our situations has changed. I can't bear to stay in Oak Haven and Nate can't bear to leave.*

It's actually straightforward, she thought, *if only I'd let it be.*

As they crested the hill, the once-majestic oak grove came into view. Scarlett's breath caught in her throat. The ancient branches sagged with an unsettling weariness; their leaves drooped, many tinged with a sickly yellow. Tiny red lights darted amongst the branches, painting the grove in an unnatural crimson haze. In place of the usual hum of magical energy, the air thrummed with the strange buzzing of the dragonflies.

But the scene wasn't entirely bleak, because the grove buzzed with something else besides flies: Oak Haven residents. Due to the current crisis, the law forbidding non-witches from entering the grove had been rescinded; it seemed like the whole town was here. Friends and neighbors, all of them ready to pitch in and try to save the oaks.

In the center of the grove, Kelly Melrose stood beneath the central tree, barking out instructions to the workers. Her shoulders were squared, her back as straight as ever. Despite her worried expression, a steely glint in her eyes spoke of generations of Melroses who'd faced worse crises than this. As she caught sight of Scarlett and Nate approaching, her features softened for a split second, as if to say, *very nice to see you*—before turning hard, as if to add, *glad you finally showed up*.

Aphra Pierre, her usual bohemian attire replaced by practical jeans and a flannel shirt, sat with a small circle of women, including Scarlett's sister Luna. They were weaving intricate cages from skeins of glowing metallic thread. Periodically, Aphra would put down her own weaving project to advise one of the other women on theirs. She smiled and waved when she saw Scarlett and Nate approaching.

"Scarlett!" Aphra called out, her voice tinged with urgency. "We need your help over here. These cages are holding for now, but we don't have much time."

Scarlett nodded. "I'll be right there."

Other townsfolk were busy with more down-to-earth tasks. The time witch Louise Demain, wearing a bulky canvas apron over her usual black chiffon, stood at the base of one of the oaks, poking at a cluster of the glowing insects with a long branch. Nate nudged Scarlett and muttered, "If I were those bugs, I'd be worried."

Meanwhile, Samuel and Belinda Chatterjee chased

dragonflies with butterfly nets, hopping clumsily here and there as they tried to bring down one or two insects at a time.

A makeshift processing line had taken shape on the grove's far edge. Once captured, the glowing insects were carefully transferred from the nets into Aphra's cages. These had been hastily enchanted to confine the creatures, temporarily limiting the dragonflies' ability to infect more trees with their chaotic sparks of magic. Once the containers were full, the volunteers of the Emergency Magic Service, led by Priti Chatterjee, took charge. Unfortunately, they were struggling to find an effective method of disposal—they tried fire, they tried water, they tried electricity. But the flies were tiny Rasputins, laughing off every attempted execution.

The townspeople worked tirelessly to contain the infestation, but it seemed that for every fly they captured, a dozen more took its place. Scarlett felt the weight of her responsibility pressing down on her, a physical ache in her chest, and Louise's words repeated in her mind—an ugly melody she couldn't get out of her head.

They passed town selectman Conrad, perched atop a ladder. Armed with his own net, he was reaching out to try and catch some flies that had taken shelter on a high branch. But he was awkwardly poised, and his ladder was shifting back and forth worryingly.

Nate turned to Scarlett and said, "I should go help Conrad before he ends up in traction."

"You do that." She nodded. "I'm going to check in with the general."

But first, he squeezed her shoulder. "You sure you're okay?"

She shrugged him off. "Don't give it a thought." She marched toward her mother without turning back.

***

Mama's lecture began before Scarlett could even offer a hello. "Scarlett, I realize you've built your own glamorous life out west . . ." she paused to direct Belinda Chatterjee ". . . that's wonderful, Bel; please take those over to the EMS team, all right? But, Scarlett, when you are in Oak Haven, you are a Melrose, and therefore—"

"*Therefore*, I have a responsibility to honor the generations of Melrose leaders who have come before," Scarlett recited. "Yeah, yeah, I know. So, do you think this is going to work? Just de-infesting the entire grove by hand?"

Mama drew closer to offer a confession. "It's a band-aid at best. We'll never be able to remove them all manually. But panic was starting to set in. People needed something to do. So tell me, did you learn anything from your visit with Louise?"

"Uh, sure. Apparently, the answer to the infestation has been inside me all along. I just need to click my heels three times and find it."

"Hmm," her mother said unsmilingly, "I suggest you get on with it then."

Scarlett noticed a makeshift refreshment table set up under a wide elm tree. A brightly patterned tablecloth was laden with steaming mugs of apple cider, a large urn of coffee, and baskets overflowing with pumpkin bread and cider donuts. Polly was manning the table, verbally sparring with her daughter, who was clearly supposed to be helping but was clearly not.

Violet spat out a list of vile insults at her mother, which she capped off with a hearty "I hate you!" before storming off. The teenager plunked down under an oak on the far edge of the grove, the hood of her sweatshirt pulled low, and her head squarely focused on her phone.

Scarlett watched this play out from a distance, debating

whether or not to approach. She had settled on *no way* when Polly noticed her standing there and gave an exhausted half-wave.

Ahhh, nuts, Scarlett thought. *I've been spotted.* She ambled over to Polly's table.

"I suppose you saw that fight," Polly said before Scarlett could greet her.

Scarlett raised her hands. "No judgment. My mother and I have really gone at it more than once or twice in public."

"It's just the age, I suppose. Do you want some cider?"

"Sure, love some. Look . . . Polly . . . I just want to say . . . About your store, and um, everything that happened there."

"I don't want to talk about it. Certainly, I don't want to talk about it with you. Your mother said she'd help me rebuild once magic is restored, so, I'll survive."

"I just wanted to offer an apology."

"Right, well." Polly looked away. "Not really wanting one at the moment."

"Sure." Scarlett nodded. "That's fair. Okay, um . . . would you mind if I tried having a talk with Violet?"

"Do I *mind*. No, I don't mind. But did you bring a shark cage with you?"

"I'll be careful." Scarlett pointed at the cups of cider on the table. "I assume this is family-friendly cider and not the hard kind?" Polly nodded, so Scarlett took two cups and headed over to Violet's tree.

The teenager didn't look up.

"Brought you some cider," Scarlett offered.

"Not thirsty."

"Okay." Scarlett sat down beside Violet anyway, putting a cup of cider beside her. She sipped her own drink for a while, watching in silence as the townsfolk worked tirelessly to contain the infestation.

Finally, she glanced over at Violet's phone. "So . . . learned any good TikTok dances lately?"

"Don't try to relate to me," Violet growled.

"Okay, fair. I won't relate to you. I'll just be blunt: what are you doing hanging out with Maximillian?"

Violet glanced up ever so briefly, but then her head swiveled back down. "I don't know who that is."

"Bullshit. I saw the two of you in town. In fact, I *followed* you both—until Max pulled some sort of magician-y disappearing act on me."

"He's nice to me," she said quietly. "He understands me."

A troubling answer. *Magicians don't understand teenage witches,* she thought. But to Violet, she said, "Sure, that makes sense," and tried to keep the worry out of her voice. "So, I'm curious about something. What do you think Max and all his magician buddies are up to anyway? You don't think they have anything to do with this dragonfly situation . . . do they?"

"What are you talking about?! Maybe the magicians just like it here. Maybe they just want a place where they can be themselves and be accepted for who they are."

Scarlett frowned. "Hmm, that doesn't make much sense. Trust me—rightly or wrongly—nobody in Oak Haven accepts magicians for *who they are.*"

"Yeah, because you're all prejudiced! Max and his friends are nicer and cooler than anybody else in this dumb town."

"Huh. Okay." As this interrogation was going nowhere fast, Scarlett stood up. "I think I'm going to go help out with the trees. Maybe you could join me? I know Oak Haven is dumb and prejudiced and all that . . . but it's still your home for the foreseeable future. And we're all pitching in to clean up the grove. What do you say?"

Violet looked up, her eyes full of rage. "Why would I? Why would I want the grove cleaned? Seems to me the oaks are getting exactly what they deserve."

"Whoa!" exclaimed Scarlett. "What does *that* mean?"

"It means I'm no snitch and I don't betray my friends." Violet stood up and kicked over the cup of cider Scarlett had left.

"What friends, Violet? Do you mean Max? Why wouldn't Max want the grove cleaned?"

"Leave me alone!" She stomped away.

"Hey," Scarlett called. "We're not done! Why wouldn't Max want the grove cleaned, Violet? Did the magicians do this? Did you help?"

Violet didn't answer—she just kept going, right past her mother, down the path toward town.

Nate must have heard the tone in Scarlett's voice from across the grove. He abandoned Conrad to his fate and jogged to her. "What's the ruckus?"

Scarlett was staring at the path where Violet had just fled. "She's mixed up in all this—she and Max."

"Which *she*?"

"Violet."

Nate turned a baffled expression on his face. "Wait—*Violet*? But why? Jeez, Scarlett, are you sure? She's just a kid."

A sudden commotion erupted near the center of the grove. Shouts of alarm and frustration filled the air as Aphra's containers faltered. With EMS unable to terminate the flies, the glowing cages were straining under the sheer number of insects they held. One by one, the delicate metallic threads strained and snapped, unable to withstand the relentless pressure of the buzzing swarms within.

Scarlett and Nate could only watch in horror as all the town's work unraveled. Aphra and Luna rushed over to reinforce the failing cages, but too late. With a final, resounding crack, the cages all shattered simultaneously, releasing a torrent of glowing red insects back into the grove. The flies swarmed the trees once more, their tiny bodies pulsing with chaotic magical energy. A crimson haze descended upon the grove with renewed intensity.

Mama shouted orders, desperately trying to rally the group, but the sense of defeat was palpable. Scarlett felt a lump rising in her throat when she saw the Chatterjees abandon their post, realizing the futility of their actions. They joined the others in a slow, disheartened retreat from the grove.

As the last of the volunteers filed past, their faces a mix of exhaustion and despair, Scarlett felt overwhelmed with loss. The once-mighty oaks, the heart and soul of Oak Haven, were mere shadows of their former selves, ravaged by an enemy that apparently could not be overcome. And she had helped make it happen.

On her way out of the grove, Luna came over to hug her sister. "I'm sorry," she whispered, her voice barely audible above the incessant buzzing of the flies.

Scarlett shook her head, her gaze still fixed on the grove. "We tried," she murmured. "We'll try again." Part of her wanted to tell Luna about Violet and Max, but her sister was already in tears. *What would be the point of telling her now?*

"It wasn't enough," Luna said, sniffling. "Translating the *Myrmex Arcana* wasn't enough, Aphra's containers weren't enough . . . Nothing is enough."

"Don't give up, sis," Scarlett said. "If *you*, of all people, lose hope, we're all doomed. See you at home, okay? We'll talk more."

With a sad nod, Luna joined the flow of people heading back down the hill.

Soon Scarlett and Nate found themselves alone once more, watching the sun set over the grove. Scarlett couldn't help but fear that Oak Haven's hopes were fading along with the dying light.

"A teenager," Nate marveled. "A teenager caused all this? I can't believe it."

"We don't know precisely what Violet did," Scarlett pointed out. "Maybe something, maybe nothing. I need to have a word with Max. Or possibly a fight."

"*You* don't need to fight with anybody. Let your mother handle it. Or the EMS. Don't just take this on alone."

"But Louise says this is on me to fix."

"No one should be putting all this on you," he said. "That's not fair."

"*Faaaaiir*," Scarlett said, perfectly imitating her mother's voice. "Child, I have seen a spell turn rain to sun. I have seen a spell turn old to young. But never have I seen a spell to turn the world to fair."

Nate smiled. "Your mom is extremely wonderful, but she can be extremely annoying." He reached for her hand, but Scarlett moved away.

"She is. Especially when she's right."

Chapter 28
Fat Man and Little Boy

By the time Scarlett returned to the inn, the joint was jumping. Oak Haven's prominent witches had gathered in the dining room to plot their next move. In the ballroom, the Gilbert and Sullivan Society rehearsed *Pirates of Penzance*, the performance that was to be the culmination of their gathering. In the lobby—dead in the middle between the scheming and the singing—Delilah manned her post at the reservation desk.

She looked up from her paperwork when Scarlett walked in. "There you are. Big meeting in the dining room—you should probably get in there."

"If it's a big meeting," Scarlett said with a frown, "why aren't *you* in there?"

"I never am." Her big sister gestured at the reservation desk. "Someone has to do *this*."

A voice boomed from the ballroom. "I am the very model of a modern major-vegetable . . ."

The piano stopped and the anguished director called out, "Try again, please!"

Scarlett moved toward the dining room—she felt poorly

about Del being left out, but she knew it was urgent to inform them about Violet.

But when she reached the doorway, the sight of the witches stopped Scarlett cold. A lot of prominent women were there: Mama, Luna, and Aphra among them, plus Jerusha and Candace, two members of the Oak Haven Elder Council. Also there was Belinda . . . and her daughter Priti . . . and also Polly.

Polly. Oh no. Polly is here.

The idea of bursting into a meeting and saying, "I know whodunit!" was much less appealing when her audience included the mom of the one whodunit.

"Shit," Scarlett said quietly.

Maybe I need proof—more than just one incriminating conversation—before I go accusing somebody's kid.

Needing a moment to assess her options, Scarlett drifted back to the reservation desk. From the rehearsal room came the baritone voice again: "About binomial theorem I am teeming with . . . a . . . pot of beans?"

"Defenestrate yourself immediately!" howled the director.

Scarlett wiggled her eyebrows at her sister. "Tough rehearsal, huh?"

"They are driving me *crazy*," Delilah moaned. "Performance is tomorrow—it can't be over soon enough for me. Mandy Patinkin's understudy is a catastrophe, as you can hear for yourself. Anyway, don't you think you ought to go—"

"Waaaait," Scarlett said, laughing. "Wait, hang on. There's a lot happening right now, but I'm going to need you to pause and explain what you just said."

"I was saying, you should really get into that meeting because—"

"No, Del. Not that. Mandy Patinkin?! You can't mean Mandy 'Inigo Montoya' Patinkin, surely."

"Well, duh, yeah. He was supposed to chair the Gilbert and Sullivan conference, but he's busy doing . . . I don't know what. Shooting *Yentl Part 2* or whatever. I have no idea. So now we're stuck with *that* dummy instead."

From the next room, the singing started up again. "With many cheerful facts about the square of the . . . hippopotamus . . . ?"

Del's sigh was like a lonely breeze through an abandoned playground. "Good God, he sucks."

"Darling sister of mine, are you telling me that Mandy Patinkin was supposed to be coming here? To Oak Haven?"

"Obviously! Mama made a big effort to get the booking. They were going to stay in Litchfield somewhere? But she called Mandy and she said, 'Look—'"

"Halt." Scarlett raised her hand. "Mama knows Mandy Patinkin? That's what you're telling me. Kelly Melrose. Is friends. With Mandy Patinkin."

"I mean . . . *friends* . . ." Delilah said slowly. "I guess . . . more like, friends with—"

"Don't you say it! If you say *benefits* right now, I'm going to lose my fucking mind."

Before Delilah could confirm or deny this gossip, voices drifted down from the second-floor landing. Maximillian jauntily descended the stairs, flanked by two top-hatted magicians, one on each side—a tall, portly fellow on the right and a short, thin fellow on the left. The big magician talked endlessly; the little one said nothing at all.

Scarlett gasped. *It's Max! Right in front of me. Here's my big chance to get to the truth.* "Hey, Maximillian—" she began.

But Delilah grabbed her arm and shushed her.

"No, Del, you don't understand, I need to—"

"Shut up, don't say a word."

Scarlett glared at her sister, then realized that Del was looking as appalled as she was. Surely it couldn't be for the same reason? Had her sister already figured everything out? *It wouldn't be the first time that Del got somewhere ahead of me.* "We need to get the truth," she whispered urgently.

"*Not now*," Del said between gritted teeth.

The magicians reached the bottom of the stairs. Deep in conversation, they swept right out of the inn without a glance at the reservation desk.

"Why'd you stop me?!" Scarlett demanded. "You know they're involved with the infestation somehow, right? I don't know how exactly, but Violet made it quite clear to me today that they did *something*. We need to question Max."

"Okay, calm down, Columbo. First of all, questioning him directly isn't going to get you anywhere—Max is too smart for that. But that's not why I stopped you."

"Then why—"

"*Because*," Del said ominously, "those two magicians with Max just now? Fat Man and Little Boy? They never entered this inn."

Scarlett blinked a few times, hoping that would help her make sense of Del's statement. "We just saw them coming from upstairs. Obviously, they entered the inn at some point, because they just now exited. I think you've been behind that desk too long, Del."

"That's my point, actually. I've been at this desk *all day*. All day, Scar, with no breaks. And yet, I've never seen those two. I'm telling you, they entered the Stargazer some other way."

Scarlett glared at the staircase as if the answer was written on the steps. "But how could . . ." Slowly, she turned back to her sister. "You're saying . . ."

"I'm *saying* . . . something is going on in Max's room."

Scarlett gasped. "You know what? I just remembered. When Nate and I checked for portals, Max wouldn't let us inside. He was adamant we not see his room. But . . ." She leaned over the reservation desk—so far over, her forehead was nearly touching her sister's. "There's no one there now."

Delilah jingled her ring of room keys. "Let's do this."

***

Delilah inserted the key into the lock, expecting the satisfying click of the tumblers falling into place. Instead, the key refused to turn. She tried again, jiggling the key with growing frustration, but it was useless.

"He must've changed it."

"That's some balls on him," Scarlett marveled. "Changing the locks on your rented room!"

Delilah bit her lip, her mind obviously racing. "I could try a spell to open the lock, but . . . we both know that's not the best idea."

"Hold that thought." Scarlett disappeared down the hallway, leaving Delilah to stare at the unyielding door.

Delilah jigged the lock again, just out of spite. "I wonder if Luna could do it . . ."

Scarlett reappeared, a triumphant grin on her face and a fire axe clutched in her hands. "I choose violence."

"Scarlett, no! You'll destroy the door! And Max will know we were in there."

"So? He changed the lock *on a hotel room*, Del! That's plenty of justification. Wait till Mama hears—she'll kick him out so fast he won't have time to pack."

"Scarlett, wait—"

But her sister was already in motion. Gripping the axe tightly, she raised it over her head and brought the blade down on the door. The sharp metal bit into the wood with a satisfying crack. Splinters flew as Scarlett wrenched the axe free, the door shuddering under the force of her blow.

"Scarlett!" Delilah glanced nervously down the hallway. "Someone's going to hear."

Scarlett merely shrugged, a mischievous glint in her eye. "Then we'd better hurry." She swung the axe again. The lock gave way and the door swung open.

Max had completely redecorated. Gone were the antique furnishings and watercolors of autumnal scenes. Gadgets and props of every description littered the space—disappearing cabinets in multiple designs, a guillotine prop, a box of wands. A collection of top hats in mildly varying designs was laid across the windowsill. Perhaps the most surprising items in the room were all the books. Some magic books, but most were unrelated. *Webster's Third New International Dictionary, Unabridged. The Guinness Book of Records. The Encyclopaedia Britannica* in thirty-two volumes.

"Huh." Scarlett poked at the books with mild interest. "Max must slay at those coffee shop trivia nights."

"Everybody needs a hobby, I guess . . ." Delilah moved further into the room. "If I were a portal, where would I be?"

"Bathroom." Scarlett was already moving toward the door.

The sisters entered cautiously, half-expecting to find a

shimmering vortex waiting to swallow them whole. But to their disappointment, it was just an ordinary bathroom, complete with fluffy towels and complimentary toiletries.

Scarlett, never one to let an opportunity pass her by, couldn't resist peeking into the medicine cabinet. She let out a snort of laughter as she pulled a bottle off the shelf. "'Enchanted Essence Aftershave,'" she read aloud. "Bleagh, I'll pass on Max's *enchanted essence*, thanks."

Delilah shook her head, fighting back a smile. "Focus, Scar. The portal's not here."

Scarlett closed the cabinet. "Only one other place it could be." She turned to face her sister, her eyes glinting with excitement. "The wardrobe."

They returned to the bedroom and approached the wardrobe slowly, their hearts pounding in their chests. Delilah reached out, her fingers hovering over the handle. She glanced at Scarlett, who nodded. With a deep breath, Delilah grasped the handle and pulled.

The interior of the wardrobe shimmered and rippled, the back wall replaced by a swirling vortex of energy.

"You wanted to know where all those magicians are coming from?" Del asked. "Here's your answer."

"Well, well, well." Scarlett smirked, a hint of mischief in her voice. "Where do you think this goes? Maybe Narnia? Shall we have a look?"

"Wait!" Delilah reached for her sister's arm. "We have no idea what's on the other side of that thing. Could be dangerous."

But Scarlett was already stepping forward, her hand outstretched. "Come on, Del! Where's your sense of adventure?"

Her sister hesitated, torn between caution and curiosity.

"What if the portal disappears on us? How will we get back?" She watched as Scarlett's fingers brushed the shimmering surface of the portal, sending ripples cascading.

"We'll find another, Del, good grief! We've got to seize the day, be brave, all that jazz."

Delilah's gaze snapped to the window, and her eyes widened in shock. "Scarlett . . ."

"You need to do a little living, Del. You can't spend your whole life behind that desk!"

"Scarlett, look . . ."

"And more importantly, this could be our chance to finally get some answers."

"*Scarlett, dammit.* Look at the window!"

Hanging from the curtain rod was a cage filled with glowing red dragonflies.

Chapter 29
The Queen's Gambit

In the dining room, the witches were drinking pinot noir and trying to figure out what to do next.

Aphra couldn't stop apologizing for the failure of her cages. "I really thought I had things under control . . . I'm so sorry I've let everybody down."

"Babe . . ." Dayo sat beside her wife, a supportive arm over her shoulder. "Nobody could have done better."

"Absolutely," consoled council member Jerusha.

"You're goddamn right!" Belinda declared. She got up and brought the wine over to refill Aphra's glass. "This isn't your fault, sweetheart."

Mama clinked her wineglass with a fork. "Ladies. Dwelling on what went wrong gets us nowhere. What is our next move?"

Seated beside her, Luna flipped open the *Myrmex Arcana*. "I did read about a parasitic wasp from Macquarie Island, near Tasmania? It lays eggs inside the thoraxes of other magical insects. Maybe that's something? Introduce wasps?"

"One question," said Polly. "What happens after the wasps have run out of dragonflies to kill?"

Candace nodded fretfully. "Will they come for my ladybugs next?"

"I hear you," Luna admitted. "I'm not sure about that. Of course, if we clean out the grove, we should get magic back so—"

The witches reacted with alarm. "Should!" exclaimed Jerusha. "Kelly, what does your girl mean, *should*? I thought everything will be normal once we clear out the flies!"

"Unbunch yourself, Jerusha," Mama said. "Luna is merely acknowledging that life is uncertain. Still . . ." Here she turned to address her daughter. "I do think the ladies have a valid concern. Introducing a new potential pest to address a current one doesn't seem especially wise."

"Luna, you're our historian here," Belinda said. "What about the old days? You said these flies originated in Ancient Egypt, right? How did they fix the plagues back then?"

"Um . . ." Luna grimaced. "How did they end the plagues . . . in the story of Exodus?"

Candace laughed. "I don't suppose you have any Chosen People you could set free, do you, Belinda?"

Mama lifted an eyebrow. "Belinda's gnomes already left," she said slyly. "So that won't help."

"Well, I was just asking!" Belinda huffed.

Into this bickering marched Scarlett and Delilah. Scarlett triumphantly placed Max's cage of flies on the table.

"Oh my goodness," cried Jerusha. "Just look at them!"

Aphra gazed at her friends. "What've you got here, gals?"

"These were in Maximillian's room," Delilah said.

Scarlett nodded. "He's the source of our problem. I'd suspected before, but now we have evidence."

Mama stood and approached the cage, pulling her readers up

to her eyes to study the tiny beasts. "Luna, these creatures had to be conjured, am I understanding correctly? He couldn't have bought these in a joke shop, in other words."

"Yes, that's right. They haven't existed for thousands of years."

"Someone created them." Mama straightened up, gazing at each of the witches in turn. "How did he manage it?"

"He had a little helper," Delilah announced. "I'm sorry, Polly."

Polly looked appalled. "What are you suggesting?! I certainly didn't assist that muppet. You can't mean me."

"No," Scarlett said sadly. "I'm afraid we *don't* mean you."

A silence fell over the dining room.

"Oh dear," Belinda said. "Oh, that poor child, what was she thinking?"

***

Violet sat on a stone bench in the back garden, jabbing angrily at her phone.

Polly emerged from the dining room, with the Melroses close behind.

"Violet." Her mother's voice was firm, but her eyes held a pleading softness. "We need to talk."

"Don't feel like it." The teenager refused to look up.

Polly stepped closer, her voice rising. "I know you've been up to something with that . . . that magician."

"He's my friend—so?! What, am I not allowed to have friends now? Thanks a lot, *fascist*."

"As it happens, no," Polly retorted. "You're not allowed to have friends who are twice your age and magicians. And what about the dragonflies?"

"What about them?"

"Where did they come from? Scarlett found a cage of flies in Max's room. But we very much doubt he could have conjured them himself seeing as he has no genuine magical powers. Violet, did you help him create the files?"

The teenager kept her head low, focused on her phone. "I don't know what you're talking about."

Polly sat down beside her daughter. With a swift and well-practiced motion, she reached over and wrenched the phone right out of Violet's hands. Holding the device up like a threat, she said, "Don't you lie to me. Did you help the magicians?"

Violet remained silent, her eyes fixed on her lap.

The rest of the witches had all gathered behind the Melroses to listen. Their expressions ran from motherly disappointment to white-hot rage . . . but none could bear to miss a word.

Polly could feel the group's judgment without needing to look at them. "I can handle this," she snapped. "This is my daughter, and she doesn't deserve to be interrogated by half the town."

Mama Melrose held up her hands in a placating gesture. "We don't mean to intrude, Polly. But at the same time, this affects all of us."

Polly returned her attention to Violet, taking her daughter's hands in her own. "Please, sweetheart. Talk to me. Did the magicians trick you somehow? It's what they do, Violet—we can all understand making a mistake. But we need you to be honest with us now. The town depends on it."

Under her mother's gentle but persistent questioning, Violet's defenses crumbled. Tears welled up in her eyes as she finally spoke. "They're nice to me." Her voice trembled. "They treat me like a grown-up. They said if I could help them with a bit of magic, they'd make things better. That the dragonflies would make Oak Haven more like a normal town. And then maybe I could have a boyfriend. Maybe Dad would come home. They said they could make everything better . . ."

"Oh, Violet." Polly was clearly heartbroken. "How could you?"

"You don't understand!" Years of anger and frustration came pouring out. "You have no idea what it's like. To have my whole life ruined by that stupid Forgetting Spell. My own dad doesn't remember I exist! I don't even have any friends! How could I? I can't have friends in Oak Haven—everyone who sees me says, *look, there's the weird girl whose father poisoned the grove.* But if I try to make a friend from outside of town, they forget me. You don't know what it's like to always be alone!"

Violet stood, her hands clenched into fists. "I just want a normal life!"

She ran for the inn, shoving her way past the witches and bursting into the dining room. Her chest heaving with sobs, she collapsed into a chair, burying her face in her hands. The witches followed her inside, their expressions grim.

Suddenly the air in the room began to shimmer and ripple, like the surface of a pond disturbed by a stone. The walls melted away—but instead of glitching to Waikiki or Studio 54, the dining room glitched to reflect the inside of Violet's broken heart.

The witches found themselves standing in a cozy living room decorated with jack-o'-lanterns and grinning paper skeletons. Warmth and happiness radiated from every corner as a young Violet twirled in a fairy princess costume. Her face was lit with joy as she showed off her sparkly wings to a smiling Polly and Bill.

Too soon, the scene shifted. The room grew dark and cold, festive decorations replaced by shadows and gloom. Polly and Bill were fighting, their voices loud and accusing. Bill stormed out, slamming the door so hard that the witches flinched. Little Violet ran to the door and threw it open, sobbing and pleading for Daddy to come back.

Scarlett leaned over to whisper to Luna. "Who's doing this? Is it Violet?"

Luna nodded. "Her emotions have gotten away from her, and the dining room is responding."

"We should help her somehow."

"I disagree." Mama leaned over to put one arm on each of her daughter's shoulders. "Let's let this play out. See what she knows."

The memory changed once more, and the witches found themselves standing in downtown Oak Haven, outside Spellbound Books. Violet, now a teenager, smiled as a handsome young man handed her a bag from the Happy Panda. The witches' hearts fluttered along with Violet's as the young man paused to chat. All along the street, window boxes burst with flowers, all blooming at once.

But the scene quickly shifted—Mr. Happy Panda returned, but this time he regarded Violet with polite confusion, no recognition in his eyes. Nearby, windows began to splinter and crack, and the sky turned dark with an approaching storm.

The memories continued to flash by, each playing out in vivid detail. The witches saw Violet storm out of the bookstore and into the street, a hammer in her hand. They gasped as she smashed the magical sigil built into the crosswalk, and they shuddered as Maximillian appeared behind her, observing Violet with a sinister glare.

Suddenly, they were in the coffee shop. The witches could feel the warmth and acceptance radiating from the group of magicians as they comforted Violet and listened to her story.

They watched as Max held out a copy of *Myrmex Acana,* his conniving smile unfurling from ear to ear. He asked Violet for something—just a little thing, barely even anything at all. The witches all felt the desperate longing for approval that drove the young girl to agree.

Throughout it all, the real Violet sobbed in her chair. Polly rushed to her daughter's side, gathering her into her arms and holding her tight. "It's okay, baby," Polly whispered into Violet's hair. "Everything is going to be okay . . ."

***

As Violet's sobs began to subside, the dining room settled back into its normal state. A whirlwind of chaotic teenage emotion just moments ago, now the room was now eerily still. The only sounds were the distant strains of "Away, Away, My Heart's on Fire," drifting in from the *Penzance* rehearsal on the other side of the building.

The witches gathered in a loose circle, their whispers barely audible as they grappled with what to do next. Aphra spoke in favor of negotiation, while Belinda leaned toward stringing Max up by his thumbs. Luna looked as though she might faint, and Mama placed a reassuring hand on her back to steady her.

The quiet was shattered by the squeak of the inn's front door. Maximillian the Magnificent strode in, his rabbit Quentin in a cage under one arm. He stopped abruptly midway across the lobby, his eyes widening as he saw the assembly of witches in the dining room.

The women turned as one to stare at him. He stared back, and for a heartbeat, no one moved.

Max's face, usually so carefully composed, betrayed a flicker of panic. He was a poor chess player who'd carelessly tumbled into the Queen's Gambit.

Swallowing hard, he took a single step forward, plastering a cheesy grin on his face. "Ladies, good evening . . ." He was too startled to even come up with an accent. "How are you all?"

The witches gazed back at him, nonplussed.

Max spun on his heel and bolted. Poor Quentin bounced unhappily around in his cage as Max raced up the stairs two at a time.

Delilah, at her post behind the desk, vaulted over the countertop in pursuit. Scarlett, the only other witch who understood the true severity of the situation, was right on her heels.

"Stop him, Del!" she shouted. "He's going for the portal!"

Max reached his third-floor room in record time. He made a beeline for the wardrobe and dove in without hesitation.

Delilah burst into the room mere seconds later, her eyes locking on to the wardrobe. She knew exactly where Max had gone, but fear made her hesitate. "Ugh! Where do you lead?" she demanded of the portal. "What's on the other side? And if I enter, how will I get back home?"

Scarlett burst into the room at full speed and gave her sister a firm push from behind, propelling them both into the abyss.

The other witches arrived at the doorway . . . too late to see anything but the empty wardrobe and a lingering shimmer of magical energy.

"Well, well," said Mama with pride. She leaned into the portal and shouted, "Good hunting, my dears! Come home safe."

Chapter 30
Beginner's Luck

Having exited Oak Haven via a modest wardrobe, the sisters reemerged into a closet large enough to qualify as a San Francisco bedroom. The space was stuffed with racks of costumes: leopard-print catsuits, baby doll blouses in a variety of pastels, ladies' tracksuits, and black Lycra cocktail dresses. An entire wall was devoted to Union Jack regalia.

Scarlett and Delilah looked at each other and shrugged. "Could be worse?" Scarlett offered.

"Sure," Delilah agreed. "I was afraid we'd end up inside a volcano or something."

Scarlett cracked open the door and peeked out.

The brightly lit dressing room was a whirlwind of post-show chaos. The room was lined with make-up tables and full-length mirrors, where five scantily clad performers were busily removing their make-up and wigs. The walls were plastered with multiple copies of the same poster:

BELLAGIO HOTEL WELCOMES
THE WANNABEs
A LIVE SPICE GIRLS EXPERIENCE

A chorus of gasps erupted as the performers spun away from their mirrors to view the new arrivals from the closet.

"Bloody hell!" exclaimed a woman who was clearly Not-Sporty Spice. "Another one?!"

"Where'd you come from?" demanded Not-Ginger Spice, false eyelashes fluttering.

"Yeah!" Not-Baby Spice added. "And why does this keep happening?"

Not-Scary Spice, the least easily rattled of the group, simply pointed at the door. "Your mate went that-a-way . . ."

"Sorry to interrupt." Scarlett knew better than to explain how they were in the closet—none of their lives would be long enough for that. "You say you saw a man go that way? With a rabbit?"

"We're very busy," Not-Ginger said defensively. "We don't have time to take down descriptions of every man who appears in our closet."

Scarlett nodded. "That's fair."

"That chap did have a bunny," Not-Baby cooed. "I noticed because I love bunnies! He just left."

"Fantastic, thanks for the information." Scarlett made immediately for the door.

But Delilah paused. "Quick question. You said this *keeps* happening. It's not just been tonight, has it?"

"Oh, blimey, no," said Not-Ginger Spice, whose lousy accent marked her as a native of someplace near New Jersey rather than anywhere near to the original. "Come through here all the time, they do. They stride into our dressing room without so much as a hello, walk into our closet, and poof. Never see 'em again."

Scarlett glanced at her sister. "At least now we know where all those damn magicians are coming from."

Not-Posh, who'd ignored them all while she cracked open a window, whirled around with a cigarette between her teeth. "Any of you got a light?"

With the instinctive grace of a life devoted to hospitality, Delilah idly snapped her fingers, and the cigarette was lit.

The performers all applauded. "Nice trick," said Not-Scary appreciatively.

"*Scarlett*." Delilah ignored the Spices and locked eyes with her sister. "I just did a spell . . . and . . . it was fine."

Scarlett's face flushed with happiness. "Magic works here!"

"Ohhhh, of course it does," Delilah exclaimed. "I can't believe I didn't think of it before. The grove only powers our town, not *all* magic. The condition of our trees doesn't impact anywhere else. Scar, you realize what this means? As long as we're outside of Oak Haven, we can—"

"Do whatever we want!"

Hand in delighted hand, the sisters moved to exit the dressing room. "I'm starving," Scarlett announced. "Should we hit the buffet?"

"Where is there a buffet?" asked Del, confused.

Scarlett pointed at the Wannabes posters. "Bellagio Hotel! That means we're in Vegas, where there's always a buffet! God, I keep forgetting you've never been anywhere . . . C'mon, follow me."

"But . . . what about catching Max?"

"I know, I know," Scarlett replied. "Let's catch Max . . . *and* find the buffet."

The sisters gingerly made their way down a dark, narrow corridor, which ended with a big black door marked "EXIT TO CASINO." Scarlett was about to push it open when a thought stopped her cold.

"Wait. I just realized something."

"Mmhmm?"

"That portal, in the dressing room. Magicians have been using it to reach Oak Haven, right? On a regular basis. Which means it's stable. The accidental portals, the ones caused by the oak grove issues? Those aren't stable at all. Nate and I went into the walk-in, ended up in New Orleans, and the portal closed behind us. But this dressing room is apparently just sitting there, open all the time."

"Okay . . ." said Delilah. "What's your point?"

"How did he do it, Del? He's just a moronic stage magician, right? Magicians have no powers of their own—isn't that what we keep saying?"

"Well . . ."

"And what about the dragonflies? Violet is a kid! Yes, she's a witch, but do you really think she conjured a biblical-level spell *alone*? That's a group spell—it has to be."

"You think there's more witches involved?"

"No, Del, I think . . . I think maybe Luna might be right about magicians."

"Ugh." Del looked nauseous. "Don't even go there."

To terminate the discussion, she pushed open the door and the sisters were slammed by a wall of noise—a sensory onslaught that hit them like a physical blow. A relentless soundtrack of electronic beeps, robotic jackpot announcements, and the clanging cascade of coins battered their ears. Mirrored tiles and pulsing strobe lights refracted the images of people, drinks, and flashing game boards into a disorienting montage. The air hung heavy with perfume, alcohol, and the adrenaline-laced sweat of desperate gamblers.

Delilah clutched at her sister's arm, her eyes darting wildly. "This is like stepping inside a concussion!"

Scarlett led her shell-shocked sister through the maze of slot machines, their progress punctuated by ringing bells and electronic whoooop whooops. A sense of reckless abandon bubbled up within her. When they approached a slot machine with a giant glowing pineapple on top, Scarlett couldn't help herself.

"A SpongeBob SquarePants slot machine!" she shouted. "This here is my destiny."

Delilah frowned. "There's no time. We're supposed to be chasing Max, remember?"

"Bah, we'll toss out a little locator spell and find him in two seconds. C'mon, Del, live a little." Humming the theme song under her breath, Scarlett dropped a quarter into the slot. With a dramatic flourish, she smashed a big yellow button in the middle of the machine, sending SpongeBob's eyes spinning. Lights flashed, and suddenly, a torrent of coins cascaded into the tray. A giant digital dollar sign flashed, the jackpot total ticking steadily upwards.

"Woo hoo!" Scarlett cried. "We did it!"

"Did what?" asked Delilah. "I don't even know what's going on!"

"Beginner's luck," Scarlett said with a wink, scooping up her winnings. "I guess drinks are on me."

They navigated past rows and rows of slot machines, the incessant din punctuated by the occasional frustrated groan or joyous shout. Scarlett paused near a large, green-felt blackjack table, its surface littered with chips and cards. Gamblers perched on their chairs, their faces lit with hope and grim determination in varying degrees. A burly man in a Hawaiian shirt perched on a stool, staring intently at the two cards before him—a nine and a four. He hesitated, muttering, "Vegas baby, it's Vegas baby, it's Vegas . . ." like a secret prayer.

The sisters watched from off to the side, mesmerized by the unfolding drama. Scarlett recognized the adrenaline cloud hanging over the table—a thrilling dance on a knife-edge between recklessness and strategy. It was precisely how she'd felt as a kid, every time she'd attempted a spell that she wasn't supposed to.

Her sister—who had never in her life attempted a spell she wasn't supposed to—shifted uncomfortably. "All that stress over a game of cards," she muttered.

Finally, the man tapped the green felt. "Hit me," he rasped.

The dealer, a woman with a bored expression and expertly painted red nails, flicked a card across the table: an eight. The man threw his arms in the air and roared. "YEAAAAAAHHHH! VEGAS BABY! IT'S VEGAS!"

People around him cheered—even Delilah couldn't help but smile. Suddenly, she grabbed Scarlett's head and turned it sharply to the left. There was Max, striding toward the buffet line.

Scarlett had to laugh. "Guess we hit the jackpot again."

The massive double doors of the buffet whooshed open with a pneumatic hiss, revealing a spectacle that rivaled the casino floor in terms of sensory overload. Mountains of golden brown fried chicken glistened under heat lamps, mashed potatoes and meatballs and shrimp scampi piled high in stainless steel pans, and an entire wall displayed a dizzying array of desserts. The air hung heavy with the combined aromas of roasted meats, buttered vegetables, and sugary pastries, and the clatter of plates and chatter of customers.

A hostess appeared, clipboard in hand: "Name, please?" she enquired with a bored smile.

"Uh . . . Melrose," Delilah hesitated, glancing at Scarlett.

The hostess scanned her list with pursed lips. "No Melrose on the guest list, sorry. Buffet is full up."

Scarlett glanced at her sister, who gave her an almost imperceptible nod. A mischievous glint flashed in her sister's eyes.

Delilah cleared her throat, taking a step closer to the hostess. Her voice was a soft, measured whisper—barely audible over the din of the buffet. She raised one hand, index finger slightly extended, like she was hailing the most mellow taxi in the universe. "Actually," she said calmly, "I'm sure you'll find us on your list. Look again."

The hostess frowned slightly, her fingers tapping nervously against the clipboard as she studied the names once more.

"Huh," she murmured. "Well, you were right. Melrose party, table for two. My apologies."

"No worries," Scarlett said with a smile. "We're not the witches you're looking for."

"Shut up," Delilah whispered.

The hostess gave Scarlett a quizzical look, then clearly decided she didn't want to pursue this inquiry any further. "Plates and utensils are against the left-hand wall. Enjoy."

"You always make that joke," said Delilah, annoyed. "*Every time* I use that spell, you make that joke. And it's never funny."

"Au contraire, it's always funny," Scarlett demurred. "Pretty sure George Lucas stole the idea for the Force from our kind. We may as well get a few chuckles out of it."

"Hush," Delilah said. "Focus. Do you see Max anywhere?"

Scarlett's head swiveled left and right. "Uhh, he's around here somewhere; we saw him come in. Look, you can't expect me to play Sherlock on an empty stomach. C'mon, just a quick bite . . . *please*? You go for the savory; I'll hit the sweets. We reconvene at the prime rib mountain in two minutes."

Delilah rolled her eyes. "All right, all right . . . but the second we see him—"

"We're following. Absolutely."

When their trays were piled high with every manner of carbohydrate imaginable, the sisters found an empty table in the corner. "So . . ." Scarlett said as they dug in, "is Mandy Patinkin gonna be our new daddy?"

Delilah rolled her eyes. "Will you let it go, Scar?"

"Well, I'm just saying—"

"Papa's been gone ten years! Mama has a right to a life."

"Really?" Scarlett shot back. "Because clearly she wouldn't say the same about you."

Delilah stared at her sister. "What is that jab supposed to mean?"

"It's not a jab, Del, it's an observation." Scarlett shoveled a forkful of fettuccine carbonara into her mouth. "She keeps you locked behind that desk 24/7. When are you gonna get out and see the world? Maybe even have a relationship?"

"A *relationship*?" Her eyebrows ascended toward the gilt

ceiling. "What, like you and Nate Williams? Yeah, I'll pass on that mess, thanks."

"Well . . ." Scarlett blushed. "Yeah. Okay. I'm not offering myself as an example."

"The two of you really are amazing. Ten years apart, and now you're right back in that *will they or won't they* nonsense from when you were teenagers. If I remember correctly, you both finally concluded *yes, you would*, and then—"

"And then we couldn't. Because of Papa."

"Well, Papa's long gone now." Delilah stabbed a piece of prime rib with her fork. "Seems to me the statute of limitations has run out on that excuse."

Scarlett set down her fork and glared. "It's not an *excuse*, Del. The situation has changed. I have a new life now. And I don't think Nate fits."

"Then tell him that! Let him go. Let Polly have him—she's certainly made her interest clear."

Ugh, Nate with Polly, Scarlett thought. *Don't think I could bear that.* But at the same time, she knew in her heart that Delilah was right.

"I suppose you have a point." She sighed. "I should tell him there's no chance." *It's not fair to him,* she thought. *All this back-and-forth, all this kidding ourselves that we have some sort of future. I claim to be Nate's friend—if I'm truly his friend, I should act like it.* "Okay. When we get back, I'm going to tell him we have to stop all that dumb flirting. I'm letting him go, full stop."

"You should!"

"I will!"

"You better."

"God, Del, I just said I'd tell him, jeez! It's done. It *has* to be

247

done. Because once the grove is repaired, I'm headed out west, period."

"*Out west*," Delilah repeated the words like they tasted of sulfur. "I still don't understand what you get out of the Normie Life. What's the point? I mean, don't you miss magic?"

"Ehh, sometimes. But after Papa . . . the fear got to be too much. You know what I mean? Giving up magic didn't seem like a burden when I felt sick just thinking about it."

Delilah shook her head. "You took it so hard, what happened that night. From the way you fell to pieces, you'd have thought that *you* were the only one whose father died. But I mean, Luna and I lost our father too, you know."

"I know that, Del. I wasn't trying to be a drama queen about it. But I mean, it was a lot different for me because—" Scarlett looked directly into her sister's eyes and stopped. *Because it was all my fault*, was the end of that sentence. But she couldn't bring herself to say it. "Because . . . I don't know why. I just felt how I felt."

"That's for sure. You totally lost it at the funeral, and then poof, you were gone."

"Yeah, well . . ." Scarlett's throat tightened. "You've always had your shit together more than me, so, nothing to see there. You're hypercompetent; I'm a mess. Just business as usual for the Melrose sisters."

Delilah bristled. "If my *shit* was more *together*, as you put it, it was because it had to be. I never had the choices you did. It was my job to take care of the two of you, and Mom, always."

"Yeah, which you've never hesitated to remind everyone about," Scarlett said. "Your job was being the boss of us, Luna's job was being the flaky prodigy, and what the heck was my job? I could never figure that out."

"Your job was being Papa's favorite, you idiot."

"What?!" Scarlett exclaimed. "No, I wasn't!"

"Of course you were. You always were. And then, when he died, you had no use for the rest of us, and off you went."

That stopped Scarlett cold. Beneath her sister's sarcasm, beneath all the snark, there was this horrible, painful, and totally untrue belief—that Scar had left because she'd wanted to. "Oh my God, Del, is that what you think?!"

Delilah stared into a murky bowl of chicken and sausage gumbo. "It's what I know," she said quietly.

Scarlett reached across the table for Delilah's hand, but her sister wouldn't offer it. So she said, "It's not true at all. I felt like I had to leave. I didn't *want* to."

"Well," Del replied, "all I know is, you sure didn't want to stay."

Silence settled on the table. The weight of their feelings hung in the air, heavy and tangible. They pushed their food around on their plates, suddenly no longer hungry.

And then, like a crazy ray of sunshine cutting through clouds, Scarlett saw him. There was Max, striding purposefully through the buffet, forcefully shoving carrots into Quentin's cage as he headed for the exit. "Look, there he is! He's about to leave!"

"I see him." Delilah tossed her spoon on the table.

Scarlett jumped up so fast that her chair nearly tipped over. "Let's go."

Chapter 31
What Happens in Oak Haven . . .

Abandoning their half-eaten plates and half-finished conversation, the sisters raced through the maze of hungry diners. They spotted him again outside the buffet—a tuxedoed blur against the neon lights, making his way toward the exit. Max was surprisingly nimble, considering his furry burden, navigating the maze of gaming tables with practiced ease.

In the lobby, a towering wall of sequined showgirls materialized in front of Scarlett, blocking her path. By the time she squeezed through, Max had vanished.

"He went that way." Delilah grabbed her arm and pointed, just in time to see Max's tuxedo tails flutter through a bank of revolving doors.

As they burst out of the casino, the night air hit them like a slap. "Why is it so cold?" Delilah demanded. "Isn't this the desert?"

"Yeah, that's how deserts work, Del. Day equals hot; night equals cold." Scarlett spun in a circle, trying to see which way Max went. "You really need to get out more."

She rolled her eyes. "So you keep saying."

Neon signs in a tangled jungle of garish hues bathed the Strip in an artificial twilight. Towering casinos and hotels with mirrored facades lined the street as far as the eye could see. A steady stream of honking taxis and tourist buses clogged the lanes, their headlights adding to the relentless assault on the senses. Amidst the cacophony, the rhythmic thrumming of bass music vibrated from a nearby nightclub—a low, insistent pulse.

Scarlett caught sight of Max at the far end of the casino's sweeping driveway. He'd paused to speak with a disheveled man hunched over a makeshift sandwich board. The faded cardboard was covered in bold, scrawling letters that read: "MAGIC IS REAL! ASK HOW I KNOW." Max's movements were animated and full of conviction; whatever he was saying, he meant it. The sign man pointed sharply to the left and Max took off running.

Delilah raced over, but by the time she reached the end of the driveway, Max was already gone. "Excuse me!" she called out, breathless from her run. "What did you say to that man?"

The man looked up at her with bleary eyes. He smelled strongly of cheap booze. "What man?"

"The man! Who was just here!"

He stared off into the middle distance. "Don't remember no man."

"But it was literally two seconds ago. He was wearing a tuxedo? He had a rabbit for crying out loud!"

"Didn't see no rabbit."

"But . . . I don't . . ." Delilah was utterly flummoxed. "He was just . . ."

Scarlett finally caught up, breathing hard. "You move pretty fast for a desk jockey, Del," she said between pants. "Hey, old-timer, where's the magician headed?"

"He says he didn't see anyone," Delilah said furiously.

Scarlett studied him, and he peered back at her expectantly. Then Scarlett noticed a bucket by the old man's feet. "Oh, I see. Here, take this." She tossed all the coins she'd won from SpongeBob into his bucket. And then, reconsidering, she snapped her fingers and doubled the amount.

The man grinned. "He was asking me about the Vanishing Point—it's a magician hangout. That a'way."

"What the hell!" Delilah complained.

"Information ain't free," the man said simply. "Data is king."

Scarlett just shrugged. "Vegas, baby. C'mon, Del, let's go."

"Hey!" the man called after them. "It's members only, you know! You want help getting in?"

Delilah hollered over her shoulder. "We got it, thanks."

The sisters took off running down the brightly lit boulevard. Giant billboards and neon signs for different shows and attractions assaulted their senses from all directions. Scarlett and Delilah dodged throngs of tourists as they scanned the crowds for any sign of Max. They passed a squat, nondescript building with no signage—it was like a black hole in the center of the dazzlingly lit surroundings. But there was a man standing by an unmarked door—a veritable mountain of a human, decked out in a bespoke leather jacket, enormous reflective sunglasses, and a chestful of gold chains. He leaned against the building with his arms folded.

Scarlett stopped running. "Look at him," she whispered to her sister. "Does he look like the kind of guy who stands beside any old door for no reason whatsoever?"

Delilah considered this. "Vanishing Point?"

"Vanishing Point."

The sisters confidently approached the bouncer.

"Members only," he rumbled.

Delilah tilted her head slightly, lifting two fingers to her temple. She appeared as though she was about to make an incredibly incisive point, which, in fact, she was: "We are members."

The bouncer gazed at her for a moment, then nodded. "Of course you are." He pushed open the door, and they were in.

Sotto voce, Scarlett said, "We're not the witches you're—"

"*Shut up, Scar.*"

The sisters made their way down a dimly lit hallway leading to a small antechamber. The walls were draped with dark velvet curtains, muffling the raucous Strip outside. A single unmarked door stood at the end of the passage.

Scarlett hesitated, nerves abruptly getting the better of her. *What if these magicians despise witches as much as Max apparently does . . . but there's a lot of them? And even if we find Max, what will we do with him?*

But Delilah had no such hesitation. She strode up to the blank door and, without preamble, turned the handle. It was locked.

"Open sesame?" Delilah suggested to the door, but there was no response. "Shazam, perhaps?"

"Swordfish!" Scarlett exclaimed, but to no effect. "Not Marx Brothers fans I guess."

"Oh! I know," Delilah realized. "Duh. Abracadabra!"

The door opened smoothly and Delilah disappeared inside.

With no other choice, Scarlett swallowed her misgivings and followed. She blinked as her eyes adjusted to the dim interior. Vanishing Point was a small, intimate lounge with velvet booths lining the walls. Candles flicked on small round tables, and a haze of smoke hung in the air, with a hint of something herbal Scarlett couldn't quite place. A few magicians sat at the tables, quietly talking or nursing drinks. At one table, a woman levitated a series of crystal balls, making them dance in a circle like a mystical Ferris wheel.

The bar ran along the far wall, a masterpiece of dark mahogany with rows of colorful potions and elixirs lining the shelves behind it. The bartender, a dapper gentleman with a curled mustache, was mixing drinks that sparked and fizzed with supernatural energy. Around them, the bar pulsed with magic—glasses refilled themselves, playing cards shuffled in midair, and on a small stage in the back, a jazz band's instruments played on their own.

"You seeing this?" Scarlett nudged her sister. "I hate this."

"Yeah," Del muttered. "I'm currently making a list of a hundred reasons why I hate this."

"Magicians aren't just knucklehead performers, after all. At least some of them *actually have magic*."

"Yep."

"Which means . . ." Scarlett looked at her sister and sighed. "Luna was right."

"That's, like, reason number three on my list. Hey, look over there."

Max was perched at the bar, with Quentin's cage beside him.

"Right," Delilah said. "So . . . um. What now?"

"What do you mean, *what now*?" Scarlett whispered urgently. "Back at the buffet, you were all gung ho!"

"Hey, you were, too!"

"Well, we're doing it. So . . ." Scarlett shrugged. "Let's . . . just . . . sit down and talk to him, I guess. Act like a magician—

254

he won't remember us now that he's out of Oak Haven. Let's just get him chatting and go from there."

"Okay," Delilah said reluctantly. "But I just want it on the record that *you* pushed *me* into the portal."

"So?"

"So, you started it, Scar."

"No, Del, you started it."

"No, you—oh, never mind." Del folded her arms over her chest. "I don't like this."

"What, you and me bickering? I *love* you and me bickering—I didn't realize how much I'd missed it!"

"No, I don't like pretending to be somebody else. I'm no good at it. I was never good at it."

"Oh, don't worry, you'll be totally fine," Scarlett assured her. On the inside, though, she was worried. Even as a kid, Delilah had been lousy at playing pretend. When they played 'doctor' with other kids in the neighborhood, Delilah would invariably diagnose everyone with terminal cancer. "Just follow my lead. And remember the old rule: with good improv, the response is always 'Yes, and . . .'"

Scarlett and Delilah took a deep breath and approached the stool where Max sat. He sipped a neon blue cocktail and absentmindedly shoved carrots inside Quentin's cage.

"Hey there," Scarlett said, sliding onto the barstool beside Max, and Delilah hovered awkwardly behind. "Nice rabbit."

Max glanced at her suspiciously. "Do I know you?"

"Yes, and?" Delilah said confidently.

"Uh . . ." Scarlett made a face. "We're just a couple of magicians passing through. Heard this was the place to be." The bartender leaned over, and Scarlett indicated they'd have whatever concoction Max was having. "So, what brings you to Vegas? Do you perform here?"

"No, no. Actually . . ." Max chuckled into his drink. "Actually, the truth is, I have no idea what I'm doing here."

"Ahh, yes." Scarlett shook her head sympathetically. "One of those rough Vegas weekends—I know the feeling. I guess that's why they say, whatever happens in Vegas, stays in Vegas."

"This is stranger than that. Last thing I remember, I was on the East Coast. I'd been entrusted with a secret mission, you see. I went deep undercover—I used an accent and everything . . ."

"Just the one?" Delilah muttered. "I bet it wasn't just the one."

"Shhht!" Scarlett shushed her as subtly as she was able.

"But from the moment I arrived? I remember nothing. I don't even know if I . . . Oh, actually . . . wait . . ." Max squinted like he was trying to pass an eye test. "I *was* there. Yes, I do remember, just little flashes. There was an inn . . . and . . . scarecrows. Ugh, scarecrows all over the place."

Scarlett turned to face her sister, mouthing, *What the fuck?!*

He remembers! Delilah mouthed back.

Scarlett leaned forward, putting her elbow on the bar and fully turning her body toward Max. "So, Secret Agent Man . . . I'm not sure I'm following this story. You went on a mission to a place . . . that you don't remember . . . except you do, a little bit?"

Max smiled. "I'm afraid I can't share details, dear. It's all very high level, you understand."

"Yes, I do understand." The bartender delivered the two screaming blue martinis and Scarlett nodded her thanks. "I understand perfectly. *Maximillian*."

His expression shifted from confusion to shock, his eyebrows shooting up and his mouth hanging open. "You know me? But how?"

"Your mission was in Oak Haven, correct?" Scarlett asked, her tone gentle.

Max gasped as recognition dawned. "Oh! Oh, my . . . are you my handlers?" His voice was filled with relief. "I knew I was supposed to make contact with someone once I got out, but I . . . Oh, I'm so sorry if I was rude earlier."

"Not at all, Max." The corner of her mouth twitched upward as she tried not to betray herself. "Let's move this conversation to a booth, shall we? You may consider yourself officially handled."

Chapter 32
. . . Stays in Oak Haven

Nestled in an overstuffed velvet booth with two beautiful women he understood to be his superiors, Max was happy to be forthcoming about his adventures. Or what he could piece together anyway. Quentin sat on the table, chewing away on his fourth carrot of the evening.

"Clearly, you ladies already know all about my assignment, so I can skip that—"

"Well . . . *of course* we do know it all," Delilah offered. "But you should begin at the beginning anyway."

Scarlett nodded, and with her eyes, she tried to tell her sister that *yes, that's the idea.* "Part of our report will include an assessment of your ability to understand the broader context. So. Have at it."

"Yes, Max. Contextualize it for us."

Max glanced from one woman to the other, his expression baffled but game. "Uh, sure. Whatever you say. So, the broader context is, of course, the situation in Jacksonville. The city is completely denuded of magic—dried up completely. The local magicians are all desperate to relocate. But it's tough because so many magical sites have already been claimed. However, there is this little New England oasis called Oak Haven, which sits on a veritable oil well of pure magical power that nobody is using. And—"

"Well," Scarlett interrupted, "not *nobody*, right?"

"Sure, but not anybody who's a somebody, if you catch my drift. The town's run by this posse of postmenopausal *witches.*"

Both Scarlett and Delilah couldn't help noticing that when Max said *witches*, he seemed to intend a different word entirely. They very much did not care for it.

"This place could be an absolute gold mine," he continued. "Have you seen what's been done with Salem, Massachusetts? Witch museums, witch walking tours, witch-themed restaurants and hotels, witch-themed T-shirt shops . . . If exploited correctly, Oak Haven could be all that and more. *Someone* stands to make a fortune—why not us? But there's one problem, which is this vexing amnesia-like spell protecting Oak Haven. Makes for a terrible marketing campaign: *Come Visit Oak Haven—Make No Memories Whatsoever!*"

"And yet you seem to remember it." Delilah was sounding more confident by the moment. "How is that possible?"

"Well, everything I've told you so far—all that *context*, as you put it—I already knew before I left. Alas, I recall very little of what happened once I arrived. *But!* We were working on this problem, you see. Because it turns out—and this really is clever, I do give those old witches credit—the amnesia is caused by these constant psychic blasts of meaningless information. The enchantment prevents memories from forming. But we have found a weakness: you can steel yourself against the onslaught by training your brain to file away these factoids before they can harm you. It takes a great deal of practice—it's not easy, don't misunderstand! But if you study hard, it can be done."

Scarlett's own memory suddenly flashed to Hexpresso Yourself—that conjuration of magicians inside, and the jaunty chalkboard sign outside—QUIZ NIGHT, it had said, SHOW OFF YOUR MAD TRIVIA SKILLZ. She remembered all those reference books they'd found in Max's room, and the time she'd found him studying World War II facts in the dining room.

"Trivia nights," she said suddenly. "You trained your minds to fight the spell by means of regular trivia nights."

"Exactly!" Max said enthusiastically. "We, um . . . Well. Actually, I'm a bit fuzzy on how we went about it. But I do recall finding myself in some sort of public venue . . . a bar, perhaps? Maybe? Or . . . was it a Starbucks?"

"Don't *even joke*!" Scarlett exclaimed. "Oak Haven does not have and will never have a fucking Starbucks."

"It'll have three by the time we're done with it!" Max swiveled his head from Scarlett to Delilah and back, seeking affirmation. But their unsmiling faces gave him pause. "Erm . . . are you *sure* you're my handlers?"

Delilah knitted her fingers together, making a little church with her hands. "Let me make sure I understand. You discovered that the more skilled a brain becomes at filing away irrelevant tidbits, the less power the spell has over that person."

"Exactly! So . . . I think . . . what I did . . . I'm not sure about this part. But I *think* I used to sit for hours, training myself. Just learning facts. You know, like, the Beatles' first gig was at the Marquee Club in 1961."

"So much for your training." Scarlett frowned. "The Beatles' first gig was at the Cavern Club. You're thinking of the Stones."

"Oh. Ah. Amnesia spell strikes again, I suppose." Max blushed uncomfortably. "Still, you're all ready for a visit, sounds like! Say, shall we order another round of drinks?"

"I don't think so, Maxie Boy," Delilah said, suddenly dropping into Bad Cop mode. "I have more questions. Tell us about the dragonflies."

"Well, it, uh . . . sounds like you already know about the dragonflies."

"Yeah," she replied, her anger rising. "*But what do* you *know, pal?!*"

Scarlett subtly lifted her hand, as if to say, *Okay, Del, cool it.*

"Well, the plan going in—and, remember, I cannot testify to what actually occurred once I got there—but the plan was to infect their oak grove with these ancient magical flies that render their magic source unstable. That would cause chaos in the town, set witches against one another, presumably? While the women were distracted, we could focus on our trivia training and destroy the amnesia spell."

"But this doesn't make sense," Scarlett mused. "The infestation makes the magic unusable. If you spoil the magic source, then what's the point?"

"Exactly!" Delilah pounded the table repeatedly. "What do you gain, Max? *What do you gain?*"

Jesus, Scarlett thought, *I've created an improv monster . . .*

Max stared at the women, mystified. "We have a plan to fix it, *obviously*. From the beginning, the plan was that we'd be the heroes who came up with the cure. Those old biddies would be so happy to have their magic working, they probably wouldn't even fight us on the Starbucks thing. We magicians could just take over. And then . . . wait . . . hang on! I just realized something . . .

I'm sitting here. I left Oak Haven. So . . . maybe it's done? Maybe it worked! Did it work?"

"It absolutely did not work," Delilah said darkly.

"Yeah . . . yeah, I'm afraid you failed big time, buddy." Scarlett gave her sister a subtle nod. Best to let Max assume the big plan had gone wrong. "The witches figured out the cure on their own."

"Ohhh calamity," Max said sadly. "Yes, that was always the potential weak point in our plan. That they'd suss it out before we were ready. Ah, well. So tell me, what did the cure turn out to be? The bosses wouldn't say—I suppose they were afraid I would drop hints unintentionally. By any chance, was it blackbirds? Please tell me it was blackbirds."

"Blackbirds?" Scarlett asked. "I don't understand."

"The oak grove is an ecosystem, no? Which means it's all a big food web. Why do flies exist, really, except to become dinner for something bigger? We had a betting pool in the office, actually—we all wagered on which animal would be used to clear out the flies. I put all my money on blackbirds. A friend of mine bet on chuckwallas, which are some sort of desert lizard? I said to him, 'Brian! Oak Haven is in New England. Why would it be desert lizards?' But I don't know . . . Brian just likes chuckwallas, I suppose. Now, Cindy the intern, *she* bet on bats—I thought that was clever. Witches, bats . . . would make sense . . ."

As Maximillian babbled on about his precious wager, Scarlett touched her sister's hand. "We should get home right away, start conjuring predators," she said quietly.

Delilah nodded. "Sounds like a good Luna job to me. Let's get back." She slid out of her side of the booth.

"Wait, where are you going?" asked Max.

"We're busy." Delilah shrugged. "And you bungled it. You failed. And those *bosses* you mentioned? Do they strike you as forgiving types? I suspect not so much."

"Leave the bill," Scarlett told her sister. "Take the rabbit."

Delilah picked up Quentin's cage and tucked it under her arm.

"Not Quentin, no," begged Max. "Please . . . please don't take my Quentin."

"You keep him locked in a tiny cage all day. And then you took him to *a bar*. In Vegas, of all places. I think Quentin deserves better care than that, wouldn't you agree? There's more to a bunny's life than being shoved into hats and pulled out of them again."

"But I don't understand . . ." Maximillian the Magnificent gazed around, suddenly as denuded of magic as a Jacksonville oak tree. "I mean . . . if the plan failed . . . and you're leaving . . . what do I do now?"

Scarlett left the booth to stand beside her sister. "You fought witches, and the witches won. And in a situation like that, there's really only one thing you can do." She leaned over the table, and she stared into Max's soul with witchy eyes full of fire. "*Hide*."

Chapter 33
Cane Toads

Scarlett and Delilah let themselves into the shuttered Spice Girls Experience theater, traveled back through the portal, and found themselves returned safely to Max's room. Delilah gently placed Quentin's cage on the queen-sized bed and let him out. "I'm going to find you a much better living situation. No more of those ridiculous performances." She gave him a good scratch behind his ears. "Don't you worry, Q."

They went downstairs to find the lobby dark and quiet—the actors must have knocked off for the evening, and many of the witches had gone home. Eventually the sisters found Mama, Luna, Aphra, and Priti, still huddled around a cast-iron table in the back garden, still trying to work out a solution to the town's problems. Their worried faces were accentuated by the candlelight, but a happy cry went up when they saw Scarlett and Delilah returned.

Luna leapt up to hug them. "I was so worried! Mama said not to, but I couldn't help it."

"Aw, that's sweet." Scarlett had to smile. "Mama was confident we could handle ourselves."

264

"Not especially," their mother corrected. "But if you failed, we're probably doomed, so what's the point of worrying?"

"Right. Great."

Aphra beckoned the sisters to come join their circle. "We've been sitting out here trying to brainstorm more oak-rescue ideas."

"Not getting very far," Priti said. An open bottle of white wine was on the table, and Priti offered them both a glass. "Please, improve our evening and tell us you found something."

Scarlett and Delilah glanced at one another. "We did . . ." Delilah said hesitantly.

"Yeah." Scarlett nodded. "Whether it improves your evening or not remains to be seen."

They explained the surprisingly stable portal Max had created and how he'd been moving magicians in and out for some time. They talked about the Vanishing Point and their discussion with Max—about his Secret Agent Man identity and quiz nights at the coffee shop. About the magicians' plans to turn Oak Haven into Salem. About the creation and intended destruction of the flies.

"Okay, awesome," said Priti. "So we need to figure out the right predator to clean out the flies and Bob's your uncle." She tilted her head. "What a dumb expression, *Bob's your uncle*. Why do people say that, anyhow?"

"Bob ain't *my* uncle." Scarlett chuckled.

"Nor mine," Priti agreed. "Who around here has an Uncle Bob?"

But Aphra wasn't in a joking mood. "I don't like this one bit."

"Aw, c'mon," said Priti. "How about you lighten up and take yes for an answer." She abruptly turned back toward Scarlett. "Now, that's an idiom I can get behind. Take yes for an answer."

"*Priti*," Aphra said warningly. "Think this through. The magicians are our enemies, apparently. Frankly, I don't care for the idea that *anyone* in Oak Haven has an enemy, and yet it seems we have a whole pack of them. The predator solution came to us from our enemies. Why would we use their method? Why would we want to act like them in any way?"

Scarlett frowned. "But . . . it's a good idea. Why not seize a good idea, regardless of the source?"

"*Is* it a good idea, though?" asked Luna hesitantly.

"Exactly," Aphra agreed. "There's a long history of people trying to solve one pest problem by bringing in a worse pest."

Luna nodded. "Cane toads. I saw them all over Australia when I was there. Cane toads were imported to *only* kill the beetles that were harming Australian sugar cane crops. Instead, cane toads kill everything in their path."

"Look, I hear what you're saying," Scarlett said. "But until we have our own genius solution—which you all just admitted to me we absolutely do not—I say we at least consider Max's."

Delilah reached for more wine. "Remember this, too: magic will return to normal once the dragonflies are cleared out. Then, if we need to remove cane toads, bats, or whatever it might be, we'll have our powers available to do it."

"A lot of assumptions there, Del," said Aphra. "Like, that magic definitely will come back—we hope it will, but we've never dealt with this before. Also, you're assuming the cane toads won't make things even worse in ways we can't think of right now."

Priti held out her glass for more wine. "I think we all agree, cane toads are out."

Scarlett nudged Delilah. "I wonder which intern took cane toads in the office betting pool?"

266

Delilah shook her head. "Don't start."

But it was too late. Mama leaned forward, sensing trouble. "What's this about an office pool?"

Scarlett explained about Max gambling on sparrows, dummy Brian with his lizards, and clever Cindy, the intern. "That aspect does bother me," she admitted. "What *office?!* Magicians have an office?"

Delilah nodded. "Also, Max talked about his *bosses*—what they would tell him, what they wouldn't. So . . . somewhere there's a group of hierarchical magicians with an office and an internship program?"

"It's like no matter what we do," Priti joked, "we can't get rid of Ricky Gervais."

Scarlett laughed. "They keep their *wands* in jelly instead of staplers."

Mama rapped on the table, her longtime signal for *cut the shit*. "If you girls had questions about the bosses, why didn't you ask Max?"

"Well," Scarlett said defensively, "we were pretending to be his handlers. So there was a limit to how much ignorance we could show."

"You don't know what it was like, Mama," Delilah said.

"He was already deeply suspicious of us," continued Scarlett. "We got him talking with this whole 'handlers' ruse but he started doubting us pretty quickly."

"Why?" Mama demanded. "If you'd put a solid hypnotic spell on him, he wouldn't have *doubted you* if you'd pushed him into traffic."

"We did the best we could, Mama!"

"Oh, well, thank you so much, Scarlett. I'll be sure to let the people of Oak Haven know—when our unpredictable magic has caused all their houses to explode and the magicians have returned to put a McDonald's in the middle of the town green? I'll be sure to let them all know that *Scarlett Melrose did her best*."

"Oh my God, Mama," Scarlett groaned. "If you're such an expert, why don't you go fucking ask him yourself!"

"Hey," Luna said gently. "Let's not—"

"No," Scarlett said fiercely. "I mean it. Go ahead, Mama. The portal is right upstairs. I'm sure a witch of your caliber will have no trouble locating one sad-sack magician in a town of, what, less than a million people."

Mama's expression went stone cold. "You left him out there?"

"What the hell did you think we were gonna do, arrest him?"

"*Why the hell not?*" Mama shot back. "He could have given us names, locations, all sorts of useful details."

"We wanted to get home and tell you all about—"

"You were reckless, Scarlett. Reckless and thoughtless, as ever." She stood up, signaling the conversation was over. "Luna, I want you to figure out which predator we need—perhaps the *Myrmex Arcana* contains a clue. Aphra, you work on new enchanted cages where we might keep these predators in check for as long as possible. And girls, I want both of you to know that I do recognize the wisdom of your words. You are smart to be cautious. But as *Scarlett* has so kindly pointed out, we are dangerously low on options at the moment. Priti, I'm sorry but I'm afraid we must depend on you and your EMS service to continue to respond to incidents wherever necessary. Delilah, you see to the guests—even in times of trouble, we are still an inn, and we still owe our customers good service. I will be upstairs in meditation." She turned and stalked back toward the dining room.

"And what about me, *Mama*?" demanded Scarlett. "*Whatever shall I do*?"

"How about you stay out of everyone's way and not continuously make the situation worse. Can you handle that?"

Scarlett flinched as though she'd been slapped. She stood, fighting back the tears that threatened to spill from her eyes. Without another word, she turned and stormed back inside.

She paced the lobby like a miserable tiger in a roadside zoo. *Reckless, thoughtless . . .* the same goddamn criticisms her mother had been leveling at Scarlett since childhood. *Kelly Melrose needs some fresh material.*

After all, if it weren't for me, we never would have found Max in the first place. Delilah was just standing there in front of the portal, staring into the blankness—like some highwire performer without the guts to go over the edge. I'm the reason we have all this information. I'm the reason we have some idea how to fix it.

Scarlett saw herself reflected in the lobby's dark windows. *You're also a major reason the town is in this mess in the first place,* her reflection seemed to say. *So yeah, maybe you sorted out how to fix it. What do you want, a medal?*

She was still standing there when Aphra entered, her coat over her arm. "You all right?"

"Fantastic," Scarlett said bitterly.

Aphra wrapped her arm around Scarlett's elbow. "Well I'm off—I'm headed home, Dayo's waiting up for me. You want to come along, just for the walk? A little fresh air might do you good."

"Yeah . . . I need to visit Nate, anyhow."

"Ah." Aphra smiled. "There we go. Nate will cheer you right up."

But Scarlett shook her head sadly. "No, not this time."

***

Scarlett and Aphra ambled down Main Street side by side. Despite the current chaos, the people of Oak Haven were embracing the coming of Halloween with a theatrical fervor. Porches were strung with strings of lights shaped like jack-o-lanterns. Cardboard cut-outs of dancing skeletons hung on doors, and everywhere were handmade scarecrows in a variety of spooky get-ups—mummies, Draculas, Frankensteins. Meanwhile leaves crunched underfoot, and bare branches, like skeletal fingers, clawed at the night sky. Overhead, a gibbous moon peeked through the swirling clouds, casting an ethereal glow.

"It's so beautiful," Aphra sighed. "I love how everyone gets excited about Halloween. You'd never know there's so much trouble brewing in the grove."

"It's Disneyland on the surface and *Buffy the Vampire Slayer* underneath," Scarlett murmured.

"Listen . . . about your mother . . ." Aphra's voice was hesitant. "She can be a bit . . . tough on you, can't she?"

Scarlett shrugged. "Tough? That's putting it mildly. She's like Smaug atop his treasure hoard, except the treasure is criticism and every once in a while she chucks a fistful at my head."

"I think she's just worried about the town. There's a lot of responsibility on her shoulders as a Melrose. The rest of us don't have statues of our families in the center of town."

"Don't I know it," Scarlett grumbled.

"She loves you, you know."

"Doesn't always feel like it."

Aphra reached out and squeezed Scarlett's hand. "You're perfect just the way you are," she said, her voice filled with warmth and sincerity. "You and Delilah did a great job in Las Vegas—not one of us could have done better, Kelly Melrose included."

They continued on their way, their footsteps echoing on the lonely cobblestone street. The closer they got to Williams Hardware, the more Scarlett's heart lifted at the thought of seeing Nate, even if it was for a terrible reason. *Delilah's right,* Scarlett thought. *I have to let him go. But at least I can do one thing right today—I can do right by my best friend. I can feel good about that, if nothing else.*

But something wasn't right. The usually welcoming porch lights of Williams Hardware were dark. The windows were black and empty.

"That's strange," Aphra murmured. "Nate always leaves a light on. Even when he's closed, you never know when the Earls will be out here playing chess or some such."

Scarlett nodded, a knot forming in her stomach. "Something happened."

Exchanging a worried glance, they pushed open the door, the rusty hinges creaking in protest. The darkness within was absolute, the air heavy with a strange, metallic scent.

"Nate, it's me," Scarlett called out, her voice echoing strangely in the oppressive silence. "Nate, are you here?"

A faint moan, followed by a muffled *goddammit*, came from the back of the store. Scarlett, heart hammering, raced toward the sound, with Aphra close behind. She nearly tripped over a rack of rakes, their metal tines glinting faintly in the sliver of moonlight filtering through a window.

There, lying in a heap near the storeroom door, was Nate. He was clutching his head, and covered head-to-toe in black soot.

"Oh no!" Scarlett knelt beside him. "Nate! Nate, are you all right?"

He blinked slowly, his eyes struggling to focus in the darkness. "Scarlett?" His voice was raspy, as if he'd inhaled a mouthful of smoke. "I . . . I saw a light. Under the storeroom door. It got brighter and brighter. Blinding. And it kept spreading, farther and farther past the door. It moved across me, across the store . . . even outside, I guess? And then there was this whoosh sound and . . . this eye-gouging flash of light and then it all went black."

Aphra had found a camping lantern and turned it on; the sudden bloom of light revealed the extent of the devastation. The storeroom door hung open, its frame charred and blackened. Inside, every trace of magic—the herbs, the crystals, the enchanted tools—had been reduced to ash.

"I'd been picturing your storeroom as being akin to uranium," Scarlett said, her voice shaking. "I guess that was more accurate than I thought."

Nate, still dazed, pulled himself to his feet. He poked at the ashen remains. "Is it over?"

Aphra made her way to the center of the bombed-out storeroom, and tears welled in her eyes. "There's nothing left. Oh, Scarlett, how will everyone protect themselves? There's nothing left at all. Priti and the EMS will be helpless."

"It's going to be okay, Aphra . . ." Nate went to her, wrapping her in a friendly hug. "I can restock," he said encouragingly. "I'll call my contacts in Boston tomorrow—they've got everything."

"It could be too late."

He shook his head, uncomprehending. "Too late for what?"

Aphra sighed and hugged Nate again. "Scarlett can explain everything. Me, I'm going home. I miss my Dayo. I want to make out with my wife and run a hot bath, not necessarily in that order. Scarlett, I'll stop by the inn tomorrow so we can keep talking."

When she'd left, Nate turned to Scarlett. "Look at us. You and me, alone in the wreckage. Yet again."

"Seems like it. You're right, though, you can restock."

"Should I though? I mean, I know—I just told Aphra I would but . . . maybe bringing in fresh supplies to this situation is a bad idea." Nate idly nudged a charred herb barrel with his boot. "The grove is getting worse, isn't it?"

Scarlett chuckled bitterly. "Yup, the grove is getting worse."

Their eyes met, and Scarlett felt a rush of emotions—pangs of regret and guilt, but also something deeper, something she wasn't quite ready to name.

Nate, his face covered in soot but his eyes filled with affection, reached for Scarlett's hand. His touch sent a jolt through her. "What brings you back to my now even-more-humble-than-usual abode?"

"Yeah. Um. Well. Nate, the truth is . . ." She paused, hoping he couldn't hear the tremor in her voice. "The truth is . . . I came here to say something to you. Can we sit and talk somewhere?"

Nate studied her carefully. "I'm not sure I want to have whatever conversation this is."

"I know," she sighed. "Me neither. But we have to."

Chapter 34
The Room

Moments later, Scarlett found herself trailing behind Nate as he led her up a narrow staircase at the back of the store. She'd never visited this part of the store before—when they were kids and Earl Twelve ran Williams Hardware, the upper floors were for storage only, and children were strictly forbidden. Her curiosity battled her exhaustion as they reached the landing. Nate pushed open an unremarkable door, revealing an unremarkable bachelor pad.

He left her alone momentarily to change his soot-covered clothes and wash his face. Looking around, Scarlett was surprised to find his living space was almost monastic; it was quite a surprising contrast to the hoarder aesthetic downstairs in the store. Sparse furniture—a worn sofa, an overstuffed easy chair, a simple table, and a neatly made bed—accentuated the feeling of openness. His rough-and-ready bookshelves, assembled from boards and bricks, were stuffed with paperbacks by Ray Bradbury and Octavia Butler. There was a stark efficiency here, a sense of someone more focused on function than frills.

Although it shamed her to do it, Scarlett's gaze instinctively scanned the space in search of any feminine presence. A stray lipstick, a hairbrush, lacy knickers?

There was nothing to see.

It's none of my damned business anyway, she reminded herself sternly. *Remember: you're going, he's staying. That's all there is to it.*

Still, something by the window did catch her eye. On a small table crowded with crafting supplies—the only part of the room that looked actively used—sat a nearly finished model of a balsa-wood ship trapped within a glass bottle. Scarlett approached, a smile spreading across her face as she realized what it was: a pirate ship with the Jolly Roger flying proudly. Earl Twelve was still inside Nate somewhere, hiding out.

"Yeah, I'm building a ship model." Nate's voice broke softly into the quiet room. "And yeah, it's a pirate ship, and no, I don't care to analyze what that might indicate."

Scarlett spun around, her face a picture of mock innocence. "I certainly wasn't going to say anything."

Nate lifted an eyebrow. "Uh-huh. Anyway, you wanted to talk." He plunked down in a well-loved armchair and gestured at the couch, inviting her to sit. "What's up? What was Aphra all upset about?"

Scarlett offered the highlights of her adventure in Las Vegas, focusing on the successful aspects of her and Delilah's interrogation of Max—the magicians' plot, their trivia games, and the mystery predator that might save the grove. She left out the many inadequacies and mistakes detailed by her mother.

But her judicious self-editing didn't matter because Nate understood everything, as he somehow always did. "So you let Max go free, then . . . ?"

"Yep."

He laughed. "Ooh boy, I bet Kelly's pissed."

"You said a mouthful there, mister."

Nate brushed the matter away with a casual wave of his hand. "She'll get over it. So. Predators, huh? Okay. What do we do next?"

Scarlett lifted an eyebrow. "We? What do we do?"

"Yeah, we, of course." He shrugged. "You think I'm going to leave you in the lurch now? After all this? I'm Team Scarlett, remember? Hell, I was Team Scarlett a couple of days ago when everything seemed like it was your fault. Now that you're about to play hero, you think I won't be along for the ride?"

Ah, Scarlett thought. *Shit.*

Breaking things off had seemed like an easy decision while sitting at a buffet in Las Vegas. Breaking things off had seemed perfectly logical on the walk over here. But now, up in Nate's apartment, with those black pirate eyes taking her in . . . things didn't seem so obvious. Not when she was sitting about ten feet from Nate's bed.

"You know . . ." she said, stalling. "Maybe this isn't the right moment. It's late, we're exhausted . . . you just survived an Oppenheimer at White Sands sort of situation. We can postpone. I should probably get back to the inn, anyway."

Nate sat forward in his chair. "Can I tell you what I think?"

Scarlett nodded because she was suddenly unsure she could speak. All she could think was: *One slight move, and I could be in his arms.*

"I think . . . that if you go back to the inn right now, you'll find your mother and sisters waiting up for you. And I think they will hand you yet another urgent assignment. Which I think you'll accept, even though you're exhausted. And after you've finished, one of them will find you *another* urgent job. Which you'll also do because you haven't been home in ten years, and you can't say no because you feel too guilty over a hundred different things . . ."

Scarlett winced. He wasn't guessing. He knew her too well. "It's mainly the one giant thing, but yeah."

"And once you've completed that job? Hey, what do you know? Something else will come up that you have to deal with immediately. And your guilt will drive you on and on until nothing is left of you but a little green globule like a drummer in Spinal Tap. How am I doing?"

"Disturbingly accurate," Scarlett admitted.

"Right, so here's my idea," Nate continued. "Stay here. Sleep. I'm not suggesting anything beyond that. Sleep, for as long as you need."

"But—"

"When your mother inevitably calls to ask me where you are, I will say you got called away on urgent witch business and can't be contacted."

"She won't believe you."

"I don't care. Unlike most of this town, I'm not afraid of Kelly Melrose."

Scarlett's breath immediately left her body. "That is the greatest goddamn sentence I have ever heard in my life."

Nate's cheeks flushed, but he held her gaze. "Go rest. I'll take the couch." He stood and reached out to pull her to her feet. "Feel free to borrow a T-shirt if you want—clean ones are in the bottom left drawer."

She smiled. *I will absolutely be doing that,* Scarlett thought, warmth spreading through her. "Nate . . ." There was something she needed to say, but she wasn't sure how to find the words. "Sorry I'm so . . . complicated."

He laughed and pulled her into his arms. "I don't mind complicated." They gazed at one another for a long moment. Scarlett wanted so badly to kiss him but felt so strongly that it was wrong. So she just stood there, letting him hold her, trying not to move, breathe, or do anything that might cause the moment to end.

Finally, he smiled and brushed a strand of hair from her face. "C'mon, you should get some rest."

"Why don't you come lie down with me? Just to sleep?"

Nate winked. "You think we can be trusted to manage that?" But then his face turned serious. "I'm kidding. Of course. Whatever you need."

Scarlett quickly changed into one of his T-shirts; the soft cotton enveloped her like an embrace. She curled up on the cozy old wooden-frame bed. Nate settled in behind her, his arm around her waist. Their bodies fit together like a puzzle that had been missing a piece for a long time.

Just before she drifted off, Scarlett threaded her fingers through his. Holding on so tightly, a deep sense of comfort washed over her. The scent of Nate's skin and the sound of his breathing lulled her into a deep sleep. For the first time in years, her mind was not filled with anxious thoughts or regrets about the past. She was simply at peace.

Sometime later, Scarlett awoke to find herself still wrapped in Nate's arms. She glanced at the clock on the nightstand. They had slept for hours, and the morning light was creeping through the windows.

Nate stirred. He sleepily nuzzled the back of Scarlett's neck.

"Hey, you," he murmured.

Scarlett rolled over to face him. The look in his eyes made her heart skip a beat. She reached up and stroked his cheek.

"Hey, you," she said softly.

They gazed at each other for a moment, a thousand unspoken words passing between them.

"I should probably go," she told him.

"You should definitely go."

Scarlett leaned in closer, their faces nearly touching. "Everybody is going to be wondering where I am."

"They are," he whispered. "There is a great and terrible crisis, and you must go forth and save the day."

"That I must. Right away." She kissed him. "Just five more minutes maybe . . ."

Downstairs in the store, the phone rang.

"Ignore it." Nate took hold of her face and kissed her deeply, searchingly.

Scarlett returned the kiss, one hand in his hair while the other moved across his chest. She felt his strength and willed it to soak into her.

Downstairs in the store, the phone continued to ring.

Nate's hands slid down to her hips, pulling her tighter against him.

"You know it's my goddamn mother," she whispered.

"Let her wait."

She smiled, feeling happier than she had in a long time. For a moment, she allowed herself to forget about the grove, Louise Demain's words and even Papa—about all the challenges that lay ahead and all the mistakes that lay behind. "I wish we could stay like this forever," she murmured.

Nate kissed her again, more urgently this time. She could feel his desire growing, and her own need responded in kind. It felt like something she'd been searching for her whole life.

His hands slid down her back, his touch electric even through the fabric of the T-shirt. Her pulse quickened, a delicious heat spreading through her. Her hands slid down his chest, feeling the hard lines of muscle beneath his shirt.

Years of wanting came crashing over them. Meeting his eyes, she said, "Nate, nothing has felt this right in . . . maybe ever."

"Then let's make it count," he murmured, his voice rough with emotion.

The world narrowed. It was just the two of them, the feel of his hands on her skin, the heat radiating from their bodies. He trailed kisses down her neck, his touch feather-light yet electrifying. Scarlett moaned softly, her body arching instinctively toward his. Once their clothes were nothing but a tangle on the floor, Nate traced the outline of her nakedness with deft hands. Her collarbone, her shoulders, the curve of her hip. He gently eased her legs apart, breathing her in.

"Scarlett," he whispered, his voice like velvet over her bare skin, "you're so beautiful." Nate's touch, a slow exploration, sent shivers dancing across her skin like fireflies.

She breathlessly whispered, "You too, Nate."

But as close as he was, she suddenly felt he was much too far away. She needed him—needed him on her, in her, caressing every part of his body with every part of hers. She reached down to pull him up to her, the outline of his face stark and perfect. His lips found hers again, a hungry meeting with no more hesitation, only the fierce joy of a long-awaited homecoming. Scarlett's fingers threaded urgently through his hair as they lost themselves in the rhythm only their bodies could understand. Each kiss was a promise finally kept. The weight of him felt like a declaration, unspoken yet understood.

A choked gasp escaped her. Heat bloomed, spreading to encompass her entire being. She felt raw, exposed, yet utterly safe in his arms.

Time seemed to warp and bend, the only constant being the frantic rhythm of their hearts and the deepening sighs that escaped them both.

The room itself seemed to shimmer. Then, with a shuddering breath, Nate was inside her.

"Scarlett . . ." he rasped.

There were no more words, just a tangled mess of emotions—joy, relief, yearning, a fierce need to possess everything he was and could be. In that moment, she knew, with a bone-deep certainty, that this was what home felt like.

He cupped her face, his thumb tracing a path down her cheek. "Scarlett, all this time, I . . ." He trailed off, searching for the words.

"Don't say it," she whispered. "Show me."

He didn't need to be told twice. Time lost all meaning as they surrendered. Nate's name escaped her lips in a strangled moan, a mixture of pleasure with the vulnerability of finally letting go. And then, with a final, shuddering breath, they reached a peak that left them clinging to each other, hearts pounding in unison.

As the world slowly came back into focus, the only sound was their ragged breaths echoing in the stillness of the room.

***

Nate dozed off, and Scarlett tried to follow. But her mind was plagued with thoughts of the outside world. She'd close her eyes and see Louise Demain. Or a monstrous raven trying to peck out her eyes. Or red dragonflies darting around a dying oak tree.

Shit.

She got up and aimlessly paced around Nate's bare apartment, unsure what to do with herself. She knew she ought to return to the inn, but she also desperately did not want to face all that yet. Plus, sneaking out on Nate after what just happened didn't feel especially sportsmanlike.

She stared at Nate's bookshelves and pulled out a Philip K. Dick anthology. Unable to muster enough focus enough to even decide on a story to read, she sighed and put it back.

Scarlett plunked down at Nate's craft table to study his ship-in-a-bottle project. The pirate ship made her think about Nate's ancestor: the Great Sea Wolf, Earl of Anglia, the Terror of Tortuga. If the legends about him were even partially true, he'd committed an entire galleon's worth of sins—he had far more blood on his hands than Scarlett. And Oak Haven had accepted him anyway. If he'd been forgiven, perhaps she could be as well?

But, of course, all that spilled blood belonged to outsiders. He'd never killed a Melrose.

"Uh-oh."

Startled, Scarlett turned to see Nate staring at her. He'd pulled his jeans back on, fortunately. *If he'd been standing there naked,* Scarlett thought, *my brain would have melted and dribbled out my ears.* "What do you mean, uh-oh?"

"You have that trademark melancholy look of yours. You do realize that *that*—" he flicked his head in the direction of his mussed sheets "—is supposed to make you happy, right? Not melancholy."

"I am happy," she said, unconvincingly. "I just . . . Well, the truth is . . . I came here to break off whatever this thing is between us."

"I knew that. I'm a grown man—I can recognize an *I'm dumping you* look when I see one."

"You talked me out of it. Or, I guess, kissed me out of it."

He shrugged sexily. "What can I say? Should I put some coffee on?"

A tempting offer . . . but no. "I should get back. I've got a whole Walk of Shame to do. Best get it over with." As she gathered her clothes and dressed, she felt so confused and conflicted that it made her nauseous. The memory of last night lingered, yet the light of day brought all her doubts raging back.

Nate watched her silently. His expression was unreadable, but she could feel his gaze following her around the apartment.

"I'm sorry," she said softly, pulling on her shoes. "This wasn't fair to you. I shouldn't have let things go so far."

"I wouldn't change a thing." His dark eyes were serious but soft. "I meant what I said. You're everything I've ever wanted, Scarlett. I'm not giving up that easily."

Her heart constricted. She wanted to believe him, wanted to throw caution to the wind and trust that this could work. But a person doesn't repeat the same phrase over and over for ten years and just stop believing it. She repeated the phrase again now. "You can't leave, and I can't stay. That's it."

Nate crossed the room and knelt beside her. He gently tucked a lock of hair behind her ear. "But you're wrong, Scar. You can stay if you want. We'll figure this out together." He tipped her chin, forcing her to look at him.

"I wish it were that simple," she said, blinking back tears. "But there's so much you don't understand."

"Then help me understand. Because I'm not giving up this time. It was dumb for you to leave in the first place. It was dumb for me to let you. It was dumb to just let things stay that way for so long. And yeah, I can be kinda dumb sometimes, but ten years of dumb is more than enough, even for me."

Scarlett paused, emotions swirling. She wanted to cling to him, to believe they could build something together. But the memory of Papa's death loomed, clinging to her like she'd walked through a cobweb that she'd never shake off.

She wiped her eyes, kissed Nate on the cheek, and said, "I have to go."

Chapter 35
Toad Suck

The inn was a buzzing hive of activity. The Gilbert and Sullivan crowd bustled around the lobby, putting the final touches on costumes and props in preparation for this evening's performance of *Pirates of Penzance*. Feathered hats were adjusted, plastic swords were brandished, and vocal warm-ups echoed through the halls.

Meanwhile, Aphra, Dayo, and Priti gathered over coffee in the dining room. They were brainstorming what to do now that there were no supplies left in the hardware store—yet another challenge for the pile. Scarlett entered and joined them at the large wooden table.

"Well, well, look who finally decided to grace us with her presence." Aphra eyed Scarlett's rumpled outfit. "Wearing the same clothes as yesterday, I see."

Scarlett felt her cheeks flush. "Never mind that. What's the latest on the grove situation?"

Priti sighed heavily. "Not good. The infection is spreading faster than ever. The EMS is out of supplies, so is Aphra's store, and now so is Williams Hardware. If there's some new explosion or fire . . . I don't know what we're going to do. EMS is going door-to-door, seeking donations of whatever people can spare. Herbs, crystals, anything to sort of band-aid this whole situation."

"Do you really think the townsfolk will hand over their supplies?" Dayo asked skeptically.

"Doubtful," Aphra said. "But we have to try something. Unless anyone has a better idea?"

"What about reaching out to that coven in Boston?" Scarlett suggested. "Maybe they could lend some support."

Dayo shook her head. "They're dealing with their own magical crisis at the moment. An infestation of pixies that are turning all the beer in the city into mead."

"Oh, the humanity," Aphra deadpanned.

Just then, Priti's phone buzzed with an alert. She glanced at the screen and grimaced. "I knew I shouldn't have said anything; I jinxed myself. Another fire, other side of town. I better go check it out." She pushed back from the table and hurried out.

Scarlett suddenly felt eyes boring into her. She glanced over to see Louise Demain staring intently from across the room, her unblinking gaze deeply unsettling. Scarlett squirmed uncomfortably, then abruptly stood. "I'm going to go see what Delilah is up to. Be back later."

She found her sister in the lobby, fiddling with an antique clock on the wall. "Hey, I have a thought," Delilah said as Scarlett approached. "Why don't you take Max's dragonflies to Luna? She's gone through one of the portals to try conjuring some potential predators. We realized it would be smarter for her to work somewhere without all the anarchy."

"Which portal?"

"Broom closet, second floor."

"Aha, that'll be Toad Suck, Arkansas." Scarlett vividly remembered every portal that she and Nate had worked on. Even thinking of him made her chest tighten with emotion, but she pushed it down. "All right, I'll go find her."

She headed up to the broom closet and stepped through the portal. Scarlett found herself transported to a wooden treehouse. Crooked beams supported a spacious room, with window-shaped openings overlooking the dappled Arkansas woods. Sunlight poured through the leaves, painting the gnarled floorboards with golden splotches. Scarlett's footsteps crunched on fallen leaves that had blown through the windows.

She descended the ladder and found her sister beneath the sprawling butternut tree. Luna sat cross-legged on a woven rug in vibrant colors. Around her in a wide circle sat a menagerie of surprisingly obedient animals: bright-eyed squirrels, grumpy-looking toads, a green iguana covered in spikes, and a variety of birds. Some looked very much at home in Arkansas—the crow, the sparrow, the chicken—while others—the macaw, the bird of paradise, the quetzal—just looked confused. But regardless, every creature gazed at Luna with a reverence Scarlett found unsettling.

"Luna?" she said hesitantly. "I brought flies?" She held up the metallic cage.

Luna rose, smiling. "Perfect, I've been waiting for this. Let's see if we get any takers."

Scarlett joined her on the blanket, watching in fascination as Luna offered a dragonfly to each animal in turn. The frogs sniffed disdainfully and turned away; the birds pecked warily, then backed off, and the iguana lifted its head briefly before returning to its nap. Hope dwindled with each refusal.

"Umm . . . let's see . . . looks like you haven't done an owl?" Scarlett suggested.

"Ah, great idea!" Luna resumed her conjuring position, sitting cross-legged on the blanket, eyes closed, hands extended, and palms turned up. In a moment, the air in front of her shivered and changed shape as if Luna was channel-surfing reality itself. The shimmering slowly but surely resolved into the form of a white-faced barn owl.

The owl immediately hopped over to the cage. It studied the dragonflies from one angle, then climbed on top of the cage to examine them from another. Suddenly, the barn owl shot straight up into the air, wings flapping furiously. It flew back down, hovered in front of Luna, and shrieked furiously right in her face. And then it flew off, soaring into the woods.

"He's not that into you, I guess," Scarlett mumbled.

"I don't get it." Luna sighed, running a hand through her wild hair. "Maybe we need a more exotic predator. I don't know . . . do pangolins eat flies?" She flopped on her back, staring up at the tree canopy overhead. "It's the uncertainty that's killing me. At least when the trees were poisoned, we knew exactly what to do about it."

"The good ole days . . ." Scarlett said softly. "I wonder whatever happened to old Handsome Bill . . ."

Luna sat up, surprised. "What do you care?"

"I suppose I don't. But he is Violet's dad, after all. You saw how much pain she's in over his absence. And, I mean . . . he's an Oak Haven-er." She paused, considering. "Oak Haven-ite? Haven-ian? Whatever. He's one of us."

Luna shook her head firmly. "I'm sorry, but he stopped being one of us when he attacked the grove."

"Obviously, that was a bad choice . . ."

"Bad choice?! Scarlett, that was a lot more than a bad choice. Actions have consequences, and some actions can't be forgiven."

Scarlett's heart sank. For just a moment there, she'd wondered if she might confess to Luna that it was her mistake that killed Papa. If Luna knew what had really happened that night when Papa died . . . Could Scarlett be forgiven? But clearly the answer was no. She swallowed hard and changed the subject.

"Maybe we should try spiders next? They eat flies, right?"

Luna made a face. "You know how Mama feels about spiders. If I cover the grove in black widows, I'll never hear the end of it."

They brainstormed a few more bird ideas—a red-tailed hawk, a meadowlark, an eastern wood peewee—and Luna easily created them all. But none would have anything to do with the magic-tainted dragonflies. At one point, Luna even conjured up a black bear cub, which promptly tried to use the cage as a soccer ball. Adorable but unhelpful. The sisters slumped in defeat.

"Hey," Scarlett said suddenly. "Did you try a starling? Starlings are major bug-eaters, aren't they?"

Luna looked aghast. "No way, no no no. Starlings are an invasive species. We only have them in the U.S. because a bunch of dum-dums decided to import every bird mentioned in every play by William Shakespeare. They released about a hundred starlings in Central Park, and boom, before you know it, there were millions of them. They take food from other birds, and they evict other birds from their nests . . . just terrible things."

"Dunno, maybe they're just clever survivors," Scarlett said with a shrug. "Maybe that's exactly what we need."

"Clever? I was in South Moravia one time, and I saw a flock

289

of starlings destroy an entire vineyard overnight. Overnight, Scar. No, I don't want to replace one invader with another. Plus, they look weird. What are you, starling—are you black, are you brown, are you purple, green . . . what's even going on?"

Scarlett laughed. "But they're super smart, right? They're the ones who fly in those groupings—what are they called, murmurs or something?"

"Murmurations," Luna corrected. "Giant twisting clouds of starlings. Very creepy."

"Dunno, it seems like telepathy to me. Which is . . . *kinda* like magic? So who knows, maybe they won't be so offended by eating magic dragonflies. C'mon, Lulu, do a starling."

Luna made a face. "*You* do a starling, if you want one so much."

"Well, maybe I will." Scarlett pulled herself up to a kneeling position and closed her eyes. She focused her mind on the complex markings on one of nature's smartest and yet most unwanted birds. She visualized the iridescent sheen of the starling's feathers and the sharpness of its clever eyes. She felt energy flowing through her as she summoned the bird's essence. A faint popping sound made her eyes open.

A starling appeared on the ground in front of her. It stared up at Scarlett curiously, then turned its attention to the enchanted cage. It hopped closer, eyeing the tasty treats within. With a quick flick of its beak, the bird snatched one up and gulped it down. Satisfied, it ate another. And a third.

"Hey!" Scarlett said happily. "Luna, look! We're in business! Now we just need our own little murmuration."

But Luna looked despondent. "We can't do it. The only way to get rid of one pest is to create ten thousand more? No way."

The starling squawked angrily at Luna and fluttered up to perch on Scarlett's shoulder.

"Sorry, birdie," Luna sighed. "I shouldn't judge you for being a starling—it's not your fault."

"How about this," Scarlett offered. "We conjure the starlings, then send them through a portal when the job is done."

"To where, though? To become someone else's problem? That's not right. When you conjure something, you're responsible for it. And look at the mess I've already made right here." She gestured at the adoring crowd of creatures she'd created. "I'm responsible for these goofballs now. A lot of them I can just let loose in the woods, but it's going to take me hours to find a good home for a *quetzal*. No, I'm sorry, Scar—we can't bring a bunch of starlings to Oak Haven without a clear plan to dispose of them."

At the word *dispose*, the starling let out a loud, disapproving squawk. With an affronted flap of its wings, it took off for the dense foliage of the nearby trees, continuing to tweet its complaints as it flew away.

Scarlett gave a little nod. "You just got read to filth by a bird, Lulu."

Her sister sighed. "Occupational hazard."

"Well." Scarlett stood up, brushing bits of grass off her jeans. "I don't know why my solution can't possibly be the right solution—is it just because it came from me, the family embarrassment?"

"Oh, don't take it like that. I just want to solve our current problem without creating a new one."

"But why are starlings any different from these other beasts you've conjured? Oh wait, I know. Because you made them, right? Luna the expert instead of Scarlett the screw-up."

Luna's eyes went wide. "No, of course not! Starlings truly are devastating for ecosystems that can't defend themselves, Scarlett. They tear through foliage, spread diseases like salmonella, drive out other birds . . . Starling droppings are *highly acidic*, Scar, I'm not even kidding. Look, I'm not trying to be difficult, I swear. I just don't want to introduce something that I can't—"

"You know what? Never mind. Fine. Hate starlings if you want. Best of luck with your pangolins. I should get back to the inn." Scarlett scanned the clearing, looking for an exit. "How do I portal back?"

"Wait." Luna stood to face her sister. "Scarlett . . . I promise, I'm not saying no to starlings because they were your idea. I'd have the same concern with any predator that's considered invasive. Before we settle on an animal that could destroy the entire grove, I want to keep looking, make sure we've considered all possible options."

"All possible options . . . except mine."

"But that's not what I—" Luna stopped, chewed her lip for a moment, then started again. "I'm sorry. Please, Scarlett . . . We've been apart so long. I don't want to argue."

Scarlett's expression softened—the sadness in her sister's voice melted her frustration. "Me neither. And I understand, you're just trying to do the right thing."

It struck Scarlett that, given how badly she had messed up with magic, she really had no right to criticize her sister. If Luna wanted to be cautious, she was probably right. "After all, you've been traveling the world practicing magic for ten years, while I've been sitting at a desk and fixing broken URLs on websites." She smiled. "So I *guess* it's *possible* that *maybe* you know a little bit more about it than me."

Luna flung her arms around her sister, squeezing her tight. "We'll figure it out. And who knows, maybe we can find a way that starlings could work. I shouldn't reject your ideas so quickly."

"It's all good. So can you hook me up with a portal home?"

"Ah yes, this is a good one. You run as fast as you can, directly at the trunk of the tree. And just as you're about to crash into it? Portal opens."

Scarlett turned to stare down the stout, gnarled tree trunk. "I'm supposed to run, full speed, directly at this tree."

"Yep. It's a faith-based portal. So, no hesitation. If you hesitate, it won't open."

"What happens then?"

Her sister grinned. "Then I expect you end up with quite a headache. So don't hesitate. You need a running start—go stand about ten feet that way."

Scarlett did as instructed, but somehow the distance made the tree look even more intimidating and ouch-inducing than before. Nevertheless, she knelt like a runner at the starting blocks. "Okay, here I go! One . . . two . . ." She paused. "You know, these portals are pretty great, aren't they? I know we need to fix magic, but it'll be a shame when they're gone."

"You're stalling!" Luna laughed. "But you're right, maybe we should keep a portal or two."

"Definitely. The inn could offer day-trips through a portal, a nice little income stream. Let's see some Marriott or Hilton offer *that*! Of course, there's a downside." She kept riffing, enjoying every moment that she was not running face-first into a butternut tree. "A witch would need to go along on each trip, to keep the guests safe and make sure they get back okay. Can you imagine Del doing that? Trying to play tour guide, with *her* questionable people skills?"

"Yes," Luna said with a knowing smile. "That sounds like a terrible job . . . for *Delilah*."

"Oh, stop it. You know I'm going back to San Francisco the minute this is over."

Luna tapped at an invisible wristwatch. "You're not going anywhere if you keep avoiding this portal, Scar."

Scarlett glared at the tree. *Fuck my life,* she thought. "I hate this."

"Nah, you got this. Faith! Trust! Belief!"

Scarlett squared her shoulders, her resolve warring with her instinctive desire to protect her face. She almost took a step but then stopped. "Are you familiar with the phrase, I'm getting too old for this shit?"

"Just do it," Luna encouraged. "Unstoppable force meets immovable object, let's go!"

Her heart pounding, Scarlett let out a rebel yell and sprinted straight at the immovable tree. As the butternut loomed larger in her vision, she squinted her eyes, bracing for impact.

Chapter 36
Sous Chef

The impact never came. A wave of disorientation washed over Scarlett, and when she opened her eyes, she'd been safely returned to the second-floor broom closet.

She stumbled out, landing in a heap on the worn, wooden floor. She just lay there for a moment, drawing in the familiar scent of lemon oil and old magic. A wave of unexpected contentment washed over her.

As she pushed herself to her feet, a childhood memory flickered in Scarlett's mind, so strong she could almost see it— she and Luna, racing down this very hallway, a whirlwind of laughter and untamed magic. Their father, emerging from his study, scooping a giggling Scarlett into his arms as she nuzzled into him. Back then, the inn had been a place of safety, not a reminder of loss and unwanted obligation. For the first time in a very long time, that feeling was returning.

Bite me, Thomas Wolfe, she thought, *turns out you can go home again.*

The good feelings evaporated as Scarlett looked up to find

Louise Demain standing in the hallway, her spectral eyes staring into Scarlett's soul.

"Oh, for crying out loud," Scarlett muttered. "What do *you* want?"

"I desire naught but the void," Louise's voice echoed. "My presence serves as a mere reminder of the cosmic duties that bind you. A destiny inescapable and unrelenting."

A surge of resentment rose within Scarlett, and she met Louise's gaze with a defiant tilt of her chin. "Listen, lady. I just returned from the delightful town of Toad Suck, Arkansas, where I spent the afternoon trying to help Luna save the stupid grove. She's still out there, conjuring animal after animal, but not one of them has the slightest interest in those flies. Me, I conjured a starling that sucked down those files like a starving aardvark on an ant farm. But Luna's not interested. I tried, and I got shot down. So before you start in on *my* destiny, maybe check your sources, okay?"

She turned and strode away, but Louise's spectral voice drifted effortlessly down the hall. "Your father wishes it."

Scarlett whirled around. "Don't you dare—"

"He told me as much."

"Oh my God. Get lost, you creepy old woman!" She stormed blindly down the hall to the stairs. But as she descended to the lobby, Louise's words stubbornly stuck in her ears.

Your father wishes it.

He told me as much.

Your father wishes it.

He told me as much.

"I don't know how!" she shouted aloud without thinking.

The crowd of actors in the lobby stopped and stared up at the hollering lunatic on the first-floor landing.

Scarlett stared back at them, embarrassed. "I don't know how . . ." She awkwardly turned it into a song. ". . . to looooove him . . ."

"Wrong show!" the major general called up.

"Yeah, you're not even close," agreed the maid. "That's from *Jesus Christ Superstar*."

Scarlett scurried down the stairs, blushing. "Oh well . . . musical theater isn't my genre really." She dove for the swinging doors and the safety of Zahir's kitchen. Scarlett was immediately enveloped by the rich, comforting aromas of fresh herbs and simmering sauces.

Zahir looked up from his stove, a wide grin across his face. "Well, well. Grab an apron, your supreme witchiness. I need some potatoes peeled."

Scarlett rolled her eyes but couldn't suppress a smile as she tied an apron around her waist. At last, here was a job she understood. She picked up a peeler and went to work.

"So-o-o-o," Zahir sang conspiratorially, "from whom are we hiding?"

"Me?! No, I'm not hiding! Why would you say I'm hiding?"

"Because I've met you. When we were growing up, the only times you voluntarily helped in the kitchen were when you were in trouble with your mother."

"Ah." Scarlett had to laugh. "Right. Okay, from whom am I hiding, you ask. Well, let's see. Actors. Time witches. Other witches. My mother. Nate."

"Wow." Zahir nodded. "That's quite a list. Good thing I have a lot of potatoes."

They worked in companionable silence, and yet again, she felt that powerful, seductive feeling of belonging. *Groucho*

Marx always said he'd never join a club that would have him as a member, she thought. That policy had served Scarlett well for ten years . . . but the temptation to rejoin Oak Haven was becoming overwhelming.

After a while, Zahir spoke again. "Uhh hey, just for the record—" His tone had an uncharacteristically defensive edge. "I don't have anything against Spam."

"Oh Z . . ." She paused her peeling to look at him. "Are you still ruminating on that? It was just one bad night."

"Ho ho, says the girl who has spent a decade dwelling on her own *bad night*."

"Wow!" Scarlett's eyes went wide. "Cheap shot!"

He winked. "Cheap, but fair—my specialty. Anyway, I think I get a few weeks to wallow in *my* one bad night, if that's okay with you."

"All I'm saying is, you are the *only* person still thinking about that Spam thing."

"Maybe, maybe not." Zahir shrugged. "I just need to clarify. Some time ago, we did a luau in the dining room? I made Spam musubi, and it *kicked ass*. Oyster sauce, nori, furikake seasoning on the rice? I'm telling you, it rocked. I can make Spam sing if I choose to."

"Z, I don't think anybody thinks you have it in for Spam, okay?"

"It's just . . ." his stirring became more aggressive ". . . if I cook scallops, I want them to taste like scallops. If I cook meatballs, I want meatballs. Sardines should taste like sardines. Et cetera. Oh! That reminds me." He brightened a little. "What did you think of the Scarlett Honorary Sardine Dish? I never got your review."

"Amazing! I used to think I hated sardines, but now I love them. Thank you so much for doing that for me."

"Well, Scar, it is a famous story around here. I had to pay homage. I don't think I've heard of any other witch *ever* taking a risk like that. Turning herself into a bunch of animals, wilding out for a little while and then turning herself back. It was crazy magic, but also beautiful magic and very, very *you*."

Scarlett's peeler clattered to the counter. She felt the entire universe shift, and she thought, *He's right.*

It was crazy. It was beautiful. And it was the answer.

"That's it!" she exclaimed. "That's how I do it."

"You lost me. Do what?"

She turned to stare at him in shock. "We don't need to conjure *actual* starlings. We don't need to invite an invasive species into the grove. Don't you see? I am the starling. *I'm the solution, it's me.*" She dropped her half-peeled potato in the sink and practically leapt at Zahir, throwing her arms around him. "You're a genius!"

She could do it. She could turn herself into a small murmuration of starlings, consume the dragonflies, and then transform back into herself. That way there'd be no invasive species and no risk to the grove's ecosystem. Just Scarlett, wielding her magic in the craziest, most beautiful way possible.

"I gotta go! I have to tell Delilah and Luna!"

Without waiting for a response, she raced out of the kitchen, leaving Zahir alone at the stove with a pile of unpeeled potatoes and a bemused smirk on his face. "You'll never make it as a sous chef," he hollered.

Chapter 37
The Dork Debate

When Scarlett was fourteen, she had secretly applied to and been accepted at a six-week computer-programing summer camp, hosted on the grounds of a *mildly respected* university in Cambridge, Massachusetts. The question of whether or not to permit young Scarlett to leave the witches of Oak Haven to walk among the nerds sparked a family argument that dragged on for five days. The Harvard Dork Debate, as Delilah had named it, was one of those endurance-test rows—a multi-hour verbal slugfest where opposing teams would periodically take breaks and return to their corners to steady themselves. It was like one of those marathon games of Risk, where the incomplete board sits on the dining room table for weeks, and friends stop by to offer strategic advice. Except in this case, the ultimate prize wasn't Kamchatka—it was Scarlett's life.

The Harvard Dork Debate—with Scarlett and Papa in the *Pro-Camp* camp, Mama and Luna in the *Anti-Camp* camp, and Delilah solidly in the *Who Cares About Camp* camp—was unquestionably the most intense conflict the Melrose family had ever experienced . . . until now. From the moment Scarlett brought her starling idea to her mother and the other witches, it was clear that this Murmuration of Scarletts Debate would make the Harvard Dork Debate look like a mild difference of opinion. It would probably make the Battle of Stalingrad look like a mild difference of opinion.

But Scarlett had history on her side: she'd won the Harvard Dork Debate and by God, she'd win this one too.

***

"Absolutely not!" Mama slammed her teacup down so hard, it sloshed Earl Grey onto the tablecloth. The debate had been raging for some time—this was Mama's third cup of tea—but her determination hadn't flagged. "A flock of birds? Have you lost your mind, Scarlett?"

The dining room of the Melrose inn had been transformed into a war room of sorts, with witches crowded around the large oak table. Scarlett stood at the head, her chin lifted defiantly as she faced her mother's fury.

"As I have said *repeatedly*, it will be a telepathic murmuration, not just any old flock. And it's the only way."

"It's sheer lunacy!" Delilah chimed in to agree with Mama. But in her eyes, Scarlett thought she saw a flicker of reluctant admiration.

"Scarlett, this is madness. If even one starling doesn't return, you'll be trapped forever. I won't allow it."

"Luna, tell them." Scarlett appealed to her baby sister for support; Luna had far more street cred concerning magical decisions than she ever would.

Luna leaned forward, her voice calm but urgent. "Mama, believe me, I understand what you're saying. But—"

"But?!" Mama repeated. "Oh good grief, Luna! Don't tell me you support this!"

"—*but* if we don't stop the dragonflies, the grove will be destroyed. Starlings seem like the answer, but wild starlings will most assuredly destroy the grove. Scarlett's plan might be our only hope."

Mama shook her head. "You don't understand. I have an entire presentation on the perils of wild animal transformation—I have slides! Let me show you all the slides."

Scarlett smiled affectionately. Just last night, her mother had been shouting *at* her. Today, she's shouting *about* her. This was better. "I don't need to see the slides, Mama. I inspired the slides, remember? I've lived the slides."

Lounging in her chair, glass of pinot in hand, Belinda Chatterjee waved dismissively. "Oh, let the kid try. What's the worst that could happen?"

"*The worst that could happen?!*" Aphra's voice quivered with emotion. "We could lose Scarlett forever. No, it's much, much too dangerous."

Violet bounced in her seat, eyes wide with excitement. "It's totally metal! Scarlett, you have to do it!"

Jerusha, one of the elderly witches, cleared her throat. "In my day, we respected the dangers of magic. The young always think they're invincible. But transformation spells are not to be taken lightly."

"This is so." Candace nodded sagely. "But with that being said . . . might we consider that perhaps Miss Luna should perform the spell? I believe she is, well . . . how shall I put this . . ."

Scarlett lifted an eyebrow. "Better at witch shit than Scarlett the screw-up?"

"My word!" The old witch huffed. "I would never use such language!"

"Dear old Candace . . ." Luna patted her hand consolingly. "We all appreciate your wisdom—"

"Speak for yourself," muttered Scarlett.

"—but Scarlett's abilities aren't in question here. After all, she's the only witch in this room who has successfully performed this spell before."

"Beginner's luck!" Mama pounded the table again. "That was just a case of God looking out for drunkards and fools."

Scarlett made a face. "*Thanks, Mama.*"

"I don't want *any* of my girls participating in this nonsense, no matter how skilled they are."

"Kelly," said Jerusha firmly. "You know as well as I that magic demands a price. And the grove must be preserved."

"Oh, the grove, the grove, blah blah blah." Mama threw her hands up in exasperation. "I am so sick of hearing about the grove. What about Scarlett? One errant bird, one gust of wind, one . . . I don't know, one cruel boy with a stone . . . and we'll lose her forever!"

"If you think about it . . ." Polly examined her nails with a bored expression. "Scarlett has been lost to us for ten years already. So . . ."

Mama turned a murderous glare on Polly. "So *what*, exactly? What precisely is your point, Miss Polly Practically Perfect?"

Polly blanched. "Nothing, I just . . . I'm just saying . . . if she's willing to try, who are we to stop her?"

Louise Demain, who had refused a seat at the table as she preferred lurking ominously in the shadows, abruptly stepped forward. "In the cosmic abyss," she intoned, "the desires of mortals are but fleeting whispers, drowned out by—"

Mama rolled her eyes. "Oh, and you can shut the fuck up, as well."

The elderly witches gasped at the bold language of Kelly Melrose, while her daughters had to suppress delighted giggles.

"Sounds like Louise casts her vote in my favor," Scarlett said. "It's hard to tell, but—"

"I favor nothing," she declared. "I am the voice of a cold, indifferent universe."

"Put a sock in it, time witch," Mama shot back. "I don't recall inviting H.P. Lovecraft into my dining room."

Zahir entered from the kitchen with a tray of sandwiches and opinions of his own. "It's a terrible idea. Reckless, foolhardy, and likely to end in disaster." He set the tray down and met Scarlett's gaze. "Which is exactly why you'll do it, no matter what anyone says. Here, I made you a tuna sandwich."

Scarlett reached for the treat, then paused. "Did you put pickles in? And hot sauce?"

"Of course, and lime zest." He spread his arms wide. "Who do you think you're talking to?!"

She grinned and dug in hungrily. "I understand everyone's concern," she said with her mouth rudely full. "But this is happening."

"It most certainly is not!" shouted her mother.

***

More time passed—more debate, more discussion, more of the same points made over and over. Neither Mama nor Scarlett showed any sign of weakening.

304

Then they heard the front door open, and Mama muttered, "At last, the cavalry has arrived . . ."

Scarlett's eyes narrowed. "What exactly does that mean?"

Nate strode into the dining room. The debate fell silent, all eyes turning to him as he made his way to an empty chair at the table. Scarlett stared, but his expression was unreadable.

Mama rose from her seat, a triumphant twinkle in her eyes. "Darling boy, thank you so much for coming . . ."

"What did you do, Mama?" Scarlett demanded. "Did you call him over here? How dare you drag Nate into this—it has nothing to do with him!" She felt a knot of unease tighten in her stomach. *Is he Mama's secret weapon?* The thought made her heart sink. Because honestly? As secret weapons go, he was a good choice. If there was anyone who could talk her out of this plan, it was Nate.

"We're so glad you could join us," Mama continued. "Please, sit. Belinda, would you be a dear and pass our newcomer a sandwich?"

Scarlett locked eyes with Nate and spoke directly to him. "This is none of your business. You should stay out of it."

Belinda Chatterjee jumped to her feet, eager to play hostess. "Of course, Mama Melrose. Nate, we have tuna, turkey, and grilled veg, I think. What's your pleasure?"

Nate settled into the chair, his eyes never leaving Scarlett's face. "Is the tuna done Scarlett-style?"

"Of course," Belinda announced. "Truth be told, it's impossible to get Zahir to make it any other way."

Nate nodded. "Then tuna's fine, thanks."

Mama leaned forward, her eyes glinting with satisfaction. "Nate, I'm sure Scarlett has told you about her ridiculous plan."

"She didn't, actually. *You* did, when you summoned me over here."

"Be that as it may. We were just discussing how utterly foolish and dangerous it is. I knew you'd want to be here to help us talk some sense into her."

Nate stared at Scarlett over his tuna. She met his gaze, her eyes pleading silently. *Don't do this to me,* she thought at him. *You definitely could . . . but please, please don't.*

"Scarlett," he began, his voice soft but clear, "I know you. I know your heart, your strength, and your determination. And—"

"Yes, of course," Mama said soothingly. "That was never in question."

"If you'll let me finish."

"I'm so sorry," she said. "The floor is yours."

"Right." He returned his gaze to Scarlett. "This is a grave decision. No one in the room wants to lose you after finally getting you back after so long."

"But Nate . . ." Scarlett pleaded. She sensed some hardcore emotional blackmail was coming and didn't like it.

"Listen to me, Scar." He paused to gaze around the table; all the witches sat on the edge of their seats like this was the last sixty seconds of the World Cup Final. "If you truly believe this is the only way to save the grove . . . then I support you, completely and without reservation."

The dining room erupted. Mama's face went slack with shock, her eyes wide and disbelieving. "Nate, how can you say that? Don't you understand the risks?"

He raised a hand, silencing the clamor. "I do. But I also understand Scarlett. She wouldn't suggest this if she didn't

306

believe it was essential. We need to trust her, to believe in her abilities."

Scarlett felt a rush of relief and gratitude wash over her. She suddenly felt like she could take on the world.

Around the table, the witches erupted into a renewed frenzy of arguments and counter-arguments, their voices rising to a crescendo. All the while, Scarlett and Nate just stared at one another, smiling.

Just as the debate reached a fever pitch, the stage manager of the Gilbert and Sullivan crew burst into the room, his face flushed with annoyance. "Ladies, please!" he cried, waving his arms for silence. "The performance is about to begin. You don't have to attend, although, of course, your presence is desired. But for the love of all that is holy, you must quiet down! You're disturbing everyone!"

Duly chastised, the witches stood, most of them heading to the ballroom for *Pirates of Penzance*. On her way out, Mama turned to Scarlett, her eyes narrowed in determination. "This isn't over, young lady. We will discuss this further."

Scarlett nodded, her expression polite but resolute. She knew, deep in her heart, that the decision had already been made.

As the witches filed out, Luna and Delilah pulled their sister aside. Del grabbed Scarlett by the shoulders and pulled her in, so they stood forehead to forehead. "This is stupid, and reckless, and a terrible mistake . . ."

"Don't care," Scarlett replied.

". . . and I love you, so don't fuck this thing up." Del abruptly turned and fled the room.

Scarlett turned to her baby sister and lifted an eyebrow. "There's nothing like a Delilah pep talk, is there?"

"Listen carefully. I'll keep Mama off your back for tonight." Luna's voice was low and urgent. "While she's at the play, you should get ready. Go upstairs to our old bedroom. Meditate, prepare yourself mentally for the spell. We'll go tomorrow morning—anything I can do to help, I will." The sisters hugged, and Luna joined the other witches in the ballroom.

When the dining room was empty of witches, Scarlett flew at Nate. She threw her arms around his broad shoulders and pressed her lips against his, hoping to convey a depth of gratitude far beyond what she could express with words.

When they pulled apart, breathless, he said, "That was not the kiss of someone who's about to dump me."

"But I *am* dumping you," she said with a grin. "I'm turning myself into birds and flying away. Maybe forever if my mother is correct."

"Well, that is the most extreme breakup method I've ever heard of." He pulled her close and whispered into her hair. "Forget your mother. *I know* you can do it."

One last embrace, and then Scarlett slipped out of the dining room and made her way to the lobby stairs.

Nate followed her out. "Hey, Scar." His voice was tinged with a forced lightness. "I'm not going to wait around, you know. I just want to make sure that's clear. You go do this bird thing if you want, but you better come right back."

Halfway up the stairs, Scarlett turned back. Despite everything, a smile tugged at her lips. "As you wish."

Chapter 38
Streaming Service

While the witches of Oak Haven enjoyed the tale of Frederic among a band of pirates with oddly stringent apprenticeship requirements, Scarlett was sitting cross-legged on the worn wooden floor of her childhood bedroom. Flickering candle flames cast dancing shadows on the walls, and the air was heavy with the scent of sage and lavender, the herbs burning slowly in a small brass bowl beside her. As a teenager, she'd scoffed at all the mood-setting accessories of meditation—the candles, the herbs, and all the rest. Tonight, however, she wanted all the help she could get.

Scarlett focused her mind, slowly letting go of all the worries and fears that had plagued her for so long. She visualized her thoughts as leaves floating down a gentle stream, each one drifting away until her mind was clear and still.

As she sank deeper into her meditation, Scarlett felt a tingling sensation spread through her body, starting at the base of her spine and radiating outward. It was as if every cell in her being was awakening, alive with her own power. She embraced the feeling, letting it fill her until she felt like she was glowing from within. *I can do this,* she told herself.

Hours passed, and the world outside the inn faded away until there was nothing but the steady rhythm of her breath and the hum of magic in her veins. When she finally opened her eyes, Scarlett was shocked to see that the room was dark, the candles long since burned out. Luna snored gently in the bed across from hers.

Scarlett rose to her feet, stretching her stiff muscles as she made her way to the window. The inn was quiet, the guests long since retired to their rooms. Her stomach grumbled, annoyed at having been ignored for so many hours.

Making her way down the dark staircase toward the kitchen, she was flooded with memories. Of the countless times she and her sisters had raced up and down these stairs, giggling and shouting as they played. Of the sleepless nights when she would sneak downstairs, only to find her father already there, a mug of hot chocolate waiting for her. They would sit together in the dim light, talking about everything and nothing until the first rays of dawn crept through the windows.

It was a relief to remember happy things about her father. Over the past decade, most of her thoughts had not been so sweet. Ten years ago, she had gone to the grove to cast a spell, and instead, she had lost the most important person in her life. And her own carelessness was the cause.

Then, just a few days ago, she'd returned to the grove and messed up yet again. And now here she was, going back for a third try.

Well, she thought to herself as she passed through the lobby, *maybe the third time will literally be the charm. And if not, at least this time, the only person I'm going to destroy is me.*

Scarlett was startled to see her mother pulling leftovers from the refrigerator. The kitchen was dimly lit, the stainless steel appliances gleaming in the low light. It was a space designed for bustling activity and the clatter of pots and pans, but in the stillness of the night, it felt strangely intimate.

Mama looked up, somehow not at all surprised to bump into her daughter in the kitchen at three o'clock in the morning. She gestured for Scarlett to sit. They dug into some of Zahir's leftovers—a hearty stew, the rich aroma of herbs and spices filling the air as they ate in silence.

Finally, Scarlett broke the quiet. "How was *Pirates of Penzance*?"

Mama sighed, shaking her head. "Frederic was all right, I suppose. But the major general was a disaster. He didn't come close to what Mandy would have done with the role."

"So you and Mandy, huh?" She whistled suggestively. "I had no idea."

"Oh, stop," Mama rolled her eyes. "Delilah has no idea what she's talking about. She vastly exaggerates the whole thing."

"Well . . . maybe I can meet Mandy if he comes next year."

"Maybe you can."

Mama's words hung heavy in the air. They both knew that if Scarlett's spell went badly, she might not have a next year.

They lapsed into silence once more, the only sound being the clink of their spoons against the bowls. Scarlett took a deep breath, steeling herself for the conversation she knew she had to have.

"Mama, listen . . ." she began, choosing her words carefully, "I respect your feelings about the transformation spell. But it's happening. Luna and I are going out to the grove tomorrow, and we're going to try. And the fact is—"

Mama raised her hand, silencing her daughter. Without a word, she rose from her seat and fetched two wineglasses and a bottle of merlot. She poured generously, the dark liquid swirling in the glasses as she handed one to Scarlett.

"Continue," she said, taking a sip.

"The fact is, Luna conjured an entire zoo's worth of animals, and not one of them would eat the dragonflies. Me, first time out, I made a starling and it worked." Scarlett swallowed hard, the wine warming her. "And then there's what Louise Demain said about my destiny."

"Bah. Louise Demain is an absinthe-addled gooney bird."

"Definitely," Scarlett conceded, "but has she ever been wrong?"

Mama sighed. "Never."

"So there you are. I understand your point of view, I swear. And God knows you have every reason to doubt my abilities. But—"

"What are you talking about?" Mama interrupted, her voice sharp. "I don't doubt your abilities, not for one moment. This was never about that."

Scarlett scoffed, muttering, "Well, that's stupid."

"Excuse me?!"

"Honestly, Mama? You *should* worry! You should worry very much about my powers. You'd still have a husband if it weren't for my powers."

Mama stared at her daughter, shocked. "What does that mean? What happened to your father wasn't your fault."

Scarlett laughed, but it was a bitter, humorless sound. "See! You think you know everything, but you don't. It was totally my fault. Look at you—the all-seeing Kelly Melrose—and all this time you never even knew."

"What are you talking about?" Mama's voice was soft, almost afraid.

The words poured out, a torrent of guilt and grief that Scarlett had held inside for far too long. "You know, I didn't even want to go to the grove that night! Nate and I had just decided that we were maybe, possibly, *finally* going to have a real date. Plus, Papa had a shipment of tulip bulbs he wanted us to put in the garden before the frost. There were a hundred things I wanted to be doing that didn't include sitting in the woods pulling toxins out of fucking oak trees. But *ooh, it's the grove, we've got to protect the grove, we're Melroses, we have responsibilities*, blahdy blah. So there we are, sitting on the ground, and it was cold, and my trousers were wet, and it was taking forever—you were doing some kind of incantation that just went on and on and on, and I was so fucking bored. And I let my mind wander and . . ." Tears streamed down Scarlett's face, her body shaking. "And right then you said something about a vessel, but my mind wasn't focused on the actual vessel, it was entirely on Papa, and all the poison went into him and he died! And I haven't come home because I can't face you. Or Del and Luna! How can I ever look them in the eye, if they knew I killed Papa?"

"Oh child . . ." Mama's own eyes were wet with tears. "Oh no, oh you precious girl, come here to me." She rose from her seat to wrap her daughter in a tight embrace.

They held each other for a long moment, the silence broken only by the sound of their shared grief.

Finally, Mama pulled back, cupping Scarlett's face in her hands. "Beautiful girl, that's not why. That's not why it went wrong. Sweetie, no. I was leading that spell, not you. The miscalculation was entirely mine. I should never have brought you girls along in the first place—I knew you were all too young. What I *should* have done was drag Jerusha and Candace out to the grove to help me instead. But I just . . . well . . . the truth is I fucking hate Jerusha and Candace! But I love you girls. I was being selfish, don't you see? I wanted to share that experience with you. You were all growing up so fast . . . and I thought, who knows how many more opportunities I'll get to do collective spells with you. But the whole time, instead of truly focusing on the task, I was paying attention to you girls—how you were doing, and if you were all right. And *my* mind drifted. I started thinking about the five of us—our lovely family of Papa and me and you girls. My angel, it was my focus that was off; that's what made things go so wrong. I'm to blame. Not you. Never, never you."

They cried together, holding each other tight as years of pain and guilt washed over them. When the tears finally subsided, Scarlett sniffled. "I guess I should have brought this up sooner."

Mama laughed and cried equally. "You foolish girl. Oh, my foolish girl, I love you so." She took Scarlett's hands in her own, her expression fierce with love and determination. "Listen to me. Tomorrow, we will all go to the grove as a family. And you will perform the spell and those goddamn starlings will murmurate all over the place and you, my darling girl, will save this town."

Scarlett wiped at her eyes. "Are you sure?"

"Very much so."

"Thanks, Mama. I promise I won't let you down. I'll prove to you that I can do it."

Mama shook her head. "You don't need to prove it to me. Maybe you need to prove it to you, but not to me. And listen to me—when this is over? If you want to go back to San Francisco because that's where you *truly* want to be, then go with my

314

blessing. All I ask is that you don't wait ten more years to come visit us. Okay?"

Scarlett nodded.

"And, of course—" here Mama had a mischievous glint in her eye "—if you decide that there is *somewhere else* you truly want to be? I won't mind that either."

The hour was late, and Mama declared that it was time for them to get a couple hours of sleep. As they made their way up the dark staircase, Scarlett paused.

"Mama? Remember when I first got home? We sat in your office and you told me that phone sabotage is one of the most-cast spells?"

"Published in the *Acta Diurna Magus*, yes of course."

"Well, I gotta know . . . what are the others?"

"I must tell you—" she sighed "—the popular spells these days are embarrassingly small-bore. Let me think . . . clearing highway traffic is one. Password retention is another. Locating lost 401ks. Oh, there's a spell that lets the recipient immediately know which *streaming service* a particular program is on? I don't even understand that one."

Scarlett's eyes widened, excited. "Ohh, I do. That's a good one. Those all sound quite good."

Mama frowned, unimpressed. "When I was your age, the most-cast spell involved the Berlin Wall, but . . . sure. Streaming services." She paused at the top of the stairs, turning to face her daughter. "Sweet dreams, my dear. Tomorrow, you save our world."

Chapter 39
Floaty Candles

The early morning sun cast a soft, golden light over the oak grove as Scarlett made her way up the hill, her mother and sisters by her side. The air was crisp and cool, and the dew-covered grass sparkled like diamonds beneath their feet. Despite the seriousness of the task at hand, there was a sense of warmth and unity among the women as they walked together, their steps in perfect sync.

Over her shoulder, Luna had a satchel filled with candles, herbs, and other mystical tools to help amplify Scarlett's power. Delilah carried a few soft blankets and a couple of folding chairs, while Mama had a large basket overflowing with food and water. They were prepared to stay by Scarlett's side for as long as it took. Also, Kelly Melrose had never once in her life turned down a picnic.

As they approached the edge of the grove, they weren't surprised at all to find Nate there waiting for them. Without a word, he fell into step beside the women. His hand found Scarlett's and he gave it a reassuring squeeze.

But as they entered the grove itself, the mood shifted

dramatically. The trees were even more sickly and withered than ever, their leaves drooping and bark peeling away in large, brittle chunks. The air was tinted a vague, unsettling red, the color of rust and decay, and it was filled with the constant, droning buzz of countless glowing dragonflies. The insects flitted from tree to tree, their wings leaving trails of crimson light in their wake. The stench of rot and disease was almost overwhelming.

Scarlett made her way to the center of the grove, where the largest and oldest oak tree stood. Its mighty trunk was gnarled and twisted, its branches reaching up and out like the grasping fingers of a crone who'd lived far too long. Luna began to arrange her herbs and candles in a circle around the tree—her hands moved with practiced grace as she sent the candles floating into the air.

Delilah approached Scarlett, her eyes shining as she pulled her sister into a fierce hug. "You're an idiot," she whispered. "But you've got this."

Luna came next, her smile soft and encouraging. "Remember, Scarlett," she said, "you are stronger than you know. Trust in yourself and in the magic that flows through you."

Luna squeezed Scarlett, who whispered into her sister's wild hair, "Thanks for not calling me an idiot."

Mama stepped forward, her jaw set with determination and love. "My brave, beautiful girl. I am so proud of you; I know your father is too. You can do this. Just remember, when you're zipping around in the sky, stay the hell away from mean boys with stones. And don't get so enamored with flying that you forget to return to the ground."

Scarlett nodded. "I promise I won't."

Finally, it was Nate's turn. He pulled Scarlett close, his arms wrapping around her in a tight, desperate embrace. "I love you," he whispered.

She couldn't begin to process that statement, so she made a joke instead, "*I know*."

Nate shook his head, chuckling. "A moment like this, and you're going all Han Solo on me."

"You better believe it." Scarlett kissed him fiercely and then said, "I love you, too. Now back up and let me do this."

Scarlett settled herself against the tree trunk, surrounded by Luna's herbs and her enchanted candles. "Hey, wait," she said suddenly. "I just remembered: Luna, you never showed me how to do the floaty candles thing."

"Well then." Luna forced a smile. "I guess you have a reason to return to us."

Scarlett's gaze shifted to Nate, and she winked. "*Oh, finally*, a *good* reason to return." Nate winked back.

She closed her eyes and let her mind drift. She found herself floating back through the years to the countless memories she shared with Papa. There he was, standing in the garden, his hands caked with dirt as he carefully tended to his beloved delphiniums. There he was, sitting at his big carved desk, surrounded by books. There he was, dancing with Mama in the living room, their laughter echoing through the house as they twirled and swayed to "Blue Moon."

She could feel her father's presence all around her, his love and strength flowing through her. Where before these memories had been tinged with guilt and regret, now Scarlett felt only joy at feeling his spirit twinned with her own. Under the ancient oak tree, surrounded by her family, both living and not, Scarlett knew that she was exactly where she was meant to be now.

Suddenly, a burst of blinding light illuminated the forest, and a ferocious wind tore through the air. Scarlett's human form shattered into thirteen starlings, each one glimmering with silver flecks like tiny jewels against their jet-black feathers. With a synchronized flutter of wings, they soared into the sky, their movements fluid and graceful as they weaved through the trees. The sound of their trills filled the grove, echoing off the ancient oaks.

The starlings flew in in perfect unison, creating an intricate and mesmerizing display against the blue sky. As if controlled by a single mind, they twisted and turned, their path forming an intricate, spiraling pattern like a glittering black tornado. They descended upon the unsuspecting dragonflies with a furious hunger, devouring the insects with precision and grace.

Scarlett's family watched in awe as the starlings feasted. They laughed together as the birds swept through the trees.

"Look at her go!" Delilah exclaimed, her eyes wide with wonder. "I've never seen anything like it!"

Mama unfolded one of the chairs and sat down, back straight as always. "That's my girl."

***

In the shadow of the oak grove, a man and a woman in top hats and capes lurked behind some shrubbery.

"Are you seeing what I'm seeing," hissed the gentleman magician.

"That I am," his companion whispered back.

"This is bad. This is very very bad. What should we do?"

"Don't fret," said the lady magician with a wink. "I know exactly what we do."

Thirteen starlings versus a thousand dragonflies was an epic battle, and not a brief one. Ever patient, the family gathered on the blankets to watch the show.

As they snacked on the sandwiches Zahir had sent, conversation turned to the future and all its many possibilities.

"So, Nate," Delilah said with a mischievous glint in her eye, "when are you going to make an honest woman out of our sister? I mean, you can't very well burn down Polly's store every time you want to fool around."

Nate coughed, his face turning pink. "Well, uh . . . You heard about that, huh?"

Mama frowned. "What's this about the bookstore?"

"Nothing, Mama." Luna giggled, nudging her sister with her elbow. "Leave the poor boy alone, Del."

"I'm just saying," Delilah continued, undeterred, "if he's going to be part of this family, he might as well make it official. We've all been waiting for it for years."

Slowly but surely, the tide turned against the insect invaders—the starlings had them on the ropes, swooping and darting through the branches of the old oak trees. The red tint that had suffused the grove began to fade, replaced by the warm, golden glow of the afternoon sun. The air grew fresh and sweet, the stench of decay dissipating like a bad dream. The trees themselves seemed to stand a little taller, their leaves unfurling and their branches reaching toward the sky with renewed vigor.

By sunset, the grove was dragonfly-free and utterly transformed. The starlings, bellies full and wings heavy with exhaustion, returned to the base of the great oak tree, settling into the circle of candles with soft, contented coos.

"Look! It's worked!" Luna cheered.

Mama, Delilah, Luna, and Nate all rose to their feet in applause. They had so much they wanted to say to Scarlett, so many words of love and pride. They wanted to sweep her up in their arms and never let her go. They stood happily and watched the starlings peck the dirt, and groom themselves.

As the minutes ticked by, the starlings remained huddled beneath the tree, a sense of unease grew. Where was she? Why hadn't she returned to her human form?

"Luna," Mama said, concerned, "what do you know about the timings here?"

"I . . . I don't know anything. I mean . . . this isn't a common spell, so . . ."

Delilah turned to Nate. "Do you remember when she did it with the fish? It happened pretty quickly, didn't it? Didn't she come back pretty soon?"

"Could something have gone wrong with the spell?" Luna asked. "Mama? Did something go wrong that we didn't notice?"

"I . . ." She shook her head. "I don't know . . ." Mama stepped forward, her brow furrowed with concern as she approached the circle of candles. She counted the starlings one by one.

Twelve. There were only twelve starlings beneath the tree.

Mama's hands trembled as she counted the birds again. Twelve. Only twelve starlings returned.

A choked sob escaped Delilah's throat as the horrible truth set in. "No," she whispered. "No, it can't be!"

Luna's knees buckled, and Nate quickly moved to catch her before she collapsed. His face was drawn with anguish and disbelief. After finally getting Scarlett back, the thought of losing her again was too much to bear.

"This isn't happening." His voice was raw and broken. "She'll find a way back to us, I know she will." But even as he spoke the words, doubt crept into his heart.

Mama stood frozen, her eyes fixed on the starlings. Tears streamed down her face, but she made no move to wipe them away. "My baby," she whispered, her voice so soft that it was almost lost on the evening breeze. "My darling girl. Where have you gone?"

Chapter 40
The Thirteenth Starling

A bitter wind whipped through the oak grove, scattering the autumn leaves and chilling the air as the witches walked slowly back to town. Their overwhelming loss was written plainly on all their faces, their expressions haunted and distant as they trudged back to the inn.

But Nate remained.

"She's coming back," he declared. "And she'll be pissed if we've all left."

He settled beneath the ancient tree, his eyes scanning the sky for any sign of the thirteenth starling.

***

As dawn broke on the following day, the Melroses led an army of witches back up to the grove, all of them decked out in birdwatching gear. They combed the area, searching high and low for the elusive starling. But to no avail.

Aphra brought materials to create an enchanted cage, and Nate helped her construct an enclosure beneath the big old oak tree. The idea was to ensure the twelve starlings stayed safe and close . . . just in case the final one returned.

"*When* the final one returns," Nate reminded her.

"Yes." Aphra nodded solemnly. "When."

Once the work was complete, Aphra gently suggested to Nate that there was no more to be done, no more to be asked of him, and no more to be gained from him living in the grove alone.

But Nate remained.

***

As the days passed, ever-smaller contingents of witches returned to continue the search. One by one, they began to accept that Scarlett had given her life to save their own.

Perhaps we should erect another statue, the witches whispered to one another. *A beautiful stone Scarlett in the center of town, right beside her ancestor, Goodwife Melrose.*

Kelly Melrose would glare at the women with homicide in her eyes. "My daughter does not require a statue," she'd say. "My daughter will return." And the witches would go quiet.

***

Periodically, Zahir brought food to the grove for his old friend. He'd sit beside Nate, attempting to engage in friendly conversation. Zahir would ask if Nate cared to know the latest news from town, or if he wanted to hear about a particularly zany guest who'd visited the inn, or if he was even *slightly* curious about what was happening at Williams Hardware in his absence.

And Nate said, "Not really. Thanks anyway."

As the sun dipped below the horizon, Zahir always attempted to persuade Nate to join him in Oak Haven for a beer. But Nate remained.

Down in Oak Haven, the restoration of magic breathed new life into the town. The glittering colors were back, the scents of pumpkin and woodsmoke were all around, and the streets were adorned with gourds as far as the eye could see. Even the miscreant squirrels with magnificent tails had returned, many sporting jaunty new berets. The Road Work Spell Committee worked diligently to mend the damaged sigils, and their magic permeated the air.

Meanwhile, Spellbound Books stood fully restored. Polly sat in the front window every Wednesday, reading stories to groups of enraptured children. She'd conjure parades of ducks to march around the store, eliciting squeals of delight.

***

As the last autumn leaves clung to the trees, two magicians—one male, one female—sat together in the front window of Hexpresso Yourself. The coffee shop had become the magicians' refuge and makeshift headquarters, where they gathered to study trivia, drink cappuccinos, and (these days) feel very sorry for themselves. Most didn't even have the heart for trivia practice anymore—not since their leader, Maximillian, had disappeared without a trace. They were feeling lost, bitter, and uncertain of their futures. Not an ideal state of mind for memorizing Elton John lyrics.

"We should kill that fucking bird." The male magician's eyes narrowed in frustration. "It's stupid to just keep it hanging around. I'm so sick of listening to it chirping day and night."

His partner shook her head. "Bosses said not to hurt it. They want to run tests, figure out how it works. Maybe we can learn that spell, too."

"Sure, but it's *evidence*. Keeping it around just proves that we interfered." He took an angry swig of his coffee. "You just know those witches will be here any minute to kick us all out of town. And if they find out we've been keeping that thing—"

"They won't," the lady magician assured him.

"We should get the hell out of here while we can. To tell you the truth, I don't see why we haven't all cleared out already."

She tilted her head sympathetically. "I know, it's been rough. But the bosses say stay put. The bosses say they're working on a plan B, and we should sit tight and await further instructions."

"*The bosses say, the bosses say* . . ." he muttered. "Who cares what the bosses say."

"Uhh, I'd rather not piss them off. Know what I mean?"

"Yeah. Yeah, I know. It's just . . . The whole situation makes me so mad. Ugh, those goddamned witches."

"You can say that again," she agreed.

"No, you don't understand." He pointed out the window. "Out there. Goddamned witches, *right goddamn now*."

A phalanx of witches, led by the determined Priti Chatterjee and her EMS team, were marching down the street toward the coffee shop. Panic erupted among the magicians inside, their eyes wide with fear as they frantically gathered their belongings and fled, desperate to escape before being caught by the powerful coven. The sound of clattering objects and fleeing feet echoed through the shop as they hastily retreated.

The lady magician snatched up her top hat and dashed to a low cupboard in the back of the shop. That cupboard contained a very precious item, which she alone had been entrusted to protect at all costs. She grabbed the item, bundled it with her cape and a few essentials, and sprinted out the back door.

"Wait for me!" her companion shouted after her, but there

would be no waiting today, not for him or anyone. She had a solemn responsibility to escape with the evidence, no matter what.

The magician's heart pounded as she sprinted down the cobblestone streets, the sound of witches' cackles echoing behind her. She followed the winding road that led out of town, her breath coming in ragged gasps. When she reached the covered bridge, she felt a glimmer of hope—but halfway across, three more witches materialized at the far side, blocking her escape. The magician skidded to a stop, knowing she was trapped. Desperate to hide the evidence, she tossed her bundle into the river.

The witches closed in, surrounding her.

"I'll never talk," the magician spat out. "You can torture me all you want. But I'll never comply."

Priti laughed, her eyes glinting with amusement. "My goodness, you magicians are *intense*! Nobody's torturing anybody! We're going to toss each of you in a portal to a different location. By the time you all figure out how to get home, you'll have forgotten about Oak Haven completely. That's all. We don't want to hurt you; we just want you all gone."

"*Whatever*. Our bosses won't forget about Oak Haven. You'll see. They'll just send more of us to try again."

"Maybe so," Priti said amiably. "But we'll be ready for you next time."

And with that, the witches dragged the magician away.

Beneath the old bridge, the magician's possessions floated along the sharp rocks. There was a change of clothes, a dog-eared copy of the *Farmer's Almanac*, a travel backgammon set . . . and a small, gilded cage holding a vibrant starling.

The little bird sang urgently. But as the cage floated in the shadow of the old covered bridge, her trills went unheard.

***

One Sunday, Earls Nine through Twelve marched up to the grove to visit Thirteen. They brought a tent, a few changes of clothes, and materials to build a solar oven. They sat with their heartbroken descendant, hoping to distract him with epic tales of the Great Sea Wolf, Earl of Anglia, Terror of Tortuga. Nate enjoyed the old men's stories, and welcomed their company. But when his beloved ancestors raised the issue of coming home?

Earl Thirteen remained.

***

Most evenings around sunset, Delilah and Luna would head downtown, recreating that stroll they'd taken that very first evening Scarlett had come home. Eventually they'd find themselves on the town green, staring up at the statue of Goodwife Melrose.

"I shouldn't have been so hard on her," Delilah would say every time. "Remember, Luna—I accused Scarlett of running away, just like our ancestors from Salem. But she didn't run, did she?"

Luna would wrap her arm around her sister's and rest her head on her shoulder. "No," she'd say sadly, "she didn't."

***

In his misery, Nate took daily walks to try and clear his head. He'd amble down the hill from the grove and pause beside the babbling river. And he would gaze sadly at the covered bridge. The very bridge where Scarlett once jumped, brave and reckless and as beautiful as anyone he'd ever seen. The very bridge that had been the backdrop of their first and only date.

At the same moment, the starling sat trapped in her golden cage, which had become wedged between two large rocks beneath the bridge. She was surviving on meager rations of beetles and minnows that happened to float past. Not much, but just enough.

The starling could sense when Nate was nearby, and she would sing for him. She'd warble and whistle and trill as loudly as she possibly could.

But all Nate heard was the rushing water and the breeze rustling through the trees.

When he couldn't bear the painful memories a moment longer, he'd turn his back to the bridge and walk in the opposite direction.

***

The first flakes of snow drifted down in mid-November. Luna went up to the grove to visit Nate. She, unlike everyone else in town, never asked him to come home. Instead, she sat cross-legged on the ground, meditating for hours until she'd conjured for him a tiny but lovely one-room house.

***

Thanksgiving arrived, and all the Mrs. Earls marched up the hill to beg their son/grandson/great-grandson/and-so-on to come home. Just for one day. For a family Thanksgiving. Please.

But Nate remained.

Zahir made him a plate and brought it up to the grove. The men sat on the stoop of Nate's little house and watched the sun set in silence.

***

Time marched on, and winter arrived in earnest. Nate chopped firewood and scanned the sky, his beard growing ever longer.

He noticed that the starlings seemed to require almost no water and very little food. They just carried on somehow. He hoped this was meaningful. He hoped they were waiting for Scarlett, too.

Under the bridge, the starling shivered in her little frozen prison. But although her voice was growing weak, she continued to sing.

***

Oak Haven was transformed into a winter wonderland. Buildings were adorned with enchanted icicles; they glowed in warm neon hues, as though the Northern Lights had settled permanently over the town. The street lamps sang Christmas carols whenever prompted, and the snow that blanketed the streets was always perfectly white.

Delilah trekked up the hill on snowshoes, bringing supplies to Nate in the middle of a fierce winter storm. She didn't bother asking if he'd be willing to come home.

***

Before too long, spring arrived. Under the bridge, the starling's cage thawed but still would not release her.

Meanwhile Nate tended to his daily chores around the grove, a sharp cry pierced the air. A young fox pup had become entangled in the brambles near the river's edge, its tiny paw caught in some thorny vines. Nate rushed to the pup's aid, carefully untangling the frightened creature from its prickly prison. In his haste, Nate scratched his hand on the brambles, which left bloody marks across his skin.

"Ow, dammit!" he muttered. But then he looked into the pup's eyes and had to smile. "Sorry, it's okay—don't be scared. Hey, are you somebody's girlfriend, by any chance? My girlfriend is a bird. You haven't seen her, have you?"

The pup made no reply.

Despite the pain and the steady trickle of blood, Nate gently cleaned the little fox's wound and released it, smiling as it bounded away to join its family. He wrapped his own hand with a strip of cloth torn from his shirt and returned to watching the sky.

***

Summer came, and Nate fished in the nearby river, cooking his catch over a fire. On clear evenings, the Melrose family would join him at the grove, sitting around the fire and sharing stories about Scarlett under the stars. When morning came, they packed up to leave. But Nate remained.

***

Autumn returned to Oak Haven, and with it the glittering leaves and colorful gourds and pumpkin spice scent in the air.

One morning, Dayo and Zahir pulled up outside the abandoned building that once housed Hexpresso Yourself. Dayo's truck was packed tight with kitchen appliances and crates of barware. Dayo went inside, opening windows to air out the musty space, while Zahir affixed a sign to the front door.

COMING SOON TO THIS LOCATION
OAK HAVEN'S FIRST BREW PUB:
DOUBLE, DOUBLE BOIL AND TROUBLE

The two friends and new co-owners spent the day cleaning and moving appliances around. They were packing up to go home when Dayo noticed one final cupboard in a dark corner of the empty shop.

"Hang on, we haven't seen what's inside that cabinet over there. Maybe the magicians left us a pile of spare magic wands, that'd be fun."

Grinning, Zahir knelt down beside the cupboard. "Or how about some of those gold coins they're always pulling out of people's ears." A small knob on the cupboard door refused to turn. "It's locked . . . somehow . . . I don't actually see how, but . . ."

Dayo rolled her eyes. "Magicians and their goddamned enchanted locks." She grabbed a hammer and smashed the knob.

The door swung open. Inside lay a half-full bag of birdseed.

"Well," Dayo said, "*that's* disappointing."

"Birdseed?!" Zahir poked at the bag. "What did they need birdseed for?"

"Somebody's gotta feed all those doves they conjure out of their top hats."

"Okay, but why bother enchanting the cabinet? Why go to that much trouble?"

"Dunno," Dayo shrugged. "Special, magical birdseed?"

"Huh. I mean . . . maybe?" Zahir frowned. That didn't *feel* like the right explanation. But he couldn't think of a better one.

***

At the grove, the oak trees turned spectacular colors—everyone in town said it was the best leaf-peeping season they'd ever seen. But as a weary and lonely Nate tended to his chores, the spectacular autumn display meant nothing to him. Over the past year, he'd trained his mind to remain blank; he'd run out of thoughts that weren't painful.

Today especially. Because today was the first anniversary of Scarlett's great sacrifice. A Murmuration of Scarletts, she had playfully called it. But to Nate, it was the Beginning of the End.

He took his daily stroll as always, walking down the hill to the river and staring mournfully at the bridge. And as always, he turned away, to walk in the opposite direction.

But today, something stopped him. Perhaps it was the anniversary. Or perhaps Nate was sick of letting that bridge loom over his life like some epic wooden monster. Whatever the reason, today he did something that had been unthinkable for the past 364 days.

Today he walked toward the bridge.

As he approached, a high-pitched trill pierced the air, the all-too-familiar sound of a starling's call. Nate didn't even register the noise. After all, he spent every day listening to the caged starlings that lived outside his cabin, and he spent every night listening to the missing starling in his dreams.

The trill sounded again, louder and more insistent, demanding his attention. A flicker of annoyance crossed Nate's face. He glanced around, looking for the source of the noise. A glint of something metallic caught his eye.

Nate's breath caught in his chest. There, nestled between two large rocks, sat a tiny golden cage. Inside was a vibrant starling— bedraggled and starved but alive.

"Scarlett . . . is that you?"

The bird tweeted impatiently.

He scrambled across the rocky bank, stumbling in his haste.

Reaching into the water, he grasped the cage and lifted it out. The starling hopped up and down, chirping at her rescuer.

"How did you get here?" Nate murmured in wonder. He undid the latch to free the little bird, cradling her gently in his strong hands.

The starling let out a triumphant trill, her little body quivering with exhaustion and relief.

As if under a spell himself, Nate carried the bird back up the hill to the grove. There sat the far larger cage, where the twelve starlings had waited for so very long. He opened the cage, and the birds burst out. The thirteenth starling fluttered from Nate's hand to join them in mid-air. The birds all took to the clouds, forming a mesmerizing star-shaped twister that spun faster and faster until thirteen had become one, and Scarlett's body tumbled from the sky.

Nate raced to her side as she lay in the grass, dazed but unharmed.

"Hey." She reached up and tugged his beard. "I thought you weren't waiting for me."

He chuckled, blinking back tears. "I was just about to give up, actually. I hate tardiness."

"Sorry," Scarlett grinned, "I got held up."

Their lips met in a long-awaited kiss, the grove's ancient trees the sole witnesses to their reunion.

As Nate and Scarlett's kiss lingered, the world around them seemed to fade away. He cupped Scarlett's face in his hands, as if to reassure himself that she was truly there, flesh and blood. Tears of happiness rose in his eyes, mirroring the glistening droplets streaking down Scarlett's face.

She reached up and stroked his chin. "You grew a beard."

"Yeah, kind of by accident. Do you like it?"

"Not at all." She laughed and so did he, and they held each other tightly, afraid to let go—afraid the moment might shatter into a cruel dream.

As the sun began to set, casting a warm, golden glow over the grove, Nate and Scarlett finally disentangled themselves from each other's embrace. He took her hand and helped her to her feet.

"C'mon," he said gently. "Your family's been waiting for you. Actually, the whole town has been waiting. Oh—uh, although . . . maybe not San Francisco? San Francisco might not have waited for you. Your mother told me that your job sent your final paycheck to the inn. And I think you might've gotten evicted from your apartment."

Scarlett just laughed. "Yeah, spending a year trapped in the form of a bird is not a great career builder in Silicon Valley. Makes no difference to me." She threw her arms around him. "Everything I want is right here."

Nate took her hand to lead her down the hill. "Let's go see everyone."

But Scarlett stopped him. "What are you, nuts?" She flicked her head in the direction of Nate's quaint little cottage. "Is there a bed in there?"

"Well yeah, but . . . your mom, your sisters . . . ?"

"They waited this long; they can wait one more day. *But we can't.* C'mon, Earl Thirteen, let's do this."

Nate's laughter, deep and genuine, echoed through the grove. He scooped her into his arms and carried her across the threshold.

Chapter 41
A Deep-Fried Pirate Thanksgiving

It was Thanksgiving Day, and the usually tranquil Oak Haven town green was filled with the laughter and chatter of families gathered to celebrate the holiday. The aromas of hot apple cider and spiced pumpkin lattes mingled in the crisp autumn air. Long tables had been set up around the perimeter of the green, all draped in warm, autumnal colors. Pumpkins of various sizes and shapes adorned the tables, their carved faces grinning mischievously at passersby. Enchanted cornucopias overflowed with an abundance of fresh fruits, vegetables, and magical treats, their contents spilling onto the tables in a display of the very particular bounty of Oak Haven.

Townspeople were gathered around the town gazebo, which was decorated with streamers, balloons shaped like pilgrim hats, and an enormous banner: OAK HAVEN TURKEY TROT. Polly and Violet stood on the steps, surrounded by a sea of eager kids. Each child clutched a piece of paper featuring a hand-drawn turkey.

"All right, everyone!" Polly called out, her voice filled with enthusiasm. "It's time for the Turkey Trot! Let's see those beautiful turkeys come to life!" Polly smiled at Violet, who—for today at least—had decided to participate rather than glower. Mother and daughter held hands, closed their eyes, and cast an enchantment over the sea of eager young faces. The hand-drawn turkeys sprang to life, leaping from the pages into the world. Their paper feathers rustled as they darted and wove, while their little creators chased them around the green.

Scarlett and Nate stood off to the side, watching the festivities with big dumb grins on their faces. Thanksgiving represented everything they loved about Oak Haven, where traditions were honored, where magic and wonder were celebrated, and where the bonds of family and friendship were strong.

Scarlett rested her head on Nate's shoulder. "I can't believe it's my first Thanksgiving home in ten years."

"*Eleven*," he corrected.

"Right, eleven. I forgot to count my Bird Year."

"Gotta count your Bird Year." Nate chuckled. "Anyway, you'll make up for lost time today, that's for sure."

"Yeah, what is it, *four* Thanksgivings? Dinner at the inn first, then at your parents', then *another* dinner at your grandparents'— why those two can't be combined, I'll never understand."

"Aw, it's a Williams family tradition at this point. My dad is insisting on deep-frying the turkey this year, but my grandparents say that's a sin against poultry. My great-grandparents sided with my dad, and they all ended up arguing, and voila: two separate dinners. Be glad it's only two this year—for a while, they were all battling over mashed potato recipes, and we had to do *three*."

"Good grief." Scarlett laughed. "Remind me to never challenge pirates about their food preferences. Anyway, after all that's done? Then we're expected at the inaugural Thanksgiving feast at Zahir and Dayo's pub."

Nate grinned. "You know that any meal at Double, Double Boil and Trouble is going to be incredible."

"Zahir's skill is not in question. But that's way too many Thanksgivings! How are we ever going to eat four Thanksgiving dinners?"

"I guess we'll just have to pace ourselves. Skip the rolls, probably." Nate kissed Scarlett on the head. "But there's nowhere else I'd rather be than right here with you."

"Unfortunately . . ." she glanced at her watch ". . . we actually have to get back. It's time for your class, holiday or not."

As they made their way back to the inn, the aroma of roasting turkeys and freshly baked pies wafted from every window, mingling with the laughter and chatter of families and friends reuniting for the holiday. Enchanted decorations adorned the storefronts, with animated cornucopias spilling their bounty and tiny, glowing pumpkins floating in the air.

They ambled up the walkway to the Stargazer, the inviting glow of the inn's windows beckoning them inside. As they approached the front door, an elderly couple exited the inn. The elders paused to greet this vision of their younger selves. "Happy Thanksgiving," said the old man.

"What a lovely young couple you are!" exclaimed his wife. "When are you two getting married?"

"Oh, you know . . . I'm holding out for a destination wedding," Scarlett said, smiling. "But he has to pass his exams first."

"Isn't that charming," the woman said. "And what are you studying, young man? Are you in medical school or such like?"

"Trivia school," Nate said. "Packing in as much useless information as I can."

The old man's eyebrows furrowed in confusion. "I have no

338

idea what that means, young man, but I'm sure you'll make it work."

"Are you enjoying the Stargazer?" Scarlett asked.

"Oh, absolutely," the old lady enthused. "We just happened upon your inn by chance, and we've been so delighted with everything. In fact, we were just saying—as soon as we get home, the first thing we're doing is calling all our friends to tell them about Oak Haven."

Scarlett and Nate exchanged glances. "Not much chance of that," Scarlett said kindly. "But Happy Thanksgiving to you both!"

***

At the Stargazer, Nate headed off to the dining room for his class while Scarlett joined Delilah at the front desk. "All right, little sister," Delilah began, her tone a mix of gratitude and stern instruction, "I'm trusting you to keep this place running smoothly while I'm gone. Don't screw it up."

"Your unyielding support never ceases to amaze," Scarlett replied.

"Yeah, yeah, whatever." Del grabbed her by the elbow and dragged her behind the desk. "C'mere, did I show you the reservation book?"

"Only a hundred times!"

"Well, I have a system, Scar! I don't want to get home and find out you messed up my system."

Just then, Luna breezed up to the front desk, her travel bag slung over her shoulder. "Ready to hit the road, Delilah? The world awaits!"

"Actually, I haven't packed yet."

"Delilah!" Luna shook her head. "How can you not have packed?! We're leaving right after dinner, remember?"

"Well, there's a lot to think about! I have a lot of responsibilities, you know. I can't just throw two pairs of knickers in a bag and vanish like you do."

Scarlett felt a sudden lump in her throat, the reality of her sister's departure hitting her. "You'll write, won't you? Keep us updated on all your wild escapades?"

Delilah laughed, a rare but genuine sound. "Wild escapades? Who do you think I am, *you*?"

Luna grinned, winking at Scarlett. "Oh, I have a feeling Delilah's got a few surprises up her sleeve."

"Hang on, though . . ." Scarlett fidgeted with a pen, trying to find the right words. "Delilah, I . . . I just wanted to say—"

She held up a hand, cutting her off. "Don't get all sentimental on me now."

"I know, I know. But still, I need you to know how much I appreciate everything you've done. For me, for our family . . . just . . . taking care of everything. Staying here with Mama when Luna and I weren't around. I just want to repay you for all that."

Delilah shrugged. "You can repay me by making sure the Stargazer is still standing when I get home."

"Yeah, I think I can manage that much."

Luna wagged a finger at her sister. "No s'mores in the bedrooms."

"Oh my God," Scarlett groaned. "*Six! Years! Old!*"

Mama Melrose breezed past them at the desk. "Scarlett, join me in the office please."

Scarlett's heart skipped a beat. *What'd I do now?!* Her sisters laughed and made *oooohh, uh-oh* . . . faces. She sighed and followed her mother, bracing herself for a lecture.

Instead, Mama gestured to a large basket on her desk full of gift-wrapped boxes. "It's high time you got all this junk out of the office."

Confused, Scarlett peered into the basket. "What junk is this?"

"Well, not junk, exactly. A decade's worth of your birthday presents." Mama's voice softened ever so slightly. "I never forgot your birthday, Scarlett. I always held on to hope that you'd come back to us. So every year, I'd get a little something, and put it away for your return."

Tears welled in Scarlett's eyes as she hugged her mother. Mama, ever the stoic, patted her back and cleared her throat. "Yes, yes, that'll do. There are Christmas presents, too, but you can wait till next month for those. But do get these out of my way."

Scarlett carried the basket out to the lobby, her heart full. Impulsively, she ripped open one of the gifts, finding a chef's jacket with "Stargazer Inn" embroidered on the cuffs and "Melrose, Sous Chef" over the breast pocket. As she pulled it on, she thought, *I gotta show Zahir.*

In the kitchen, Zahir was a human tornado, putting the finishing touches on the inn's Thanksgiving dinner while simultaneously beginning the prep for tonight's festivities at his and Dayo's place. But despite the frenzy, he looked happier than Scarlett had ever seen him.

"You better earn that jacket," he said before she could get a word in. "Take these appetizers out to the scholars in the dining room."

Scarlett entered the dining room where Conrad, the town selectman, was leading a trivia workshop.

It had been the ever-practical Delilah who'd realized that the witches should be using Maximillian's trivia idea for their own ends. If the Forgetting Spell could truly be mastered through trivia exercises, Oak Haven could keep its anonymity without forcing the non-witches to remain eternally trapped in town. And so, the trivia workshops began. Nate and his father Twelve, Sam Chatterjee and his son-in-law Raj, and a handful of other Oak Haven men spent several hours a week engrossed in a lively exchange of pointless minutiae, their laughter filling the room.

"All right, gentlemen!" Conrad called out. "Time for a speed round. Let's hear those unique collective nouns. We'll go alphabetically, one at a time, starting with Twelve."

"Aardvarks, armory of!" shouted Twelve.

"Bats, flutter of!" offered Nate.

"Cobras, quiver of!" Sam added.

And on it went. Once the group had achieved "zebras, dazzle of," Conrad moved on to randomized questions. The men eagerly shouted out their answers.

"Who wrote an entry on 'conjuring' for the *Encyclopaedia Britannica*?"

"Harry Houdini!" called a gentleman in the back.

"What is the longest bridge in the United States?"

"Lake Pontchartrain Causeway in New Orleans!" another voice rang out.

"And in the world?"

Raj was on it. "China's Danyang-Kunshan Grand Bridge."

"When was the margarita invented?" Conrad asked, a mischievous glint in his eye.

Nate's hand shot up. "Trick question! The recipe was first published in 1937 by the United Kingdom Bartenders' Guild, but it was called the Picador at the time, not the margarita."

Scarlett grinned. *That's my man.*

As the lessons continued, Scarlett's mind wandered to the future that lay ahead. With Nate in memory training, the possibility of travel and adventure beyond Oak Haven's borders was tantalizingly close. For now, they had their happy responsibilities—Scarlett running the inn and Nate his hardware store. But the world was full of endless possibilities.

Scarlett looked around the room, taking in the faces of her loved ones, the warmth of their laughter, and the magic that filled every corner of her hometown. She knew that no matter where life took her, Oak Haven would always be home. And with Nate by her side, anything seemed possible. The future stretched out before them, a blank page waiting to be written with love and far too many Thanksgivings.

Acknowledgments

No writer is a solo act, no matter what she pretends. I want to sincerely thank everyone at Avon for deciding they wanted to produce this strange little book and trusting this strange little writer to create it. Thanks above all to my editor Elisha Lundin, who not only provided the initial spark for this story but also offered tons of thoughtful insights and suggestions along the way. She made this story stronger, clearer, and, I hope, highly enjoyable.

I also want to shower all possible levels of praise and affection on my agent, Courtney Miller-Callihan (or, as she is known in my house, SUPERAGENT COURTNEY). Without her support and protection this book would never exist . . . not least because I would have given up on this business years ago. Everyone who does not have a SUPERAGENT like mine should be very jealous, indeed.

Thanks also to my immediate family / constant readers, Mark and Jonah. And extra-special thanks to my mother who has been telling me to write exactly this sort of book for years. I love you almost as much as I hate it when you are right.

I want to acknowledge just a few of the stories that I referenced in the course of telling my own. Most importantly, there is a certain American television program set in a certain Connecticut town, with a certain woman-centric cast, which provided endless inspiration, laughs, and lots of cultural references I had to look up. Imitation truly is the sincerest form of flattery and I very much hope their lawyers agree.

The subplot about Violet, who orders takeout over and over in hopes of catching the eye of a handsome delivery boy, is a deliberate nod to Justine Biagi, a character on the wonderful, gone-too-soon program, *GLOW*. I've also tipped my hat to the office wager scene in one of my favorite films, *The Cabin in the Woods*. And the beleaguered rabbit Quentin is of course my ode to the equally beleaguered hero of Lev Grossman's The Magicians.

When I was a child, there were certain stories I read over and over, and those stories made me want to invent my own. One of my favorites was James Thurber's *The Thirteen Clocks*. Thus it was inevitable that when I wrote my own fairy tale, the starlings would number thirteen. Thank you, Mr. Thurber, wherever you are.

And last but definitely not least, thanks to *The Princess Bride* for existing.

Speaking of which, may I remind you that this is a work of fiction. Names, characters, and implications about Mandy Patinkin's marriage are products of the author's imagination, devised for entertainment purposes only. Any resemblance to Mandy Patinkin's actual romantic history is entirely coincidental. We don't know his life.

—E.G.